A DISTANT FLAME

ALSO BY PHILIP LEE WILLIAMS

FICTION

The True and Authentic History of Jenny Dorset

Blue Crystal

Final Heat

Perfect Timing

The Song of Daniel

Slow Dance in Autumn

All the Western Stars

The Heart of a Distant Forest

NONFICTION

Crossing Wildcat Ridge

The Silent Stars Go By: A True Christmas Story

CHAPBOOK

A Gift from Boonie, Seymour, and Dog

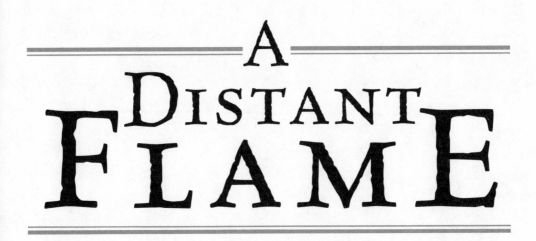

A DISTANT FLAME

PHILIP LEE WILLIAMS

Thomas Dunne Books
St. Martin's Press ☙ New York

THOMAS DUNNE BOOKS.
An imprint of St. Martin's Press.

A DISTANT FLAME. Copyright © 2004 by Philip Lee Williams. All rights
reserved. Printed in the United States of America. No part of this book
may be used or reproduced in any manner whatsoever without written
permission except in the case of brief quotations embodied in critical
articles or reviews. For information, address St. Martin's Press, 175
Fifth Avenue, New York, N.Y. 10010.

www.stmartins.com

Design by Jamie Kerner-Scott

Library of Congress Cataloging-in-Publication Data

Williams, Philip Lee.
    A distant flame / Philip Lee Williams.—1st ed.
        p. cm.
    ISBN 0-312-33252-1
    EAN 978-0312-33252-5
    1. Georgia—History—Civil War, 1861–1865—Fiction.
    2. Sherman, William T. (William Tecumseh), 1820–1891—Fiction.
    3. Sharpshooters—Fiction. 4. Soldiers—Fiction. I. Title.

PS3573.I45535D57 2004
813'.54—dc22   200409077

First Edition: September 2004

10 9 8 7 6 5 4 3 2 1

For my parents,
Ruth and Marshall Williams

I sing to the last the equalities modern or old,
I sing to the endless finales of things,
I say Nature continues, glory continues,
I praise with electric voice,
For I do not see one imperfection in the universe,
And I do not see one cause or result lamentable at last in the universe.
O setting sun! though the time has come,
I still warble under you, if none else does, unmitigated adoration.

—WALT WHITMAN,
from "Song at Sunset"

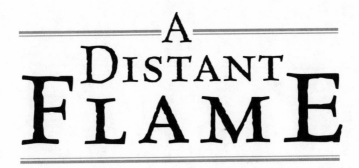

A Distant Flame

Prologue

BLOOD SPILLED DOWN THE man's neck in crimson runnels, and Charlie prayed, kneeling beneath the murderous flight of lead, that the convulsions and fear would end soon. The twelve-pounder Napoleons on both sides gnawed the air into tatters. The dying man blinked, coughed twice, spoke in bright red syllables. Charlie leaned close, heard nothing but Enfields and artillery. He looked around helplessly for aid.

"Don't move!" Charlie screamed, but his own voice might have been the silence of graves. His fingers felt swollen from the heat. A stench drifted across the field—horses and men, sweat, fear, gunpowder, blood, bone, excrement. The dying man's hair hung from his face in black curls. Shrieking minié balls displaced the air near Charlie's left ear. He felt the heave of tears again, a shoving of the breastbone from inside, like a violent hand thrusting outward to catch or push.

The smell arrived and left, arrived once again with more urgency. The oven air swarmed with shot and the distant, then closer, crump of Napoleons and Parrott guns. Charlie knew he must stand and go for help, but the space above his kneeling form held a sea of fire, thousands of bullets, fused balls, shrapnel ripping through brambles, lifting earth upward in small spikes. So Charlie lay down and held him and wept as one red claw rose from the dark-haired man, rose toward Charlie, then fell onto the sweat-fouled shirt and lay there, motionless.

Men swarmed past him then, and one knelt over them and spoke, but the syllables swam away in gunfire. Charlie rolled to his side and saw the wounded man's eyes blink once, his tongue come out as if searching for water or speech. Then his eyes opened wider and stayed that way, dust already settling on the glazing eyeballs, and the tongue, covered with the words of its own blood, did not slide back. A small stream of liquid spilled from the corner of his mouth and flowed just beneath his left ear, then down his neck.

"Don't move," choked Charlie. He shook the man gently, then with increasing urgency. "Don't move, don't you move, don't you move!" The gray-coated soldiers who had flowed past him were fleeing backward now, and one grabbed Charlie beneath his arm, pulled him up, screamed. The air filled with angels. They were sentient, fair as young girls, with smooth skins and the song of morning. Charlie could not feel the ground with his feet, and he thought he might be drifting toward or away from something. He looked down, and his feet were three inches off the ground, and he could steer on the currents of gunfire. Strands of rifle fire braided beneath him into a warm walkway. He stepped upon it. He was heading into the maw of a battery from Arkansas. General Cleburne stood to one side holding a chessman and smiling. Charlie felt fear release him.

Then he was not moving, and the Federals had gained, were now spilling him over the field, but none dared touch him. They gave way as he rode the highway of screaming fire. He rose above tree level, then came back down, avoiding bristling spikes of abatis that drew scars around the city. He drifted above the smoke then back into it, but the dust did not choke him; instead, it was a tonic, a shearing of agony and exhaustion. He sipped it sweetly. Charlie came back to the wounded man and folded into stone by his side.

"Get up, and I will lead you," whispered Charlie, and the man blinked blood three times and stood beside him, dusting caked blood from his chest. "You knew I would come back and get you, didn't you?"

"I always knew that," said the man. Charlie touched his hand, and the man's feet rose, too, and they came east over the lines toward home. July knelt, stunned with heat and noise. Broken bodies, bent into strange, inhuman shapes, crowded below them. Down the blue line of Federal artillery, unbroken rows of men stood and fired, ripped ramrods out to reload, and the cannon spoke with a singular core of violence, a giant's roar, the prelude to earth's ending. Charlie and the man rose higher, and he seemed uninterested in stopping their flight. The noise began to hum like a distant storm.

"Look down there," said Charlie. They looked below them, and the gently rolling green countryside broke into patches of field, stitched together with rail fencing. "There is a pattern to it."

"I don't see any pattern," said the man. "I don't see any pattern at all."

Charlie laughed and saw the world blue as water, green with renewal. Tree crests brushed the bottom of his brogans. He turned and saw that the man was gone, and he knew this was right. *This was how it should be.* He wondered where he was for only a moment, lifted by a great sense of exhilaration and buoyancy.

Life did have meaning, and sorrow fell backward in retreat. He saw his father coming up a distant hill, and Charlie summoned him with the warmth of memory, the smell of his winter coat, the laughter at their table. Just past him, Charlie's mother walked through a sea of campfires, bearing in her hands a cup spilling with spring-fresh water. He motioned for them, then he looked beyond them for Sarah, but he could not see her, though he strained and turned one way and then another, through the dusted sunset, through stars, through blooded hands.

She must be on her way home, bearing his name upon her lips.

CHARLIE MERRILL LAY IN the mahogany four-poster bed, wrapped in a clot of damp sheets, remembering. Light crept into the sky through the tall windows facing east, and the panes shuddered with a freshening wind. He blinked the memory away, but it was never past. It came at least once each week just after he awoke, bearing old horrors shaped in new narratives of flame and blood. He pushed himself up on his elbows and looked around the second-floor bedroom. For a moment, the familiar sheared into picture-book oddness. Whose room? Whose castle? Whose city?

Today, he thought. *This is the day.*

He stood on thin legs and walked across the wide floorboards to the window, his dressing gown drooping to his ankles as he stepped softly. Charlie raised the window, and a pleasant breeze lifted his white hair, fluffed it behind his ears. He rubbed his hand on the unshaven cheeks

and looked down across the Georgia Railroad tracks toward the cemetery. He turned to his left and saw the book on the table and smiled as
he lifted it, opened it to the title page, and felt himself alive with boy-
hood: *Rowena: A Novel of the Southern Life* . . . The title went on for
another line or two. He closed his eyes and thought of his father's foot-
fall on the steps as he ascended with the volume when Charlie lay
bedridden that summer. Charlie read it for days, studied relationships
and plots, places and names. One character was a doctor who was always talking about astringents, narcotics, cathartics. He dreamed of
thoroughwort and boneset and Osage orange and styptic weed. His
mother would bring him plants from the railroad banks, and he would
try to discover their properties by description alone.

He put the book back down and went to the window. An automobile came puttering past on Main Street, out early, he thought. Then: an
aroma of bacon from downstairs, and he knew Mrs. Knight was already
cooking his breakfast, that she would be singing "Aura Lee" or
"Lorena" as she flipped and stirred, her voice gliding off key, repeating
phrases without regard to flow or meaning. She was a wide and flush-
faced woman, careless in her dress and speech but an able cook who
held pride in promptness. Her son Nathan, who sold hardware,
dropped her off each morning at six and picked her up each evening at
six. Nathan was unnaturally tall, and Charlie pictured him now with no
chin and a knot of Adam's apple, cheering too hard at town parades,
wildly childish and unmarried. Mrs. Knight was very sad about that.

The railroad bisected the Branton City Cemetery. The town had
started burying its dead on the other side of the rails in the midnineties
when the older section had filled its neighborhood of coffins. He
watched as the light sifted through the higher branches of water oaks
planted there decades before. The morning train would arrive soon,
heading toward Atlanta, rattling and swaying between the dead, but
not disturbing them. He tried to imagine them whispering in the night,
returned from heaven or hell to share secrets with the honeysuckle or
verbena.

Time wore on him, slumped his shoulders, turned his hands parchment thin and mottled. Mrs. Knight whistled from the kitchen, but not
to a dog, not to Charlie, simply to herself, in a tuneless and repetitive
way, like wheels on a long stream of summer rails. Birdsong spilled below him. He took one of the lead soldiers from the table and turned it
gently in his palm: a kneeling man, brave bayonet thrust out but bent,

broken. He remembered when his father brought them to his bedside, hopeful eyes, kind hands, toys for one too old for play, too young for Manassas. He had lined them, small and heavy, across his sheets, dreamed victory and glories. Now he held his wounded soldier in the morning's sharp light, turning it, remembering the man slumped against a hickory tree at Chickamauga.

"Spare me, friend," he gasped. "Brother, please spare me." Charlie saw the blue-gray heap of entrails spilling on his lap, where he held them in a trembling left hand. Charlie knelt and put the mouth of his canteen upon the man's lips and tipped it, but he convulsed, went vague, choked, fell heavily dead to one side. The snakes of his intestines fell into the hot dust. Flies came. The menace of Chickamauga had been dense and breathless, populated less by rage than a vast and deeply shared fear.

"Dear God," said Charlie out loud as he remembered. A whistle swept west with its clattering overtones: *On time today.* He put the lead soldier back on the table and walked slowly to the sideboard and poured the basin full of fresh water from a white porcelain pitcher. He foamed his brush in the shaving cup, stropped the shimmering blade, and pulled it straight across his left cheek. The train had come through Branton, picking up a clacking speed, and he felt the thrum of its movement in his hand as he shaved. He watched himself in the small wall-mounted oval mirror, turned his face between its lathered sides, saw his father in his cedar pulpit with its dark gloss.

"Mr. Charlie? You awake in there? You remember what day this here is, Mr. Charlie? You got your speech wrote?"

"I'm awake, Mrs. Knight," he said. "I'll be down directly. I'll take my coffee in here if you don't mind."

"You don't sound good, Mr. Charlie. Not good at all. Have you gone and caught a chill? God help me you caught a chill. Half the town be blaming me if you caught a chill."

"I'm perfectly fine. Just bring me my coffee, please."

She left in a soft trail of muttering, and her steps creaked the stairs. Yes, I remember what day this is. He thought of her straw-colored hair. He remembered how she read Keats and Shelley and Jane Austen with soft unsentimental tones, how she would cross her ankles, and one boot eyelet would tap another, that metallic reminder of her presence. Her eyes were pale blue-gray, sky against new snow, but they could shade darker when she was troubled or ill. She could not abide the fields of death, denied certainties, spoke of Boston's sacred and sun-stained spires with love.

Charlie shaved his cheeks and chin as the train's last car swayed west behind the house. *She will not come.* He knew that much anyway, with far more certainty than what he might say at the celebration. She would not step from the return train. She would be fragile and gray now, even long gone to those northern ancestral sepulchres, which she made real in words. He washed the last lace shred of foam from his face and dried with a hand towel. A slow tread on the stairs, uncomposed whistling, then leaning with a groan to place the silver tray and its steaming cup on the floorboards of a dark hall.

"Hit's out here, and you be down in ten minutes or you breakfast be cold," said Mrs. Knight. "Go on and drink it, maybe you fighting a chill already. You go on and drink it."

"I will, Mrs. Knight. Bless you."

"Bless me. I could take a blessing . . ." her words trailing down the stairs like a scent of spice at someone's front door, promises and traps set. Charlie, still in his gown, opened the door, and the wind, lifting through the open window of his bedroom, belled the cotton gown as he knelt for the cup and saucer. He came back into his bedroom but left the door open to a fine breeze, which blew back the pages of *Rowena*. He sipped the coffee and walked once more to the table, put the cup and saucer down, snugged his eyeglass wires around his ears. He lifted the book to read. How did we receive messages? From the chance flip of a page in a freshening breeze? Did the inside of anchorites bear more witness? He cleared his throat and read aloud. Dr. Perry was reciting cures to a patient: *Morus rubra, L. Mulberry. Grows along rivers and swamps; vicinity of Charleston . . . The fruit is laxative and cooling, and a grateful drink and syrup are made from it, adapted to febrile cases.*

Charlie laughed, taking off his glasses, lifting the blue transferware cup to his lips to sip the fragrant coffee. His grandfather's cup, the last of its kind, yet uncracked, familiar as rain. No great messages in mulberry laxatives. Then: A great rush of wind and the small silver bell hung on the front door pulsing pure tones, footsteps fast and hollow on the stairs. Morning came through the tall window, and most of all Charlie loved the morning, its promise spread in infinite shades of gold and blue, with cool winds and the fragrance of possibility. He turned to see Barrington Avery lean breathless through the open doorway, his straw boater askew. The aroma of his shaving lotion did not stop as he did and blew into the room, sharp and lingering, like spiced fruit.

"You're not dressed yet, sir? Forgive me. It *is* very early."

"Come in, Barry. Would you join me for breakfast? Mrs. Knight says I'm overdue at the table already."

"Is she coming back up here?" He removed the hat and fingered it nervously, looking back, then stepping into the hall for a brief glance.

"She's not coming back. She may shout again. She shouts very well."

"Her son Nathan's mad at me. He said he had the first open cotton boll of the season from that little farm of his. But he twisted the boll, an old trick, to make it open. I believe you are the one who taught me that."

"I believe I am," said Charlie. He smiled warmly at Barry. Yes. He was most certainly the right one to buy the *Eagle*. A good decision, one of my better ones. First open boll of the season and a free year's subscription.

"Anyway, I talked to the other three, and they're willing to wear their uniforms, all but T. D. Varnell, who won't fit anymore, as you know. I want a photograph, Mr. Charlie, and the uniforms would be splendid, I think. After fifty years and all that, old comrades."

"I don't have my uniform," said Charlie. "I threw it out after the war, burned it with kerosene in the backyard. You could get a picture of me standing by the spot where I burned it."

"Ha, yes, well." Barry was embarrassed but had to ask. He was not tall but thin and blond, hair plastered back but scattered and sharply parted.

"Mr. Charlie, your breakfast won't stay hot all day and still be fitten to eat." Mrs. Knight shouting from the foot of the stairs.

"I'm coming now," Charlie yelled back. Barry crept to the door like a spy and peered nervously around the frame.

"Well, anyway," said Barry. "You wouldn't happen to have an extra copy of your speech so we could start setting the type?"

"I haven't written it yet."

"But the thing is *today*. When are you going to write it?"

"I may just speak from the heart." Charlie grinned.

"Right. Well, then, I'm off. Oh, by the way, the Augusta paper this morning has dispatches from Europe. Looks like a war certain over there. Doubt they can stop the whole place going up in flames since they killed the archduke. But really none of our affair."

"Perhaps not," said Charlie Merrill.

Charlie dressed as Barry walked with morning stealth down the stairs and out the front door, the silver bell shivering only twice from the motion. Charlie put on a starched shirt but no collar, dark trousers, and bright red suspenders.

He stared at his face in the cool surface of the mirror and he turned back past the town and its orderly cemetery, beyond the scars of Georgia, to a land bright with snow.

Winter, 1864

NEAR DALTON, GEORGIA

MERRILL'S BRIGADE OF THE Eastern Army stood at the flank and stamped with cold, breath feathering the sharp blue March sky. Not far ahead, the Western Army waited, newly armed, for the assault. Snow lay on the ground in a thick, icy shroud, and even the sunlight did little to melt it. If Merrill's Brigade could turn the right flank, they might send the Western Army back into the center of the lines where Johnston's men waited. Jaws of a winter-spun trap.

"Ah, Charlie, it's pretty," said Duncan McGregor. "It's the first damned movement that's felt good since Chickamauga."

"Keep your head down," said Charlie.

"It ain't my head worries me," said Duncan. He laughed, a stuttering, stomach-shaking burst of genuine relief. Charlie smiled at him.

The line went solid. Men began to move forward, most in a fine mood, the best since November at least. Sensing the flanking movement, the Western Army closed up and began to move toward the center of its line, forming a skirmish point in an angle.

"Come at us and get yourn," said a soldier in the Western Army.

"No, *yourn*," said Bob Rainey. He was in line next to Charlie Merrill, who far from being a real brigade commander, was a private in Govan's Brigade of Cleburne's Division of Hardee's Corps of General Joseph Johnston's Army of Tennessee. They called themselves Merrill's

Brigade as a camp joke because no one had known anyone quite like Charlie, just a boy, but a deadly shot with his Spencer rifle. (Govan's Brigade had captured half a dozen or more breech-loading repeaters during the Battle of Chattanooga, and Charlie had earned one.)

"Go, boys!" Charlie cried. A wailing scream rose from both sides of the line. Some of them were laughing, but most weren't, bearing down by then, honing their aim. Merrill's Brigade, having failed to turn the flank, attacked straight forward anyway, the lines holding together until they were no more than ten feet apart. Unwilling to hold their defensive position, the Western Army moved to the engagement, drew bead, and raised their arms.

The air exploded with the frosted haloes of snowballs.

As soon as they unloaded, the boys leaned quickly into the heaps of wet snow and scooped up more, rough red hands on white balls, threw again. The air rang with laughter and curses, and a few angry words when a snowball loaded with a rock or a minié ball found a half-frozen cheek or neck. From the north Georgia hillside, Charlie looked down the lines and saw hundreds—no, thousands—of men engaged in the frontal assault. Some people from Dalton, even ladies, had come out to watch, and they stamped against the cold up on the high ridge behind the lines, having a wonderful time. He was turning to point out the spectators to Duncan McGregor when a loaded snowball hit him on the side of the head. He felt the stun, saw expanding, elliptical stars, fell to his knees. A rock in that one. Pay more attention. For a moment, the snow felt good on his knees, salved them after all the drilling of the past few days, but then the cold spread into his bones. Duncan was helping him up.

"You got pasted, but I got the son of a bitch," said Duncan. A man from the Western Army was sitting on his rear in the ice, mouth open, showing snow on his gums. He was the one who had hit Charlie. He looked very tired, maybe worn past recovery. You could see it in their eyes when the time had come. He didn't have much strength, but he'd used all he had to hit Charlie.

"Too bad I'm not General Sherman," said Charlie. The soldier in the snow laughed but seemed as if he might cry. Charlie noticed that the perspiration and snow had frozen in the man's beard, making it look like tree moss, fragile, easily broken.

✧ ✧
✧

THE SNOWBALL BATTLE HAD been approved (though soldiers started it) by Confederate General Joseph Johnston when the Southern army had moved into winter quarters in the north Georgia mountains south of Chattanooga. The men loved Old Joe as much as they despised their former commander, General Braxton Bragg. Johnston had found the army in desperate condition: undisciplined, disorganized, poorly fed, and sick of war. Desertions had become rampant. The hospitals were choked with men suffering from measles, pneumonia, and the lingering effects of battlefield wounds. Some days they died of disease as fast as they had in battle at Chickamauga the previous September. The clothing of the troops was in tatters, and winter quarters found the men with little resolve and much less fighting spirit.

At least twice a week, Charlie jerked awake from the memory of Chickamauga. It had been his first fight after he'd joined the Confederate troops, and the carnage was ghastly, thousands falling, no one able to stop for the wounded. He had shown up from nowhere with his rifle, a boy riding the rails up from Atlanta, rocking in the heat and stench of a boxcar, afraid but saying little. Charlie had attached himself to Cleburne's Division just before battle, and during combat he seemed unafraid, firing at Yankees, dropping them from stunning distances, until Duncan McGregor, a bantam whose parents had come from Scotland twenty years before, had pushed him forward and said, "Aye, God, son, you're the devil's own marksman, but a fool for that." Charlie felt himself drift through the screams of the dying and wounded, dreaming it, watching Federals fall before his firing.

The Federals thought there was a gap in their lines, but there was none, and when troops were moved to cover it, the Confederates rushed through, wailing their scream in a skin-shivering shriek that did not seem to penetrate Charlie's resolve. He kept moving, kept firing, kept dropping the enemy from great distances. A little later, he saw a Southern soldier lying beneath a tree, the snakes of his entrails intertwined in his lap.

No one knew who Charlie was or where he came from. Later, when the Confederates had been routed from Missionary Ridge overlooking Chattanooga, driven back cold and grieving into Georgia for winter quarters—only then did a few of the men find out about Charlie. Now in March, he was beloved by the troops, especially by Duncan McGregor, with whom he had grown very close. Charlie laughed and cleaned his gun around the cold sputtering campfires, awaiting spring. Sometimes, he would take out the letter and read it:

Dear Charlie,

I write you with great sorrow from Savannah where I wait to board a ship for London. It was not my idea to leave with such urgency—this you must believe. I have wept the whole time, and now that an ocean will separate us, I can only hope Death will come for me soon.

It is not enough for me to say that I love you, dear Charlie. You are the star of my life, the only true joy I have ever known. I had no sister or brother as a child. When I was sent to Branton, I felt the most perfect hopelessness that it is possible to know. My uncle and his stupid Specific shamed me, and his loud ways were no better than what I heard in Boston.

I very nearly believe that I dreamed myself into your arms. I was alone and full of sorrow, and I asked God for a boy to take me as his own. At first, I asked God what He could mean—you were frail and ill, though Jack was such a fine friend to you. I loathed Branton, but then I did not mind it so much when God sent you to me.

This war is a kind of madness as you told me. My father writes that he shall not return to America because it holds war and my mother. I might have hoped he was leaving on some principle—abolition, unity—but in fact he left for convenience, and my Uncle is sending me away for the same reason.

I wept when I was told. I said that I had to get to your house to tell you goodbye. Uncle said I'd spent entirely too much time with you already, much, he supposed, to my detriment. But Charlie it was not to my detriment. I felt a light in my soul that could not have been condemnation. I cannot believe a just God would deny happiness to those such as us who are alone and broken in the world. If it was wrong, then I shall admit such when I stand before God.

I shall try to write you when nature manifests itself, but each day I cradle the thoughts tenderly, and I weep as I see your face before me. The only salve I have is that I met you at all. Perhaps it has been ordained that we meet and part, and

*that only in death will we be joined again. I will never forget
the joy I found with you or the peace I saw in your eyes when
we loved. My heart will ever be yours.*

*Now I must post this in haste for they are calling me to
the ship, and I cannot know what will happen next. But as I
sail, I will love you, and some day I will come back, and we
will share that love God intended for us.*

All my love,
Your Sarah

IN MIDAFTERNOON ON THE day of the snowball fight, Cleburne's Division paused for the execution of Private Evan Cason. Evan had gotten as far as Smyrna. When they caught him, he had a pone of cornbread, two knives, one without a handle, an empty canteen, and a kepi caked with dried blood. He was sitting on a stump watching a creek when the detachment came on him. He denied nothing, and then they took him straightaway back to Dalton, providing Evan with a horse. The day was very cold, and snowflakes rolled into his mouth on a north wind. There were two corporals, a sergeant, and a lieutenant in the detachment. Evan had been hiding since Chickamauga, and that was several months now, and he spent part of it in an abandoned shack near Villanow, but that was no good. He was in Ringgold for a time, but they were all around him, so he decided to head south—he might get to the Gulf and then back up the river to Arkansas. He made it about sixty-five miles.

When the firing squad shot him, he failed to die, and he sat up in the slush and begged for mercy. The sergeant was ordered to finish him with a pistol, but it misfired. Then the squad had to reload and shoot the prisoner all over again.

Charlie watched it pensively, saying nothing, feeling as if each thud of lead had wrecked his own heart.

NIGHT CAME, AND WITH it a few flurries, and Charlie sat before the campfire, sipping coffee, the tin cup so heated it almost burned his fingertips.

"Aye, God, they orta give us the victory this afternoon," said Duncan McGregor. He talked with a piece of hardtack moving up and down in his mouth because he was cleaning his gun, and that took both hands. He looked at Charlie with kindness, affection. "Some of them boys ought to have had their sweet arses kicked for puttin' rocks in them snowballs, eh, Charlie?"

"They got hard feelings," said Charlie quietly. The cold seemed blacker than the night, an ache that began deep inside the earth.

"I never thought we'd get the spirit back, but Old Joe's done it," said Bob Rainey, an older man with a gray-flecked beard. "I'm near about ready to send some bad news to a few Yankee mothers."

"Blasted damn cold," said Duncan. He swallowed his cracker, the mass going down hard, then turned his Enfield toward the fire and seemed satisfied with the look of it. In the past week, many of the men had begun to clean their rifles again. Some had only shotguns, and Charlie had even seen a few ancient flintlocks. The men used percussion caps on them instead of flints (the guns had been altered to use them), and the guns fired but were wildly inaccurate. The smoothbore muskets that not a few soldiers had were useless at more than two hundred yards. Duncan's Enfield was deadly, but though its range was longer than Charlie's Spencer rifle, Charlie was much more accurate at short ranges.

"It's not long until the sun comes out for good," said Charlie.

"Blasted cold ruins my head and keeps my rifle a mess, don't you see, Charlie," said Duncan. "Don't you think them Yankees is having it no better, though, 'cause it's worse in Chattanooga, and I don't have to remind you of that." The flurries got no harder, but they didn't stop, either. "Old Joe's got a plan, boys, and when he sets us to it, it's gone be like fire through a dried-up cornfield."

Charlie had been considering the dead and the snow and the heat from the fire, trying to think of nothing, to empty himself in a kind of wakeful sleep. Sometimes it worked, sometimes not. Bob Rainey was much older than Duncan, maybe in his late thirties or even forty. He never said his age and wouldn't tell when asked, but his cheek shone with scar tissue, creased by a Yankee shot at Ringgold Gap in late November and having healed poorly. Where the ball had plowed his face like a fertile field, no beard would grow. Bob Rainey never showed fear, never seemed to reflect on anything that gave him pause, much less trouble. He was from Carolina, he said. Charlie thought it was South Carolina, which was odd, since most boys in this division were from Arkansas or Texas. But Carolina, anyway, and Charlie thought it was

South Carolina, and Duncan thought it was the other one. The Confederates had suffered less than five hundred casualties at Ringgold Gap, and Bob was one of those, though he was only in the hospital tents for two days before he got up and went back to his company. He scoffed at the wound as a scratch, but it was worse and festered. He suffered silently in the tent until the scab came off and winter air helped heal the slash.

Major General Joseph Hooker of the Union forces had sent wave after wave of Yankees against the Southerners at the Gap, five hours' worth of assaults, but the Confederate lines held. Bob Rainey reckoned he had killed five Yankees by himself.

"How's your head, young Merrill?" asked Bob Rainey. When he called him that, Charlie felt a closeness to the older man. "We wouldn't have you spent out over a snowball what was built around a stone, now would we, young Merrill?"

"We would not," said Charlie.

The camp seemed very quiet just now. Men were bedding down, exhausted after the mock battle, tired of fearing what might come in a few weeks. There was much blessing in thinking of it. You could die of malaria or a fever, any fever. Slim Madden had died of the clap when they were up in Tennessee. A terrible thing, to die of the clap. He wouldn't get treated until it was too late, and he was bucking like a stung horse in the hospital when his heart just stopped beating. You could die in the summer of heat stroke. One of the Branton Rifles back in Sixty-One had died from the heat in a boxcar two days out of town, and they buried him in a pasture on the side of the railroad tracks in North Carolina. The artillery could cut you in half. Or a picket or a sharpshooter or massed fire. It was all the same.

"I reckon this snow's gone end here directly," said Duncan. "You think so, Charlie?"

"Always has," said Charlie. He said nothing more, and though his mind drifted over his mother and Martha, he thought mostly of Sarah. When night came, he always did.

July 9, 1861

☆ ☆
☆

LIMPING, JACK DOCKERY CAME into the firelight carrying a half-rotted tree limb. One end had dissolved into a crumbling ruin. The other held the shape of an old break. Wind-cracked during a storm, Charlie thought, or perhaps a simple snap from age.

"It's worse," said Charlie, "I mean it's hurting worse today. Aren't you still using Dr. Sartain's ointments and pills?"

"They don't do any good," said Jack. "I'm all right, stumbled in the outhouse doorway this morning. Stupid thing, really. You reckon this is gonna burn? I'm thinking it will go all smoldery for a bit then catch on."

"Possibly," said Charlie. "But it *will* be smoldery."

Jack knelt with the log, offered it to the small blaze. Night was very near now, and a whip-poor-will sang his three notes relentlessly, deeper in the forest. The boys had spread their bedrolls in the clearing, and eaten beans, peeled waxed paper back from dried beef that Mrs. Dockery had packed for them. Now, it was time for talk. The log turned the small flames smoky, and Charlie shrugged and sat on his bedroll and listened to the coming night sounds. He could not remember the first time he'd met Jack Dockery, but it must have been in church when they were both very small. Charlie's first memory was the funeral of Jack's grandfather, when they were six years old. Jack's mother was controlled, already accepting her loss with finality if not equanimity. She was a large woman who did not weep easily. Jack leaned into her and sobbed, his damaged foot in a special boot. Jack's father seemed unmoved. Charlie had sat with his mother and Tom, eyes sharp upon the open coffin lying below the pulpit. He scanned the stained glass windows, especially the one with Jesus on the cross, and a thunderstorm breaking around him, indifferent soldiers nearby along with the first Christians, dumbstruck with horror and grief. *The little boy with the hurt foot.* That's how Charlie thought of Jack until they met in town a few weeks later. Jack was carrying a sack of groceries, struggling with the burden.

"Let me help you with that?" asked Charlie.

"You're too little," said Jack.

"Your foot is hurt is all," said Charlie. "I was sick when I was a baby."

Jack had stopped, and a kind light rose in his eyes. "So was I. Born this way. We only moved here a year ago. Your daddy's the preacher at the church did my grandpa's funeral. Maybe we could take turns."

They carried the burlap sack of groceries to Jack's house near the railroad tracks. His mother sewed curtains and dresses, anything a lady in Branton might need, and his father owned a hardware store. Since then, Charlie and Jack had been inseparable, swimming in the Branton River, which sliced through the town from north to south over a shoal of boulders large as carriages.

"You're right, it *is* smoldery," said Jack. He limped to his bedroll and sat on it and pulled his clubfoot up beneath him. "Maybe it'll keep any stray Yankees away from here. I'd hate to have to kill one tonight. Then we've to bury him, and we didn't bring a shovel."

Charlie looked at their shotguns, propped low against a punky hollow log. Once here, a possum had wandered up toward the fire deep in the night, and Jack had shot it. Charlie felt himself sicken at the small strange animal in its death thrashings and had walked out of the firelight and vomited. Jack comforted his friend and apologized. *I was rash, he said. I've been rash in my life.* It was just past dusk, which invited nostalgia, an evocation of memories.

"But it *will* burn," said Charlie. "You get a fire hot enough, anything will burn. I've heard that in India they burn up people when they die, and they get a fire so hot there's nothing left but ashes like a fireplace."

"I never heard that. It's kind of sickening. When the Camak place burned, they said you could still sort of tell who everybody was, but it was a sickening thing. And that house was the biggest fire I ever saw. You want to play chess?"

They always brought the board and pieces, but Charlie had to cheat to make the games pleasurable because he was so much better than Jack. Charlie shook his head. The last light was gone now, and night sounds had begun, and he loved and feared them. Once he had told Jack the night must be like dying because it was fearful, but it should be loved if you were going to heaven.

"I wouldn't shoot a Yankee," said Charlie.

"I would. I think I could kill a Yankee. Maybe not. I don't know." Jack was quiet for a time. The log still spread a dense white smoke into the clearing, drifting high into the limbs of oaks and poplars. Then: "I heard something you won't believe."

"What?" asked Charlie.

"You'll think I'm lying."

"Try me."

"I heard two men talking about it at Daddy's store. I was dusting the bins, and they didn't see me. They said there was a man down near Macon who was asleep on the railroad tracks, maybe he was drunk, I don't know. Anyway, he was on the tracks, and the train came, and ran over him and cut him half in two."

"That's terrible," said Charlie.

"That's nothing," said Jack. "This one man told the other one that a fella on the train saw the man's top half crawl twenty feet with his hands after he was cut in half." Charlie felt his stomach heave, and he turned away from Jack. Was that a sound in the forest? Someone might be stalking them, about to attack. Enemies could be much closer than you thought.

"I don't believe that. It's just a story."

"That's not the worst part."

"What?" The log's smoke was thickening, and night birds gathered.

"They said he had time to take out a pencil and a piece of paper and write down the words *I love Maggie* before he died. But he didn't write his name."

Charlie felt his skin go clammy, and he stood and walked to the fire. He formed a picture of the severed man, the upper half crawling away, the lower half left behind, and in between the blood of slaughterhouses, sinews, and organs. He had cleaned chickens himself, knew the slick insides of a living creature.

"That couldn't be," said Charlie.

"It was. They said it."

"They must have been making it up, just a story. That couldn't be. That's the most sickening thing I've ever heard in my life." Charlie felt the blood fill his face. He was on the verge of screaming, maybe running into the woods. Nothing had ever made him feel so afraid.

"It's hard to know what's true and what somebody's made up. They say there's going to be a big battle in Virginia. Everybody's saying that the war will be over by August. My daddy said he couldn't understand all this over a bunch of niggers. It's only people like the Sheltons and the Holmeses that even need all the slaves. He says boys who haven't got any truck with niggers are the ones who will die over them."

"I've heard that. Every other person you ask has a different reason for wanting to go fight, but everybody's hot on it. It's the slaves or it's not. It's states' rights or it's not. It's the Constitution or it's not. I don't know a durned reason why, but it seems like everybody's been looking for a reason for a long time. But you know about half the people in Branton don't even want this war at all. This whole town's divided. But, Jack, I'd surely love to have me one of those uniforms the Branton Rifles wore when they left in April. And a good gun that was sighted so sharp you could hit a gnat at two hundred yards. I'd like to be able to shoot better."

"Aw, hell, you're the best shot I know, Charlie. You're the best shot in town."

"But that thing in Macon—that couldn't be. I feel like . . ." Charlie shook his head, trying to shake the image loose, but he could not dismiss it.

"Well, I believe it."

"Then you're stupid." Charlie turned, face flushed from the smoking fire and his own thoughts. He swallowed hard and for some reason saw before him ranks of soldiers marching into lines of cannon, being blown into body parts, like the frosty hog slaughter on sprawling plantations and small farms.

"I just said what I heard. Don't call me stupid for saying what I heard."

"You're stupid if you believe it."

"I'm stupid because I believe something I can't prove? Can you prove somebody nailed Jesus to a cross? You can't prove that."

"It's in the Bible. That means it's proved."

"What if somebody way back then made it all up for a joke? What if it's a story like Mrs. Stowe's book? Maybe it is a lie and maybe it's not, but you don't know and neither do I."

"Shut up, damn it, Jack. Just shut up. I don't want to think about it anymore."

The log suddenly burst into flame, and the white smoke disappeared. The fire rose four feet above the shaft, engulfed its entire length. Charlie held his palms out, trying to get hotter and hotter, to feel the world's rock flow liquid around him, to prove that hell was present in everyday things.

July 22, 1914

T HE SUN STREAKED ROSE and silver along the rails. Charlie stood in the window of his bedroom again, reading from *Rowena.* He smiled and closed the book, set it back on the table. The novel was poor, but if anyone read half a sentence from it, he could likely finish it. He thought: *She will not come. She has not responded to the advertisements. I know she will not come.*

Barrington Avery would be in five places at once, planning for the interviews and the photographs of the old soldiers' return today, the fiftieth anniversary of the Battle of Atlanta. He was a good boy, ambitious, neat, with elegant manners. Charlie missed writing the *Eagle,* but not very often. Now he would sit in the sunshine of his screened side porch and reminisce. So many had gone before: The cemetery was the fastest-growing neighborhood in town. If he wished, he could sit in his room all day, any day, and think or write. Old age was for restoring childhood, its certainties of faith and love and harvest, not for flight but for the amplitude of rest.

"Are you wanting more coffee, Mr. Charlie?" Mrs. Knight asked. She loomed in the doorway wiping her hands on a damp cloth, emitting the odor of breakfast and Rinse-O-Brite. "You ate next to nothing and on a day you're to give a big speech. It ain't right, you ask me."

"No."

"No what? No, you don't want no more coffee, or no, you ain't working on your speech? I hear Mr. Avery's going to wire your speech to the Atlanta papers, and it might even be in the papers up north, and you are standing here watching the sun come up and not eating nothing of the fine breakfast I fixed for you. I might as well be fired."

"All right, Mrs. Knight, you're fired."

"What? You can't fire me for telling the truth."

"Correct. You're rehired. I'm going to take a brief constitutional now, and when I return, I may wish a cup of coffee, but not now. And you're right to hector me about my eating. I don't seem to have much of an appetite these days. I feel like I'm missing things."

"Well, I'm going back to the kitchen afore you fire me again," she said, smiling. Charlie fired her at least once a week, then hired her back instantly, in a game of affections of which neither seemed to tire. She turned to go and stopped in the doorway, then stepped back, eyes narrowed, shoulders drooping in apology.

"Yes?"

"You never said a word to me in all the years I been here about what it was like in that war. Not a blessed word. And you in the middle of it from Chattanooga to Atlanta. It must have been a horror to see all that death and them Yankees driving us straight to Atlanta like they was rolling down a steep hill. It must have been a horror. Was it a horror?"

He closed his eyes and turned to the window and felt the sun butter his cheeks. The wind was rising again, and a green shimmering spread across his yard to the home of Mrs. Dalton Conner, a wizened widow whose memories were all demonstrably untrue. She remembered a fierce battle taking place with the Yankees just east of Branton, trench lines, artillery, cavalry charges, the earthquake of shells from their first crump until their fused explosions in the gardens of Branton's whitewashed mansions. Except none of it ever happened, and Charlie and everyone else knew it. History, he thought, was who had the loudest and most persistent voice. Slocum's Corps of Sherman's Army had marched through Branton in one day that November, turned south toward Eatonton, done little more than burn a few stores and steal some silver. History was a collective imagination, not the truth. It was the story of our stories, solidified into stone.

"I never talked about it much," he said. "I was only a boy then. Everything was different then. I have appreciated your never asking."

"Well, it being the fiftieth anniversary and all."

"When my mother was dying, she asked for my forgiveness," said Charlie, turning to Mrs. Knight, who saw the sun's rays spread around his head like an engraving of an Old Testament prophet. The sharp light seems to penetrate Charlie's face, come through and out his eyes, and a tense half smile lingered on his face.

"For what?"

"I didn't ask her. A woman's got a right to beg forgiveness for all her sins, exclusive of time and place, doesn't she, Mrs. Knight?"

"She was the wife of a preacher. What would the wife of a preacher need to ask her son for forgiveness for?"

"We all must ask forgiveness for every act we committed or did not. We cannot move from sorrow to solace unless we do."

"Why would you ask for forgiveness for an act you didn't do? You're losing me, Mr. Charlie. I may have to just quit instead of getting fired. I was just asking about the war. People would be interested in that history. I would myself."

"I wasn't involved in history," he said. "I was involved in death. We reach a point where we look around and realize that death is the only thing left to achieve. We begged for a slaughter, and it was given to us."

"I'm going back to the kitchen. You're sounding like a old man. Like a old man."

"Fancy that."

Mrs. Knight shook her head and whispered philosophies as she descended the stairs wiping her fat hands in the damp towel.

COME ON, YOU LAZY hound. You're acting like Methuselah." Charlie whistled, and Belle, his small white dog with one black ear and a tipping gait, caught up with him. He walked with the teak cane surmounted with a silver lion's head, given to him when he sold the *Eagle* and retired two years before. Mrs. Penelope Allen, a young-looking sixty, saw him, waved from her porch, beneath the cool shade of four Ionic columns that fluted upward two stories. She was not properly dressed to meet a visitor, and Branton was the Heart of Propriety or no place was. Others, from more distant towns, called it charm.

"Morning, Mr. Merrill. Your animal is looking well. Sometimes he chases after my cat Isabel."

"I apologize on behalf of myself and my sorry animal, Penelope. But I shouldn't worry much. She couldn't catch a rabbit in a round room."

Mrs. Allen tittered, pulled the neck of her morning gown together with her left hand.

"John dislikes my cat anyway," said Mrs. Allen. "He told our grandson he could shoot it if he took a shine to. We had a tremendous row about it. Perhaps you heard all the pitching of crockery and such." She was laughing now, teasing him. "Our grandson wouldn't shoot a duck on the wing. He's a gentle child like his mother and his grandmother. He doesn't even own an air rifle."

"Belle could not catch your cat. In her earlier days, perhaps, but not now. She has lost her agility and on some days her reason. I believe she has learned it from me."

"Oh, pooh. And we are so looking forward to the celebrations today. Shooting the anvil, fireworks, the Branton Brass, speeches, all our local idiotic politicians, especially the mayor, who has not yet written a word of his speech, the fool." John Allen, her husband, had been mayor of Branton for seven years.

"Speeches will be the least of it, I assure you," said Charlie. "I'll make sure that Belle doesn't bother your cat anymore."

"Everyone is most looking forward to *your* speech. Heaven knows they don't care what John says." She took a few steps toward the front of the porch, and the breeze moved the hem of her gown, and Charlie was surprised to feel aroused, wondering. "They say that a big war is coming in Europe. I hope we have the good sense to stay out of this one. I'd say we've had enough war for one lifetime. Of course, I was only a little girl during the War Between the States, but I remember what it felt like when they said we had lost and it was all over. I thought the world had come to an end. But it didn't. Here we are still. Amazing. I'm not properly dressed to receive you, or I'd offer you coffee."

"I've had my coffee. Come on, Belle."

"You're looking thin," she said, waving, then going inside. Charlie smiled and nodded: Yes, Branton almost knew how to act, almost knew what to say.

He turned on to Dixie Avenue in the fragrance of boxwood hedges and well-tended flower gardens. Dapper stalks of sunflowers bobbed in the sun-drenched side yards. A wealthy man named Steiner, who had moved from Atlanta a few years back, stood motionless in his clear-paned greenhouse, peeling dead leaves off a potted heliotrope. He wore heavy gloves and a tie. Wearing a tie to work among plants, thought Charlie. *The Heart of Propriety. Orange daylilies in a bed, a fig bush at-*

tended by hovering dark-winged birds. He saw the familiar green shape next to Bob Lamont's house: *Magnolia grandiflora . . . This magnificent tree grows abundantly along the seacoast and in the streets of Charleston . . . grows in Georgia also.* He thought of his bedside table and the books upon it. Then he thought of Duncan.

The pain began first this time in his left arm, a numb throbbing, rising up through his shoulder then down his chest, and he tried to comfort it, reason with it. Belle walked slowly ahead to a new Hudson parked on the street and sniffed its tires. This is my wound, he thought, the sourness of age, the flecks of pain that surge through my ribs. He closed his eyes and leaned on the cane and waited for what would come next. *She* would come next. He must push it back, as he waded through the murderous fire at Chickamauga and the air shaved breathless with shot in Decatur. He tried to put his mind on other things, on automobiles, and their leathered glories, the goose-honk of their horns, the others coming today, the absolution, the friend who died in his place, the rain and the fire. An icy breath came from his lips. He felt faint, then the feeling passed, and a surge of strength entered his long bones, and he felt Cleburne nearby, whispering.

Cleburne. Charlie remembered his gray eyes, steady in command, turning bright as he spoke of his Susan, the wound not hidden, as he hoped, beneath the wisps of beard. Charlie remembered Cleburne's love of Keats and the River Bride, his affection for Arkansas and a green rainy land where children starved. Most of all he recalled chess matches with Cleburne, the draws, unsolvable riddles, the stench of rain-ruined wool in his tent at night. Charlie recalled the slaughter at Kennesaw Mountain, when the Federals rose straight up the slopes into their deaths, almost as if they welcomed it. But mostly Cleburne: shot up and leaning in exhaustion among the whorls of poke and sumac, shouting for battle, for blood.

Belle stood looking up at Charlie, and he smiled down at the dog and realized the pain was gone, and in its place an unexpected euphoria had risen. It was morning, another morning. The day was a bouquet of gifts. Time was inexpressible by numbers or watches, and those numbers, by which men lived, seemed stale and vapid, for a life might be judged in the hours between starvation and violence.

I know she will not come.

April 19, 1864

DALTON

THE SNOW MELTED IN Cleburne's winter camp nine miles north of Dalton, and Charlie Merrill exulted in the warmth of late April, feeling strong, easy on his feet. Officers drilled the men, tightened discipline, worked them hard. The trees shot out green, and horses regained weight on forage as it grew. Spring was the season for sun-warmed amnesia, a time for men to deny the death rattle of winter limbs, to plant and pretend their escape was permanent and irreversible. A religious revival threatened to sweep the army, though it didn't quite get to Charlie's regiment. At night, the men still played poker and twenty-one, faro and chuck-a-luck. Sick call found fewer and fewer with rheumatism, pneumonia, scurvy, erysipelas, or jaundice.

This day, there had been a grand review of Johnston's entire army, forty thousand men with a snap in their stride. General Patrick Cleburne rode at the head of his seven thousand men, who marched with their own battle flag. Ladies from Dalton came out and fluttered handkerchiefs at the dazzling movement, the boys sharp in butternut and gray, most with shoes, and all well fed and rested. Johnston had been pleased, but behind his smile, the small, neat general, almost a dandy, knew a force of Yankees more than twice the size of his army was no more than twenty miles north. Now, in the camp twilight, Charlie sat hunched on a rough stump and finished a letter he was writing for Private Thomas Flournoy of Crossroads, Tennessee. Flournoy, a small man with no lips and enormous ears, stood nearby. This is what he had given to Charlie to "make pretty":

> *Der mother,*
>
> *I tak pin in hand to writ you now. Wel, iff you wory aboun me, you are not in need of it none, becas we are fed good on cornbrade and beefs are you etin good I hope so we her rumors of gen's Lees caught that old ape linkin now that would be the end of this war well maybe it aint tru a man here don't know here they say we will have a us a big fought soone and I am so redy.*

It ended there, a scrawl down a stained sheet of lined paper, thick marks of pencil. The effort had almost exhausted Flournoy.

"I just want you to pretty it up," said Flournoy. Charlie had done it several times for other men, and now they were coming to him, standing in line sometimes, offering him rations, which he refused.

"Then it won't sound like you," said Charlie. Thinking: *He doesn't want to sound like himself; he wants to sound like a thing he is not and never can be.* No matter. Charlie looked at the man's gray teeth, and a warm kindness rose in him. *Father, he thought. O my Father.* This is what Charlie wrote:

> *Dearest Mother,*
>
> *Do not worry about me, dear Mother, for I am safe, and the Army of Tennessee is gaining strength by the day. With God's grace, I shall survive until the end of this war, and I will come home and be with you.*
>
> *I am eating very well now, and most of us have shoes. The cold is over, thank God, and we expect to move into battle any day. I know that God will guide us with His strong hand and give to us the victory that must be ours . . .*

Charlie went on in this vein for a page and its back in fine print, giving a small amount of news wrapped in sentimental platitudes the men thought made them sound educated. When he got through, he read it to Flournoy, who was overcome with gratitude and mumbling emotion.

"I didn't know I could never sound nothing like that," he said.

"You *don't* sound nothing like that," said Bob Rainey in between gulps from his canteen. "That letter's got perfume all over it, Charlie."

"I suppose it does," said Charlie softly. He felt his own letter in his breast pocket. Sarah would be close to him when death came; he only hoped for thirty seconds to think of her bow-shaped mouth, her blue-gray eyes, her lovely blond hair. Thirty seconds would be enough, then he would fall downward into darkness.

"So, it's a damned fine thing for you to provide this service for young Flournoy and a fine thing for us to watch," said Bob Rainey. "After this war, they'll think our army was too ed-e-cated to have won, that's all."

"Ah, boys, it ain't education wins a war, and it ain't artillery and it ain't your flanks and charges," said Duncan McGregor.

"Read it back at me again," urged Private Flournoy.

"It's *fear* what wins a war, fear of dying," said Duncan. Bob Rainey sucked on his corncob pipe.

"I tell you one thing," said Rainey. "It ain't cornbread wins a war. I'm getting a mought sick of cornbread and blue beef."

"Read it back at me again," said Flournoy, and Charlie did, and then he gave the sheet to the Tennessee boy, who went away in slight awe of himself for such fine sentiments. Charlie stood and stretched and was about to say something about the weather when a horseman came riding up to their tent and dismounted. A major. The men stood, and Charlie thought: Not from our company, not from our brigade, but maybe from Division. The evening was blue and green and filled with the smoke of campfires and the smell of cooking, and there was the soft and pleasing jangle of cooking gear and tin cups. A light wind fluffed the major's rich, oily beard. Men played checkers and cards, and a number, including Charlie and Duncan, had running chess games, often with hand-carved pieces.

"General Cleburne sends his compliments and asks if Private Charles Merrill is hereabouts," he said. McGregor and Rainey looked at each other.

"Begging the major's pardon, but what has that fool Merrill done now?" asked Bob Rainey. "We never know from one day to the next what he might be about."

"I'm Merrill, sir," said Charlie. A sergeant came up in a dust cloud, riding a black horse and leading a mount. The major had a cold eye, but the sergeant looked relaxed and happy.

"General Cleburne sends his regards and asks to see you," said the major. Charlie felt that the message was wrong; a general officer does not *ask* to see a private. He *orders* him to appear. He does not send compliments, either. That was for fellow officers. But it was difficult to read Cleburne, a native Irishman who had lived in Arkansas for some years. He was fearless, and had been shot in the face during the Kentucky campaign, and his men trusted, even loved him. And yet there was something exotic about him, a clouded light behind his eyes, the knowledge of a lost and distant land.

"I'm at his service," said Charlie. The major cocked his head toward the empty horse, and Charlie swung himself up on to it. He had not been on a horse in some time, and in truth rode poorly, but the mount seemed easy, clopping in no special hurry through the camp, sidestepping men and fires. Charlie rode alongside the sergeant, who sang "Lorena" in a loud, off-key voice that cracked with roughness. Charlie winced.

"You ain't a music lover, private?" asked the sergeant, grinning.

"I am," said Charlie.

The sergeant laughed, and his tongue came out and shuddered twice. His beard was yellow, and his body seemed nothing but muscle. They were riding down a swale, and then uphill, past thousands of huts, of men all appearing to do the same things. The country was magnificent now that the rain and cold had left, and Charlie tried to take it all in from horseback. The sergeant sang a phrase or two of "Annie Laurie," but a phrase or two was all he knew, so he sang them over and over.

"I allays said one er these days, this army was gone have a fine mess with its rifles cause the Springfields take fifty-eight caliber, and the Enfield's a five-seventy-seven," the sergeant blurted. "Them five-seventy-fives fit 'em both but it's a fine damned thing to have sech a mess, ain't it, private?"

"Sir," said Charlie.

"I'd as lief have one of them pikes of Joe Brown's as an Enfield that's gone blow up on me. Or a thirty-pounder Parrott gun. I'd blow me some Yankees to kingdom come."

The officers had lived in small log huts during winter quarters, but Major General Patrick Ronayne Cleburne, thirty-five, was ready to march, and so he had moved into his normal field tent. The major pulled up before it, but the sergeant went forward. Charlie stopped with the major.

"Private, dismount and await orders," said the major.

"Yes, sir," said Charlie. He did, handing off the horse to a black groom who took it away, speaking softly to it and patting its long muzzle. Officers walked past in groups, and Charlie had never seen so many in one place, lieutenants, captains, majors. The major had pulled back the tent flap and disappeared inside for a moment, then the flap whipped back, and the major stood before him.

"Private, General Cleburne will see you now," he said.

"Yes, sir," said Charlie, saluting. He tested his emotions to see if fear was present, but it was not. Charlie went into the tent and saluted the tall, thin, gray-eyed general, who was smiling in the light of two lanterns.

"Private Merrill," said General Cleburne, rolling the R's. Sometimes, when giving orders, his Irish accent would vanish, but at his ease, the soft burr would come back, and he would seem wholly Irish. Everyone knew that Cleburne, who had been a cold-eyed commander from Shiloh to Missionary Ridge, was in love. He had gone on leave in January with his friend General William J. Hardee to Hardee's wedding in Mobile. There he had met Susan Tarleton, the maid of honor, a lovely twenty-four-year-old. Before he left to return to the cold hills of north Georgia, he had proposed, but Susan had demurred, though she said he could write, and promised to write him back. In early March, unable to stay away, he had traveled back to Mobile and proposed again, and this time Susan said yes. When Cleburne came back, he was changed, softer and more generous, dazed with happiness. Still, his eagerness for the spring campaign filled him with energy and hope.

Cleburne's belief in the Southern cause was complete, because he felt that Arkansas had saved him. He and most of his family had left Ireland at the height of the famine, and they arrived in New Orleans to find a country ripe with promise. He had been an apprentice apothecary in Ireland but had never earned the right to practice alone, and so when he heard of an opening for a drugstore employee in Helena, Arkansas, a town on the Mississippi River, he applied and won the job. Later, he read law and became an attorney before joining Yell's Rifles, a local company, at the outbreak of war. Now, through three bloody years of battles, through the horrors of Shiloh and the death fields of Chickamauga, Cleburne had grown in stature. Even President Jefferson Davis had praised him.

The inside of Cleburne's tent smelled of leather and coal oil, and Charlie saw a half-written letter lying on his camp desk, the pen flat across it like a sword on a family crest. Cleburne smiled slightly. He was not handsome, and he was missing two teeth in his left jaw from the face wound in Kentucky. The wispy beard did not hide his wound, and Charlie noticed at once how thin he was. And yet there was a kind light in his eyes, a gentleness around his mouth, that made his presence warming. Charlie had once been about a hundred feet from the general but no closer. He was certain there must be some confusion here.

"Reporting as requested, sir," said Charlie, saluting. Cleburne returned the salute.

"At your ease, private," said Cleburne. "Please." He pointed toward a campstool and Charlie removed his field cap and sat down. Cleburne rested in his chair and crossed his legs, his eyes glistening. A chessboard lay at one edge of the field desk, and a game was in progress, with the black pieces bearing down toward a victory. "You must wonder why I sent for you. You know, it took me some time to find out who you were."

"I do wonder, sir," said Charlie. "If I may speak freely."

"You may indeed. Would you like some coffee?"

"No, thank you, sir."

"Would you mind if I did?"

"Not at all."

"Buck?" cried Cleburne. The captain walked slowly into the tent and waited for orders. "Would you mind getting me a cup of coffee with some sugar in it?" Cleburne rubbed his hands together like a small boy ready for mischief. "I've a taste for it."

"Of course, General," said Buck. "Food, sir?"

"Not at present, but thank you, Buck."

The captain disappeared, and Charlie tried to sit straight on the campstool and await the general's pleasure.

"Private Merrill, you have developed quite a reputation in your brigade at such a tender age," said Cleburne. The word *brigade* came out *brrrigade,* and Charlie loved the music of the general's speech. "You arrived out of nowhere just before the fight at Chickamauga, a Georgia boy, with a rifle and a fearlessness. As I recall, we all but had to drag you off Missionary Ridge before our redeployment."

"I wanted to do my duty," said Charlie.

"Well done, Merrill, certainly well done," Cleburne said. "General Govan has spoken to me of you, and at first, he was considering a brevet promotion for courage under fire. But then he watched you in practice shooting with the other boys. He says you are one of the best shots he's ever seen."

"I thank General Govan for the compliment," said Charlie.

"Son, you may be less formal. Please. I would ask you, as a favor to me, please be less formal. Tell me about yourself."

"There is not much to tell, general. I will be seventeen this April. I was ill for much of my childhood though I managed during that time to become a good shot. Last summer, after Vicksburg fell, I gained strength and finally came to Atlanta in September and rode a boxcar north to our army. The first brigade I came to was the one now commanded by General Govan. After that, I have served in the ranks."

"I am told you are quite literate and even know something of literature," said Cleburne. "I'm a lover of the written word myself." Cleburne cleared his throat and struck a declamatory pose.

> *Now, Lycidas, the shepherds weep no more;*
> *Henceforth thou art the genius of the shore—*

Charlie broke in softly, looking into a lantern flame.

> *In thy large recompense, and shalt be good*
> *To all that wander in that perilous flood.*

Cleburne's eyes turned glassy with delight. Captain Buck came back with the coffee, and Cleburne sipped it with evident pleasure. Sounds of men laughing and talking filtered into the tent, and Charlie hardly knew what to say.

"Enjoy Milton, do you?" asked Cleburne.

"A great deal, though not so much as Keats," said Charlie.

Cleburne's voice had an odd hiss because of his missing teeth, and when his voice rose it was unpleasant, and he clearly knew it, so he kept the tones mellowed, low. He said:

> *A thing of beauty is a joy for ever:*
> *Its loveliness increases; it will never*
> *Pass into nothingness, but still will keep*
> *A bower quiet for us, and a sleep*
>
> *Full of sweet dreams, and health, and quiet breathing.*

"*Endymion,*" said Charlie. "That has always been one of my favorites. It was a great favorite of my father's in his youth."

"Well, I suppose the time for poetry is drawing to a close, but I have felt the urge to recite of late," said Cleburne.

"We have all heard of your happiness, general, and the men wholeheartedly approve, if I may say so."

"You may certainly say so," said Cleburne. "You most certainly may. Now, I know you must wonder why I have brought you here. Let me show you something." He went to a corner of the tent and reached into the shadows and lifted a rifle by the muzzle and brought it over. "Do you know what this is? Here." Cleburne handed the rifle to Charlie, who inhaled sharply as he took it.

"It's a Whitworth," said Charlie. "A sharpshooter rifle. Accurate sometimes to seventeen-hundred yards."

"Two thousand, at times, I'm told," said Cleburne.

"Magnificent," said Charlie, turning the burnished stock toward the light. All of the men in Cleburne's command, including Charlie, knew of his longstanding interest in sharpshooting teams. There were competitions to see who would be eligible, and the duty was dangerous but coveted, because the men had no camp duties and often ranged far on their own, picking off artillery soldiers from vast distances. Cleburne had been given two dozen Whitworths, and they were loved by all soldiers who valued accuracy, who yearned to be in the middle of unsupported danger. "It uses a forty-five-caliber twisted hexagonal bullet." Charlie held the heavy rifle up and looked down the barrel. "Telescopic sight."

"Our boys have used cylindrical bullets with only a small loss of accuracy," said Cleburne. "Molds for the twisted hexagonal bullets are hard to come by. How does it feel in your hands?"

"Like bread to a starving man," said Charlie. "I thought they were all designated to our men."

"The man who used this one has, alas, just died from pneumonia in the hospital, and as we are likely to move soon, I have no time for another contest to find a sharpshooter to handle it. We have twenty Whitworths and ten Kerrs. Quite a prized possession." Charlie could not quite grasp the meaning of the words. Was he being asked for an opinion? "I have asked Generals Polk, Lowrey, Govan, and Granbury who they think would be best, and General Govan without hesitation suggested you."

A faint happiness played in Charlie's eyes. He looked up at Cleburne, whose cheeks were bright with joy. Charlie could not remember seeing a happier man in his life. Perhaps that is what love did for a grown man—give him an invincible shield against all fear.

"This would be my rifle, and I would join your sharpshooter company?" asked Charlie.

"You would be the youngest by several years, but I trust your character. I have asked urgently about your character. You write letters for the men. You ask nothing. You allow others to defeat you at chess even though you are by all odds better than they are. I am right that you do play chess?" Charlie thought of Jack Dockery for the first time in days, of their endless matches, of laughter, kicking over a losing board, tactics and attacks.

"I play chess," said Charlie.

"This board here, for example," said Cleburne. "Do you see a way for the white pieces to claim victory?" Charlie looked at the board, and in a glance could see many moves ahead, could judge feints and maneuvers.

"I do not see a way for the white pieces to claim victory," said Charlie. "But I believe a defeat could be forestalled for some time."

"Precisely," said Cleburne. He set down the nearly drained cup of coffee and crossed his arms across his chest. "Then it is decided. You shall have the last Whitworth, Private Merrill, and you shall join my sharpshooter company. You will be able to work with others in the company or alone as you see fit, taking care to stay at least four hundred yards from the enemy. I should warn you that there is hardly a more dangerous duty."

"I shall take care to protect myself," said Charlie.

"You are what they say of you," said Cleburne. "Now is there anything else you would require? We will always give you ample ammunition. When the hexagonal rounds are available, they shall be given to you, but a cylindrical forty-five caliber will also fire. You are to kill as many of the enemy as you can. You will be killing men all day, possibly for weeks at a time. Are you up to that?"

"I will try not to mind," said Charlie. "There is one thing I might ask."

"Certainly."

"I have a friend named Duncan McGregor who has shared my tent since Chickamauga," said Charlie. "He is not a fine shot, but he is a good soldier and would amply assist me. We've been close as brothers since Chickamauga. He would guard me well."

"Then I will see that both of you are in the company. He can assist you as a scout. Can he use your Spencer?"

"Certainly."

"Finally, I would like for you to report to me in the evening and to sleep in a tent near my headquarters as the whole sharpshooter company does. Lieutenant Schell will be your commander. He's a good man, detached from the Second Tennessee Regiment. I should very much like to have a running game of chess with you and be able to speak of literature. There are few in this army who can do both."

"At your pleasure, General Cleburne."

"You should take the next few days to practice shooting the Whitworth. I think you will find it altogether remarkable. Now, I have a letter to finish. Captain Buck will escort you back to your camp. You and this McGregor may move here in the morning." Charlie stood and saluted.

"I'm grateful for the chance, General," said Charlie. "I will not fail you."

July 26, 1861

A **HEAVY RAIN SPILLED** off the roof of Grace House, dripping clear strands down the siding. Charlie sat at a third-floor window and watched the pecan trees wave and float in the strong wind. He had awakened the night before and heard the rain coming, like a distant army marching, thunder and wind, and suddenly, his room's curtains had been sucked into the frame, then blown back outward into the room. Since then, the rain had come hard, and Betsy Clark Merrill had brought Martha to the ballroom on the third floor to play with dolls and sew. Charlie was reading *Ivanhoe* for the third time. He could recite the first sentence from delighted memory: *In that pleasant district of merry England which is watered by the river Don there extended in ancient times a large forest, covering the greater part of the beautiful hills and valleys which lie between Sheffield and the pleasant town of Doncaster.* Charlie was on chapter 29, but his mind wandered.

Martha sat idly, watching her mother sew button eyes on a homemade doll. Martha was blonde, unlike Charlie, with huge brown eyes, dimples, and a calmness that rarely seemed to change. Her beauty astounded visitors, and her talent as a pianist amazed many, though she would not turn seven until November. She sat in a rocking chair and watched her mother sew, eyes not wandering, concentration complete. Charlie liked to sit and watch her, and most of the time she was gentle, but sometimes a mood would shake her, and her eyes would flame, her voice grow deep and resonant, her feet stamping, her hands reflexively hardening into fists.

There was a clomping on the stairs, one hard step then a softer one, like someone dragging something. In the late Forties, this had been the ballroom of Grace House, where Branton's lights came for dances, but after the Baptist Church bought it in a fit of Fifties prosperity, dancing was forbidden. Now it was a playroom, a rainy-day hideaway.

"Jack," said Charlie.

"I expect," said Betsy Clark Merrill. "Lately it looks like his foot is worse. I do wish there was something could be done for that boy."

"He never says anything about it," said Martha. "It must not hurt."

"It hurts, but he never says anything about it," said Charlie.

"Maybe he has a thorn, like the lion with his paw. What was the man who took out the thorn, Charlie?" This was Martha, turned to look with level love at her older brother.

"Androcles," said Charlie.

Jack hobbled up the last step and into the ballroom, his face flushed with the effort. He leaned on his good leg and looked down at his stockings.

"See, Mrs. Merrill, I took my shoes off before I came inside with mud. I'm much better behaved than Charlie."

"Jack, you're a prince," said Betsy Merrill.

"My pleasure, ma'am," said Jack, bowing low and sweeping an invisible hat, with invisible feathers sweeping the polished floorboards.

"This is making me ill," said Charlie. Jack walked to him, sliding his clubfoot along the floor behind him, smiling and humming.

"You're reading what again?" asked Jack.

"*Ivanhoe,*" said Charlie. "And how did you know I was reading something *again?*"

"You always read everything again. I never read anything more than once. I read *Hamlet* once and that was enough for me. I read a book about President Jackson. Very boring. Then I read a book about the indignities being heaped on the South. Now the war may already be over, and we won't be able to make soldiers."

"We can't say anything for sure," said Betsy. "Word is there is some fighting out to the west, and Mr. Lincoln is sure to use the men he's called up. I believe those who say the war is going to fall apart before it really starts may be quite wrong. I read books more than once. Maybe that's where Charlie gets it. I read *Ivanhoe* to him aloud when he was seven. He would seem to be sleeping, but if I stopped, he'd open his eyes and say, 'Mama, don't stop reading the story. I want to know what happens next.'"

"I don't understand make-believe stories," said Martha. "That doll Mama is sewing the eyes on, Jack? I don't make up stories that have her speaking of her prince or anything. I know she's nothing but cloth and buttons."

"A realist," said Jack.

"Come on, let's go to the front porch," said Charlie.

"Have you ever looked to see if there is a thorn in your foot?" asked Martha.

"Martha Merrill!" cried her mother.

Jack slid over to them, laughing, and Betsy saw that his smile was soft and genuine, almost as if his face had lost its focus. She knew from the way he carried the foot that it pained him, and yet he showed nothing. She felt her vision blur.

"I was born with a sick foot," said Jack. "Like you were born with dimples, and Charlie was born with no brain. No use bucking against the way things are. Like your older brother Tom was born to have opinions."

"Is that a philosophy?" asked Martha. "Papa is always talking about philosophies."

"Something Jack knows nothing about, alas," said Charlie. "Come on, let's go sit on the porch now."

"Good day to you, ladies," said Jack.

"I'm not a lady, not yet," said Martha, giggling.

"Soon," said Jack, "you will be. Mrs. Merrill." He bowed again and limped to the stairs, and Charlie descended behind him, their unmatched footsteps on the hollow-sounding stairs, and the rain harder than before and dampening the floorboards near the open windows to the north.

MAIN STREET WAS MOSTLY deserted beyond them, with an occasional slow-walking horse swaying in the mud. Once, a sun-splintered brougham, now streaked with rain, rattled past with hissing wheels in the damp ruts. The driver held his reins loosely. Those inside had lowered the curtains against the water.

"Hasn't been this cool since early spring," said Jack.

"No," said Charlie.

"I wonder what it was like for them in Virginia, fighting the Yankees all the way back to Washington City. My daddy says the French and English will come in on our side any day, because they have to have cotton. They won't have any clothes without our cotton."

Charlie didn't answer. He was thinking of his father and wondering what he might say in his sermon tomorrow. Contributions had begun to dry up, and his father still visited the ill and the hapless, but the light in his eyes seemed shuttered, unsupported by his soul. His health had faded.

"Did you hear about Joe Hopewell?" asked Jack.

"What?"

"He got drunk on his daddy's bourbon and then was sick right at the courthouse on the sidewalk. His old man whipped him with a razor strop right in front of everybody there. It made Joe cry, and you know what a big tough boy he is."

"I didn't hear that."

"You ever had a taste of it?"

"Liquor? That's the devil's brew. Papa's told me that since I was little. I don't want to wind up like Henry Brown staggering drunk all over town. Have you tasted it?"

"Not yet."

"Then you might?"

"I don't know. I don't know what I might do in the future. You think you know what you'll do, but we don't know until it happens. Let me ask you something. If you had been in that battle in Virginia and they were coming at you with guns firing, would you have stood there and died or run off? How would you know what was right? What if God meant you to save souls later?"

"I wouldn't do the wrong thing."

"You lose at chess to keep me from feeling bad. That's not honest."

"I don't do that."

"Sure you do. Never mind. Who do you think the first person from Branton will be killed in the war?"

"Jack, you're running on at the mouth."

"Okay, then who's the prettiest girl in Branton?"

Charlie knew the boundaries of this game well enough. For years, when camping or walking down the street, Jack would ask him the same question. They would debate the merits of this Ella or that Jane, plantation daughters, merchant girls. Blondes or brunettes. Blue eyes or brown. Now they spoke, too, of shape, the spilling curves, the blush of a cheek. Neither had had a girlfriend, and Jack, with his obvious deformity and Charlie, small and prone to illness, expected none soon. They attended Mr. Marker's School, an academy in a once-fine house on South Main Street. The schoolroom, for boys and girls, was overheated in winter by a potbellied stove, and pleasant in spring and fall with its tall windows thrown open to a cross breeze. Jack was as excellent at mathematics as Charlie was poor.

Charlie watched the rain and thought of the picnic that ended school in the spring. He had found himself standing near Susan Meadows beneath the limp whips of a willow tree in the academy's side yard. Mr. Marker was, for once, not walking around with his pale, emotionless eyes glazed on their movements. He sat on a blanket with his new wife, who was small and looked afraid all the time. Susan: light brown hair, green eyes, a ready laugh. She was new to town, and her father had delicate manners and sold clothing at Mr. Rosenbloom's. She and Charlie had talked of nothing, but the sun caught her hair, blew it shimmering, until it seemed almost a pale mist. Now, he thought of her, thin and sweet, leaning to whisper in his ear a single sentence before she ran across the academy yard: *I like you, Charlie Merrill!* What, exactly, did that mean? Perhaps it was borne on the edge of pity, or did she find his face attractive and worth love? Charlie went home that night and looked for a long time in a mirror, and he saw changes, his face longer and a new maturity around the eyes, but perhaps it was his imagination. Maybe Susan hadn't said anything. Dreams took him sometimes, and he awoke unconvinced that they were filmy suppositions. He had not seen Susan for nearly a month now, and thought of dropping around to her house, but he could not make himself. She was too pretty, too particular. Perhaps it was merely kindness.

"I don't know."

"You don't know who's the prettiest girl in Branton? Well, I do," said Jack. "It's Mary Singleton. Her chest is growing faster than the corn in July. I'd like to thrash about with her in a hay barn."

"You're dreaming," said Charlie, grinning. "No girl in this town would have you or me, either. Every other boy older enough to shave's off being a hero in the war, and we're just boys sitting on a front porch in the rain, you with a sick foot and me skinny as a book page. We got nothing to offer a girl that's she'd exchange for holding hands, much less thrashing about in a hay barn. We'd have to pay a girl to let her kiss us."

"It's just my opinion, sir, that some girls would like a man with a sturdy limp," said Jack. "I think it adds character. That's what my mother has always told me."

"She *has* to lie. She's your mother."

"Of course, you are too thin for any girl to want. That part is definitely true."

Richard Powers, a deacon of the church, rode up, tied his horse and came past them, grim-faced, heading inside. Charlie's eyes narrowed.

"Well, here's to good lies and soft girls."

"You're hopeless," grinned Jack. "Utterly hopeless."

THE NEXT DAY WAS warm and dry, and Charlie and Jack stood behind Grace House near the grape arbor that shimmered in a tense wind. The heat cramped them, oppressive, but Charlie leveled his musket and raised it toward eye level.

"Hit that from here, and I'll give you a thousand dollars in gold," said Jack.

"You don't have five cents in copper," said Charlie.

"Okay, I'll give you the entire contents of my pockets."

"Oh, boy."

"Which includes," said Jack, reaching in and removing his pockets' contents, "a penny, a loop of packing string, a key to nothing, and my piece of lucky amber."

"A key to nothing?" Charlie lowered the gun and looked at his friend.

"I found it in an alley," said Jack. "I have a theory, sir, that the most valuable keys in this kingdom are the keys to nothing."

"*That* makes sense."

"It does, sir. It makes as much sense as you do. A sickling boy who shoots as if his gun had eyes. I think your varied sicknesses are caused by poisoning from gunpowder. And take this string. It could be a hangman's knot or the binding of a book which tells the secrets of the world."

"And I suppose your lucky amber has some special meaning, too."

"Certainly, sir," said Jack. "It is the guarantee that one side or the other will win this war. I promise it."

"Your logic is breathtaking."

"Applause," said Jack. "Okay, then. My penny says you cannot hit that can over there across the tracks."

"Ah," said Charlie. He brought the gun back up, and the effort made his arms shake slightly, but then a deep calm settled into his upper body, and he squeezed the trigger, and the can, two hundred yards away, screamed upward, as if tossing itself for fun. Jack sighed and flipped the penny toward Charlie, sun on sun on sun.

"But you're not getting my key to nothing," said Jack. Charlie grinned, nodded.

July 22, 1914

⚝ ⚝
⚝

CHARLIE STOOD IN THE the library of Grace House looking at the names along the spines of books, familiar and leather-struck, gilt shining in the sharp morning light. These were his last and best friends, foxed pages, steel engravings, volumes that marked the passage of his days. He took out a black volume and opened it: *The Life, Speeches and Public Services of James A. Garfield . . .* The title wandered on for another seventeen words. Published in Boston by B. B. Russell. The flyleaf had grown the brown speckles of an old man's hands. President Garfield, in his engraved portrait, looked bored or even petulant, face hidden in a beard that was now lost to fashion. After Lincoln, it seemed American presidents were doomed to violent deaths.

The library smelled of leather and dust, mostly history and biography. His tastes ran to Greece and Rome, to the early years of the Great Republic. On his desk lay a familiar oversized book: *Merrill's History of Branton County,* which had been struck in an edition of three hundred. All of them were eventually sold, but it took four years. Charlie looked at the book and knew it contained statistics, stories, and family lies. During his years as a newspaperman, he had written five books and achieved considerable national fame. Three were novels, and their long stories, of families bearing sorrow, of loves achieved, brought letters from all over the country.

He walked across the room to his globe, an expensive blue ball sunk in the half circle of a mahogany frame, where it could be turned. He pushed it around to Europe, looking at the white bristles on the back of his hand, the yellowed fingernails, the slight tremor. Barry said that war was near, and Charlie believed it. Soon enough, men would have enough of peace anywhere, in place or time. They would feel an unassailable urge to destroy everything they had made, to spill blood, wreck cities, purge ideas. They would line up against each other and scythe down strong young men with murderous weapons—the teeth of an animal grown more perfect and voracious each year. Charlie felt the shadow again, hovering near him and whispering his name. He could do little else about it now.

Only one other person could know what he felt. *But she will not come.*

Small, rapid footsteps came down the hallway, paused, then turned into the library, and Charlie craned back and smiled broadly.

"Catherine," he said. "I'm so happy to see you this morning, dear."

"Papa, Mrs. Knight said you ate nothing, took Belle for a walk, and haven't written your speech. She called me on the telephone and said you were acting strange. Barry said you refused to pose for a photograph in your uniform. You've kept it in good condition in the attic all these years—what are you waiting for, the *hundredth* anniversary of the battle?"

Catherine Phillips stood in a fierce pose of love, arms down. She wore a fashionable green dress, not the high-collared affairs of her mother, but more comfortable, easier to manage with two children. She was not smiling but seemed more nettled than worried, her chestnut hair moving as she spoke. Always, Charlie recalled, she was an animated child, dancing along the hallways, running into rain with her head up, mouth open, as if she could inhale all nature. She was a force, a dimpled wind that lifted everything before it. He walked painfully to her, not showing the discomfort, of course, and he grasped her shoulders and kissed her on the cheek. She smelled of rosewater and freshly cut fabric.

"Cath, you look lovely this morning."

"And you are changing the subject this morning. What were you doing walking the dog in this heat? Looking for a weed in the family plot?"

"Just me," he said, laughing out loud.

"I worry about you, Papa," she said. Her voice was gentle and edged, like book leaves blessed with gold. She shifted from one foot to another, impossibly restless, loving motion as a young animal does, impossibly fit to frolic. He felt only a need for poise and slow motions. Perhaps he would turn into a statue one day, and that would be death.

"I'm not wearing some ridiculous uniform for a picture. Barry had to ask, and I had to say no. I will be firing Mrs. Knight as soon as you leave for being quarrelsome beyond bearing."

"Again?" said Catherine.

"She *should* be fired again. I've already fired her once this morning. Sometimes I fire her five times a day."

"Papa, is it true you haven't written a word of your speech?" There was a sound from outside, and Charlie walked past the globe, past the leather ranks of books, to the open window and saw Marianne and Lewis, his grandchildren, chasing each other in the grass where dew had now dried away. He leaned on the whitewashed windowsill and inhaled the fragrance of morning and loved the vision of their happiness. Marianne, a head taller, was explaining the rules of some secret game to her brother.

"It's true, and I'm going to have to fire Mrs. Knight for that, too. I must have mentioned it to her. Darling, don't worry about me. I don't think anybody much is going to come anyway. That battle happened before most people in town were born. I was just a boy myself. I don't know what else there is to say. It's hard to remember what all the fuss was really about. Everybody had his own reason for wanting to fight, and maybe I'll think of something to say before this afternoon. Marianne looks just like you did as a little girl."

"Are you all right? That's all I worry about. People get . . . wandery . . . sometimes when they are, uh . . . ."

"Old? I'm fine, Cath. Really. History's just a succession of wars we fight to create a sense of history. We scratch ourselves to see if we can still bleed. Being able to be mad and then bleed means you're not dead yet. Then it gets to be an epidemic. I'm overflowing with aphorisms today. Mr. Darwin would be sickened to know how little we've changed as a species."

"You're a tease, Papa. Stop with the evolution stuff. You know I don't believe it."

"I believe in God *and* Charles Darwin. And men of good will believe with their hearts in war. Science, death, religion—everything fits,

Cath. Revenge, murder, blood sacrifice—it's all part of a great myth we carve to remind us that we have been alive. But what if this is all some fever dream of a giant? What if the suffering and the monstrous lies are nothing more than fancy stories?"

"I think I feel an oration coming on," said Cath. For the first time since she'd come in the door, she felt better. This was her father, the town's conscience, the intellect, the man who would consider any idea, even the most frightening.

"No more orating." Charlie turned back to the window. Out there, Marianne and Lewis were playing tag on a summer morning. That's the edge of happiness, and from there it's all worry and bother. The greatest gift is the wonder of the childlike. Catherine stared at her father through a blur of tears that she quickly wiped away while his back was turned to her. All her life, he had been speaking this way, perhaps damaged by an unseen misfortune, a captive to his mulling, a man whose columns in the *Eagle* had been reprinted all over America for two decades. Now he had chosen silence, and the soul he had sought to repair through words was complete or not reparable. She loved him enormously, thought of his death, felt she could not bear it. When he vanished, her vitality would slip away, too, into his faraway pain.

She came to him and put her arms around him from behind and rested her head on his back, and through the shirt, she felt his bones, the cage of his ribs, the heart still speaking in its sluggish thumps. Charlie felt himself rise, felt his soul grow larger than his body, drift upward over Grace House in a moment of pure repose. He wondered if we choose our epiphanies or if the map for all life was scripted distant centuries past.

April 20–May 8, 1864

DALTON

CHARLIE AND DUNCAN STOOD high on Rocky Face Ridge near Dalton, staring across the green-bearded mountain at a plank seventeen-hundred yards away that Duncan had emblazoned with a large X. Charlie gauged the heft and displacement of the Whitworth rifle after he'd loaded it, ramming the cartridge down the long hexagonally rifled barrel. It was heavy, but there was a certainty about it, its solidity a promise of accuracy. The day had risen lovely and fair, and a soft warmth filled the sky high above Dalton. Drilling had increased, but Charlie and Duncan no longer marched or performed camp duties. They reported to Lieutenant Schell of the sharpshooter company, which was camped near Cleburne's Division headquarters, and took a tent there, met the other men. Most of them were cool and disdainful of the young new recruit until he'd fired a few rounds from his Whitworth and hit a target consistently at twelve hundred yards.

The army seemed more ready for battle every day, certain of its desire for motion. When Joe Johnston had taken over from Bragg, the army was in tatters, sick and deserting. Freezing and coughing men vomited, squatted at the edge of camp with violent diarrhea, picked lice and bedbugs. The camp's smell annoyed some of the Dalton ladies and a few of the gentler men. The hospital was full of dying men, embarrassed that they lacked wounds. One man, near death from typhoid, begged a friend to sneak him a pistol, and then blew his own brains out.

Little by little, their strength had returned, both in numbers and health, and the spring campaign, which would start soon, would be bloody and decisive. The soldiers had no idea which way things would go; some bet on a new push into Tennessee to retake Chattanooga, while others, knowing Sherman outnumbered them nearly two to one, saw only retreat toward Atlanta.

Now, with morning drill over, a few boys from Charlie's old company in General Daniel Govan's Brigade stood on the ridge and watched. Bob Rainey could not see the wisdom in climbing this peak just for a little target practice, until Duncan explained the range of the Whitworth rifle and the inadvisability of firing it anywhere near troops. There were troops on Rocky Face Ridge, but they were lower and farther south this morning.

"I don't think there's a man could hit that plank with a Parrott gun," said Tyree Baskins, a nearly bald man in his late thirties from near Little Rock. Baskins chewed a plug of tobacco, and the oily residue dripped into his beard. A boy named Isaac Kennon stood not far away, scratching his head and holding his Enfield, butt to the ground. Kennon had been afraid every day for the past eighteen months and ran away for a time at Chickamauga then came back, begging forgiveness. One of his own men was about to turn him in to the officers when that man took a minié ball in the nose. Afterward, when Kennon lay wounded himself, with the meat of his left forearm folded back in a bloody flap, everyone forgot his brief desertion.

"I don't reckon *God* could hit that plank with a Parrott gun," said Bob Rainey. Isaac Kennon laughed nervously.

"Boys, meet God," said Duncan McGregor. "Not meaning anything disrespectful nor nothing of the sort."

Charlie lifted the gun, and its weight was astonishing. Trading a light, rapid-fire Spencer for this seemed an odd swap, but he already knew the Whitworth's value. He held it shoulder high, pushing his muscles against the long weight of the rifle, judged the distance with his sight, looked through the telescope, saw an X on the plank. He squeezed his trigger, and the Whitworth gave a ferocious bark, and a smell of black powder drifted over them. They saw a shudder in the plank, but it had not fallen.

"Goddamn, he missed the whole plank," said Tyree. "Isaac, run down there and get that thing and bring it back." Isaac was not afraid now, and pleased to be doing something, he handed his rifle to Bob

Rainey and walked the crest of the ridge. Charlie lowered the Whitworth and waited. He dreamed of standing high on Rocky Face Ridge or perhaps lying down, looking into the valley below. He smiled lightly.

Isaac Kennon walked rapidly back to them with the plank under his arm, a three-foot-long slat that shone dully in the morning sun. Tyree leaned over slightly and spat a long, sticky stream of tobacco juice, almost hitting Duncan's brogan. Below them, far down, the drill had long ended, but thousands of men were moving with no discernable pattern—no, thought Charlie, *tens* of thousands.

"God*damn*dest thing I ever seed in my life," said Isaac, walking up to them, now breathing hard. His clothes were stitched up roughly, as if sewn by a drunken tailor. He held the board before him, set it down in the sun-warmed pine needles. A cool wind tousled Charlie's curly black hair, but little expression creased his face.

"Jesus Mary Mother of Christ, won't you lookee here," said Bob Rainey. "Boys this ain't our young Charlie, this is damn Davy Crockett."

A clean forty-five-caliber hole had splintered the board at the cross of the X. Isaac, standing behind the board, stuck the little finger of his right hand through the hole and waggled it.

"Stick your pecker through it, Isaac," said Bob Rainey. "It'll make the hole look bigger." The men laughed, and even Isaac grinned, taking no offense at the joke. Charlie laughed out loud, but they had no reason to bring the board to him. He knew where the bullet had gone, where it would always go with this rifle.

CHARLIE SAT AT THE chessboard and stared for a long time at the pieces and then back up at General Patrick Cleburne. The general's chief of staff, Major Calhoun Benham, came in and out of the tent, and sometimes Cleburne would step aside to speak with him, to look at a map, to write orders or receive them. Sometimes Captain Irving Buck came in or Major J.K. Dixon, assistant inspector general. Cleburne's aides, Mangum and Hanly, had been with him since Helena, and they silently went about their business, bringing coffee, offering Charlie a cigar, which he declined. A hazy smoke lay over the army's winter quarters.

"I suppose we will be moving soon, general?" asked Charlie.

"I cannot say, as I am forbidden," said Cleburne.

'I understand, but the men are ready. I'm ready. The Whitworth is a fine instrument."

"I hear that you have astounded the rest of my sharpshooters with your accuracy. My only wish is that you stay a quarter mile from the enemy. Experience tells me that when a man has a gun that will kill from such a distance, he is more eager by the minute to use it. They will train fire from artillery batteries on you. Their own sharpshooters will watch for your puff of smoke and then target you. And of course you know by now the loud pop the Whitworth makes. It is distinctive, if heard."

"I am not so afraid of dying," said Charlie.

"We must not be afraid to die in this fight, for it is that, certainly, a great and majestic cause, Mr. Merrill." Cleburne moved a bishop forward three spaces and held it for a time before removing his hand. "Perhaps you might wish to join the Comrades of the Southern Cross, which I founded. Have you heard of it?"

"Yes, sir," said Charlie. "Perhaps." Though a number of officers felt compelled to sign an oath, Cleburne's organization, modeled on the Masons, of which he was a member, drew little support and mild derision in the ranks.

"I detect a reticence, if I may say so," said Cleburne. "Please speak freely. I do so enjoy your company, and I have no wish for you to feel pressure."

"I have a belief—call it a dream, sir—that I shall be witness to something in the coming campaign that shall change me," said Charlie. "I cannot imagine what it is, but something will change me, and I will never be the same again."

Cleburne's gray eyes narrowed, and he rubbed a single finger down the scar on his face. "You are only a boy, but boys are not the only persons who change," said Cleburne. "I only know there are things one must live for. You must have a mother and a father, perhaps a sweetheart at home." Charlie smiled ruefully but said nothing. "One must have a lady in this world, Mr. Merrill. One must have a reason to bring this war to a successful close some day."

"Do you think it will have a successful close?"

Cleburne's eyes continued to smile, but his mouth went slightly slack, and he turned and stared into a lantern flame.

"I suppose that depends on what General Sherman does," said Cleburne. "We receive reports that his army is very large indeed. We must feint and thrust like a swordsman. I have full trust in General Johnston. He will look after his boys."

"The men think him almost a god," said Charlie. "He has restored hope, no small thing for a man, young or old."

Cleburne's smile returned.

"You are wiser than your years, Mr. Merrill," said Cleburne. "Might I ask what they think of me?" Charlie could not quite believe he was asking, but the truth was easy enough to repeat.

"Your men all wish they had half as much courage and a fraction as much knowledge of war and compassion," said Charlie. Cleburne laughed and shook his head.

"What I have learned as a soldier I have learned on horseback," said Cleburne. "You needn't say it. I *know* I always ride a slow horse, but I'm only an adequate rider, my boy. In my youth in Ireland I rode only rarely, and so now I am wary of being thrown. Great generals are not afraid of being thrown from their mounts. Do you know what I was before the war?"

"I have read that you were an attorney in Arkansas."

"I was once shot on the streets of Helena while standing by for a man in something of an ambush. And he wasn't even my best friend. I nearly died. Shot through the back."

"I have never yet been shot," said Charlie. "And you were wounded in Kentucky."

"With these teeth lost, I hiss, I fear," said Cleburne. Charlie advanced a pawn two spaces. "I have the devil's own pride, though. I want to live for my Susan, not die in some pointless charge, and God grant that we never be called upon to do such a thing. I have never in my life been prouder of my men than I was at Missionary Ridge, when we were the last standing and the last to leave. I am near tears in the face of such sacrifice, Mr. Merrill."

"We did not break," said Charlie.

"Your tactics on the chessboard are not those of a man seeking death," said Cleburne. "I believe you will see what must change you."

"I am not afraid, sir."

"When we were the last division to leave Missionary Ridge in Chattanooga before we came south to this place, you fought on with the best of them," said Cleburne. He considered moving a rook down his line of defense then took his hand away. "It is true that, up close, fear and courage sometimes look the same. Nevertheless, I shall be counting upon you as the spring campaign begins. Please know that I would not want to lose you."

"There are only so many things one can lose, general," said Charlie. "I will do my best to honor your trust."

"Protect yourself well," said Cleburne, putting his hand briefly on

Charlie's shoulder, then taking it away. He looked to one side, and a mist seemed to film his eyes. "When I was young, I would sit and watch the water in the River Bride and wonder where it flowed and whence it came. Boys are given to such philosophies, as if they have discovered the world and all its treasures alone and for the first time. But then the blight came, and all the potatoes in Ireland died, and I saw them starve about me, thousands of little girls and boys, old men and women, the foul and profane and the saintly and kind. And I knew that we are not vouchsafed a clear passage in this life, and that in the end we must have done our duty as we see it. I believe God will always show us the way. It was God no doubt who caused me to attend General Hardee's wedding where I met Miss Susan Tarleton. We must remain as witnesses if we are able, Charlie. Witnesses to the justice of God."

"When the time comes, I will be ready," said Charlie. Cleburne stared at the chessboard, but he was not seeing it.

"I was ready at Shiloh," he almost whispered. "I was ready, Charlie Merrill. Almost every officer in my brigade past captain fell in that terrible fight. My command was nearly erased from the earth, and I stood in the midst of it like a feather in a storm, and I was unharmed. The charge we were ordered to make that April was nothing short of a command to suicide. And I rode back and forth, hoping that my death would inspire the men, but the bullets seemed to part around me like the Red Sea around Moses. I cannot think why unless God was sparing me to greater glory. But God! Ah, God! Those boys who will never walk again!"

"I can only tell you that I will try to guard my fear," said Charlie. "I have reasons for wishing to live." It was Charlie's move, and he raced a rook the length of the board and cornered Cleburne in an awkward, if not fatal position. Cleburne stared at the board for a moment before a mild grin spread across his face.

"Most boys would lose on purpose to a general," he said. "Especially the highest ranking foreigner in the Confederate Army. Being so far away from my homeland and all. Most boys would lose and be done with it."

"I suspect you would think the less of me for it," said Charlie.

"Indeed I would, Mr. Merrill," said Cleburne.

Cleburne showed Charlie the map spread on his field table. Starting at Dalton, Cleburne drew his finger south over the towns of Tilton, Resaca, Calhoun, Adairsville, and Kingston and then to the Etowah River.

He kept dragging it from Allatoona to Acworth and then Kennesaw Mountain. Atlanta lay next. Cleburne lifted his hand, scratched his face, and glanced up at Charlie. Benham came into the tent.

"Sir, General Johnston requests the pleasure of your company at his headquarters," said Benham. "As rapidly as you can get there, sir."

"Very well, Benham," said Cleburne. "Thank you."

Charlie stood and dusted off his pants and prepared to leave. The Whitworth leaned against the general's tent pole, and he lifted it, enjoyed the weight with a quiet pleasure.

"I shan't resign from this game just yet," said Cleburne. "We will remember our positions and take it up again when we can. I shall send for you as I have time."

"With pleasure, General," said Charlie.

"Might I ask one question before you leave?"

"Certainly, General."

"When writing a young lady, should I say her eyes are like moons or like the sea? Which in your mind is better? I am an awkward man with a pen in my hand." Charlie smiled at the general's timidity, saw a blush spreading up the dark skin of his neck.

"I should think we might say her eyes are like moons, low over a calm sea," said Charlie. Cleburne bit his lip slightly and nodded.

"Well done," he said. "Quite. Moons low over a calm sea. I shall let you know if it has the requisite effect."

"Sir."

TWO DAYS PASSED, THEN three, and Charlie watched with growing excitement the snap and stride of the men, their new order and resolve. He and Duncan took target practice each day with the Whitworth, and Charlie felt more and more certain of the weapon's capacities. He spent time with another sharpshooter in the company, an Alabamian named Walter Bragg, a decent fellow who could also bear down on a target with his Whitworth to fine advantage. The Kerr rifles seemed to have slightly less range, but they could also shatter board targets at fifteen hundred yards. Target practice, which had been going on for all the infantry, continued each day.

The weather warmed even more, and rumors spread through the camp—that Sherman was marching into Alabama, that Longstreet would arrive soon with his corps to strengthen Johnston's Army. Hundreds of men took their baptisms from ministers before the campaign began. Earlier in the winter, near Dalton, there had been a revival, and ten men had come to a mourner's bench to confess their sins to God and be saved.

"This huge tree'd been burning nearby for two days, all a-smoldery from lightning," said Duncan. "And when the ten men sat upon the bench, there was a great creak and crack, and the tree fell with the speed of thunder across them and kilt all ten at once. They buried each in a coffin. They had asked God to take them, and he had. Such ways are strange indeed."

Charlie knew about the ten sinners' deaths, but men retold the same stories over and over to test their truth. To soldiers, the idea of a coffin was strange, exotic. They had seen hundreds of their fellow soldiers buried without a shroud, and beasts had dug up the carrion before the flesh had fallen from the bone. There was no peace for a soldier's body. Now, as they sat at their campfire, drinking coffee, Duncan and Charlie cleaned their rifles and listened to the murmur of thousands. A great swath of firefly camp lights spread up the slope of Rocky Face Ridge, and attenuated bursts of laughter fluttered from flame to flame.

"Do you think about dying in battle?" asked Duncan. "I cannot stay the thought, Charlie. Each morning, I think it shall be the day of my death. And I think of all the world before me that I shall never see. Ah, God, I would be a witness to this majesty. For that is what it is—a majesty we shall never see again."

Charlie looked at his companion, felt a kind sadness. Duncan seemed rather old, weary, and impatient to see the journey's end.

"I feel a great sorrow for it all," said Charlie. "And I have had this dread of dying, Duncan, of the shot coming for me. It is in great heat, in summer, and I fear I will know, for a moment, that a shot is for me and that I will never get home."

Duncan looked down the barrel of his rifle one last time and set it aside. He sipped cool coffee from his dented tin cup. A man not far away seized up with hacky coughing, spitting phlegm and wheezing as he walked.

"Brighten up, my boy," said Duncan with his Scots burr. "Any man who sees a death in war will never find it, God is my witness. We needn't suffer more than God made us for."

"We all suffer anyway," said Charlie.

"I believe in protecting my country," said Duncan, "but I've no sympathies with the rich landowners. Our people was never but the poor, and I know that when I die, it shall be for a rich man and not for my country. But no single man can sway the course of history. I am swept along in it, and I cannot gainsay it, Charlie."

"I think the entire war is a tragic mistake," said Charlie quietly. "I think the South will lose, and I think it deserves to. Slavery seems monstrous. I'd appreciate it if you kept that opinion to yourself as I don't wish to be staked out and shot before the war starts again." He laughed, but it was not genuine.

"You're lucky to have a friend in me, son," said Duncan. "And watch your tongue, or the world will treat you ill." They were quiet for a time. "The men speak of your meetings with Old Pat. They cannot quite understand how a mere boy has been taken to friendship by one of the best generals in the whole Confederate army. And him an Irishman to boot. Understand, I can *bear* your Irishman. I wish no man ill will. But they are by and large a sorry lot, unfit for fierce battle, and moved by petty hatreds."

Charlie laughed and set the Whitworth gently aside.

"But you were not more than a boy when your parents moved here from Scotland," said Charlie.

"A Scotsman don't lose his patrimony when he moves, son," said Duncan, grinning. "All of us carries with us every relative and ancestor of ours, and that is a call to honor. Poor Evan Cason found that out."

"All he did was run away because he was afraid," said Charlie. "Being shot three times for being frightened seems a terrible wage for it."

"That's sedition, and I'll remind you again how proud you should be to have a friend in yours truly," said Duncan McGregor. "I will always guard over you. I will do that." He looked away, embarrassed, full of emotion.

A loud argument over cards erupted not far away. Someone was probably cheating, Charlie thought. He looked at the campfires, was glad Duncan held nearby.

DRILLING INTENSIFIED WITH THE heat. For three nights running, Cleburne was far too busy to resume the chess game or send for Charlie, who spent his time on Rocky Face Ridge firing his Whitworth and listening to others in the sharpshooter company give hints for a clean kill, to avoid overshooting, when to move back after an officer falls.

"Sometimes, men in an artillery battery will watch one of their own crumple and fall, and they will poke him to see if he has fainted, not even having heard the shot that killed him," said Lieutenant Schell.

"I'd like to see that," said Isom Bedgood, a South Carolinian who had been sick all winter but was now strengthening, though still hollow-faced, globe-eyed. He coughed, stood wracked, then hoicked, spat. Bedgood was a deadly shot but new to the company. Charlie watched him with amazement, for he must have been past fifty, and his beard was brushed with white and gray. He was also unnaturally tall, with his upper body at a weary angle to his legs, making him seem unlikely for this duty. But Charlie had seen him split a target at nearly two thousand yards, and his hands held their burden of steel and wood easily.

"I've done it many a time," said Walter Bragg, the Alabamian. "It takes them a minute sometimes even to come look, but when they see that clean forty-five-caliber hole, they know right away, and they start looking to higher places around them, watching for the glint on a barrel or another breath of smoke. And I've seen our own boys picked off by sharpshooters on the other side. It's a fearsome thing, boys. Worse than having an artillery shell blow you to bits. Because then there's no dying. I've hit a man in the head clean a few times, but mostly it's the chest and once in the throat, and there's all manner of shock and suffering."

"We all need to realize that casualties in this company are usually high," said Lieutenant Schell. "We will be operating in teams without support, looking for opportunity, not standing with massed fire against a charge or a flanking."

"Lieutenant, ain't this gone be the end of it?" asked Tommy Wallace, a courageous Texan who had been in Granbury's Brigade. "Ain't we gone chase them back into Tennessee? My fields is gone two years without seeing a plow, and there's apt to be trees there if I don't get home soon."

"It won't end even this year," said Charlie. They all turned and looked at him. Duncan touched his sleeve.

"That's for the will of God and General Joseph Johnston," said Lieutenant Schell. "I believe both will make good use of us. I want you all to stay alive and inflict what damage you can—that's all you can do. There's a hundred men out there in the ranks who'd take your places. No camp duties, no drill, and sometimes not even marching twelve miles one way and turning around and marching right back. We report back each night to division headquarters and camp there. If you're where you can't move, then come in the next day, but stay alive. And scout and kill. General Cleburne has the eyes of several thousand men upon us—he will know what we have done before we report it. Duty demands our best work."

"What in the hell is that son of a bitch doing?" asked Isom Bedgood. Down the ridge, a feebleminded man named Holtzminger was moving the target board back to the edge of the crest, a little more, Charlie thought, than two thousand yards away.

"Ain't a man living could hit that," said Wallace.

"Merrill? You want to have a go at it?" asked Lieutenant Schell.

"I do," said Charlie. A deep calm settled over him. The wind was warm and flowing, a river that raked the pine trees bristling along the rocks. Axmen had felled many trees atop the ridge, though, and the sharpshooters held a clear line of sight to the edge where Holtzminger had placed the target.

"Pretend it's that Ape Lincoln," said Bedgood.

"Naw, pretend it's old Billy Sherman," said Bragg, who was very tired of being asked if he were kin to the lately deposed and much unloved General Braxton Bragg.

Charlie rammed the powder and cartridge down the barrel of the Whitworth. He lifted it, loving the weight and balance of it. He put his right eye to the telescope mounted on the left side of the stock near the trigger. Then he sighted the target, exhaled, visualized the flight of lead, squeezed. The loud cracking pop of the Whitworth echoed down Rocky Face Ridge then back up. More than a mile away, Holtzminger was looking at the target, hopping up and down and pointing like a madman. He put the plank under his arm and walked double time toward the sharpshooters, who moved forward as one organism on many feet, fast, then faster. A few minutes later, they met on the ridge beneath a hot sun, and Holtzminger was babbling in a language that might have been English.

"For the love of God, would you look at that," said Tommy Wallace.

"You ain't a Cleburne sharpshooter, you're the god of all shooters," said Isom Bedgood.

"Let me see it," said Lieutenant Schell. He took the board, and a clean small hole had gone straight through the center of the bull's-eye with barely a splinter. "Private Merrill, you are a wonder at that. You and McGregor should be on the north end of the ridge when the Federals come."

"Don't put me nowhere near *them,*" said Bedgood, laughing. "Anybody what shoots that good will be drawing fire from the whole Yankee army."

Charlie smiled easily. He was looking down from the heights at the Confederate army that lay before Dalton, thousands drilling and marching, preparing for war.

July 27, 1861

REVEREND MERRILL, I'D LIKE you to meet my niece from Boston, Miss Sarah Pierce. She was visiting with us when all this began, and we have thought discretion the better part of valor in her return. We are presuming that she will be able to return soon, but we shan't be happy to lose such a decorative part of our lives."

Dr. Sawyer Pierce, fat and fifty-seven, stood not far from the piano in Grace House and curved his arm around a thin girl with blue-gray eyes and blond hair. She smiled once, but the smile was a gesture that could not hold. She wore a red and blue ribbon in her hair, scrolled and draping down the corkscrew curls. Charlie turned his head to listen, for he had not seen her before. Dr. Pierce was not a medical doctor, but a dispenser of herbal remedies of his own concoction. One tonic, created with sassafras root and alcohol, which he called Pierce's Specific, had made the family rich, and they lived in a mansion half a mile farther west, on Dixie Avenue.

"Miss Pierce, welcome to Branton, and I am so grieved that it has to be under such circumstances," said Reverend Merrill.

"Ah, the circumstances," said Dr. Pierce, patting his stomach. "My brother Roger took it into his head to live in the North years ago, and he has raised his family there, this lovely girl and her brother Herman, who I regret to say now bears arms against us."

"My word," said Betsy Clark Merrill. "Would anyone like more punch?"

"I am pleased to be received in your lovely home," said Sarah, curtseying slightly.

Introductions all around. The room spilled with laughter and singing. One Sunday evening a month, the Merrills opened Grace House for a party, and in fine weather the families who came milled outside, the men sneaking into the sheltering branches of a magnolia for swigs of bourbon from silver flasks. Baptists, of course, spoke with a stern harshness about the evil of liquor and then turned a blind eye at the proper time. They were here tonight: Craveltons, Potters, Syncoles, Jacksons, Westfields—the merchants and lawyers who made Branton a town of grace and prosperity. Tom Merrill sat on the stairs smiling merrily, speaking with no one, watching the hands on the grandfather clock in the front parlor. Mrs. Letitia Syncole sat at the piano playing with a romantic flourish, checking constantly to see if anyone was looking at her with admiration. Not enough. Never enough.

Mothering house slaves who had come with their owners watched over children, chided them, gave orders. When the children fell into patterns, the slaves then backed into shadow and spoke of plantations and rifles, of the war. Away from their owners, they whispered seditions, opened their bitter honesty.

"Sarah, we are so happy you are here," said Mrs. Merrill. "This is our son Charlie. You must be about the same age. This must be difficult for you, being in the South while all this is going on." Charlie heard his name called with a swelling embarrassment.

"They *are* the same age, hah!" said Dr. Pierce, "even though Charlie's a bitty thing, ain't he? He was always a bitty thing, and the Lord will have a job for them what's bitty as well."

"Oh, he's not that small for fourteen," said Charlie's mother.

"Punch?" asked Reverend Merrill to no one in particular. "He's one of the best rifle shots you've ever seen. Steady hands." Reverend Merrill turned his back and tugged on his collar.

"Well, at least Sarah can say she's visited a foreign country when she gets home, haw!" cried Dr. Pierce. She blushed, and Charlie's eyes smiled at her. Her uncle said her name as *Say-ree,* and Reverend Merrill said *Sah-rah,* exotic and vaguely English. Charlie's mother said *Say-ruh.* Charlie felt a stirring, a clammy nervous energy close to pity. He had always possessed a terrible affinity for helpless things, for sick animals, for lost children, for the sick and dying. His nature did him little good, and he often despised it as a weakness. Even now, as he watched his grinning older brother Tom sitting on the staircase, Charlie imagined his strong body laid out, washed and dressed for burial, perhaps battle-drained of his life and blood. Earlier in the day, Tom had announced secretly to his younger brother that he was leaving in the morning for the war. Charlie did not believe him.

Charlie scanned the large room, saw much of his Branton County family: his Aunt Jenny, square and genial, his mother's only sibling, unmarried and unwilling; his father's brothers, Garland and Stuckey. Garland's wife, Nancy, had died in childbirth in 1857, and Garland had been left wan and shapeless, bent and whey-faced. Garland listened to the piano and sipped punch, bent and hollow-eyed. Laughing near the mantle: Uncle Stuckey and his wife Lottie, and through the room and spilling outside, their children, oldest to youngest, Michael, Gil, Melinda, and Dorothy. Michael and Gil, eleven and nine, banged on each other with a genial insistence. Melinda seemed damaged and irritable, trying to rearrange every scene of her life to some hidden purpose. Sweet Dorothy was only seven, and she loved Charlie's sister, Martha, in a quiet, beautiful way. Charlie's father also had a younger sister named Cynthia, and she was there with her husband, Byron Cooney, and their children, John, Anna, Zachary, and Leah. The children began to slip outside into the lightning-bug twilight, poking and giggling, and the chiding insistence of slaves corrected them, chastened them. Charlie's mother's mother, Grandma Irene, refused to act her age and giggled with stories and games in a children's conspiratorial corner. The room seemed to rotate on an axis of family and church and town, and yet many were missing. Many families in Branton Baptist had sent a son to the army, and a few letters had arrived, but most mothers trusted in God while their husbands awaited hideous news with grim finality.

"Charlie, dear, why don't you take Sarah outside with all the young people," said Betsy. Charlie wanted to get away from his mother, but he was always obedient, and so he nodded.

"Yes, ma'am." He smiled weakly at Sarah and nodded for her to walk ahead of him, as any gentleman would. He watched her, the pale white dress that clung to her thin shape like a half-forgotten shadow, her yellow hair, the silent slip of her movement across the room, weaving through the laughter. They went outside and walked down the broad front steps. Children were screaming, running, calling out games, making rules. A few older men smoked their pipes placidly at the porch end. Crickets screamed to be heard among the cicadas and children. Small hands grasped at lightning bugs, but there were thousands of them, sparkling in a molten lilt.

"I'm sorry you got sent to tend me," said Sarah, her voice full of un-spilled laughter as they reached the shadow of a huge live oak. Charlie wondered if she was mocking him. Her accent was almost unknowable, odd and foreign, yet American. "I know you're rather be with your friends than tending a strange girl from another country."

"Boston's not another country," said Charlie. He felt heat in his face. An irritation lifted his head a little. He wished Jack had come, but the Dockerys were Methodists and held to their own.

"My uncle says it is. Of course, my uncle's a pompous blowhard a great deal of the time."

Charlie stopped the motion of his awkwardness and smiled. "I have an uncle who's a pompous blowhard. My Uncle Stuckey. He's too re-spectable to get shot, so he didn't volunteer." A shriek from the back-yard: then an argument, getting worse.

"I'm *not* here just visiting. My parents are getting a divorce, and I was sent here until things at home are cleared up. Now there are, as we know, greater entanglements."

"You talk as if you are a reader, Miss Sarah." Charlie said *Say-ruh,* which made her giggle.

"I pronounce my name *Seh-ruh,*" she said. "It's all right. Most peo-ple in Branton think I'm speaking French or something. And you don't have to put the Miss in front of it. Everything in the South seems de-signed to take longer than necessary. Dawdling is what takes the place of life here, no disrespect intended."

"Well, I dawdle a respectable amount, Miss Sarah." He said *Say-ruh* again. "You might even say we've raised dawdling to its rightful place among the arts. But what did God do but dawdle when he spent six days creating the earth? Surely if He was God, He could have done it in fifteen minutes."

"Then God must live in the south of heaven," said Sarah. His laugh-ter was almost girlish, and he coughed, cleared his throat, and looked around.

Later that night, as he lay still and sleepless, Charlie thought of Sarah and wondered if she felt alone and torn with grief.

July 28, 1861

✧ ✧
✧

AN URGENCY: VOICES.
Charlie rolled over in bed and looked out the window, and the sun was just up, and he could hear his father's righteous ebb and flow below them, mixed with cries and excited sobbing. Stunned and knowing, he slipped from his nightgown into clothes and came down the stairs in a morning dream. They were in the front parlor. His mother was still in her nightclothes, and Reverend Merrill's unstrung suspenders hung down his trouser legs. He walked back and forth with a sheet of unfolded paper in one hand, running the other over his face.

"Charlie, your brother's left us and gone to the war," said his mother. He felt a rush of disbelief, even fear and guilt. Her sentence lingered, lasted thirty seconds, and he wanted to hold her. Martha must still be asleep in her innocent dreams, and the thought she'd awaken to Tom's absence tore at Charlie's heart.

"A letter! He only left us a blasted letter!" said Reverend Merrill. "I'm on my way to the telegraph office to send cables to Atlanta and Augusta. I checked and he didn't take his horse." Charlie couldn't believe his father had used the word *blasted,* which was close enough to swearing. Missy, their house servant, slow and worried, came into the room.

"Honey, did your brother say anything about this?" she asked.

"Yes, ma'am, yesterday, but I thought he was joking," said Charlie.

"What? What? You knew that he was leaving, and you didn't come and tell me your brother had a mind for foolishness?"

"I thought he was joking," Charlie repeated, his voice rising. He stifled the panic, pushed back a shout of sorrow. "He said he was going to go fight. He told me when we were walking on the railroad tracks. I don't know where he was going to be with them, I don't know. I don't know! I thought he was just saying it to seem like a man. Please don't be angry with me, Mama. I don't want you to be angry with me!"

"Oh, sweet boy," she said, opening her arms. Charlie rushed into them, felt small and childish. He could feel his father fuming, stepping closer.

"If that's not the stupidest thing I've—Charlie stand up here, son! Stand up like a man!" Through the open window, Charlie saw a double-rigged phaeton coming down Main Street, and he thought: Mr. Wittich. Bankers sometimes arrived at work in lamplight.

"Leave him be, Charles," said Betsy. "Leave him be. It's not his fault Tom got caught up in all this. Charlie's just a boy."

"It's his fault not to tell me so I could stop it. Tom never had a lick of sense, but you do, Charlie, and I have held high hopes for you—the law, the ministry. You could be a physician. You have *capacity*. But this—this is monstrous. This is disrespect for me, do you hear, for my position as an important man in this town!"

He looked weary, sorrowful.

"Don't you see, I've lost everything," said Reverend Merrill. "Don't you see that? They're—they're taking the house from us. I'm not well." He walked around in a daze. Charlie looked at his mother for answers. *What could that mean—they're taking the house from us?*

"Go outside and cool off, Charles!" his wife commanded.

"Charlie, I . . ."

"Go outside and cool off, and then go send the telegram." Reverend Merrill walked slowly out the front door of Grace House and down the steps and into the summer sunlight.

"I'm sorry. I *did* think it was a joke. I *did!*"

"Hush, your father's having a terrible time. The doctor says his health is poor. There is less and less money from the church. They're selling our house, and we will have to move to something smaller and more modest. But that's all right. It's all right, Charlie."

"I'm afraid," said Charlie softly, pushing himself away. He ran from the room, through the house and out the back door, breathless down the steps, and into the shade of the pecan grove.

REVEREND MERRILL SENT HIS telegrams, made inquiries, spoke with the stationmaster, called on Sheriff Reed. As the day grew toward noon and then passed it, Charlie walked to town and found perhaps seventy or eighty men drinking from flasks, smoking cigars and pipes, and generally screaming and dancing. Rumors had been in town for a full day before the official dispatch.

"Word's in, word's in!" cried Henry Brown, drunk as usual. "We've whipped the Yankees a week ago in Virginia! The war's all but over! Place called Manassas. Can you imagine a uglier word, young Merrill, for a great joy? Praise God!" Henry's words were slurred with alcohol, and his nose ran, and he kept wiping it on his sleeve.

"Done kilt 'em ever' one!" another man shouted. Charlie thought he might be a Schelpert or a Barger, but he wasn't sure. He felt a quiet elation since, in a week, Tom would come home with his tail between his legs.

Two other men, against the war, spoke with just as much urgency. The town never seemed to settle its affections, but speaking against the war was not only common but acceptable and perhaps even growing. Savannah might be taking glory from the fighting, but Branton's allegiance was sharply divided, though everyone seemed granted a right to speak his piece.

Charlie turned and walked quickly down Jefferson Street, turned on Madison, only slowed when he found himself next to the Branton Livery Stable. Sometimes he would come here, especially after school in the fall, when Mr. Lucius Penick would give him a currycomb and ask Charlie to help him groom. Charlie loved the smell of horses, their yeasty stalls and steaming flanks. Broken horses had the pleasant talent of patience. After a combing, they would turn their long heads toward him and nuzzle him with a placid snort. He was surprised to see Jack Dockery come limping around the corner, holding in his hand a black book with gold lettering and filigree on the spine.

"I hear Tom left for the war," said Jack.

"Who told you?"

"People talking about it downtown. You know how they are—

'Preacher's boy done run off for the cause.' I think your daddy could be elected mayor if he wanted to."

"He's sent telegrams to find Tom and bring him home."

"There goes his career as mayor. Did you know he was going to leave?"

"He said so yesterday. I thought he was being brave. But they say this battle all but ended the war anyway. He'll probably be back in two weeks pretending he's a hero. I'm not worried too much. You're not reading Shelley again, are you?" Jack had never gotten over the fact that Shelley had drowned, that so much was lost so soon. Early deaths were frequently on his mind.

"History, boy. I'm well educated." He handed the book to Charlie who opened the front cover and read an inscription in a flowing hand: *To E. Van Arsdale Andruss, with kindest wishes for this and many more happy new years, from your Friend Newell McIrsey, January 1st 1857.* Then Charlie opened the book to the title page: *Great Events Described by Distinguished Historians, Chroniclers and Other Writers.* Collected and in part translated by Francis Lieber. Boston: Wm. Crosby and H. P. Nicholas, 111 Washington Street.

"You're well educated all right. Do you know I just *met* a girl from Boston who's here in town? Dr. Pierce's niece Sarah. She is stuck here until things are straightened out, I think. She seemed nice, but I can't understand what she's saying."

"Is she as pretty as Susan Meadows? Does she have a big chest like Mary Singleton?"

"Jack, you think in one line."

"You're changing the subject. Is this Yankee niece pretty or a sow?" Charlie didn't expect the question or his response, a quiet place inside, a solitude and a silence. "Are you going to answer me?" asked Jack.

"She's—she's nice. She—I just talked to her for ten minutes last night at our party." Charlie snatched the book from Jack and walked a few paces. A heavy man bearing a jouncing stomach clopped by on a mare that wore a feather in her bridle. The horse seemed very short for such a burden. Charlie grabbed Jack's second book. "Have you been reading about the death of Socrates, Jack? I see it here right in front."

"How nice is she, then?"

"Yes, here it is," said Charlie, reading: "*And thus far, indeed, the greater part of us were tolerably well able to refrain from weeping; but when we saw him drinking, and that he had drunk it, we could no longer restrain our tears.*" Charlie read it almost with sarcasm, but as he thought of his brother, his eyes welled up, and he inhaled the day, saw summer stretching before him like a line of battle.

May 8–13, 1864

DALTON TO RESACA

SUNDAY MORNING. **THE DAY** rose warmly in a blanket of still, shimmering air on Rocky Face Ridge and below in Dalton. Rumors had roiled the ranks, and long before daylight the sharpshooters were roused and sent to emplacements on the ridge, a crenellation that ran for several miles north to south on the west side of Dalton. Charlie had been close enough to Division headquarters to hear the first guesses of Sherman's movements, which would surely begin soon. Word was that Johnston believed the enemy would attack in force at Dalton while sending a flank toward Rome. Everyone knew the Yankees vastly outnumbered the Confederates, and flanking was not a suspicion but almost a certainty.

Now, on May 8, Charlie and Duncan sat on a boulder and looked north, watching intently, listening for the creak of caissons, the tramp of hoof and brogan. Duncan lazily chewed a plug of tobacco and spat brown sticky streams on the edge of the boulder, from where it dripped like a chocolate waterfall.

"If this ain't a strange place to be in, I don't know nothing," said Duncan softly. "Aye, God, to be alone in groups of two or three without the army at your side. I must admit, my boy, I'm more afraid than I felt I would be. Don't you feel a fear in your gut?"

"Some, I guess," said Charlie. "I guess I'd be a fool not to be scared."

"Aye for that, son," said Duncan.

In the distance, Charlie thought he saw something.

"There," he said, pointing.

"Yeah, I see, and over there," said Duncan, pointing west. "They're on the move all right." Charlie took the telescope off his rifle and peered through it. "What is it, cavalry?"

"Looks like infantry," said Charlie. "Coming in some force. I'd say the spring campaign has come to Georgia."

"God save our souls," said Duncan.

"All our souls," said Charlie, reattaching the telescope. He barely felt the weight of his gear, cartridge and cap boxes, a few pieces of hardtack, canteen, and in his shirtfront, the letter from Sarah Pierce. Below them, a thin Confederate skirmish line braced and waited for the Yankees, who seemed to be boiling up like legendary creatures from inside the earth. Charlie gauged and waited. Suddenly the clatter and crack of musket fire broke out below them, and Charlie lifted the Whitworth, much more ready than he had been at Chickamauga, even more ready than Missionary Ridge. He sighted a mounted officer directing an artillery battery, shot him clean off his horse.

"Did you hit anything?" asked Duncan McGregor.

"I did," said Charlie, who was rapidly reloading. In twenty seconds, the Whitworth barked again, and Charlie could see a small bluecoat throw up his arms in surprise and fall over backward. Nothing had ever quite felt this strange before. He felt a penetrating sadness tinged with accomplishment. He loaded rapidly again and shot a color-bearer through the chest, and the banner fluttered downward into the dirt before another man grabbed it. The Confederate skirmish line retreated up the ridge in a crablike scramble, the Federals not far behind.

"Good God, them blue boys is rising like ants toward us, Charlie," said Duncan. "This Spencer of mine doesn't have its range yet. I'm going to scout a bit on our left."

"Watch your head. Some of those boys are probably good shots," said Charlie.

"Aye, watch yours, too, son."

Charlie watched the unfolding war below him with utter fascination. Cleburne's Division was back at Dalton in reserve, but General Benjamin Cheatham's Division was here behind the sharpshooters and the skirmish line. Like most private soldiers, even sharpshooters, Charlie knew little of what was happening on the larger scale, though rumors mumbled down the infantry lines faster, it seemed at times, than artillery shells.

Charlie shot four more Yankees, including one boy no older than himself. He tested his feelings, and he felt a spreading sadness but held his ground.

SPORADIC FIRING CONTINUED FROM below for several hours, and sharpshooters from the other side began to take Charlie's range and fire at him, but he made subtle movements, and the slugs flattened on stones and trees with a dull spattering *thunk*. Duncan was still gone. Charlie scanned the valley below and saw what appeared to be a colonel, waving his arms and giving directions. Charlie shot him clean through the throat. The colonel grabbed his neck, shook his head once as if to clear a thought, then fell off, his left boot stuck in the stirrup. The horse raced on for quite a while until a burly bearded soldier grabbed its flailing reins and pulled it to a stop. The colonel lay motionless in the dust. Charlie fell backward on his seat and vomited against a stone.

Is this right? he wondered. *How could this be right?*

Around noon, Duncan came running back, low to the ground.

"They're coming up the ridge in force," he said. "A brigade at least, Charlie."

Charlie stood shakily and looked through the telescopic sight and saw dozens of Yankees pulling themselves up the steep slope, using bushes and rocks to drag themselves along. Confederate fire into their ranks was steady but not massed, and casualties among the bluecoats appeared light. He swung the telescope upward.

"They're coming toward Buzzard Roost Pass, too," he said. "That pond will hold them for a time."

"Aye, the damned pond," said Duncan. Before he'd been detached to duty with Cleburne's marksmen, McGregor had helped build an artificial lake by stopping the railroad's drainage culverts with dirt, logs, and loose stones—a body of water too deep now to wade. Charlie smiled for the first time in two days as he scanned the pass: As its name implied, buzzards roosted in the trees, giving them the look of ebony leaves that sometimes flaked off and flew upward in the still, hot air. Firing also seemed to be coming from somewhere to the south, perhaps in Dug Gap, a man-made pass behind Rocky Face Ridge that was heavily guarded by Southern troops. Charlie didn't know it, but Cleburne's Division had been sent to Dug Gap when it was clear the Federals were assaulting it.

"An officer," said Charlie simply. He was sighting down the Whitworth. He shot a major in the abdomen, and he crumpled and rolled forty yards down Rocky Face Ridge before he caught a bush and stopped. Duncan was tugging at his sleeve.

"We'd better be getting out of this spot," said Duncan.

"Here," said Charlie. He handed the Whitworth to Duncan and rolled three large boulders down the slope, huge sharp-nosed stones that gained torque as they poured off the crest. The Yankees dodged all three, but they shouted up curses, waved their arms, fired their muskets.

"Sweet Jesus," said the Scotsman. "I'm taking you out of here, son."

"I'm coming," said Charlie. A few of the Confederate defenders saw Charlie's stone-rolling and also began to push boulders down on the rising Yankee troops, and at least one severely injured two corporals, but the Federals would not stop, and so Charlie and Duncan ran up the slope to the topmost crest, where Cheatham's men fired down into the ranks and prepared to move back along the thin summit of the ridge, knowing there was no way to defend the land in such a narrow defile.

"Damn me," said Duncan. A bullet whipped through the tree limbs and blew a hole in the left sleeve of his coat, not touching flesh. "I should say we must move faster, or we'll lie here tonight as a feast for the buzzards tomorrow. And I do not fancy having my flesh snipped off by carrion birds!"

Charlie grinned, and they scrambled up the slope as rifle fire pattered around them and the heavy sounds of artillery rolled in the distance. As darkness neared late in the day, Charlie and Duncan passed Cheatham's division, which had given up a lodgment to the Yankee troops that now held three-quarters of a mile on Rocky Face Ridge.

IT TOOK CHARLIE AND Duncan several hours to find Cleburne and two of his brigades, Lowrey's and Granbury's, on the ridge above Dug Gap. There had been a furious Union assault late in the day, but Cleburne's seasoned troops had thrown the attacks back, and now, with night hard and cool upon them, all firing had ceased. Duncan needed food and sleep, but Charlie felt like a lit fuse, trembling with the desire to move or run. Most of the sharpshooter company was still scattered over

Rocky Face Ridge, taking the night at their own pace, sleeping beneath the stars. Charlie and Duncan found that Walter Bragg had made his way back, but the others, including the lieutenant, were out there in the darkness.

Cleburne sat by a fire, meeting with General Hardee and discussing the day's events, which they agreed had gone rather well.

"A one-sided victory," Cleburne was saying as Charlie and Duncan walked into the camp. A surgeon not far away was working over a number of groaning men, who prayed aloud, begged for water or help. In the lantern light, Charlie saw a boy vomit blood, shudder, and then go still.

"Except the enemy has a hold on the northern end of the ridge, and we keep getting reports they are moving in great numbers west of here," said Hardee.

"General Johnston still believes they are moving on Rome," said Cleburne. "I believe we are sufficient to counter that threat."

"There is word they may be moving on Snake Creek Gap," said Hardee.

"I believe that is much too narrow for such a movement, is it not?" asked Cleburne. "And is that gap not guarded?"

The generals and their staff officers spoke for a long time, and it was late when Cleburne noticed Charlie still standing at the edge of the fire-light, holding his Whitworth.

"Private Merrill," said Charlie, saluting. Cleburne smiled and returned the salute.

"Ah, Mr. Merrill, and how did your day fare as a sharpshooter?" Duncan McGregor came out of the darkness, struggling, it appeared, to stay awake.

"He hit at least six I counted," said Duncan. "General, the man is an artist with a Whitworth rifle, and by my count that includes a colonel, a major, and varied other officers and a few private soldiers. Then he rolled rocks upon them."

"Rolled rocks?" said Cleburne, laughing. "That sounds rather biblical." Cleburne's chief of staff, Major Calhoun Benham, watched him with amazement, for Cleburne was usually serious to the point of coldness. Something in this young Georgia soldier awakened his own interests.

"Aye, it was biblical, and if he could have, he'd've parted the lake we built at Buzzard's Roost and let the blue-bellies enter and then drowned them, General," said Duncan. Even Benham grinned.

"I'm glad you came to me," said Cleburne to Charlie. "Well done. You know I take great interest in what my sharpshooters do. You are the real van of this Division. As you can, come to me. I fear we cannot continue the chess game tonight, but if we have time, we shall. I believe that in the next few days, we will force a battle from Sherman that will send them back into Tennessee as we did last fall at Chickamauga. It is in God's hands."

THE NEXT MORNING, CHARLIE and Duncan moved rapidly north again on Rocky Face Ridge and took up positions in front of Cheatham's men. Firing had already begun between the Federal forces atop the northern end of the ridge, and Charlie could see through his telescopic sight that the Union troops were hauling artillery to the crest of the ridge.

"God, they will blast us to bits," said a skirmisher named Otto Schnill, who had been with Cheatham for a long time. He came past Charlie heading to the rear. "There's a rumor that the Feds are moving west of us. We're being flanked sure as God is a Christian. We are going to get cut off here and flayed into hides."

By noon, the fire into the Confederate ranks had grown almost intolerable, constant rifle and sharpshooter fire from below, and now with the unlimbering of caissons, artillery fired straight into Cheatham's Division. Charlie and Duncan moved back with them among heavy boulders, and the acrid stench of gunpowder, the haze of smoke, drifted through and over them. Now the Federal batteries were open full on the Southerners, and General Cheatham issued a call for all sharpshooters, and Charlie and four others were assembled.

"Boys, take out what you can from those batteries," he cried in the din.

Charlie positioned himself among a grove of boulders and drew down on a man shoving a long-poled barrel sponger down the throat of a twelve-pounder Napoleon. Charlie gauged him at thirteen-hundred yards, fired, and the man fell, writhing. Loading and firing quickly, Charlie killed a captain and severely wounded two privates. The other sharpshooters, seeing his rapid loading and firing, did the same, and a sense of chaos erupted in the Federal batteries, and soon they began to pull back out of range, beyond where even the sharpshooters could reach. Union troops who had gained a nearby position fell back. A few yards in front lay a wounded boy, shivering and writhing.

"Oh, my God" said Charlie. "What should I do, Duncan?"

"Ah, leave him alone, son," shouted Duncan. "That not being part of our job and all."

Charlie felt a knot of horror. He reloaded and fired in the general direction of the enemy and then turned and knelt to comfort the boy, who looked up, begging with his eyes.

"You there, what are you doing?" asked a major with a huge beard that covered his chest like a bib. Charlie rose and walked away, through so many bullets they hummed around him like harp strings. Duncan crept, and Charlie moved, bent beside him.

"A soft heart but a fine shot," said one of Cheatham's men, speaking of Charlie.

"Strange lad," said another.

"You there!" cried the major, but Charlie and Duncan slipped through the trees and down the west side of the ridge and sat in a quieter sector. Duncan was breathing so hard, his lungs wheezed in a ragged rhythm. Charlie stared below him.

"I won't see you shot, boy," said Duncan. "Don't ask me to see you shot."

"I'll be careful. I'm sorry." Duncan stood, cocked the hammer on his rifle and fired just over Charlie's head. A Federal scout, coming up the ridge toward them, gave a dull *unnnhh* and fell backward into the leaves. Charlie gasped, stood, and walked down toward the man, who was still alive, middle-aged and not wearing a coat and so bearing no rank. His beard was flecked with white and gray. He lay on his back blinking, blood pouring from his mouth.

"Aye, God, look at this," said Duncan.

"Where are you from?" Charlie asked the wounded man.

"Boston," said the man. "Nearbouts Boston. My farm. Water." His eyes rolled into his head, and then they came back down. "A brace of plow horses." Then he slumped, dead. Flies arrived from nowhere. The man's bowels let go, and the stench was overpowering. His bladder released in death.

"Aye, God, look at this," said Duncan.

THAT NIGHT OF MAY 9, General Joseph Johnston, having heard that the Yankees were rapidly filing down Snake Creek Gap behind Rocky Face Ridge, ordered two brigades of Cleburne's Division at Dug Gap, along with the divisions of Generals Walker and Hindman, to march rapidly, starting at midnight, to Resaca, a small railroad town to the south. Charlie and Duncan, having regained the Division, marched with them in the night, staying close to men in front of them, saying little.

Charlie wondered if the man from Boston who had died on Rocky Face Ridge knew Sarah. Perhaps Sarah's brother was fighting for the Federals in the field of combat. The Whitworth felt light to Charlie, and the muscles in his legs flexed and bulged as he walked. He tested his feelings again, and a flicker of warmth passed by, like the sun escaping clouds in winter and buttering a front porch with soft heat. Soon enough, a pity swept upon him, and when they reached Resaca near dawn, he and all the men collapsed, some on unrolled blankets but many on the ground where the march ended.

"God preserve us from generals," said Duncan as he settled for sleep.

A STIRRING CAME FROM his dreams. Charlie swam upward from a brief, deep sleep. Morning clouds littered the sky, but the hump of sun still lay below the horizon. Men coughed, moving. A few stood where they were and walked to bushes to urinate or defecate. An officer on a black horse was riding back and forth speaking in a loud voice.

"Prepare to move out, men, prepare!" he shouted. "In a quarter hour's time! Prepare to move out, or you will be left. Get ready to fall in ranks."

"And where would we be going?" asked a tall soldier with a bald head.

"God help us, we are going back to Dug Gap the way we came all night," said the officer.

"That's a damnable offense," muttered Duncan to Charlie. "What have they in mind, to run us to death before we meet the enemy in open battle on our own ground? They ask us to give up our lives to fight, and then they turn us into pack mules. Aye, God, this is a fine thing, Charlie."

The two brigades marched north again, but Hindman stopped at Dalton and Walker at a small town called Tilton. Cleburne's men marched all morning, reaching Dug Gap in the afternoon, past exhaustion. Charlie and Duncan met with Lieutenant Schell and the company of sharpshooters, and he knew they were useless now and so told them to sleep as they could for a few hours. The men slumped down in the stifling, heated air, sticky and stinking with sweat.

Charlie dreamed of Jack. They were sitting on a winter's day in Charlie's bedroom at Grace House, playing chess and speaking about poetry and about girls. Jack seemed to be made of vapor and light.

"I have to go back now," said Jack.

"Where is it you go?" asked Charlie.

"To the land of the dead," said Jack. "Don't worry. Nothing can hurt you there. You are indivisible from love."

When Charlie awoke, it was nearly dark and the sky was rumbling, and he thought artillery was limbering up on their front. It took him a moment to realize it was thunder. He had held the Whitworth in sleep, and he still cradled it. He stood, looked at the heights of Rocky Face Ridge and the black clouds that lowered through the mountains to the north.

"General Cleburne asks the pleasure of your company," said Major Benham. He was standing in front of Charlie, looking weak and tired. A gamy smell rose from him like heat off a flat road. "His tent is but a hundred yards. There." Benham pointed, and Charlie followed him, his legs heavy with the weariness of two forced marches in the past twenty-four hours.

"There goes the general's boy again," said a soldier named Hicks, who spoke the words with good humor, if not affection. "Tell him that if wants us to go back to Resaca tonight, he can ship us there himself by rail." A few of the men chuckled, but most were too tired to respond. With a storm coming, and without tents, they would have to spend the night in misery, and they knew it. Cleburne strode back and forth in front of his tent, which had been pitched and covered with an oilcloth against the coming rain. He had gone and returned on horseback, and his eyes were bright with possibilities.

"Ah, Mr. Merrill, welcome," said Cleburne. They exchanged salutes. "Mangum, would you get my guest a fresh cup of coffee and some dried beef?" Mangum touched the bill of his cap.

"You are generous," said Charlie. "We are all exhausted. We all presume there is a reason for this."

"The same reason as in all wars," said Cleburne, leaning close and whispering. "The Yankees do not quite know where we are, nor do we quite know where they are. With these mountains in such excess, almost exuberance, an entire army could move undetected through defiles. Guarding them all may take more men than we can spare."

"I should be out watching for targets," said Charlie.

"Rest easy, my boy, rest easy," said Cleburne. "I do not fancy the look of that sky. This will be a long campaign, and you will have ample time for sharpshooting. Now, I must ask you something. I have been told that yesterday you knelt to see how a wounded Yankee soldier fared."

"That is true, and I admit it and will stand any punishment the general decides is sufficient," said Charlie. "I could not bear the man's suffering."

"Now, none of that," said Cleburne. "None of that. But we must guard that we encourage our men without setting a poor example for them. Word spread fast among so many men, and the truth is liable to be lost soon enough. The other men in my sharpshooting company hold you somewhat in awe for your talent and age, and so they look to you. Be sure that what you do is for the good of your fellow soldiers always. And that any sacrifice is worthy of this calling."

"What calling?" asked Charlie.

"The calling of our Southern Confederacy," said Cleburne. "What else would I mean? We are engaged in a war to save our way of life."

"I never thought of it that way," said Charlie. "With so much death, it seems designed to *lose* our way of life."

Cleburne, instead of being outraged, accepted it with grace. "You're but a boy, and a kind one, though a very fine marksman," said Cleburne. "I was much the same myself. Ambitious as the devil, wanting my family to have food and clothes on their backs. Willing to leave my own country and take up with another for it. And Arkansas is the country that took me in. And she deserves my full measure, Mr. Merrill. Anything less would be a terrible lack of gratitude."

"Sir," said Charlie.

The thunderstorm began to crack above them, roiling down the mountains, and with the clouds, heavy, loud pellets of rain began to snap at the earth, hiss in fires. The men sat beneath blankets and oilcloths. A few curses rang out, a few laughs. Charlie thought: *Causes. Our way of life. Something to be distrusted, disbelieved.*

"Look at this. Is it not in some ways as majestic as it is miserable?" asked Cleburne, eyes bright. "Oh, we would have the storms back home in Ireland, Mr. Merrill. We would have great rumbling massacres of lightning that would rip across the land. And old women who saw omens in every crow would fall upon their knees and weep for protection from God."

"Do you believe in omens?" asked Charlie.

"I believe in God and in His strong right hand," said Cleburne. "And I believe in the word of Miss Susan Tarleton. God and love are one and the same, and cannot be divided. Remember that when you face death, my boy."

"I will do my best, sir." Mangum returned with a cup of hot coffee, and though it was bitter, its heat poured through Charlie, awakened him more fully. He took the dried beef and ate it quickly and held his free hand over the barrel of his Whitworth so rainwater would not pour down its twisted tunnel.

"I must be about my work, but I wanted to speak with you. I hear that you are doing a fine job and have slain a number of the enemy, and it always gives me pleasure when my decisions are proven out."

Charlie looked around at the storm, at the men in small bouldered shapes, beneath tented blankets.

"As majestic as it is miserable," said Charlie.

"When we have an evening without orders or movements, we shall continue the chess game," said Cleburne. "I look forward to seeing your next move."

"As I do yours, General Cleburne."

THE STORM REELED AROUND them all night, like a drunken man, and, without tents, Cleburne's men lay in blankets two inches deep in water, spent with marching, fireless. Some slept as though their time on earth were over, while others sat up beneath waterproofs, shedding some of the storm, but never all. Charlie did his best to keep the Whitworth dry. He cared about nothing else but Sarah's letter, which he protected well. In the dry of early morning light, he took it out, and the ink was intact, though bleeding lightly around the edges.

CHARLIE AND DUNCAN SCRAMBLED back up Rocky Face Ridge, even after the order to assemble and prepare to march was given. They had taken ample ammunition from the supply train, dry percussion caps, a few crackers of hardtack. Charlie's light black beard was now spreading across his cheeks, and he was thinner, thought Duncan. All morning, Charlie shot toward the Yankees, and though he often missed, he dropped at least three, finally drawing fire from Union snipers around ten.

"Get back behind some boulders, for the love of God," said Duncan. He was humped behind a great clot of granite. A shot hit a hickory tree with a sharp thwack, and Charlie looked at it and thought: Whitworth or Kerr. An Enfield could splinter six boards at four hundred yards, but its large soft lead bullet had a different pattern. This was forty-five caliber, a sharpshooter's tool.

Just then, all of Cheatham's men began to abandon the ridge, and with the Federals lodged at the north end, Charlie knew that they were giving ground, backing off.

"Let's get out of here," said Charlie.

"Now you're coming, thank the Lord, to your senses," said Duncan. Gunfire hastened their movement, and going down the sharp slope of Rocky Face Ridge for the last time, Charlie watched Duncan with a kind of blank pity, wondered how he'd wound up as a scout who scouted nothing. By late in the day, the orders had been given to march back to Resaca, where the enemy was said to be massing from a flanking movement through Snake Creek Gap. Charlie and Duncan fell in to march with their old company.

"The graybacks is about to bite out my private parts," said Bob Rainey, scratching at his crotch. "If lice has sense to camp where there's action, why come our generals doesn't? Tell me that, you bloody Scotsman."

"You've been around long as I have, you old fool," said Duncan, grinning. A red sun streaked the sky, like a strip of infection, toward the west. "You've marched enough to one place and back again. The army is not a matter of sense to you or anyone else. It is an animal whose motions cannot make sense but to those who see it whole."

"Damn, McGregor, you done turned philosopher since you been a scout," said Bob Rainey. "Hope I don't never get so smart."

Charlie turned and glanced back at the summit of Rocky Face Ridge, and blue troops were spreading across it, like triumphant insects on the corpse of a giant.

CHARLIE AWOKE BEFORE DAWN as always, but now back at Resaca, knowing what the Federals would have found when they entered Dalton this morning: corpses from both sides, men dying in the hospitals the Confederates could not empty. They would find a warehouse full of cigars and peanuts, or that was the rumor. Charlie and Duncan ate lightly and moved into position on a hill north of town to await the coming of the enemy.

"They say General Sherman will flank the devil to get into heaven," said Duncan. "I have to admit I believe it. I know enough of tactics, Charlie boy, to get myself shot. But I believe we face a far greater force than our own. A general willing to flank with a far greater force cannot lose."

"No," said Charlie. "Here we go."

"Here we go what?"

"Look."

Duncan turned and saw, not more than a mile away, a great crawling beast, appearing black at first, then dark blue, hundreds of mismatched and creeping legs. Charlie looked through the telescope of his Whitworth, scanning right to left. He stopped with a jolt when he saw what was clearly an officer riding a brown stallion. Without waiting, Charlie lifted the Whitworth and held it steady before him. He aimed for the officer's chest, but when he shot, he saw the man grab his thigh and fall from his horse, immediately surrounded by staff officers. A high-ranking one.

"Did you hit anything, Charlie?" asked Duncan.

"A general, perhaps," said Charlie.

"Ah," said Duncan. "Then we'd do well to take a bit of cover."

Charlie watched through the telescope, and a swarm of staff helped the officer. The wound did not seem mortal. Just as well, thought Charlie. He will live long and as an old man speak of his wound, engrave a fancy filigree around it, embellish, rewrite. Return fire started as a light skittering and quickly grew into a whistling roar. The Southern skirmish line shot back, but Charlie could not quite believe the sheer numbers of Federal troops that boiled up now, thousands it seemed, and for a tender moment he thought of his mother and of Sarah. Several infantry skirmishers scuttled along the ground near them, one-handing their Enfields low to the ground.

"Boys, we're going to have to back up now," said a slab-faced, sunburned man with a flat nose and widely spaced teeth. "No way we can hold it. We've got strong lines dug in already back there. Don't go and get yourselfs kilt." The man kept moving.

"Which I'll take as good advice," said Duncan. "I'm supposed to be a scout, by damn, I'm going to move left and see what's over there, Charlie. I'll see you later."

"I understand."

"Take care of yourself, son."

"And you."

Charlie felt a rush of pride in his solitude. The crack and roar were starting to deafen. He moved to his right behind a large pine tree and peered out and saw a mile-long Federal line moving steadily, a majestic undulation that was just coming out of a heavily wooded area into a vast field. Behind him, Confederate artillery opened fire, and shells shuddered overhead, but they were sighted too high, and they blasted far back in the woods behind the advancing troops. Union artillery batteries whipped their caissons around and began returning fire, and Charlie's hearing ceased; the noise was beyond anything he had ever felt, and he thought of the town's name again: *Resaca.* He wondered if it had a meaning. He stepped from behind the tree and leveled his Whitworth and aimed at an artillery officer three-quarters of a mile away and shot him in the heart.

Now, walking at a pace that he knew was foolish, he moved back toward the Confederate lines, up a long sloping ridge called Bald Hill, refused to move faster as Federal musket fire began to whistle past him, refused to move faster as the Northern artillerymen began to find their range. The minié balls, fifty-eight-caliber soft-lead monsters, made a peculiar whistle and whirr as they spun around him, and for a moment he dreamed they could weave air, concoct blankets from their pattern. The afternoon heat was oppressive. Someone was grabbing Charlie's sleeve, and there was a commotion and a movement: an officer shouting at him, but Charlie heard nothing, saw lips. Charlie turned and saw the Federal lines moving forward steadily across the open field, saw the puff and recoil of artillery. Already, the Confederate batteries were hooking up their horses to their field pieces, and one gelding nearby steamed and stamped wildly.

"Fall back!" the officer screamed, and Charlie read the words on his lips. The smell of gunpowder stung, burned his eyes into a blinking. Charlie felt a kind of fear, but more a sadness, as he moved down the back side of Bald Hill with the retreating skirmishers and artillery units toward the bristling Confederate fortifications. Huge numbers of men in butternut and gray appeared to haul off the remaining Napoleon and Parrott guns from Bald Hill. Ahead, the earthworks, spread out from an existing fort, were almost magnificent, and the sheer numbers of troops stunned Charlie—thousands in both directions.

He and the retreating skirmishers came up a slope to the fort, entered it, and in the center of the lines, entirely by accident, he knew, Charlie found Cleburne's Division—hell, Hardee's whole corps, it seemed—Cheatham and Bate, too.

"—take a fight here we can whip the lot of 'em," said a short private soldier. His eyes were wild with fear and the need to have done with it. Charlie looked around him: Yes, these were Granbury's Texans, one of the wildest of Cleburne's brigades, battle-toughened Westerners who said they had just as soon die as eat.

"—don't let them cross the Oostanaula, then—hell," another man was saying. The words seemed to rise and fade in Charlie's hearing. For the first time, he wondered what had become of Duncan. The Federal troops were now on Bald Hill and looking at the Southern fortifications, and Charlie looked through a rifle gap in a log wall, drew down on an artilleryman and fired. The man crumpled like a sack dropped from the back of a wagon.

Firing continued until dark, and though Charlie could not see it, and none of the Confederates knew it, the Yankees were already rushing pontoon bridges through Snake Creek Gap, heading toward the river for a crossing, to flank.

July 22, 1914

⋆ ⋆
⋆

HEAT BLISTERED THE STREETS, though it was not yet ten o'clock. Charlie Merrill, sixty-seven years old and feeling an ache in his groin, sat upright in the Buick.

He said to his young friend Tyrone Awtry, "My idea being that I just want to see what the dais looks like and how far I will have to project and what have you."

"Say again?" The motor seemed badly timed, firing oddly in a clanking arrhythmia. Awtry was thirty-six and wore his hair greased with a part sharp as a carpenter's line. He had been slender until his late twenties when he turned to fat like his father, and now he sweated through his white shirt, poured rivulets from his armpits down his side, puddling in the seat beneath him.

"I want to see how far I will have to project my voice," Charlie shouted, smiling. He'd hired Awtry just out of school as an apprentice, and through stubborn pluck he'd learned to set type. His nails curved back black from ink, but otherwise he looked reasonably turned out. Charlie regarded him with mild amusement. They drove west on Main Street, which had been paved with concrete only two years before, and the Buick clattered along, passing one car after another. When cars had first come, men doffed their hats as they had always done from buggies or wagons when passing another driver on the road, but after a few wrecks, the practice passed. One gas lamp remained in front of the Branton Graded School, which loomed above its clean-swept dirt yard like a castle. Electricity now powered the other street lamps, that White Way being Charlie's final civic push with his newspaper. Few people knew the white house next door to the Graded School had once held the Branton Female Academy, or that from its front yard the soldiers marched off in April 1861. Ancient history, Charlie thought: Greeks and Romans, Salamis and Marathon. Fifty years—half a century. In that time they'd passed in their dozens, and those left were relics of bloodshed that no one could quite believe, even now. Had they lined up and blown each other away with such cavalier disdain? Yes. A species of madness had infected the country, but, he mused, men always looked for that madness and coveted it fiercely. Few in the South said it was about the slaves; that was a side issue, a conjuring from a few abolitionists. But slavery *was* the issue, he knew. It was. We could not *wait* for that war, thought Charlie. My own brother could not *wait* for that war.

Ezra Atkinson Park was at the western edge of the town, a green pasture with willows and water oaks and stands of pines whose needles spread their carpet in a brown shawl along the hot earth. Charlie smiled and remembered: good to walk on but hard to do it quietly. Here churches held picnics and boys stroked baseballs all summer.

"Look there," said Awtry. "Looks like they're expecting a crowd." About thirty men and women spruced the bunting, touched up its drape and shine. The platform was about thirty feet wide and ten feet deep, set up in left field of the Branton baseball diamond. The slow rich smoke from roasting pigs filled the air, and Awtry inhaled, smiling.

"They won't fill to the third base," said Charlie. "People aren't that interested anymore in an old war."

"In the Battle of Atlanta?" said Awtry in a high-pitched voice. He turned off the Buick and parked on a dusty side street, off the concrete and back on hard-packed dirt. "You telling me people have forgot the Battle of Atlanta? Hell, we didn't even lose to them goddam Yankees there, we just got outflanked by a number twice ours. General Sherman was a sure bastard." Awtry was quite exercised, and Charlie watched his ignorance with amusement. He was prone to swear, and the newspaper business did that, anyway, made a mild man prone to swear with invention and passion. Awtry's face was red, but Charlie couldn't tell whether it was from the sun and the heat or the anger. People still bristled at the mention of Sherman's name, even though the general himself hadn't come through Branton. Thousands of his troops under a general named Slocum had, but they stayed only one day and were generally well behaved. Burned a little, looted in a minor way.

"People who like history will always remember history," said Charlie. "Most people don't like history."

"What's that?" Awtry was wiping sweat and checking his pocket watch.

"I said most people don't like history. It reminds them they're going to die. People don't want to be reminded they're going to die. That's why they watch baseball games and make love and memorize the Bible and travel." Charlie felt himself growing limber and stronger. It always took a while in the mornings. "That's why we have wars, so we can pretend, until death starts in a big way, that we can't die, not even before great cannon or massed muskets. We are always trying to prove that death's illusory."

"I thought it was just a picnic and a few speeches," said Awtry. "I didn't know none a that was going on. For me, it's just set the next damn paper. And my wife complaining all the time I smell like ink. Your wife ever complain you smelled like ink all the time?"

"No, she never complained," said Charlie. "I appreciate your bringing me over. Barry could have done it, but you know what Barry's like. Can't concentrate on anything but the paper for more than five minutes."

"He's a good man, mite wild in the head."

"I've seen it. Take me downtown so I can fetch my mail, and then you can take me home."

"Sure." Awtry cranked the car, and its valves ground with furious resistance, whined, cut off, started again. He drove back to Main Street and bumped back on the strip of concrete and drove slowly beneath the canopy of trees east toward the downtown area.

"Do you know who Ezra Atkinson was?" asked Charlie.

"Who?"

MORNING, MR. CHARLIE," SAID Harris Brooks, leaning from his stool at the postal window. A few amiable widows smiled as they retrieved their mail and walked slowly outside. In here, the heat was stifling, even though the windows were open. Brooks was about fifty and wore dark charcoal circles beneath his eyes. He sat smoking a cigarette and squinting through his glasses at an address on a package.

"A problem, Harris?"

"Damn if I can read this," said Harris. "Looks like Merguns Flensvan, Branton, Georgia. What do you think?" He turned the package, and Charlie took his glasses from his breast pocket, put them on, and leaned forward.

"Merguns Flenspar," read Charlie slowly. He took off his glasses and looked at Harris, who was shaking his head.

"Who in the name of hell is named Merguns around here? We're all looking forward to your speech out at Ezrie Atkinson this evening. You got it wrote out all nice and pretty?"

"Oh, yes," said Charlie. "I always prepare everything far in advance. You may be the only one there. I doubt anyone is going to be interested in four old men."

"I heard T. D. Varnell's wife is trying to let out his old uniform. Personally, I don't think there's that much 'let' in the whole South. You going to wear your uniform? I don't think I ever saw you in it."

"I never had one. Just wore whatever. I expect this evening I'll just wear whatever."

"Hang on." Charlie had a key to his mailbox, but he liked to ask for it at the window, and Harris didn't mind fetching it. A few men came in, all of them farmers, rough and sun-reddened, smelling of fields and mule dung. The world had been inherited by machines. They would drive to the European war in automobiles. Maybe fewer horses would die.

Charlie thought: *He will come back with the letter today. It will be small and perhaps of a personal nature, the name well scripted, the stamp squarely placed, for women take care with such things. They wrap Christmas packages as if their souls depended on the elegance they achieved. Perhaps there will be two bills and a paper from Eatonton or Monticello, but folded in will be the letter, finally here on the last day it could come.*

"Nope, nothing today, Mr. Charlie," said Harris. He exhaled a gout of smoke, quickly rolled a cigarette and lit it from the butt of the dying one. Harris dropped the nearly finished smoke to the floor, crushed it with his foot. "Merguns Flensvan don't even sound like an American, does it? Sounds more like—I don't know—a Dutchman or something. You hear of a Merguns Flensvan, you ring up and let us know, Mr. Charlie."

"I will," said Charlie, distracted. He felt as if he might fall. The heat was insufferable. He turned and started walking back outside, and Harris was saying something to him, but Charlie could not make out the words, in their shape or meaning. He thought of her and knew it was impossible. It had always been impossible from the beginning, like great battles with uneven forces.

August–September, 1861

F OR TWO DAYS, CHARLIE lay death still. His illness had taken him
again that summer. Dr. Merrill lifted him, carried him upward
to his bedroom, where he lay in sunny disarray with his eyes
closed. Betsy tenderly bathed him, helped him urinate into a jar. She
was startled by the size of him, the crop of black hair, but she knew a
body must function to live, and there was no shame in a mother's love,
no matter how intimate. Reverend Merrill sat beside Charlie and spoke
to him, then went to prowl the telegraph and post offices for word of
Tom. Perhaps it was in the plan of Providence that Tom be gone for a
soldier, because no one reported seeing him. A number of Brantonians
stopped the preacher in the street to congratulate him on Tom or share
their sorrow for Charlie.

News spread that Charlie had little time to live. It was typhoid or typhus. He had received a phantom horse-kick to the skull, the kind that
cannot be detected but is always fatal. His insides had been mortally
rearranged at birth, accounting for his small size. The preacher's wife
was out of her mind with grief. The little girl was being untended and
had gone wild. The only good thing Reverend Merrill knew was that the
church deacons had balked at selling the house to raise cash. Disbelieving much of the war rhetoric, he roamed the house, torn, sorrowful, ill
much of the time. Notes were due on improvements in the sanctuary,

and so little money was available, forfeit seemed a foregone conclusion. Now they were arguing that the fortunes of war would keep them solvent. Charles worried a furrow in the territory between his eyes.

On the following Thursday, when Charlie was still very ill, Jack Dockery limped slowly into the presence of his best friend, brushed with fear and impossibilities. In sickness, people changed, he knew. They might sweat or swell, change color or seem a different animal altogether. Jack's Aunt Mary Jean Clancy had had stomach cancer two summers past, and the last time he saw her, she was bloated and vague, stunned into silence by increasing doses of morphine. Her face turned pale and circular, and the eyes caught on him and seemed furious, though she could not speak. They were bringing him to see her one last time, and both of them knew it. They shoved him in the bedroom door, and after looking at her for thirty seconds, he fled, actually running, until the pain in his foot, and a boot full of blood, stopped him.

"Charlie? Hey, it's me," said Jack. A cool rain blessed the morning, came straight down on the roof of Grace House and dripped into the yard. "I would have come over sooner, but you were too sick. How are you feeling?"

Charlie heard Jack and knew who he was, but from this distance, it was impossible to speak or move. Charlie lay on the bottom of some vast lake, stern with a steel resolve. He could not rise. He would never come up again, so tired of being sick. Here there was a certainty of silence and deeper water.

"He comes and goes," said Betsy Merrill, then resting her hands on Jack's shoulders. Jack felt embarrassed and pleased at the same time, and he did not move to shrug her off. For the first time he could remember, such a touch was beyond maternal, made him feel strong and wise.

"He will," whispered Jack. The silence in the room was now sacred, sepulchral. "He will open his eyes and speak."

And Charlie thought, *No, I will never again open my eyes, and I will never again speak, for I am so weak. Has God made me sick? Has He done this to me?*

"He has run a high fever, it's broken now, and though the doctor says he cannot say what it is, my Charlie seems to be far away from us," she said. Her voice trembled lightly, and she massaged Jack's shoulders absent mindedly. "I have read to him. I've read some of his favorite novels and, and his poetry. I've read Keats to him and have just started *The Taming of the Shrew.* That one always made him laugh. Or should I have done *The Tempest* again, Jack? He's so far away, and I want him home with me."

"I should think any of those would be fine," said Jack. "He has a volume of Wordsworth, too, I believe, and he may gain some comfort from that."

Rev. Charles Merrill came into the room, and Jack felt Mrs. Merrill's soft, insistent hands fall from his shoulders, and he wanted to ask her to come back, to touch him once more.

"There is no change then," said Charles. "Oh, God, this is a sadness I can hardly bear, a sadness no man should have to bear, to lose both his sons at one swoop and yet lose neither of them completely at all. Jack, can you tell me anything that would help me understand what has happened to my boys?"

"No, sir," said Jack. "The last time I saw Charlie, he seemed very well. People sicken for no reason. People pass away for no reason. I don't see the reason. There's supposed to be some kind of plan. What kind of a God would do this to a boy like him?"

"That's blasphemy, son," said Reverend Merrill, but he almost whispered it, and Jack could tell it was spoken as a kind of talisman or ritual, not from pain or sorrow.

"All I can say is that it seems true, and that the arguments of this world and its sadness are all random," said Jack. "What kind of God would allow a baby to die and a drunkard to thrive?" Charlie and Jack had spent so much time in books they seemed different in their speech.

"Let's let them be for a few moments, Charles," said Betsy. "Come on."

"Yes, that is proper." Their footsteps receded into the hall and then downstairs, and Jack pulled a chair close and sat next to his friend.

"Let's see," said Jack. "There have been more battles in the west, and it's starting to look like the war won't end before Christmas. There's a big army starting to gather in Washington City for the Yankees, too. Governor Brown is saying things I don't understand. After the Virginia battle, remember, we thought they'd quit? Doesn't look like they are. I 'spect Tom will come home in a few days. The big battle they had in Virginia was a victory for us, though. The Yankees got whipped and ran all the way back to Washington. I imagine we will keep whipping them until they sue for peace.

"They said Jimmy Perdue almost drowned at Turner's Hole, but then he didn't. Can you imagine what the Great Baboon is thinking up there in his mansion right now? But I don't know. Maybe—maybe it's not meant for things to turn out the way they seem."

Charlie's even, deep breathing had not changed nor had his expression, and Jack stopped talking and looked past him through the window that shone a sullen daylight on his bed. No. There was little left to say. Jack rose and slowly left the room and walked painfully downstairs and out into the rain to his tethered horse. Martha came in quietly and stood next to her brother for a long time, and he sensed her presence, smelled her hair. He wanted to hug her, to say it is all right, that it was not her fault to be related to a weakling.

"Charlie," she said softly. She will stay with me now, he thought, but she did not, and soon her footsteps receded, and he slipped into a deeper place and felt his body float downward to darkness.

DAYS AND SERMONS PASSED. Reverend Merrill began to weep one Sunday morning when preaching from the second chapter of Joel. He had meant to reassure the fat barons in the church of their righteousness in the war. He read: *Blow yet the trumpet in Zion, and sound an alarm in my holy mountain: let all the inhabitants of the land tremble: for the day of the Lord cometh, for it is nigh at hand.* He read on, past where he meant to, which he did often, and then he read verse six: *Before their faces the people shall be much pained: all faces shall gather blackness.*

He looked in the balcony, where two dozen slaves sat fanning themselves against the upstairs heat, their faces blank, their posture indifferent or their eyes shut tight. A silence came to Reverend Merrill as he thought: *All faces shall gather blackness.* The Bible meant whatever one needed it to mean at the time. Baptists had used their authority to support slavery as a moral right. Yet Branton was not a fire-breathing port of insurrectionists. It had been the railroad terminus long enough to gather philosophies. Reverend Merrill stood far too long, and he saw men and women looking at each other with knit brows. He looked down the long sanctuary at the richly detailed stained glass windows. His eyes stopped on the crucifixion, and he felt the agony of a pierced side, of nailed hands, of breath growing more faint by the moment. He saw the centurions casting lots for the cloak of Our Lord. He cleared his throat, looked down and read once more: *Before their face the people shall be much pained: all faces shall gather blackness.*

"Reverend Merrill, this has just come in," said someone from the back of the sanctuary. All heads craned, and they saw Richard Key, an old man wearing an ill-fitting militia outfit. "Oh, Lord, this has just come in."

"Come forth, Brother Key," said Charles. Betsy craned, felt sure it had to do with Tom's death, though why it should be on a sheet of paper she could not imagine. She pulled Martha to her, and the child trembled. Key walked with exaggerated health down the aisle, his heavy boots hard on the floorboards.

"It just come at the telegraph station," he said. "I was there, and Mr. Jenks, he made several copies for us to take to the churches. It just come in. I can't hardly think on it." He mounted the altar and handed the paper to Reverend Merrill, who put on his glasses and read it first to himself. An expression of such pain entered his eyes that the congregation flinched, prepared itself for terrible news. War news, no doubt. Some great battle lost? Betsy fought a terrible urge to rise and run for Charlie. She turned and saw their house servants Cephus and Missy in the balcony, and Cephus slept, but Missy leaned over the rail and looked down on the white congregation with concern.

"My dear friends," said Reverend Merrill. Key left quickly as he had come, not wanting to hear. "I have here the contents of a telegram arrived just this morning. It says the following: 'I regret to inform you that Ezra Atkinson, drummer boy of the Branton Rifles of Cobb's Legion, succumbed this morning to a fever in camp near Richmond, Virginia." A gasp rose from the men, and women began to weep outright. There was a soft moaning from the balcony. "He was a brave boy and did his duty. We regret his loss and shall send home his body by rail for rapid and proper burial. May Jesus bless you in this time of trial. Sincerely, Thomas R. R. Cobb, Commander."

Reverend Merrill held the lectern for balance. Betsy wept with relief and sorrow. The Atkinsons were Methodists, and there would be tears right now across the street. Choir members behind Preacher Merrill wept openly. He felt a speech rising in him, the kind of extemporaneous speech at which he was very good. But instead of comfort, the words challenged and condemned. Instead of balm, they offered a charge of complicity. Though he had preached hard for the Southern cause for several months now, most knew his moderate sympathies, and many in the congregation agreed. Most, however, believed in the new nation, and the plantation owners, no more than ten of them, who rode their buggies to town Sunday morning for services, expected the right words, the right support. They were the hereditary monarchs of the land, the ones for whom Ezra Atkinson had died.

"Just a boy," said Reverend Merrill finally. "Ezra Atkinson was just a boy who liked to bang the drum. I am told that many of these drummers are orphans. I am told that many of them come from heaven knows where and are brought into line because they have nowhere else to go. Ezra Atkinson was no orphan. He was our boy. He was from Branton, and his family has been here since the beginning. He was our darling boy."

Reverend Merill began to tremble. Betsy came halfway out of her seat and then sat again. Martha cried quietly, reaching for her mother. He began to sob, and he looked down, and his composure broke like sunlight through a cloud, and a great bull groan escaped his mouth, and a gasp rose from the congregation as men rushed forward to catch him if he fell or to escort him away. Slaves in the balcony were whispering *Oh, Lord,* and *Lord Jesus hep* over and over. He caught himself.

"Let us pray," he said. "Eternal God, the God of children and lambs and small broken things, protect the soul of Ezra Atkinson and bring him peace. Bring his family peace. And God bring peace to this land. Amen."

Many of the planters, who had urgently wanted war and who followed the news in Virginia and Kentucky with the greatest interest, seemed somewhat baffled. Too old to fight or too respectable to be held accountable, they glanced at each other almost with a shrug. Merrill was soft, but much of the town was. That would mean nothing. Independence was won, and no government anywhere would be able forcibly to bring millions back into a fold they'd voluntarily fled.

"In light of this terrible news, let us adjourn services so that we can begin to mourn, each in our own way," said Reverend Merrill. "In the name of the Father, the Son, and the Holy Ghost, amen."

They drifted out on a tide of tears and mumbled words, remembering sunny May and the boy who left them heading north.

IN MID-SEPTEMBER, CHARLIE HEARD footsteps on the stairs. He had lost weight but had begun to sip chicken soup regularly, though he only whispered sentences. His father would sit beside the bed in the evening and read him back issues of the *Atlanta Intelligencer,* including its sentimental poems, ads for dyspepsia cures, political reports from the State

House, and war news. Governor Joe Brown seemed to be at odds with the new Confederate government on many issues. Indeed, the state of Georgia had been divided in its vote to secede from the Union. Betsy read Charlie chapters from *David Copperfield,* and even at the funniest parts, Charlie showed only pale smiles. Dr. Dexter visited regularly, prescribed balms and plasters, but none of them helped. Jack stopped by and told jokes and stories, repeated gossip about the Battle of Manassas. The stubborn Union troops had run away, but now they were regrouping. They were too stupid even to know they were licked.

Charlie heard the footsteps today without interest. Two pair, both women. He lay pale and distant.

"Charlie, I've brought you a visitor," said Betsy. "I'm just going to put a chair here for her next to your bed. She will sit with you for a while. I didn't even send for her. She sent word she wanted to visit."

"Hello, Charlie," said Sarah Pierce. She stood before him in a pale blue everyday dress, and she stared with rising emotion at the small shrouded form in the bed at the window ledge. He seemed to have shrunk, but Sarah could tell he'd been well tended, for a smell of soap and hair oil rose from him, very light but pleasing. His hands lay at his side outside the covers. He did not sweat, and he was as motionless as the sleeping, eyes closed.

"This is Sarah, Dr. Pierce's niece," said Betsy. "You met her at our party. She's here from Boston until she can get home. She may talk to you or read to you. I have to take Martha to town now. And Charlie, if you can hear me, son, your father has gone off to Atlanta on the train to look for Tom. We have not had word from him yet if he is in Virginia. I believe he is all right. In my heart, I believe he is all right. Sarah, Cephus is in the yard if you need help."

"Thank you, ma'am," she said. "I won't be staying terribly long." She had driven a light gig over by herself, and Cephus was tending to the horse, watering it and speaking slow sentences of commiseration. Betsy left, and Charlie could hear Martha's arguing voice as they headed out the back door toward their carriage. Sarah pulled a chair to the bedside and sat in it and looked at Charlie, up and down. His shape barely disturbed the sheets and covers, and there was something vaguely wrong about her being here unchaperoned, but he was immobile with sickness, and only a vile person would think it improper.

Charlie felt a quickening but kept his eyes closed. A faint scent of mimosa came to him, and he tried to remember Sarah, and at first nothing came, then he remembered her blond hair and blue-gray eyes, her strong will and sardonic smile.

"This must be boring," said Sarah, sighing out the words. "You've been here for days and days. The whole town's been weeping forever over its drummer boy, Charlie, but nobody's going to quit this thing until half the boys in the country are dead. Can you hear me?"

Yes, he thought, lying in the deep lake of fog, *I can hear you.*

"Doesn't matter if you can or you can't. If you can hear me, raise one finger." Charlie tried not even to breathe. He was embarrassed for her to be here, but wanted her to stay.

"I do not, for the life of me, know how you can bear the heat here. The air is so very wet and unmoving all the time. And I am told people once moved here for the good air from Savannah and Augusta. I find that amusing. My uncle is most amusing, too. Selling his ridiculous tonic to old ladies, most of whom would die before letting alcohol touch their lips, knowing the truth and saying nothing about it anyway. It's a form of lying.

"You know what? I rather like being able to say what I please knowing that you probably can't hear me and will not answer. I could say anything I wanted. What could I say? I could talk about the people in Branton. Mr. Asaph Cole and his eye for the women. His wife is always trailing behind him with a proud glare, shooing off the women he bows to. Why isn't he gone to be a soldier? Why are so many men in Branton not gone to soldiers? Or Mrs. James R. Lambeth and her mansion, The Oaks. If her nose were any higher in the air, she'd smell the sweat of angels."

Charlie felt a shudder in his sheets, almost like laughter.

"So very many have hired substitutes already. Oh, Mr. Lincoln has fired General McDowell already and replaced him with a dwarf called McClellan. I guess he believes only Scotsmen can win the war for America. Are they Scotsmen or Irishmen? McClellan won two small battles in western Virginia, and now Mr. Lincoln thinks he can defeat the South. But do you know what will defeat you, Charlie? Time. That is what will defeat you. Oh, the Union has instituted a blockade of the South now as well, and we here are supposed to be cut off from sending or receiving goods. Everyone says Confederate ships are too fast to be captured.

"The big planters are worried that their cotton will rot in Savannah. The stores in town are worried the big planters won't pay them. My uncle is worried that women won't have the spare cash to buy his liquory specific. The women are formed into societies to knit socks and weave blankets. Ladies are supposed to keep journals and write letters. That man named Blasingale who fought in the War of 1812 who had hitched on with the Branton Rifles? He died of pneumonia before they got to Richmond."

Charlie loved the rhythm and honesty in her voice. She spoke rapidly, with a clipped Boston accent, not quite patrician, but nothing like the South, where life slowed to the pace of the weather.

"Nobody seems to know what is wrong with you. Most think a horse may have kicked you in the head. I don't believe that. I believe you are in there. If you can hear me, squeeze my hand."

He felt the warmth of her hand on his, felt her lifting it gently, almost finger by finger. She cradled her hand in his and held it, then once only, rubbed her thumb on the back of his hand. He wanted to exert the most subtle pressure, but he could not. He felt himself falling faster now, away, into the dense brambles of darkness. Suddenly, she pinched his hand quite hard and watched him closely, but by then he was far away, in distant shadows.

May 14–19, 1864

RESACA TO CASSVILLE

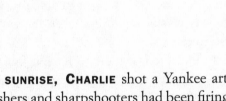

JUST AFTER SUNRISE, CHARLIE shot a Yankee artilleryman in the arm. Skimishers and sharpshooters had been firing for half an hour when the field pieces opened on both sides along the battle lines, which bristled, face to face, near the small north Georgia town of Resaca. Charlie and Duncan McGregor had strayed to the left flank of the Confederate army and were in a stand of oaks. Charlie had climbed to a sturdy oak branch and stood upon it, fifteen feet into the under canopy, and from there he could almost enfilade the Federal artillery ranks with an invisible cross fire.

"This gives new meaning to a flank being in the air," said Duncan. "Boy, you're going to be the death of me."

Charlie said nothing. He had reloaded and was looking through the telescope on the side of his Whitworth rifle, searching for a target. Sometimes he waited until he saw a scowling officer or a fuzz-faced battery commander. A few skirmishers were looking around for the source of the shot; Charlie saw what might be a lieutenant, wearing a muddy blue coat whose buttons were all unhooked, staring almost straight at him through field glasses. He centered the man's head in the sight and fired, and Charlie saw him fall. The field glasses flew backward, and there was a scrambling to turn a Parrott gun in their direction.

"Coming down," said Charlie. "They're sighting us with a field piece." He dropped his rifle down to Duncan and then squatted on the greening limb and leaped down, landing hard just as a shell ripped overhead, crashing through the upper limbs with an angry thrashing.

"You got 'em riled up something fierce, boy," said Duncan. "I'd suggest we move closer to our lines, praise God."

"All right." They scuttled low to the ground out of the small patch of woods and across an open field, and by now musket fire from the skirmishers and even some of the entrenched infantry was cracking and popping from both sides. Cleburne's Division was in the center of the Confederate lines, a distance yet, and so Charlie and Duncan, earth puffing upward from minié ball fire around them, edged into the works' left flank. A private leaned against the red-mud wall, vomiting from fright. Charlie glanced at him with compassion and passed by.

In half an hour, he and Duncan had regained Cleburne's Division and found Govan's Brigade and their old company. Bob Rainey was looking through a narrow space in the stacked-log works. He fired his Enfield, backed up to reload, cursing loudly.

"Well, for the love of God, if it ain't General Johnston's two wandering minstrels," said Bob Rainey. He was filthy and stank, but so did everyone else. There was another stench, though, the high, rising putrid aroma of carrion—horses, mules, and men—lying in the field between the lines. "Boys, have you sung any songs this morning?"

"Charlie has," said Duncan. "We separated last night, and it took me hours to find our lines and Charlie again. That will be my last individual act of scouting."

"Shall I put you down as a coward then?" asked Bob Rainey. He bit the end off the cartridge, pushed it into the barrel of his Enfield, and rammed it home.

"You may do so," said Duncan. "I've never seen much military use for dead heroes, the wishes of our officers notwithstanding."

"The *wishes of our officers notwithstanding?*" said Bob Rainey. "Ain't that pretty. They teach people to talk like that in Scotland?" He put a percussion cap on the nipple, cocked the rifle, took his place at the logs, aimed only for a short moment, and fired again.

"We value an education, unlike all you dumb Southerners. You ain't got no more idea of education than a pig does of a bonnet."

"Haw," said Bob Rainey. "Ain't you precious. So, Charlie Merrill, you have done worked for your country this morning?" Charlie smiled and looked around. The works were vast and extremely strong. Assaulting them would be the kind of madness known only in war.

"He shot two from a artillery battery far on our left flank," said Duncan. "The boy's a artist with his Whitworth rifle, Bob. A *artist.* Then they didn't take none too kindly to his art and turned a rifled gun on us. Which is why we are in this louse-filled dugout with you dog-meat soldiers rather than being out in the vanguard."

"I'll put you *both* down as cowards then," said Bob Rainey. A shell from the Union artillery exploded not far away, and Charlie saw a yellow-haired Confederate blown into three spouting pieces. The parts writhed for a moment, and the boy's face turned back and forth, glancing wildly. Then a look of consternation passed his eyes and froze in his face.

"Merciful Jesus," said Duncan.

"Bad luck," said Bob Rainey, shrugging. He loaded his rifle and fired again, and so Charlie and Duncan did the same, drawing down on Federal boys through rifle loopholes, missing, more than anything.

A BOY NAMED GARFIELD Palmer, who had been wounded at Missionary Ridge and then developed pneumonia, lay in the Confederate breastworks just behind Charlie and Duncan, coughing and shaking. He had tried to stop trembling, but as the din swelled from muskets and artillery, he held his ears and wept more.

"I won't see my town again," he said. He rolled and coughed. "I won't see my town again. Or Nana." The men in Govan's brigade pitied him, but none could spare the time to share comfort. Charlie looked back at Gar as he reloaded his rifle, and he thought: *Probably my age or even a little older. Probably won't last the day or the hour.* A lieutenant raised Gar up finally and helped him to the rear of the lines. Charlie watched until he was out of sight.

ABOUT ELEVEN IN THE morning, the Federals began to swell from their works, heading straight for Cleburne's lines. Charlie looked around for the general but didn't see him. He *would* be here. You could almost feel his presence, his light brogue, his steady gray eyes taking in the field and knitting a strategy. In the tent hunched over his field desk or the chessboard, Cleburne had kind eyes, but on the battlefield, he turned hard, even brusque, as he placed troops, studied movements. He stood in the line of fire, tall and thin, and the swept air, lead on lead, seemed to part around him.

"Here they come!" someone cried. The Union troops had to pass up through gullies of bramble and briar. Cleburne's Division—the entire Confederate works—stiffened and began pouring fire into the ranks of Union skirmishers as they preceded the infantry lines. Buglers blew calls, officers screamed commands. Gun carriages on both sides rocked as the batteries opened fire in a field of deafness. Men clutched their ears, reloaded, fired again. Charlie looked at Duncan, who was at a rifle loophole firing steadily, but Charlie was in no hurry, and he loaded the Whitworth and climbed up the trench slope and took a better position, in full view of the enemy.

"Get down, you fool!" cried Bob Rainey. Charlie shot a flag bearer, and the banner slipped from his hands and lay trampled in the underbrush. Another man picked it up, but the briars tugged it back down, released only shreds. Charlie calmly reloaded and missed the second color bearer. His hands shook, and he felt a twitch in the left corner of his mouth. Other men seemed to be screaming at him, but by now words had grown inaudible in the mass of artillery fire. Charlie looked before the Southern lines and saw old rifle pits where the skirmishers had lain in the night, and he climbed out and half fell into one and lay on his stomach, reloaded, drew bead. Duncan watched him calmly, knew he would be dead soon.

The Federals came on up the slope at Resaca. The smell of gun smoke choked them. Screaming shells arced over both lines. Charlie thought: *Resaca.* That's the name of this place. A warm day to die. For half an hour, the Union troops in their sinuous blue line wavered toward Cleburne's men, coming closer, edging back, falling in bloody clots. Charlie shot one man, and he tumbled down, vomiting blood. A rock landed in Charlie's rifle pit from the Union lines: a sign of contact and contempt. Another rock fell short, and Charlie edged up out of the pit and fired at the first motion, hitting a soldier in the back, between the shoulder blades. He did a half somersault forward, lay still as the blue lines retreated. The earth seemed to be destroying itself in a wild fit of rage and forcing the combatants to watch, stunned and sorrowful at its shattered trees and blazing fields.

The Confederate soldiers screamed and yelled, cursed the Northern troops, told them to come back, but finally they were withdrawing, and the field was writhing with the wounded, shaped by the dead. Charlie walked from the rifle pit and came over the earthen parapet and back into the earthworks. The firing was sporadic now.

"Boy, you are the dang stupidest fellow I ever seen," screamed Bob Rainey, grinning. "If you want to be dead so bad, go stand out thar about a hunnert yards and I'll shoot you myself." Charlie's eyes narrowed slightly, but he said nothing.

THE ATTACK HAVING FAILED, the Union troops brought artillery forward and began to fire at the divisions of Cleburne, Bate, and Cheatham with a steady fury. The firing was so intense none of the Confederates dared to raise their heads. A shell not a hundred yards away landed in the works and threw bodies and parts of bodies into tortured positions. Men staggered, wearing their own blood like shrouds. Trees and underbrush burst into flames, and the fire crept along, swollen and malignant. A shell struck the log rampart not thirty yards from Charlie and Duncan, and the wood splintered and began to smolder. More than twenty shell explosions a minute poured from the Union batteries, and the men lay on their stomachs. Some prayed aloud. A man who bragged he was a "Little Rock Rambler" wet his pants.

"Jesus, *get* that!" a tall soldier cried. A live shell had landed in the works, and two men heaved it over the ramparts just before it exploded. Charlie was covered with a spray of dirt and dust, and he felt a sudden, intense fear that had many origins, many meanings.

CLEBURNE'S MEN WATCHED WITH disappointment when troops under General John Bell Hood some distance away on the Confederate right began boiling out of their works around five in the afternoon, shrieking, running, howling—Cleburne's men wishing it were them instead.

"By damn, Hood's going to make a charge," said Bob Rainey. Two other members of the sharpshooter company, hollow-faced Isom Bedgood and Walter Bragg, had sidled into the area near Charlie, looking for a position to fire. Charlie was already back up on the works taking potshots at the Federal troops across the way.

"He cain't hardly wait to get him anothern," said Bedgood, who was immediately shaken with a coughing fit. "I never seed nobody so eager to kill somebody."

"Leave him be," said Bragg. "He's doing what we do, only he won't quit. He won't stop. He's got a burr in his ass. Boys, what's the burr in Merrill's ass? He so kind and yet hard sometimes."

"Well, now, it being Saturday, he reckons it's a fine time to work before the Lord's Day comes," said Tommy Wallace. "On the seventh day, he will rest. Amen."

"That's funny," said Bedgood. "I reckon that's supposed to be funny. What's Hood's boys doing over there?"

"Getting a charge," said Bob Rainey. "We sit here in these stinking works fighting off all this artillery, and then they let Hood go. Hood's a wild man, you know. Fine general, but he don't know how to stop onct he's started. That's how come he's got the one crippled arm and is minus one leg."

Even at such a distance, the Rebel yell from Hood's men spread over them. In the small spaces between muskets and artillery fire it held like a shout from the dead. Charlie held his rifle down and climbed up high enough to watch them. They ran downhill and chased away the Federal skirmish line, and there was a folding or unfolding, and Charlie was struck by its dark magnificence, the wavering lines, the screams, the knowledge of death. He knew by now that in battle you were either close to God or very far away from him. The Southerners always thought they were in the right and thus closer to God. One general, Leonidas Polk, was even a bishop in the Episcopal Church and found more satisfaction in baptism by water than fire.

The Federal lines bent back farther, then farther again, and Cleburne's men cheered, but there was a sudden sundering: Union cannon not half a mile from Hood's men opened up with a ghastly noise, like one great final explosion at the End of the Earth: the Last Judgment. Hood's men began to fall, twirling and diving or blown into shards by direct hits.

"By Jesus, that's a slaughter," said Bob Rainey. Charlie reloaded his Whitworth and scoured the artillery batteries facing Hood's men, fired at an artillery captain, but he hit nothing.

"Dear sweet Mother of God," said Duncan. Charlie looked at him, and for a reason he knew well enough, affection swept him, almost as if Duncan were a brother he had just discovered. Hood's men had retreated into a grove of trees, and over the next hour, they made three screaming charges at the Federal lines, but the cannon fire was endless. Finally, toward twilight, Hood's troops turned and ran away from their deaths. No man could bear death at this hour, when hope of reaching another day began to take shape in his mind.

✧ ✧ ✧

FOR A TIME, THE firing slowed, and Charlie thought of Martha and his mother for the first time in several days. He also thought of Sarah and tentatively touched the front of his blouse and felt the letter, knew the shape of its handwriting by heart.

About seven-thirty, Union troops down the way rushed forward and were repulsed, then did it again and again. Finally they lodged on a small hill, but Cleburne's troops were too far away to pour enfilade fire into their ranks. Besides, darkness, damp with cold, edged into Resaca, and the men lay exhausted from the day's battle. A few exchanges of inaccurate musket fire continued. The lines were so close the armies exchanged taunts, insults to mother and country, laughing charges of cowardice and stupidity.

"You boys wanted a fight, and aye, God, you had one," said Bob Rainey.

"I'm low," said Walter Bragg. "How are you fixed?"

"I've got about ten rounds," said Charlie. "I could give you three."

"All right, then."

The men who held crackers of hardtack took them from pockets and from inside their shirts. They took, ate, for this was the body that was dedicated to the Confederate States of America, Jefferson Davis, president. All those damned Virginians, Charlie thought, secure in their noble grandeur; they had brought this upon us. Even though Davis was from Mississippi, he was now steering the course of this endless war. Governor Joe Brown of Georgia had even proposed a separate peace, and the legislature at Milledgeville passed it several months before. The North Carolinians seemed even more serious about leaving the Confederacy. But it was no good. They would fight until death gave up on them. That was the unspoken truth since Fort Sumter in April 1861. This war was not being run by Lincoln or Davis but by Death, and he was a hard man to satisfy.

CHARLIE SLEPT SOUNDLY ON his arms and awoke, just after light, to a skirmish, which had already begun on both sides. Duncan sat near him, awake already, scratching his beard and loading his rifle.

"Welcome back to the glory of war, Charlie Merrill," said Duncan. "Here's the cartridges we need for our day's labor. I was thinking of writing my mother if I survive this day. Would you help me with that, Charlie?"

"I will," he said. He loaded his Whitworth. "Let's see if we can get out of this trench and get a better position."

"For once, I agree."

Bragg and Bedgood had left already, out seeking a wash or a tree from which to polish their sharpshooting into the Federal lines. The Southern lines were miles long, and Charlie and Duncan finally came to its left flank and moved out, far ahead, even, of the foremost Confederate skirmishers, creeping through rough country, looking for an artillery battery to attack. During the morning, Charlie took shots at several of them, but he was consistently firing too high, and every time he did not see a bluecoat fall, he sighed and worked his fists. Finally, near ten, he shot an officer on a sorrel horse, shot him clean off the saddle, though the man's hand convulsively reached for the pommel before he fell. In early afternoon, the Federals attacked again, but they were repulsed in a ghastly fire. Charlie looked around and saw a tall man in the saddle, and he narrowed his eyes on the scope until he was sure this man ranked; perhaps even a brigadier general. Charlie drew a bead on him and held his hands steady. Wait, wait, wait, *now.* He fired, and the officer sharply slumped to his right, and a look of pain and surprise overcame him as he began to fall, then tumbled into the arms of his field staff below. Charlie hated them for being in Georgia, but he controlled himself.

"I think I just shot a general," said Charlie.

"Bloody fine thing, because I've just been shot myself," said Duncan.

Charlie's head whipped back, and he stared at Duncan, whose arm was bleeding profusely from the left bicep. Charlie tore open the rotting shirt and saw a clean slice across Duncan's arm, no bone involved.

"Be still," said Charlie. He tore off one of Duncan's shirtsleeves and wrapped it as a tourniquet around his arm, pulling it tight tenderly.

"Ah, God, let me die of the wound, not the treatment for it!" screamed Duncan. "Help me up before I piss myself, Charlie." Charlie pulled him up, and the fire around them was heavier now, like a summer thundershower strengthening for wind and hail. Charlie looked away as Duncan pulled out his penis and urinated in a long stream, looking for blood in it, seeing nothing.

"Back down now," said Charlie.

"Back down, hell, let's get to our works," said Duncan. "And by God, find me some morphine, for the love of God. This is the fury of a thousand bees at once, and I'm not sure I'll bear it."

"Come on," said Charlie. The two rifles in his left hand weighed nothing, ounces, and he got under Duncan's shoulder and helped him away from their sniper's position amid a spattering of minié balls and screams from Federals trying to hit them. One bullet whined not an inch from Charlie's left ear. If you name things, thought Charlie, they become real, so he said it aloud: *Resaca.* The place of this death is *Resaca.*

AFTER DARK, AFTER A day when General Johnston thought the army had an opening for attack, after hundreds of deaths, and the rising stench of the dead, the Confederate officers got word that the Union army was flanking them, had, in fact, moved strongly toward the back of their works. Johnston's order to attack had been rescinded, but one group of Southern soldiers had not received the word, and they rushed into a hideous haze of spinning metal.

Charlie took Duncan to the hospital behind the lines, but they could only bandage him lightly and refused morphine. Outside one hospital tent, Charlie saw a mound of arms and legs, the offal from a slaughterhouse. A young soldier stood nearby poking at a hand to see if it would grab back. It was the same one who'd wanted to see his town the day before.

"We're moving out," someone said.

"*Now,* for the blood of Christ?" said Duncan, his face turned up in pain. Lanterns and campfires had been lit against the dark and dampness. "*Now?*"

"We can't find Cleburne tonight, so let's just find the lines and move along," said Charlie. "I'll make sure you keep up."

"God knows I *will* keep up," Duncan half shouted. "Retreating after *that,* for the love of God. Why should we have left hundreds of men in the field? Why can we not hold a position?"

"The Yankees have twice the men we have," said Charlie. "They can flank us. I suspect they have flanked us already."

"They by God have flanked me," said Duncan glumly. "I was flanked hours ago."

IN THE DARK, NEAR ten, exhausted Confederate soldiers poured across the two bridges of the Oostanaula River, one for the railroad, the other for wagons and horses. Behind them to the north, Resaca, a small but pretty village, was burning and coating the low sky with a dull red varnish. Some of the men were wounded, but most were footsore, and many had trouble hearing from the bombardment and the musket fire. The troops on the wagon bridge made a hollow clomping, but it was not a march, just a rapid unmeasured walk, without discipline. Regiments and then brigades mixed as the men moved at an uneven pace. *On the other side,* they said—we'll get back with our units *on the other side.*

Cleburne's skirmishers and sharpshooters had been ordered to stay on the north bank of the river as a rear guard, but Duncan was trembling with pain by midnight, and so Charlie helped him across the railroad bridge. There was a large river down there in the darkness, Charlie knew, but it flowed invisibly, like a rumor or a myth. Once across, the troops kept marching toward Calhoun, yet another small town, a way station in the game of flanking and retreat. Charlie knew what the Yankee troops would find in Resaca, where by some trick of God he had not died after all: rotting corpses and horses, the stench of death, wounded still in their terminal hospitals, the pervasive smell of animal and human excrement. Then: trees burning from the shellfire, like women with their hair in flames, flaring buildings, and the dirt streets warm to the touch from fire. Then they would see the bridges wearing fire like clothing.

Charlie marched, cradling the Whitworth beneath his left arm, supporting Duncan with his right shoulder. Duncan, who groaned with each step. Deep into the night, they were still marching, and Charlie was surprised to see a familiar face and then another. These were Cleburne's men, though not Govan's Brigade—Granbury's Texans maybe, but his division. No one knew the exact time when a halt was called. The men exhaled sharp breaths and many went to sleep in strange, twisted positions almost immediately. It took Duncan a while, but then his breathing changed. Charlie could see very little. They were in a pine forest, and the bed of needles was soft, but when they turned to either side, they jabbed them. Even dead things defended their territory.

JUST AFTER SUNRISE, CHARLIE awoke and sat up. In a field at the edge of the woods, the supply wagons stretched south in a long train.

"Come on, let's find our men and get some rations," said Charlie. Duncan rolled back and forth, and sat up, his beard shaking dust.

"By damn, now I think I have bites from bugs all over my body," said Duncan, scratching. "Though I will admit my arm seems to have scabbed off in a fine mood." He looked at the wound, and it had stopped bleeding, and in fact was not as deep as Charlie had thought the day before. "Still wish I could have drawn my ration of morphine, though."

"Come on, then," said Charlie. Most of them still slept, spread across dozens of acres—thousands of men who looked slain, like a Greek battlefield. This, Charlie thought, was the South's *Iliad,* and it would in the next few weeks become much worse. They walked for most of an hour before Charlie, to his delight and surprise, heard Bob Rainey's voice not far away, harrying another soldier for some indiscretion, using his normal baroque string of curses. Charlie and Duncan came up.

"Well, for the love of God, if it ain't Cleburne's minstrel boys again," said Rainey.

"Duncan is wounded," said Charlie.

"A nick in the arm's all it is, son," said Duncan, who was now walking on his own.

"You took a ball in the arm, is it?" asked Bob Rainey. "Do you remember Timmons, the boy with the sty that would never heal? He's gone to God, boys, shot in the nose. You never seen such a thing in your life as a man shot in his nose. I half disbelieve I will ever forget it, though God knows I wish I could. The brigade's drawing rations. Let's be eating. No sense denying them Yanks a fair target in our thinness."

Charlie found himself smiling. He had never seen anyone so blithely unconcerned about his own welfare as Bob Rainey. If he were alive, he would be alive. When he was dead, there would be no more marching or suffering. The simplicity of his philosophies touched Charlie. He remembered Timmons, who was always blinking from the sty, rubbing it until his eye wept and he was half blind.

THEY HAD EATEN ONLY small rations and had built few fires when the order came to move out. Men cursed lieutenants, captains, majors, colonels, generals, spat invective, not with the genial grumbling of an army in its swinging stride, but with true venom. By now Duncan was even better. Many of the men, not bothering to look for cover, dropped their trousers and defecated in the fields. Nothing else could be done, and this march could be a long one. Stragglers on such a march might be called deserters and shot.

Charlie and Duncan wandered around looking for the rest of the sharpshooter company, and they found Walter Bragg and Isom Bedgood.

"Are we holding a rear guard on the march?" asked Duncan. "Where are we placed?"

"Lieutenant says we're to march on with the boys until we take a halt and then await orders," said Bragg. "I think the whole army's headed south toward Calhoun. I heard boys who know this country say that's the next town there is."

DUNCAN WAS SO MUCH better that he carried his own gun without trouble. Before camp had broken, they had been able to get more ammunition and percussion caps from the supply train, and Charlie chafed at the retreat toward Atlanta. In March, they had half thought they would be driving the Federals back into Chattanooga, but now everything was going wrong. Word came at midmorning that while the railroad bridge over the Oostanaula had burned and collapsed into the river, the fire crews had trouble burning the wagon bridge, and it had survived. Federal troops under the command of General James McPherson had roared over the bridge and were now hot behind them, coming on, refusing to take the rest granted to the Southern troops.

"How for the love of God will we win this war if we can't burn a goddamn bridge?" roared Bob Rainey.

When they came near Calhoun, the men were pleased when they were placed in battle lines. Death on the field of combat was far preferable to them, Charlie thought, than being shot in the back as they retreated. Govan's and Lowrey's brigades of Cleburne's Division kept marching for a site two miles up the Adairsville Road, but Charlie and Duncan broke away and found a grove of trees far in advance of Bishop-General Leonidas Polk's Corps. Charlie climbed a cedar whose sticky branches brushed the ground. Cedars were not ideal sniping trees because of their spreading branch-works, but they were ridiculously easy to climb, and they were stout even in their upper reaches. Duncan went off to Charlie's left and found an open place and lay on his stomach.

Now they would wait. Charlie had a clean view of a large field and the

road that bisected it. The Federals would have to come this way. He
snugged himself in the branches and loaded his Whitworth. One sniper
who had climbed a tree with a loaded Kerr rifle in winter quarters had
dropped the gun, and when it hit the ground it fired straight upward. The
bullet entered his crotch and came out the top of his head. Ramming a
cartridge down a muzzle-loader while balancing in a tree required skill,
but Charlie did it easily, scanned the field before him with the telescopic
sight.

He would think of Sarah. He took out the letter and read it again.
Sweat stains had not smeared the ink yet, but the marks seemed fuzzier
than he remembered, as if the lines were forgetting the words they
shaped. Shakespeare's sonnets. Picnics in the pecan grove. Reading to
him as he lay ill in bed in the cold of a February day. Walks in the dark.

"Somethin's moving!" shouted Duncan. Charlie put the letter away.
He did not need the telescopic sight. Coming through the woods, on
the road, everywhere, were blue-coated troops, marching not just at
double-quick time but at a speed for engagement. Skirmishers, Charlie
thought. And just behind them, the whole damned Union army. They
were almost a mile away, but within range of the Whitworth. Charlie
drew bead on a plain foot soldier, not an artilleryman or an officer. Perhaps this was better. Officers were, after all, useless men who rarely
killed anyone, and another man would take the place of a dead man in
a twelve-pounder Napoleon battery. The skirmishers and infantry were
the fodder, the dispensable killers who were assigned death as their
duty and did it consistently if not always willingly.

Charlie shot a skirmisher whose face was indistinct. He snapped
backward, and his kepi flipped off his head. He disappeared in tall
grass. One obvious friend ran to him and knelt almost in prayer. Charlie reloaded in fifteen seconds and cocked the rifle again and then shot
the fallen man's friend. He didn't see the Union sharpshooter, but a
bullet cracked through the cedar limbs above him. Charlie ignored it,
loaded again. Now they were boiling out behind the skirmishers, coming faster, and Polk's men, who were still out of range, loosed a few
rounds of panic fire. The Federals came on up closer, took positions.
The Yankee sharpshooter took another line on Charlie, and this one
was much closer. Charlie looked through his scope into a tree line
nearly a mile away, scanned back and forth. Then: a motion. Hold on it.
A man's arms as he pulled the ramrod from the barrel of his rifle. Charlie cocked the hammer of his gun and squeezed the trigger. The man

did an acrobatic flip, and Charlie tried to follow him down, but the scope was too small, the distance too great. The shooter simply vanished. The limbs bounced for a moment then were still again.

BY DARK, CHARLIE AND Duncan had regained Cleburne's Division, and the day's action had been slight, mostly sniping, some hard firing. Everyone slept, and Charlie and Duncan fell asleep, too. Charlie did not dream, instead shifting once, blinking, awakening sometime in the night to find men moving.

"Not marching in the night *again,*" said Duncan.

"I'd liefer be dead than do another night march," said a tall soldier with few teeth. In the faint light of a few nearby lanterns, Charlie could see he was nearly bald. Most of the men coughed themselves awake. It had been a brief rest, but a rest at that.

"We may be in Atlanta in the morning," said Charlie laconically. "Maybe we can eat at a fine restaurant. I'll buy you beef and dumplings and an apple pie."

"An entire pie, then?" asked Duncan.

"Pie, my arse," said a soldier whose face Charlie could not see.

BY DAWN ON MAY 17, Johnston's troops reached the town of Adairsville, and the marching men liked the place immediately: a high ridge seemed to encircle the entire town, and from those heights, a formidable position might be held. Cleburne's men, however, marched two miles north of town before they halted. The Federals arrived early in the afternoon, and Charlie found a good position for shooting. Cheatham's Division was at the crest of a hill, but the rest of Cleburne's Division was behind it. The firing at the front was sporadic, and Charlie seemed unable to hit anything. Around three, he ran out of ammunition and began to come back through Cheatham's lines toward his own brigade. Duncan, whose wound was hurting more, had stayed with Bob Rainey. An ominous red streak ran down the shot biceps to his wrist.

Charlie saw, not far away, Cleburne himself, holding a piece of paper and shaking his head. He glanced up and saw Charlie and motioned for him to approach. Cleburne's chief of staff, Major Calhoun Benham, and his aide, Captain Irving Buck, were not far away, looking worried.

"Mr. Merrill, I see you are well," said Cleburne. "It is difficult to play chess under such conditions, but perhaps we can resume. But look here. Look here." He waved the paper. "General Sweeney of the Federal troops opposite us today sent me this letter under a flag of truce."

"Surrender, perhaps?" asked Charlie.

"Hardly," said Lieutenant Mangum, another aide who clearly disliked Cleburne's intimacy with a common soldier.

"He is likewise from Ireland, from County Cork, as it were," said Cleburne, wiping back his hair with the palm of his right hand. A merry light played in his gray eyes, and Charlie thought: *He loves this war. He absolutely loves it.* "He has proposed that after this war is over I join him in raising a Fenian army to liberate Ireland from the English. Can you imagine such a thing in time of war? What is the man thinking?" Cleburne laughed lightly, and Charlie felt the distant sliding of a burden.

"I would say he is not sufficiently attentive to the matter at hand," said Charlie. "Perhaps we can gain that attention when they attack."

"Perhaps," said Cleburne. Buck guided him away to something more urgent, and Charlie wandered up the steep slope, looking for no one, turning sometimes to see if there was a line of sight on the enemy, but none seemed to exist. What was the name of this town again? Adairsville? Perhaps this is the slope on which he would die when the artillery came up. As Charlie walked through the troops, none of whom was familiar, they seemed to part as he passed, as if they honored him. For a time, he joined other sharpshooters in an odd, octagon-shaped house whose walls were stubbled with stones, firing at Union troops, but after a while, hitting little, Charlie left and went back up the steep hill.

THAT NIGHT, THE CONFEDERATES, enveloped in a dense fog, were ordered to leave again, and the ritual curses came down. Charlie knew none of the troops near him, did not speak to them, but listened nonetheless. Rain began with the fog, and the tramp of foot soldiers began to emit splashing sounds, which joined with the rattle of belt-bound tin cups and bayonets to make a kind of music to Charlie, a music of war.

None knew of Johnston's evolving strategy: a final and triumphant battle at the town of Cassville the next day. First, he would divide his army, with half going to Kingston and the rest to Cassville. Then, when

Sherman divided his army in kind, Johnston would bring his troops together and destroy Sherman piecemeal. Atlanta would be saved, by the grace of God. Johnston knelt in the lantern light of his tent, and Bishop-General Polk baptized him in the name of Jesus Christ, the risen Lord and Savior, and Johnston's eyes filled with tears. This retreat must not turn into a rout. It must end here and now.

Charlie marched all night in the rain, feeling but not seeing the men in front of and behind him. He tried to count the number of soldiers he had killed so far, but every time he achieved a different number, and finally he realized it did not matter. He felt sick to his stomach over each one. He fell asleep after midnight but kept marching anyway. Men marched in their sleep all the time.

The next day, the Rebel army concentrated in two wings toward Cassville, with Cleburne's Division across the Western and Atlantic Railroad, south of town, opposite the Federal XIV Corps. Cleburne had reached the town of Kingston early in the morning, then kept moving, reaching his position two miles south of Cassville just after four in the afternoon.

"Damn if this ain't the biggest damn Southern army in one place I ever seen," said a soldier who introduced himself to Charlie as Jared Moulton from Memphis, Tennessee.

"Is that a fact," said Charlie, distracted. "Well, I'm going on ahead."

"Ahead?" said Moulton. "Ahead for *what?*"

"To fight," said Charlie.

"Goddamn stupid fool son of a bitch," said Moulton, genuinely aggravated.

Charlie wandered among Cleburne's men and finally sat, exhausted by the heat and humidity. Sweat dripped down the back of his stinking shirt. He closed his eyes and tried to remember the frail sick boy in Branton, but that must have been someone else, someone who feared war.

"Bless God, here's the boy sitting by himself in deep thought." Charlie turned his head and saw Duncan McGregor standing only a few feet away. "You have orders as a sharpshooter to range freely, but damn if you have orders to sit here among strangers and ignore your partner." Charlie stood and dusted himself off.

"How is your arm?" he asked.

"The red stripe is fading, bless God," he said, holding it up for inspection. "The fire is going out of her as well. It will be an ugly thing to show my grandchildren. Of course, I'll lie. I will say General Sherman himself shot me. A good lie is better than a weak truth, now ain't that right?"

"I believe you have stumbled upon an aphorism," said Charlie.

MAY 19 ROSE HOT and damp, and the men, edgy for a battle, dug their works, made rifle pits. Charlie and Duncan ate lightly. The men were assembled to hear an order from General Johnston himself, and he praised all the troops for their courage so far and said that as Confederates they would now turn and march to meet the enemy. He concluded by saying, "I lead you to battle." The men shouted and stamped. Rebel yells resounded, and Charlie felt an electric charge on his skin. So this would be the name of their pivotal battle: *Cassville*. Not a very distinguished name, but a solid one anyway: *Cassville*. Charlie and Duncan went to the right flank of Cleburne's position, behind them high up a slope where they held a commanding view. Duncan did not complain, but his wound, though clean and healing, ached to the bone. Here they did not need to find a tree, for Charlie would be able to pick off soldiers nearly a mile away, and Duncan was in no shape to scout on his own.

"General Johnston is a man of his word," said Duncan. "If he says he will lead us into battle, then he, by the rood of Christ, will do it."

"Were you ever married?" Charlie asked quietly.

"Say what, son?"

"Married. Were you ever married?"

Duncan exhaled, smiled, and shook his head. A distant softening crossed his eyes, and Charlie knew a memory had brushed past him.

"Aye, and how you could ask me that now escapes me, Charlie," said Duncan quietly. "Here we are about to see the battle spread out before us in all its glory, and you want to know of my earlier life. Look down there. It's like the world Satan showed Christ to tempt him, ain't it now? I will give you all of that if you will just worship me? Ain't it that?"

"Tell me."

"Rebecca was her name, and the prettiest thing a man ever seen in this life. Died in childbirth. A boy child who passed with her. I've not much heart to speak of it. Five years this October. Now why would you be asking that now?"

"I had a girl," said Charlie. "She was my girl."

"Many's the man who can speak them words, but few of such a tender age. So this girl, I take it, was your sweetheart then?"

"She was," said Charlie. "I don't know that I can think of her now, either."

"Well, then, there's two things we shan't speak of again," said Duncan. "By damn, I wish it would just rain and be done with it. Scots know of rain, but this hanging wetness in the hot air is something I won't never learn to love."

All morning they waited, and nothing happened. They saw no Yankee troops, and though Charlie scanned back and forth through the scope, which he had detached from his Whitfield, there was no target. Then: "There they are," he said.

The Federal troops were rapidly moving into line, just as generals were placing the gray troops further up the ridge behind the town. Shelling began half an hour later, though most of it seemed to be coming from the Union ranks. Charlie waited until they were beginning to come into range, and then he reattached his scope and fired three shots toward a clot of soldiers manning an artillery battery. He seemed to hit nothing.

"Are you hitting anything, then, boy?" asked Duncan.

"Not so far."

"Doesn't seem like our boys are getting ready to make no move. Looks to me like we're on the bloody defensive again."

"I'm going to charge," said Charlie. He felt sick and shaped with horror. Something was rising in him, and before him stood his father. Charlie was afraid and strong and weak and mad. Voices came into his mind.

"You are *what?*"

"You can make your way back to Cleburne's position, wherever in heaven's name it might be. I'm tired of this. I'm going to get closer and fight. I can't bear this." Charlie began to walk down the slope toward his lines. He saw his losses, knew what was irreparable, trembled. "I can bear no more."

"Are you daft?" asked Duncan. Charlie whirled.

"I *cannot* lose more. Dear God, I cannot bear to lose more."

'You want to be a suicide in the lines, be welcome to it, but don't expect me to accompany you!" shouted Duncan.

"I don't expect anything but a death."

Charlie moved to the right and rapidly down the slope. Brambles tore at his face, and the limbs of a cedar snapped back and scraped lines of blurred vision in his right eye. He shouted, moved faster, fell, got up and checked his rifle, kept moving. The shellfire was more intense now, but the troops on both sides seemed dug in, and the Southern lines held close to the ridge, returned light fire. No one seemed to be moving any- where, and Charlie felt a rising sorrow for the entire world, and nowhere more so than right here, right now. He walked past the line, and a few Butternut veterans shouted at him, told him for the love of God to keep his head down, but Charlie kept moving, his eyes shining with tears. He passed the skirmish line, and they screamed, told him to fall down and they'd shoot over him. *Cassville,* thought Charlie. The place of my death is called *Cassville.* He kept moving and found a scream far back in his throat, a harsh and rising howl that came out as a roar of cold fear, and he dreamed of swimming in the impatience of lead, hearing the whine, then feeling them in succession, the four or five hard slaps of death, the balls that would break bones, sever arteries, re- arrange the geography of his body into carrion.

This was so easy! *So easy!* He had not felt this good in months, and he kept walking toward them, not raising his Whitworth, almost but not quite wanting to throw it down. He thought of the perfect artillery shell, seeing it for one blinding moment, feeling the penetration of its black violent knob and the breath blown back out of him.

The blow, when it came, was from behind. He had already started to dream.

July 22, 1914

✡ ✡
✡

Tyrone Awtry dropped Charlie off at Grace House, and Charlie kept thinking of Merguns Flensvan and wondering who he might be. Someone who clearly didn't live in Branton—a mistake no doubt. Harris at the post office would send it off somewhere else. Mrs. Knight had not yet started cooking his noontime meal, so he went into his library and sat at his desk, Belle behind him. Mrs. Knight despaired when he let the dog wander in the house, but he didn't care. Belle flopped near Charlie's globe, sneezed once, and fell asleep on the cool floor.

The anniversary program would be held at seven in the evening at Ezra Atkinson Park, and Charlie thought he should begin to work on his remarks. Thinking about the Battle of Atlanta was not an agony—*that* sensation had worn off years before. But it twisted him inside, and he wanted to say something important about it. Thus far, three months after foolishly agreeing to speak, nothing had come to him. He could speak of the Battle *for* Atlanta, but he was unsure he could approach the Battle *of* Atlanta. The former was process; the latter was horror. He took paper from a desk drawer and then got his steel-nibbed pen and sat comfortably and dipped it in the inkpot. He wrote the date in the upper-left-hand corner of the paper and then stopped. He thought: *Cleburne.* How could he possibly speak of General Patrick Cleburne, the best man he had met during the war? Cleburne, who was a magnificent chess player and a man desperately in love for the first time in his life, who spoke with his soft Irish accent of the River Bride and his homeland, of the Mississippi River and his beloved Arkansas? How could Charlie reconcile that man with the fierce fighter? So little about that war made sense half a century on. Illiterate fools like Nathan Bedford Forrest had been brilliant soldiers. Intelligent, cautious men like Longstreet had somehow become villains and dupes. The nation was united, and perhaps it could not have been done without war. But the cost was staggering. Few alive knew that cost other than numbers on paper. Cleburne grew a beard to try and hide his facial wounds, but it didn't help much. He'd also been wounded in the streets of Helena, Arkansas, while defending a friend. There was an implacable ferocity about such acts and yet a wistful gentleness about him, too, as if he knew that he would not escape the war alive. He had been at Shiloh and the Kentucky campaign. He survived the rout from Dalton to Jonesborough. So much waste. And he was so wrong about the Confederacy.

Charlie laid the pen down and found himself beginning to choke back emotion. He should never have sold the *Branton Eagle* to Barrington Avery, for the *Eagle* had been his sinecure, his very public hiding place. His columns, which he kept in a cedar box along with the best letters he had received, included one he had never forgotten:

Concord
April 21, 1873

My dear Mr. Merrill,

I have to hand your essay entitled "Sacrifice," which I have read in its entirety in the New York Sun.

I would like to congratulate you on a splendidly conceived and executed example of clear thinking and fine writing. It is among the better things I have read in some time, and I can only conclude that you are a man of sensitive demeanor and exceptional talents.

It is a great pleasure to give these sentiments from

Yours most sincerely,
Ralph Waldo Emerson

When Mrs. Whitsun, president of the War Memorial League, had asked if he would give the main address on the anniversary, and he had asked why him, she had smiled, genuinely perplexed, and said, "Who else is there?" Since he sold the paper, Charlie had wandered through memory as if it were a mansion, dreaming back the days of his childhood before war came, before Tom left them for the war, before all else. Even now, he knew he could not approach that sacrifice, and he knew no matter what he did, he would soon vanish into the shadows of stone like all the family and all the soldiers before him.

Charlie put the pen down and sighed heavily and looked out the window. Cars went back and forth all day on Main Street before the house or on Dixie Avenue behind it, on the other side of the railroad tracks. Everyone had discovered motion, and with it speed, and life had gone forward with it. Twice this year already, aeronauts had flown their planes to fields just outside town and given shows, taken locals for rides, gone up so high they looked no larger than dragonflies. He wanted to slow the world back to its earlier movement, but he knew his time was evaporating. He thought, *Please, Lord, one more time,* but then he prayed no more. There was so much to write about: the ignorance and violence of the Klan; the coming war in Europe; the sorrow of survivors, the everyday love of fathers, the sweet smell of baseball leather, the glories of democracy. There was still so much to say. He was no longer the one to say it, though. He was an old man, slow and idle, and now they wanted him to speak profoundly about a battle that happened a half century ago today.

He wanted none of it. He wanted one thing only, and he knew that in this life, such glories come but once, and that fools chase their youths, never catch up with them again, then lie in tears as they fade into death and the next generation plans a healing.

Charlie walked to the table in his library and opened the Bible that lay upon it, seeking solace, thinking of his father. Often he would open the oversized book that had belonged to the minister, complete with its marginal notations, stuffed with newspaper clippings and advertisements for balms and pamphlets. Charlie would put his finger down on a verse at random and read it. Sometimes, he found subjects for his newspaper columns that way. He took his glasses from the shirt pocket and put them on and looked down. Little accident, for he knew he was in the middle of the book, where the Psalms lay, and he knew that he needed a healing and small hope. He was pointing at Psalm 86, a prayer of David:

*Bow down thine ear, O Lord, hear me: for I am poor and
needy. Preserve my soul; for I am holy: O thou my God, save
thy servant that trusteth in thee. Be merciful unto me, O
Lord: for I cry unto thee daily.*

Charlie smiled: This was no accident. He felt better and was thinking
again of his father when he heard the unpleasant sound of Mrs. Knight
at the foot of the stairs, calling his name. At first, it sounded distant and
scratchy, like metal on metal, but then it was more insistent and clearer.

"Yes, Mrs. Knight?" he called back. Too early for dinner. And I'm
not hungry, anyway.

"A visitor for you, Mr. Charlie," she said. "I'll show her into the
parlor."

"Thank you, I'll be right down." Charlie's eyes opened wide, and he
felt a rush of hope. But there was no train, and it was a long way by car
from Atlanta or Augusta, and the roads were often washed away by
heavy rains. *Be merciful unto me, O Lord: for I cry unto thee daily.*

He smoothed his hair and walked to the window, and looked at his
face in the upper half, saw an old man with foxed skin, parchment shiny
and worn. Outside, summer rose in waves of heat and greenery, and the
air was very still. Surely a breeze would rise soon. Surely there would be
no thunderstorm during the celebration to ruin it all. Or surely there
would be—perhaps God being merciful unto him. He inhaled sharply
and turned and began to walk across the room, feeling strange, almost
dizzy. He stopped to grip the edge of his desk and gain strength. From
memory, then: *Rejoice the soul of thy servant: for unto thee, O Lord, do I
lift up my soul. For thou, Lord, art good and ready to forgive* . . .

Charlie felt his strength return, and he went into the hallway and
walked downstairs and thought: *Yes, it shall be as I dreamed it.* Then: *I
have been dreaming these years, and one cannot dream the real into the
dream.* He got to the bottom of the steps, his face flushing, hands
slightly trembling. Then he walked, trying not to show the pain, into his
front parlor and saw Mrs. Murdoch Brinton standing before him,
cradling a purse in her elbow, her face a moving mask of small, impatient twitches. He smiled at his distress and almost laughed out loud. *Of
course*: Mrs. Brinton. God, after all, has His humor.

"Yes, well, I shall come to the point right away, Mr. Merrill, that
being that word is on the street that you have not prepared your remarks for the celebration this evening," she said without patience or
good cheer. She wore a heavy black dress and was perspiring visibly, a

fat woman whose infrequent smiles looked more like grimaces. She had been president of the Branton United Daughters of the Confederacy since its inception, and was growing older and more imperious by the day.

"Would you like coffee, Blanche?" asked Charlie. He had amused himself by annoying her for years, and both knew it. "Or tea. We have some very nice tea just in, from Ceylon, I believe. You can all but smell the plantations and the air of the ocean."

"No coffee, no tea," she said curtly. "Again, let me be direct. I hear you have not prepared your remarks for the evening, and I want to say that a great many people have gone to much trouble to make this the most special event in Branton's recent history. Good God, half the town consists of former Yankees now. We must attend to our own culture."

"Or jam and biscuits?" he asked, trying to look absentminded. "We have a delightful blackberry jam and fresh biscuits." He could tell she was seriously considering it; she rarely turned down food of any kind at any place. Her appetite at church dinners was legendary.

"Charlie, we have known each other too long for these ridiculous pleasantries," she said, temper visibly rising. "Do you know that two dozen ladies have been working for four months to make this day a grand thing? Do you know that? Two dozen ladies? We have been expecting a grand speech, something that we can reprint, that will go down in the annals of Branton County history. What else do we have? T. D. Varnell? A man who cannot write or read and who is fat as an autumn bear? Mr. Josiah Biggs? He can't say two words without hawking and spitting—a disgusting old man. And Mr. James Felder? I'd rather hear a snake hiss. He still pats our saintly ladies on their fannies as they pass."

Charlie laughed out loud for the first time in days.

"Maybe I shall just read for an hour from the Sears catalog," he said. "I'm so respectable that people would think it had meaning."

"Go ahead and mock me, but I've known you for forty years, and you're not some famous writer to me, Charlie Merrill," she said. "I've seen you and my late husband in your cups too often to think you are some kind of great man." She was teasing now, and he could tell it, teasing with a fey innocence that he enjoyed.

"Woman, you insult me," said Charlie.

"No, an insult would be if I called you a lazy and selfish old fool who is going to leave a town hungry for inspiration to wallow in confusion," she said in a rush. "People look up to you, God only knows why. Myself, I believe you just happened to be in the right place at the right time."

Charlie felt a sudden strange falling, an odd knowledge. The right place at the right time? No, she could not know. She could not imagine a messmate standing next to you in line suddenly vaporized by cannon fire, nothing left but a leg and a shattered Enfield rifle with a severed hand still tangled in the trigger. She could not imagine thousands of men doubled in the edge of the woods with diarrhea, vomiting from fear. She could not imagine the Federals as they charged up Kennesaw Mountain in a massive, monstrously stupid attack while the Butternuts each shot ten, twenty, seventy of them—worse than shooting dumb animals, who at least fled at the sound of touched-off gunpowder.

"My theory," he said, calming himself through effort alone, "is that we never know the right time and the right place until they have long passed. We think it is a normal day, then, years later, we discover it was transcendent, Blanche. We find that, on a certain day, everything in our lives changed, and we did not even recognize it. That we were in some fundamental way different. It could be something as large as the movement of men on the battlefield or the pressure of a loved one's hand. And we are not attuned to life enough to know them as they happen."

A gentle wind rose, lifting the white lace curtains, and they waved into the parlor. Sunlight spread in jonquil strokes across the floor. Charlie smiled and thought: more hot air. But when he looked up, Mrs. Brinton's eyes were filled with tears, and she turned away just as one spilled down her cheek.

"Will you say that?" she whispered. "Something like that? I— There was a time when Robert and I were already getting old, and we drove to Highlands. A terrible, frightening drive up the mountains into North Carolina. I complained the whole time—fancy that. And he kept laughing at me and said, Wait. Just you wait, Blanche. And I kept saying I'm *waiting* for this thing to fall off. It was the Lexington, I think. More a buggy than a car. Took us two days to drive a hundred miles. I wanted to go home, and he kept telling me to wait. And then we came to a place where the road opened up on this vista, and the world lay below us, and he pulled over and parked.

"The air tasted like honey. My legs were weak. Although I didn't know it then, he already had the cancer. And there were no other cars or horses or buggies around, just us at the edge of the world. And he put his arm around me. And he said—he said— I'm sounding like a stupid old woman."

"What did he say?" asked Charlie.

"He said, 'Blanche, this is how you make me feel,'" she said. She turned and looked at Charlie, and tears were streaming down both cheeks, but she smiled. "Sometimes, when everything changes, we *do* know it. We *do*." She wiped her cheeks and shook the emotion back into its clasped box of memory. "Now look what you did. You made me cry. I knew you were no gentleman."

Charlie was shaken, thought of Robert, missed him. He inhaled sharply to regain his balance and strength, felt the pain begin in his jaw and arm and then fade away.

"I haven't written the speech because I can't think of anything to say," he said. "My mind is gone." Blanche took a handkerchief from her purse and noisily blew her nose.

"Your mind's been gone for decades, but that never stopped you from writing all those stupid articles in the *Eagle,*" she said. "Now listen to me. We have barbecue. We have distinguished visitors. We will have everybody in the county there. My own reputation is at stake, and we all know how pristine that is."

"As pristine as a spring lamb," said Charlie. He was breathing easier now.

"Yes, well, hah, hah, and all that," she said. "Go up there now and write something down to say. You know how this town is. Word is everywhere that you haven't written a speech." Belle came tipping downstairs and walked wagging into the room. Blanche looked at the dog with barely restrained disgust. "Animals in the home. Disgraceful."

"I agree," he said. "And that's why you should be leaving now. Any longer, and I shall have to get a leash for you."

"Very amusing. Very. But I want you to know that the people of this county are expecting eloquence with their barbecue. I don't really care what you say as long as it's pretty and lasts at least fifteen minutes."

"I shall always cherish the inspiration you have given me," said Charlie, bowing.

"Oh, heavens," said Blanche, and she was shaking her head and rustling in black crinoline as she passed him and went outside, climbed in her car, and drove off. He turned and looked down at Belle.

"We have been put on notice," he said. He looked up, and in the light of the doorway, Mrs. Knight stood silently shaking her head, looking at him as she often did.

October–December 1861

ON SARAH PIERCE'S THIRD visit, when she squeezed his hand as she had done each time before, Charlie, whose illness had been worse, felt his hand squeeze back into hers. He had already begun eating solid food, though he had rarely opened his sore eyes and spoken only a little. Martha performed skits, doing all the voices. His mother read aloud from the Bible and from Bill Arp, and Charlie lay like a corpse, with his will whittling at the silence. The town wept in grief and anger when little Ezra Atkinson had to be buried near Charlotte, North Carolina, "on account of the condition of the body, which could not bear further transport south." The town bought a plot and sent to Italy for a marble statue anyway.

Across Georgia, mills roared into motion, making shoes and boots, blankets, trousers, and vests. One factory, short of wool, made clothing with cow hair. In Washington, Georgia, factory workers turned out a slick succession of waterproof oilcloth leggings, overcoats, and capes. Some towns made hats. Others fabricated butternut jeans. On some plantations, slaves were set to making shoes with wooden soles. No one knew how the Federal embargo might affect the South.

Rev. Charles Merrill had not found Tom, despite telegrams, letters, and rail messages. He wrote Governor Brown and Vice President Alexander Stephens, who had taught in Branton as a young man, and

before the war sometimes stopped for services on his way from Craw-
fordville to Atlanta. Charles continued with Sunday and Wednesday
services, with prayer meetings and visitations, funerals and even a few
weddings, mostly of boys headed for Virginia. Charles read Bible com-
mentaries to Charlie, played with Martha and took her for rides in his
carriage, meandered in the kitchen garden, speaking with God, who,
Charles was convinced, had ceased to listen. Charlie felt now as if he
were crawling inside a tunnel of fog, still almost too weak to stir. Birds
sat in the arched limbs outside and passed their days in splendid ignorance. Insects, as the evening came on, set up a somnolent drone from
yard to yard. Surely the war must be over by now, though no one had
told him much about it except Sarah. He knew the pressure of her small
feet on the steps. She would be whispering with Betsy. Charlie could
not imagine why she kept arriving, but now, for the third time in a
week, she sat beside him, and he could feel her eyes on him. She had
been talking about the stupidity of her uncle, Fort Sumter, General
Irvin McDowell, Negro sales, John Frémont's cashiering in Missouri by
Abe Lincoln—all with a kind of cheerful élan yet in quiet words. No
one else would risk upsetting him, but Sarah didn't seem to care. So
when she took his hand and held it, Charlie felt a deep warmth, like
sunlight through honey.

"Oh—oh, my God," said Sarah. "Charlie, do that again." He
squeezed her hand again, and slowly, like a sunken ship rising miracu-
lously from a great depth, he opened one eye and then the other. The
room was filled with a blasting light. He closed his eyes and blinked
them for a time. She was leaning closer, and her scent filled his nostrils
with desire.

"Sarah," he croaked. He turned his head back and forth tentatively.
He opened his eyes again, and she was there close beside him smiling,
much more beautiful than he had expected. Her eyes were wide, her
mouth opened in a faint smile.

"Sweet Jesus, you're full awake," she said. "I'll go get your mother."

"Wait—wait," he said. "Water?"

"Here." She dipped a cupful from the pitcher that Betsy kept on the
table next to his bed, then placed it to his lips and gently lifted his head.
He sipped the water, eyes opened completely now, and he felt his hands
come up and around hers. The room was warm, but he felt clean. He
knew that his mother had been bathing him and combed and scented
his hair each time Sarah came over. He fell back exhausted on the
fluffed pillows.

"I—I've heard everything you've said," Charlie whispered. "I've been very ill."

"Everyone thought you were going to die, dear God," she said. He turned and looked at her, and her eyes shone, but without tears or the shape of any fear. "But I didn't have anybody else to talk with. You're the only person since I've been here who had talked to me like I'm a person. Anyone from the North now is a low coward."

"Sarah, I—" he started and then stopped, closed his eyes for a moment, then opened them once more. "I am so glad that you came to be with me."

"Oh, I had nothing else particularly to do," she said. She took his hand again and held it, and in her eyes, he could see damage, a lack of love, a distance, and an urge. Charlie's hair had fallen into his eyes, and with her left hand Sarah gently brushed the curls back, then returned the hand to her lap, as if it had gone to his face of its own will and needed to be punished.

"I wasn't busy myself," said Charlie. Sarah was silent for a moment and burst into laughter. At the sound, Betsy and Martha appeared in the doorway, and his mother saw him, saw his face turn, his eyes open, gentle shining in his eyes, and she rushed in, shouting and falling to her knees, covering her son's face with kisses. Martha clapped and went to the window.

"Papa! Papa!" she cried. "Charlie's wide awake again!"

Sarah stood and backed across the room, and Charlie watched her, narrowed his eyes, and tried to speak.

"What is it?" asked Betsy. His throat was constricting again.

"Sarah—come back," he said. She stepped back toward the bed. "I mean come back tomorrow and sit with me."

"May I?" Sarah asked his mother.

"Of course, dear," said Betsy. "Oh, dear, dear God."

Sarah walked from the room and passed Charlie's father on the stairs, and he paused and looked at her, and she could see that he wanted to know something, to ask her anything.

CHARLIE FELT AS IF his senses had been scoured and heightened. He heard the trains from miles away, chuffing and clattering on their silver rails. He could distinguish levels of birdsong, from the subtle coughing of crows to the wild arias of mockingbirds. He would ask his mother to play the piano, and he could hear Beethoven's melodic lines worked out in grand designs. He smelled boxwood from the house next door, cookery from the Merrill kitchen, his mother's toilet water, his little sister's joyful sweat before she entered the room. He was almost strong enough to walk and so sat in a chair by the window and looked over the dozing backyard and saw the kitchen garden's last vegetables clinging to their stalks and vines. He sometimes held his chest, for it felt like butterflies or moths sparkled inside, dusting him with their wings. Jack visited more regularly, but more often he thought of Sarah. What was it that he felt for her?

Toward the middle of October, a sharp cold front snapped through Branton, and Betsy began closing the wide windows just before she kissed Charlie good night like a child. Jack came on a cold and rainy Tuesday, bearing a book, limping painfully up the stairs and into the room.

"I suppose you knew it was me from my racing gait," said Jack. "I let myself in since no one came to the door when I knocked."

"Papa's at the church, and Mama has taken Martha in the gig and gone to buy sugar and flour and such in town," said Charlie. "Cephus is probably asleep in the barn."

"A wise man who sleeps in a barn," said Jack. "I wrote that. You may use it, if you see fit."

"Is that a gift? I am tired of people reading to me. Papa is reading from the Book of Judges, which is the most boring thing on earth," said Charlie.

"Forgive me if I sit," said Jack. "I believe I injured my foot in the latest town races, and I must rest on the part of my anatomy that looks most like you."

Jack handed him the book, *The Poems of John Keats,* and Charlie smiled warmly.

"This is *my* book," he said. "You're making me a gift of my own book? You must have had it for a year."

"More than that, actually. Your fire is fading, sir. May I stoke it?"

"You may." Jack hobbled to the fireplace and took three sticks from the firebox and put them on the slow flames. A swift cluster of sparks flitted upward. "So, we hear in our pathetic little village that you are frequently visited by a Yankee girl who brings you balm in your time of anguish. We believe this makes you a traitor to the Greater Confederacy and are considering your execution. Thus far, we have reduced the choices to hanging or being smothered with kisses. There." Finished with the fire, Jack stood up wiping his hands.

"You are the great wit, Dockery," said Charlie. He had been thinking of Sarah all morning, but he knew her aunt would not let her come out in the cold rain. "I hear there is an opening for a drummer boy with the Branton Rifles."

"Scandalous thing to say," said Jack. He settled in the chair next to Charlie's bed. "You mock the South, sir. Is that why you are consorting with Yankee girls during these, our most difficult days?"

"I thought *these* were our days of glory."

"Father says that soon we'll be making coffee from sawdust if the Yankee embargo succeeds," said Jack. "We may have no principles on which we stand, but you must surely agree that a lack of coffee would doom the Confederacy to pointlessness."

"I have principles," said Charlie. "And Sarah is nice. She is very nice."

"The boy is smitten, Lord," said Jack, raising his arms like a preacher. "Let him know that consorting with the enemy is a crime, even if the enemy has gray eyes and small hands."

"How did you know she had gray eyes? Have you met her? And sometimes her eyes are blue."

"Once in Papa's store," said Jack. "She came in with her uncle to buy a coal scuttle."

"So you noticed her eyes and her hands as well?" asked Charlie.

"I was thinking to examine her for weapons. She might be an enemy spy."

"Ah, Keats," said Charlie. "Do you think it is not true that only the good and talented die young, Jack? I should have caught consumption or have been drowned at Turner's Hole."

"Not quite the same as Shelley drowning in the sea, but given our small ambitions, suitable enough, perhaps."

They had been this way for years, bookish boys in love with words and learning. The rain suddenly came harder in a liquid drumming on the bubbled windowpanes and the world beyond it, all Charlie had seen since summer, was suddenly distant, indistinct.

IN EARLY DECEMBER, THE Rev. Charles Morgan Merrill, Sr., came dashing up the stairs calling his wife's name over and over with bright excitement.

"Betsy, Betsy, our Tom is safe!" he cried. "It's Tom! A letter from our boy!" He was waving the paper, face flushed with joy. The day was unnaturally warm, and Betsy had opened the windows in Charlie's bedroom on a delightful day.

"Praise Jesus," said Betsy.

"Praise Jesus," said Martha. "Read it, Mama, read it out loud."

Betsy felt her face go liquid, and her hands seemed unable to hold the pages steady. She focused on the handwriting, knew instantly that it was her eldest son's. She sat on the edge of Charlie's bed and cleared her throat.

Camp Marion, Virginia
November 3, 1861

Dear Mama and Papa and Martha and Charlie,

I am sorry that you have been so very long without a note from me. The truth is that they have been marching us all over Virginia in the area near Yorktown, and until now I have not had time to take pen in hand to write.

I hope that you are all well and that you are not angry with me for joining the cause for which so many have already laid down their lives. Although my company has seen some skirmishes and learned to march for miles on little food or sleep, we have not been engaged in a great battle, for there has not been one since Manassas in July. We hear all sorts of rumors but I don't know as what are true and what are not.

I have a great friend now named Silas Tompkins, and he is from Arkansas but was in Athens when the war began. He serves as I do with Cobb's Legion and he is the crackest shot you ever saw, almost as good as Charlie on his best day. Silas can tell jokes without stopping for a day on foot. He keeps us all in great merriment. We call him our own Bill Arp.

We have already had cold weather, which I am not used to this early, but we have tents and blankets, and when we have marched through a town, nice ladies have given us more blankets and hats and what have you. It is very well that I fight for our country, mother, for I see now that what we fight is a tyranny. The officers say it is not about the Negros and I think that is right. It is about the Yankees coming into our country to force us to live as they do and that cannot be right.

*But mostly, it is about marching and drilling and looking
for the coming winter quarters. They say that the Yankee
army is stoppered up in Washington and shall not venture out
until spring, as General Maclelen is not tempted much to
fight at least yet. I have seen generals twice, and they are old
men and you recognize them because of their gray hair, and
there are also older men who have tried to be soldiers in this
army, but they have mostly gone home now, as they are not
able to keep up.*

*There is much illness, but I have been well except for one
visitation of troubles with my bowels. I should not put this in
a letter. But now I am fine, but I miss your cooking and
would give my rifle for a jar of your apple butter. I would ask
for you to send me some, but I do not know where I shall be
soon.*

*Please give my love to Martha and tell Charlie that he will
be a great danger if he ever grows a brain. Papa, please pray
for me, as that is not the kind of thing a boy can ask of the
others except our chaplain and he mostly prays for the dying
or the dead.*

That is all I can think to write.

Your fond son,
Tom Merrill

"I thought he was dead," said Betsy. She choked back her tears.
Martha huddled close to her and looked over the letter with glowing
eyes. Charlie lay back on his pillow and looked at the leafless pecan
branches through the window and saw high above them clouds that
looked like feathers in flight.

EVENING: THE SOUND OF a cool rain, and two boys hunched over a
chessboard. Charlie narrowed his eyes and reached for a rook, removed
his hand, grinned at Jack.

"You've accidentally stumbled into a defense," said Charlie. "I was
unaware you knew that defense was possible in chess."

"Oh, I know about defense all right," said Jack. "It's the opposite of
glory."

"So glory is what—a charge into the face of a hundred cannons?"

Jack drummed his fingers on the board and smiled with mock superiority at his friend.

"Glory is believing in something enough to die for it," said Jack. "Or in a chess game you have clearly lost but won't quit."

"What if glory means believing in something enough to live for it?" asked Charlie.

"Excuse me while I die of a vile catarrah," said Jack, who turned away from the board and made a hideous choking sound. "If you are going to present philosophies, I'd prefer you were in your right mind first."

"I'm entirely in earnest," said Charlie. "What if Jesus had lived for our souls instead of dying for them? Think how differently we would view things. No more dying for a cause but instead doing everything possible to live for one."

"I cannot continue this game, for my morals forbid me playing with idiots," said Jack. "I accept your forfeit with grace."

"What would *you* die for, then? This war? This stupid Confederacy?"

"You are hereby executed for treason," said Jack. "Bang."

"I am wounded, Horatio. Do I owe you any money before expiring?"

"Twelve dollars, not payable in Confederate specie," said Jack. "I shall take it in U.S. silver or in cotton-field labor. Take your choice."

"Would you accept my word as a gentleman?"

"A gentleman would die for his beliefs. You, sir, are no gentleman."

The rain spilled off the roof of Grace House in a pale damp shroud, and through the curtains of water, the pecan grove was as indistinct as a memory.

January–March, 1862

I N DREAMS, LINES OF battle formed, battles came. Summer sweat formed on Charlie as he thrashed and awoke to the crystal trails of frost on his bedroom windows. Then he would doze again, and he would be in some dusty trench in Virginia, rising to fire at a bristling blue line that moved up a slope through the forest toward his position. Reverend Merrill, softly and without energy, read Charlie the political news from the *Atlanta Intelligencer,* the movements of armies and suppositions for the coming spring. Then he would leave for the church and his duties, watching as membership dwindled, as baptisms grew more widely separated. Charlie read the poems of Samuel Rogers and found them dull and wanting. He slept and awakened to wonder if he would hear the soft footsteps of Sarah Pierce on the stairs, ascending to his room. Sick, then well. Charlie was never one or the other.

Missy dusted and arranged, brought him chicken on a blue plate, spoke while always shaking her head.

"Mist' Charlie, you ain't gone refresh none a you strength you ain't gone eat you food," she said. "Done been knowing you since you was a babe in arms, and you always was a small child, but you ain't 'posed to be getting no smaller than you already is."

"Okay, Missy, I'll try," he'd say, and he would struggle to swallow the biscuits and chicken, sip milk just spun from the sagging teats of their old cow. Reverend Merrill started on the Book of Numbers, but Charlie fell asleep during the Tribe of Reuben.

"It appears that it might snow today," the voice said. Charlie awoke from a strange dream of swimming in an endless river. Sometimes, he would be in the bright reflected sunlight, but often he swam for miles beneath the water, and there he could also breathe and see perfectly.

"Umm?" he said. His eyes opened to a gray smudge of light spread over his blankets. He blinked and yawned and saw Sarah Pierce standing next to his bed, wearing a heavy coat, her cheeks bringing with them messages from the cold. The seconds twisted themselves into a kind of longing; he couldn't say what time it might be, or what day. He worried that he was unkempt, but then he remembered that it must be late morning, because his mother had bathed him already. He smelled the light hint of soap on his thin shoulders. He blinked again and slid up in bed slightly.

"Were you dreaming?" she asked softly. She took off her coat and hung it on a wall hook where it dangled like the skin of a human being, slipped perfectly off. "I dream every night, fantastic things. Sometimes I dance with dragons in a meadow of flowers. Sometimes great mountain ranges are falling upon me, and I can't escape them."

"I never dance with dragons," said Charlie hoarsely. "Is the fire warm?"

"Perfectly stoked," said Sarah. "You know, by now it will be snowing in Boston. I remember a snow when I was little that was over my head. Children made tunnels through it, secret places."

"We have snow sometimes," he said. He turned and looked out the window, and roiling gray clouds hung low, and the branches of the pecan grove bobbed and scratched at them. He turned back, and she was sitting in the chair next to him, holding a book and looking more beautiful than any girl he had ever imagined. "We had eight inches one year. Tom and I built a great snowman in the front yard. This was before Martha was born, I think. We tied a scarf around his neck. It was blue with white designs. I had forgotten about that."

"My uncle says," she sighed, "that I cannot go home now until this war has ended. It is just as well. I disliked my parents' quarreling so. The choice was to stay home in that battle or come here and be with my uncle and his alcoholic tonic."

"You should not go back," said Charlie. "That is certain." He blushed, felt his face turn into a cauldron, and he tried through will to hold it back, but it spread through his chest and down his arms. Sarah smiled at him, knowing, hoping.

"Every time I come, you smell so fresh, as if you have prepared for a party," said Sarah. "Most men in the street, most boys, smell so foul one cannot be near them. I believe you may be a gentleman."

"I haven't the strength yet even to bathe myself," he admitted. "I'm here until my body decides to work on its own again."

"And Dr. Dexter . . ."

"He says that he doesn't know what has befallen me," said Charlie. "Some fever that has invaded the muscles. My cousins and aunts and uncles come by. Papa reads the Bible to me, and I am bored beyond bearing. If I rise and walk, it may be from my refusal to hear the Book of Judges."

Sarah laughed brightly, and her cheeks spread their cherry tint down her long neck into her high-collared dress.

"Well, I haven't brought you the Bible. I have brought you Shakespeare's sonnets. Do you know them? Are you sick of them, too?"

"I know them," he said. He looked out the window and wondered if the soldiers had settled into winter quarters in the north. The war news had been scant to nonexistent, and Tom had not written again. The edge of privation had seeped into Branton County, and visitors from Savannah and Augusta spoke of shortages. Women continued without fail to make clothing and bandages and blankets, though, and the Confederacy appeared strong and solid. "I have memorized several of them."

"Which ones?"

Charlie felt a sting in his eyes. He had not thought of it since he took to bed. He pulled himself up and sat in the bed. He was fully dressed and wore a light house-jacket that increased the warmth of his bed and room. Sarah sat at the foot of the bed and looked at him with wide eyes. He wanted to touch her, hold her, but he knew he was a slightly pathetic figure. He cleared his throat and spoke, looking beyond Grace House:

> *When, in disgrace with fortune and men's eyes,*
> *I all alone beweep my outcast state,*
> *And trouble deaf heaven with my bootless cries,*
> *And look upon myself and curse my fate:*
> *Wishing me like to one more rich in hope,*
> *Featured like him, like him with friends possessed,*
> *Desiring this man's art and that man's scope,*
> *With what I most enjoy contented least:*

Yet in these thoughts myself almost despising,
Haply I think on thee, and then my state,
Like to the lark at break of day arising
From sullen earth, sings hymns at heaven's gate;
  For thy sweet love remembered such wealth brings
  That then I scorn to change my state with kings.

Charlie did not realize, until the poem was nearly finished, how its mirror image reflected Sarah and the torment of his bed. He felt a shock of revelation and was ashamed. He cleared his throat and looked down. How foolish to think she would find him worth her affection. She was as inaccessible as the war, a dream of glories and bright victory.

"How beautifully you say that," whispered Sarah. Charlie looked at her, wanting to seem strong. Her mouth was a perfect bow. Her eyes caught the gloomy light and reflected it like isinglass. Before her gray eyes, the will of his disease dissolved, and he wanted to touch her hand, to say how dear her presence was. That was impossible, though. Surely he would die soon. Perhaps they had sheltered him from the knowledge. He imagined his father coming in one day and revealing the great secret, that in a few days' time, Charlie would stand before the judgment of God and should therefore bare his soul and stand straight with the Lord. He would be reduced to a distant flame on days when the sun stunned Branton into its near tropical submission.

"I don't know why that one came to mind," said Charlie slowly. "I know a number of them. I—I don't like them anyway."

"I beg your pardon?"

"I don't like them. They seem facile and too well shaped. Like schoolbook exercises. There are things I like far better." Then, believing her eyes mocked him: "They're stupid. They're all stupid."

Sarah's face very slowly spun into a sour glare.

"You're a foolish boy if you think Shakespeare stupid," she said. She stood and sat back in the chair. Charlie fell back on his pillow heavily, slightly knocking his skull on the headboard.

"Ow, drat it," he said. "Not worth a stupid sonnet to hit my head."

He stared at Sarah, and a heat spilled from his eyes, and he could not control it. She stood and went to the wall hooks, gathered her coat, and left the room without a word.

"Well, then, leave," he said. He looked out the window, and twenty minutes passed in a hard silence before he wept.

✧ ✧
✧

SARAH DID NOT COME for the rest of January, as he tried to walk again.
He struggled around the cold boards of his bedroom, with two canes,
afraid of falling. Betsy fussed over him, and he played Authors with
Martha on rainy days. In February, his father walked slowly into the
bedroom one Tuesday and said that two forts in the west, Fort Henry
and Fort Donelson, had fallen to Union forces. The armies of the
North, instead of retracting and faltering as the South had predicted,
had spread and swollen, a vast roiling blue line sweeping into battlefields with a new vigor. With help from Cephus, Charlie came downstairs late in the month and sat before the great fire in the front parlor in
a heavy chair where he sipped heated cider seasoned with a light scraping of cinnamon. He read for a time, but his eyes could not hold the
page. He summoned Cephus and asked for help getting to his father's
desk. Charlie took out a sheet of paper, dipped the steel nib, and wrote
in his most legible hand:

> *Dear Sarah,*
>
> *Forgive my rudeness and stupidity. I have been ill much*
> *of my life, and though I have tried always not to pity myself,*
> *I have lately found myself doing that very thing. I spoke to*
> *you in a rash and thoughtless way when I was in pain. If you*
> *would return and visit with me again as before, I would be*
> *grateful and promise I would not be so vile.*
>
> *If you can forgive me, please send word that you shall*
> *come soon.*
>
> *Charlie Merrill*

He folded the letter and sealed it with wax and called Cephus and
told him where the letter should be delivered.

MR. LINCOLN'S POOR SON Willie has died of a fever," said Betsy Clark
Merrill one morning as she opened the curtains in Charlie's room to a
bright day. "He was but eleven years old. Mr. Blake next door called
over and asked if I had heard, and I said no, and then he said it was
God's judgment against Mr. Lincoln for his savagery. Can you imagine,

Charlie? Can you believe that God would punish a small child for his father's actions? And the boy but eleven years old!"

"Should we pray for Mr. Lincoln, then?" asked Charlie.

"I have already," said Betsy. She sat on the bed and took her son's small hand. "Charlie, your father is unwell. He refuses to say what may be ailing him, but he sits and stares into the fire when he is not at the church. I fear for him. With Tom gone and you sick, and Martha yet so small, I cannot imagine what to say to him."

"Has Dr. Dexter seen him?"

"He will not summon the doctor," said Betsy. "Nor will he say if he has pain. I think he does not believe in this war or this new country."

"Many in Branton do not," said Charlie. "That seems to be the nature of this place."

His mother tenderly helped him bathe and announced that Sarah had sent word that she would come over in an hour's time.

"I am glad, then," he said.

"Did you quarrel with her?"

"It was my fault," said Charlie. "Should I urge father to see the doctor?"

"Speak your mind as you will," said his mother.

Missy came in not long afterward and opened the windows so a cross-breeze of cool but pleasant morning air raked the room. The day would be warm, the kind of jewel embedded in a cold season that brought hope to the old and the ill. The land, damp from recent rains, spread a rich aroma through the room, and Charlie could hear buggies and wagons from Main Street, teamsters crying to their horses, birds singing for a new season. After an hour, he was dozing and not dreaming when a voice cried upward from the backyard.

"Charlie Merrill, come down here and let's go for a ride!" the girl's voice said. He felt a clatter in his chest, his heart irregular as the sputtering of musketry. He sat up, leaned into the window, and saw Sarah Pierce below him in a light gig, the horse stamping with impatience. She was smiling upward with a dazzling insistence, and the wind blew back her light hair in tangled ringlets.

"Good morning," he said. "I haven't been for a ride yet."

"Then you shall today," she said. "I've a mind to tour your town."

"Come inside and ask Missy to get you a cool drink, and I shall be ready anon," said Charlie.

"How long is anon?" asked Sarah. "I've always wondered about that."

⚜

BETSY WATCHED THEM DRIVE away with delight and approval. It had taken Cephus and Sarah to get Charlie into the buggy, and Betsy had embarrassed him by covering his lap with a thick quilt, even though the day was warm. Now Charlie held his place easily as Sarah drove slowly down Dixie Avenue and turned on First Street. As the months had passed since the first rhetorical days of war a year before, more men had joined and left for the army; others had hired substitutes and retreated to the luxury of their personal libraries to await developments. Yards had grown the rustic disorder of winter somnolence. A few slaves worked with horses or cleaned carriage wheels.

"I could never have imagined a day in February when I could ride about in an open carriage with such pleasure," said Sarah. She held the reins lightly, and her horse clopped along the hard-packed street with a saucy eagerness. The canopy that hung over the street, rich and shady in summer, was now an interlaced thatch of arched limbs, clasping like an old man's hands.

"You see, we have things to offer here," said Charlie. "We aren't simply disease-ridden and backward people."

"Oh—I meant to tell you that my uncle came in this morning, all red faced, and said that Nashville had fallen to the Federals," she said. She did not exult, much less brag; she stated simple news she thought he should know.

"Nashville fallen," he said. "I believe that is our first state capital to be taken. Forts Henry and Donelson and now this."

"Have you heard from your brother?"

"Just the one letter. He must be in Virginia. The spring campaigns will be in full swing soon, I imagine. Perhaps that is what makes my father so ill with sickness or grief."

"I had not heard he was ill. Come on, Joe!" The horse had been slowing, and she urged him forward to a slow trot. "I hope it is not serious."

"I pray not," said Charlie, surprising himself by using his father's words. Often, when faced with hard news from congregation members, Reverend Merrill would cock his head to one side and say, "I pray not," with such genuine affection that women whispered grief just to share the balm. Then, not thinking he would, he continued. "Sarah, I was stupid that day. I was ill. Can you forgive me?"

"I believe I may," she said gaily. "I have only read your letter about once or twice or a hundred times." Joe slowed again, but this time

Sarah didn't seem to notice. He pulled the gig and his passengers with a slow walk, steady but going nowhere in particular. "I must have blushed when you recited that sonnet. You must think me a giddy fool."

"I never thought that," he said. "I—I like you, Sarah. You must know that I like you. It's just that, well, you see what I am. A sickly invalid. And you needn't feel sorry for me."

"I never felt sorry for you," she said. "I never did. I felt another thing."

Her grasp on the reins had slackened so much that Joe slowed to a stop in front of Mrs. Weymon Stiles's great house, a white mansion with twin wings and well-ordered gardens of boxwood. It had been built in Augusta several years before, then dismantled and shipped joist by beam west to Branton.

"Sarah?" He wanted to slide next to her, to enfold her in his arms. He could imagine the warm, wet pressure of his lips on hers, the fragrance of her hair, her gray eyes locked on his. Her lips were parted slightly. The breeze lifted her hair from her shoulders, and sunlight warmed it with highlights that glistened as if wet.

"Yes?"

"I like you very much," he said. He looked down at the knotted fingers in his lap.

"I like you very much, too," she said. Then: "I wasn't wanted, you know. My parents did not want me, nor did my aunt and uncle. I have never known where I belonged or did not. You are the only friend I've had since I came here. The girls I meet despise me for the accident of my birth in Boston. I don't know." She looked away, down the street, then across it, then back at him. "All we want is comfort to face death, and so many never find it."

"I do not fear death. It has been my companion since I was born." Sarah smiled beautifully at him, reached out and took his hand. Charlie felt so quickened that his breath went ragged, as if his lungs were slipping into sleep.

"Do you know sonnet forty-three?" she asked. A cloud passed his face as he thought and could not remember. Sarah spoke:

> *When most I wink then do mine eyes best see*
> *For all the day they view things unrespected;*
> *But when I sleep, in dreams they look on thee,*
> *And, darkly bright, are bright in dark directed.*

Charlie nodded eagerly; yes, he remembered. Yes, he nodded to her, go on.

> *Then thou, whose shadow shadows doth make bright*
> *How would thy shadow's form form happy show*
> *To the clear day with thy much clearer light,*
> *When to unseeing eyes thy shade shines so!*
> *How would, I say, mine eyes be blessed made*
> *By looking on thee in the living day,*
> *When in dead night thy fair imperfect shade*
> *Through heavy sleep on sightless eyes doth stay!*

Charlie cleared his throat, spoke the ending couplet aloud with her.

> *All days are nights to see till I see thee,*
> *And nights bright days when dreams do show thee*
> *me.*

They looked down, away from the other's face, at the coupling of their hands. There was a sudden rush, the sound of a woman shouting, and their hands fell apart as they saw Mrs. Weymon Stiles, fat and trying to run, a lithe dog trotting away with a large blue sunbonnet as if it were fresh kill.

"Bring that back, you cur!" she shouted. "Bring it back now!" She stamped her foot, and when she did, a ripple coursed through the layers of her face, like a great shudder in the water when a boy jumps in a summer pool. Sarah snapped the reins, and she and Charlie laughed for the length of two more blocks until silence overcame them.

May 22–31, 1864

ALLATOONA TO DALLAS

ACH TIME **CHARLIE THOUGHT** he was awakening, a gray, crowding cloud would descend upon him, elemental and roaring, full of voices and horses, hail on a shingled roof, artillery caissons creaking on bridge slats. Once he thought he smelled apricots, rich and tart. Someone said, "Bloody flux," and another said, "Crack in the cascabel." Then he was descending again, frayed, awkward as a spring colt. The sound of water ran close beneath him on a swaying bridge, pouring like an open wound across the countryside, but there were also insect sounds, so they moved in silence, in darkness.

Charlie awoke finally into darkness. He tried to sit up, but his skull was monstrous and clotted. He was in woods at the edge of a field, and below him thousands of campfires blinked like dying stars. Then, a drone: prayer. He pushed himself up on his elbow and fell back, did it again, and the blast shattered his skull, a heavy pain, and he thought he would vomit. He flailed and found himself on a litter, on the ground, with a blanket over him, and his crotch itched a little, and the pestilence spread up into the hair in his armpits. He breathed through his mouth for a long time, and then tried to sit up again, and this time he managed, but his head fell forward, and only with a groaning effort did he raise it.

Thousands of men knelt behind their clasped hands. Not far away, a soldier without a coat dripped water from a dented tin cup on the heads of soldiers, moving down the line, just a few drops each. Charlie balanced, felt the crusted bandage on his head. Then the throbbing took him, but he decided to bear it. After a few moments, the stench came, sweated clothes, urine and excrement, and something else, a hint of rot or worse. A man next to him on the ground groaned and shuddered, and Charlie looked at him, a fellow too old for war and who bore a suppurating wound in his chest. When he wheezed, air squeaked from the hole in his lungs. A coughing broke out, contagious, it seemed. Charlie looked down at his chest and his legs and saw no blood or shattered bones, felt no pain from them as he shifted in the blanket. The night was stifling, as if a thunderstorm were near. Charlie saw no stars.

"For the love of God, would you look at this," a voice said, sounding far away at first then coming very near. Charlie lifted his head, but the effort was exhausting. He focused on a man striding toward him, stepping around the wounded, perhaps even the dead.

"At *what,*" said Charlie, but his throat was so dry the words cracked off his tongue, seemed to spill down into his lap. He crawled backward on his elbows and lay down. He realized only then that he had wet his pants, no doubt more than once. Nothing worse, perhaps.

"Charlie, boy, it's your lord and savior Duncan McGregor, who brained you afore you could have yourself shot at Cassville," he said. "And it's some effort for a man with a shot arm to brain a friend, I'll grant you that."

"What's happened?"

"What's happened is just as we were about to go forth under General Johnston at Cassville, the bleeding Federals flanked us again," said Duncan. "Now we're south of the Etowah River and they say not fifty mile from Atlanta. Nothing's happened for two days, but they say there's a battle aborning tomorry. As to what happened to you, I believe that in the heat of things you'd lost what little reason you had, and I rushed forth and tapped you a mite on the back of the head with my rifle butt. But in my holy errand I seemed to have tapped you a mite harder than I had planned."

"My head is killing me."

"I'm sure it is that, and it was only with the compliments of the kind General Patrick Cleburne himself that we have kept you off your pain with morphine, but there's little left to share now. Most of the wounded and sick have been evacuated to Atlanta. We hear it's overrun with the dead and dying."

"*Where* are we?" Charlie put his right hand on the band around his head and tried to loosen it a little, but it was dried into a binding.

"Camped near the railroad at a place called, for God's sake, Alla-toona," said Duncan. "And there's a great revival spreading again among the men. When death is close, men huddle up to God. When it's far away, they will lay with their wives' sisters. Are you bearing the pain, son?"

"Bearing it, no more."

"The towns and the country are empty of people, too. Refugees streaming south toward Atlanta in a great line, whipping their horses senseless, their piled possessions falling from wagons and caught by stragglers before they hit the ground."

"*You* hit me in the head?"

"Do you remember nothing, boy? You were making a charge by your lonesome on the Union lines near Cassville. Seems you'd decided to die in glory, except nobody was fighting for a position. Just your skirmishers and some artillery, and then word comes to pull out, for the love of God, that General Johnston ain't gone lead us into glorious battle as he said. We hear he was so angry he like to blowed the feather on his hat all the way to Chattanooga."

"You saved me, then."

"At my own peril. You owe me greatly. Though with the way things is going, we may all be chatting with St. Peter by tomorry night. Would you like to stand up?"

"I would. I can't lie here. This is a terrible place."

"An offense to the nose, but these poor boys. Oh, these poor boys."

Duncan knelt and pushed Charlie up, and though the pain was terrible, Charlie steeled himself to rise, and he scrambled up into Duncan's grasp. He was dizzy. He cleared his sight and saw again the firefly campfires, heard the soft chanting of prayers.

"Take me away from here," said Charlie.

"Well, the general has asked after you, and he told me personally as the other member of your sharpshooter team to bring him word if you perished. And contrariwise, to bring him your person should you survive."

"I am not presentable," said Charlie.

"That you are not," said Duncan.

They walked slowly for a time, Duncan helping Charlie to regain his footing.

"What is a cascabel?" asked Charlie.

"A cascabel? Why, that's the knob at the base of a cannon breech, I am thinking," said Duncan. "An odd word and an odd question. Are you still daft?"

"No more than ever," said Charlie Merrill. Duncan laughed, and a few men nearby, praying and trembling, tears dripping into their beards, looked up, their eyes full of questions.

THEY HOBBLED INTO THE light of General Patrick Cleburne's tent, which was clotted with his aides, who were looking over written orders, maps, troop placements.

"General, it's Private McGregor, bringing, as you asked, whatever is left of Mr. Charles Merrill of your sharpshooter company," said Duncan. "There is not much left as you can see for yourself, but what *is* left is here at your service."

"Ah, Mr. Merrill, I am pleased to see you among us again," said Cleburne, smiling. "During your sleep, we have been on the move, and it's just as well you missed it. Little for sharpshooters to do but guard our withdrawal. Gentlemen." The aides left his tent one by one.

"I'll wait outside by the fire with your permission, General, to retrieve Charlie should he become sick or insolent," said Duncan.

"Permission granted," said Cleburne, laughing.

Charlie came in and sat on a campstool and saw that Cleburne had set the chessboard back up and that the men were in their same squares from the last game. He could barely focus on the board. Cleburne handed him a large piece of dried beef and a canteen, and Charlie took them and ate, lightly at first, then with growing hunger.

"Everyone is getting baptized," said Charlie. "Forgive my condition, general."

"Indeed, quite a sight. Have you been baptized, Mr. Merrill?"

"I have. My own father baptized me in the Branton River."

"And did you feel the Holy Spirit when you rose from those waters?"

"I gagged and spat out water," said Charlie. "I trust that I did not spit out the Holy Spirit as well."

Charlie could not understand why Cleburne seemed so strong, even eager for the coming fight. Time was not the soldier's greathearted friend. It was his enemy, the epic holder of artillery fire and the rattle of musketry. The men feared bayonets above all, the idea of the rush and thrust, the hideous pain, but lasting only perhaps for a minute or more. Charlie wondered if the dead knew they had passed, if lost soldiers perhaps stayed around in their soft shades, awaiting orders that never came. Finally, they would drift away, out of formation, headed for whatever came next.

"The Holy Spirit is yet within you, my boy," said Cleburne.

"We were set to attack at Cassville, but then we didn't, as I understand it."

"We have had misfortune in the few weeks of this campaign so far, but as I believe in the right and believe in the God of Abraham, we will prevail. Many's the time I have seen defeat turn into victory and victory turn into defeat. And the men are suffering the forgiveness of God now. It is a great thing."

"Why suffering?"

"The admission of sin is always a suffering," said Cleburne. "No man lived but Christ who did not groan betimes with his sins, Mr. Merrill. Even a boy like you must have some things of which you must repent."

"Perhaps," said Charlie Merrill. "You have set the chessboard back up for us. I see you wish to resume the game."

"Studying the possible moves offers a general officer insights," he said. "Yes, I've looked at the board and considered your moves, and you are more devious, I believe, than General Sherman or his boon companion General McPherson, even General Schofield, though I think the less of his abilities than either of the former."

"The word spreads that the Federals will flank us all the way into Atlanta."

"That shall never happen. *Never.* I trust in God and in the men. If the entire Army of Tennessee were half as good as my men from Arkansas and Texas, why this war would have been over already. You are in a strange land here as a Georgia boy, fighting with us as it were by accident since Chickamauga. After that fight, I saw to it that you stayed."

"Just as you are in a strange land, away from Ireland."

Cleburne's gray eyes glowed in the light of two lanterns. Charlie thought: It was the right thing to know and the right thing to say. He turned to the board and studied it for a while, but not long, for an avenue appeared, a move that could not possibly have such symmetry, such perfection as he first thought. He studied the avenues of attack and escape, the next few moves by both sides, then, farther, he saw the possible notions of defeat and retirement. Yes, he thought. Simple enough. He moved a knight.

"Ah, I believe you have left yourself open here," said Cleburne, eyes alight. He reached for a bishop, almost took it between his slender fingers to move it, then stopped. He did the same thing, stopped again. He backed away perplexed, nearly touched his remaining rook then removed his finger as well. He glanced up once at Charlie and saw his eyes had gone flat and calm, assured. For some time, Cleburne reached for a piece then took his hand away as if he'd suddenly discovered he was pressing it against a hot stove. Finally he sighed. "The devil take me!"

Charlie almost smiled. He had never heard anything approaching a curse come from Cleburne's lips, though only the most sullen old maid would consider that a curse.

"I accept the General's compliments," said Charlie.

"Might I ask how many moves ahead you make, Mr. Merrill? For it seems to me that you have seen your way out of each angle of attack. Perhaps you should take command of my division, and I should hie me back to Arkansas."

"A chess game is not played with men's lives," said Charlie. Instantly, he knew he had said the *wrong* thing, for Cleburne's fine mood vanished, and he sat back and looked away, and Charlie could see that he grieved, felt an established agony, an emotion he could touch but dared not in the midst of battle.

"Indeed," said Cleburne. "Give me some time to study this board. We have plans for the morrow."

"I regret what I said. It was unkind and indiscreet." Cleburne softened and smiled distantly, still looking away.

"Go outside and get some coffee and more food," said Cleburne. "McGregor attends your Whitworth. Clean yourself and take some sleep. We have hard fights coming. I shall need you. We all shall need you." Cleburne looked at the board and shook his head. "Remarkable. Really remarkable."

Charlie stood, dizzy, and saluted, and Cleburne returned it.

After he'd eaten and bedded down near Duncan, Charlie slept until morning, as if in a vast neighborhood of the dead.

✧ ✧

THE SUN ROSE IN blood on May 23, and the troops, marching in loose lines, steamed beneath the fire-blast of late spring in Georgia. They knew soon enough they were headed south again, and the mumbling and cursing bubbled down the lines. Dark eyes glared over their shoulders, almost hoping commands would come, bugle calls for a fight. Charlie marched in the ranks of his old company, for he was still too injured to hold back and find a position to cover their retreat.

Duncan carried Charlie's Whitworth for a few miles, but then Charlie took it back, and soon he began to feel better, and the lingering fog evaporated from his eyes, and the throbbing in the back of his skull went dull, though it did not pass.

"God don't love men havin' to march in this kind of a scorch," said a filthy private named Daws, a limber-limbed Kentuckian who regularly cursed the indecisiveness of his home state. "This kind of a scorch will burn the brain offn a man. This kind of a scorch will make the death of you. Goddamn if I had not rather march in a storm, whether of hail or bullets I don't goddamn care."

"Shut up there in the ranks," said a sullen captain named Hixon. His eyes were painted round with the black circles of sickness.

"Just complimenting the heat on a fine job, Captain," said Daws. "Must be Yankee heat because it's meant to kill us."

That night, they camped near the town of Dallas, and Charlie and Duncan ate their small rations, sipped coffee, waited. In the morning, Charlie drew ammunition and caps from the ordnance wagons, and he told Duncan he was going to head back through the lines and see if there was a position where he could see the Union lines as they advanced.

"Oh, for the love of God, Charlie, let's rest while we're able and have no real orders," said Duncan. "You are much the better sniper than I am a scout, and perhaps my job is to keep you alive. Have you considered that, son?"

"Being of use is my best hope."

"Aye, God, your best hope for what?" cried Duncan. "Well, then, let's be off. But you have to promise to save my own pitiful life a time or two."

"I will save your life," said Charlie, and he pushed away a tender thought of his mother and sister Martha, stood and began to walk through the Southern lines toward nowhere he could yet see.

✧ ✧
✧

CHARLIE MOVED TO THE Confederates' left flank, far ahead of the skirmishers, and late in the afternoon, he and Duncan stood in a pine forest and listened in the windswept silence for a long time.

"They say you and the general is playing a game of chess. Could that be true, for the love of God?" asked Duncan.

"Ssshh," said Charlie. "There." Duncan turned his head back and forth to catch a sound, but he heard nothing but wind.

"Not a blessed sound."

"How is your arm?"

"The ache is become my boon companion," said Duncan. "I cannot imagine how I could live without it." Charlie almost smiled.

"There. Hear that?" Charlie scrambled through the woods straight ahead, Duncan close behind. They came up a slope and saw before them what looked like the entire Yankee army, a division at least, marching in a long line across an open field.

"For the love of God, let's fall back," said Duncan. "We'll be enveloped and captured or shot right off."

"I have the range," said Charlie. He knelt and loaded the Whitworth and aimed at a man on a horse three quarters of a mile away, held him through the sight, trying to gauge rank or importance. The explosive pop from the Whitworth always startled Duncan, and he flinched as Charlie shot and watched the horseman buckle in the saddle, draw one shoulder to his ear, shake his head as if to deny he was wounded, then fall headlong off the horse into the field. Men scrambled to him, ants spilling from a kicked-up hill. Charlie could see the line's skirmishers glancing wildly back and forth for a shot.

"You knocked someone off a horse, did you?' whispered Duncan.

"I did," said Charlie, who was reloading before he realized the motion of his arms might be seen from the Union lines. Five shots seemed to go off at once, a distant pop, and the heavy Enfield slugs plucked dust from the field before them, crackled in the limbs high overhead.

"They're getting our range, and I'm getting you out of here," said Duncan.

"Not yet," said Charlie.

"For the love of God, there come some cavalry. There, mounted and coming at us from the hill." Charlie did not look at Duncan or see him pointing, just knelt again and shot a color bearer, who dropped like a chopped tree. The banner, with its stripes and stars fluttered down into the dust. A shot whistled not three inches from Charlie's head, and he felt exhilaration, a readiness for engagement. Duncan was grabbing at his arm and pulling him up.

"Yes." Charlie heard the sound of his own voice. Now they were running back through the woods, and they could hear the gallop of cavalry not more than a few hundred yards behind, and the air here was still and wet. In less than three minutes, they regained the Confederate skirmish line, passed it, slid into dugout rifle pits. When the cavalry reached within three hundred yards, the Confederates opened fire, shooting at the riders and their mounts. Horses fell writhing in the blood of their deaths, and men fired, were shot, rode back to regroup.

"Well, you got 'em all heated up," said a thickset soldier with few teeth and a red beard. He was barefoot, Charlie noticed, and there was an oozing sore on his left leg that bled through his shredded trousers. For a moment, quite unexpectedly, Charlie felt an immense pity for the man, for the South, for those who were broken and lost. "You sharpshooter girls get 'em all riled up and bring 'em to us. I reckon that's a fine thing. There ain't a good day spent unless I kill a man. It puts the electric in my blood."

"This is no damn place for such a tender boy," said Duncan, who loaded his rifle and waited for a target to present itself. Charlie's head turned slowly to the left, and he looked at Duncan and saw that he spoke without rancor or irony.

UNTIL DARK, THEY FIRED at each other, the Butternut skirmish line and the dismounted Federal cavalry. Then, a tense waiting took them. Behind, the sounds of troop movement spread for what sounded like miles. Charlie watched Duncan's face in the small light of night, saw a softness and worry spread from cheek to cheek.

"You were married, you said."

"Aye, I was married. Lost her in childbirth. And the child as well."

"How can you go on every day? Didn't you want to die with her?"

"Die with her? I wanted to choke God to death on his damned clouds and streets of gold with my bare hands. I would have suffered a thousand tortures, died a hundred deaths in agony, if she could have lived but one more day. Or the child slept through one hour at his mother's breast."

"What did you do?"

"I cried like an old woman. I cried and I screamed and I moaned as if the life of me were like a hot stove. When I awake in the morning now, I still have the smell of her hair in my nose, the shape of her back on my chest. She had hair the color of spring sunshine and eyes blue as the bluest lake. And she loved me. She loved me as no woman e'er loved a man before, complete and with all her lovely heart. Oh, she was a fine lass, and she was my sun and my moon and my stars.

"And I took to a wandering flight. I thought to drink myself into a death but could not, for it sickened me. I considered jumping from a high place to break my fool neck. I even asked a friend to shoot me."

"You did?"

"I did, and do you know what he did? He hugged me like a maiden, and I fought at him, but he would not strike back. He would not strike back at me. And I fell in a hard silence to the ground, Charlie, and of a sudden I felt her spirit with me."

The Southern skirmishers were vigilant but almost silent now, hoping to catch a few moments of sleep before the morning. Charlie could only see his friend in the faint light.

"Her true spirit?"

"I am a simple man and do not know the ways of God. But if she was not with me, I am no Christian man and no Scotsman, either. I did not see her, son, but she was with me, and she whispered in my ear that I was to live, and I could smell her hair, and the burden of her loss passed from me in that place. And I rose whole and ready to move away from that sorrow which had ruined me. Such is the whole truth of it."

"I have not been able to bear such losses in my own life," said Charlie. "I suffered such losses and ran away to this war. Not of the same kind, not in the same way, but losses, Duncan. Why are we to suffer so terribly? I cannot even see the truth of things. God is judging me for the men I have killed, and I do not even know why I kill them. I thought I should never shoot more than cans by the railway track."

They were quiet for a time.

"Leave it be, Charlie."

"Did you love your father, Duncan?"

"Me father? Aye, a good strong man killed when I was but twelve when a steer rolled on him causing a suffering to the brain," he said. "Sometimes I wonder why they came here to this country, from one country with fierce warriors only to find ourselves in a battle again. There's a feeling of distance to everything in my life, Charlie, a certainty that I will have given nothing to this world afore I shed it. It's a strange thing, but I try not to be bitter on it. So far as I can understand the ways of God, this is it: If we are not meant to do great things, at least we can help them what can. In any way we see fit.

"I am not fighting the Federals from a hatred of them, but because they have come into our land. I could care less for your colored man as a slave. Free them all. They could scarcely be more poor than I am. But me father, aye, I loved the man insensibly. And I grieve that I am not a father to be loved in his own molding."

Charlie waited for more, but the even breathing of Duncan's sleep soon filled their rifle pit. Charlie took Sarah's letter from his shirt, but he could not read it in the dark. He tried to summon the aroma of her yellow hair, her smile, the pressure of her hand, but they would not come. They would not come all night, and only two hours before dawn did he drift off, and even then he did not dream.

TROOPS MOVED ALL THE next morning, reinforcing positions, preparing for battle. The lines formed around a log structure called New Hope Church at a crossroads northeast of Dallas. Hood's Corps held there, but the rest of the Army of Tennessee settled nearby, ready for the attack they feared but hoped would come that day. Charlie and Duncan moved away from the skirmishers and looked for sharpshooting positions all day but found most exposed to enemy fire. Charlie could not stop thinking of Duncan's wife with hair the color of spring sunshine. The day was so hot, the air so absent, that even veteran soldiers gasped from the effort, and Charlie watched them drip and steel their faces for the fight as he moved north along the lines, hoping for a vantage point to fire. Late in the day, Charlie and Duncan rested near a rough piece of ground, rocky and brambled, and a dense wood before them filling with the sound of Federal troop movements. The Confederate breastworks here were magnificent, Charlie thought, bristling with logs and dug deep into the red soil, and he was amazed once again at how quickly men would dig their way into the earth. Cannon opened on both sides. Clouds had moved in during the day, and now they hung low, gray as ash, bulging with storms.

"We must get into the works!" shouted Duncan. "This is going to be a bloody field soon." For once, Charlie followed him without dissent, crawling up and over into the trenchworks, where ill-clad Confederates prepared to fire. If Charlie thought the thundering of cannon had been loud, he was startled to hear the sound double in volume, triple, then quadruple. The Federals' aim was high, as it usually was when they were sighting their Napoleons and Parrott guns, but soon they would get the range. Lightning raked positions to the north, but if there was thunder, it failed to penetrate the shellfire. Then: a peculiar sound chattering through the rumble.

"Bugles," said Duncan. "Aye, God, it's their bugles pushing them to the forward."

"Here they come!" screamed two soldiers at once. Charlie watched the men take firing positions in the works, and he did the same and saw the magnificence of it all: a long blue line coming at a steady step across the field toward the Southern troops, beneath the occasional arc of artillery, into the flash of lightning from the coming storm. They seemed to move as slowly as in a child's game, but there were thousands, stretching out of sight, perhaps tens of thousands. Then they knelt in ranks and the firing began in earnest, and most of the rounds on both sides were too high, Charlie saw, but he shot one private soldier, then another, and finally an officer of some rank urging his boys onward. Charlie glanced at those wounded, and they writhed, all but the officer, who had taken his shot in the head.

"Come on, you bastards!" someone was screaming. "You damn son a bitches! Come on!"

"I can't get me a shot!" Duncan screamed. "Moving down!"

Charlie nodded and stayed behind the logworks and slipped the barrel of his rifle up and over, fired, missed. He realized as he loaded again that he could hear nothing but an internal growling, ceaseless, like a waterfall. He came over the parapet and fired without aiming and did not stop to see what he had hit, did not load again and could hear nothing now, not even the thunderstorm that was rolling upon them, not the artillery batteries open full on both sides of the field around New Hope Church, not the rifle fire or the screaming and dying of men.

He felt no urge to charge, no need to run away.

His hearing came back, and a grinning soldier who brought up a sneer like vomit sat beside him, nodding.

"You know how far we is from Atlanta, boy?" he asked. Charlie looked at him and said nothing. "You deaf, boy? I said you know how far we is from Atlanta? Twenty-five goddamn miles! Twenty goddamn days into the campaign, and we're *twenty-five goddamn miles* from Atlanta! We cain't win. There's no goddamn way we can win."

✿ ✿
✿

THE STORM BROKE JUST after seven-thirty, a wild downpour full of hailstones and raking winds. The Federal troops retreated across the field, where hundreds lay dead or dying, and in the Confederate works, dozens sat cramped into the shape of death as well. Charlie and Duncan sat in the muddy trenches and bore the hail and rain.

The next day they skirmished for hours, and Charlie moved with Duncan down the South's right flank where Cleburne's troops were stationed behind a brigade of Georgia troops. Artillery let loose from time to time, but mostly skirmishers and sharpshooters took wild shots from their cover; Charlie could not say he hit a target all day, and he bore the frustration that night when they could not reach Cleburne's position and had no supper or a decent place to sleep.

"Aye, God, when neither side moves away, then there's a fight aborning," said Duncan. "I've felt as useless as dancing shoes on a rooster, son. I'm thinking we should work a little less together and a little more for the Confederate States of America." No storms rolled across the landscape tonight, but the weather was unsettled, foul. Charlie sat in a gully behind some Alabama troops, glaring into the darkness so hard he wondered whether his eyes glowed. Smells came: pine, grass, an unseen wildflower, and the faint whiff of carrion, which seemed to follow them like a ghost, haunting every step, every attempt to sleep.

"What should we do then? I believe this is all a kind of madness," said Charlie.

"A fine way to speak to the man who kept you alive for the greater good," said Duncan. Charlie heard the soft, wry affection in his voice.

"You're right, Duncan, but I would not, for the love of God, die on purpose for the Confederate States of America."

"Then is it honor?"

"Honor? The dead are the dead. They have neither honor nor peace. All this howling is useless and will be seen so long after it ends."

"You're tired after a frustrated day of missing all your targets, I ken," said Duncan. "Leave it be, then. We're not to understand another man's motives in this life since we can hardly understand our own. Just leave it be."

Charlie felt his lips tremble, and he wanted to fall weeping into the mica-littered soil, to eat grass, be mad, run screaming. For the first time, he thought of deserting. It would be so easy. Head away as if to find a position, then ease into the woods and walk away. He could find his way to some house, alight. Being only seventeen and not bound by law to fight, who would notice? Better than this: leaving Branton for war only to wind up marching backward toward home. Neither of them spoke again, and a few minutes later, Duncan slept. Charlie was awake most of the night, thinking.

ARTILLERY AT DAWN: BOTH camps opened fire when light spread up from the east. Charlie left before Duncan awakened, sliding down the lines to the south, moving into a copse of tulip poplars and pines. Poplars were useless for sharpshooting because they had few lower limbs, but perhaps he could find a cedar or a white oak. Shinnying with a Whitworth rifle and its shells was hard work; getting down was worse. So when he climbed he stuck to laddered trees if he could find them. The problem with cedars: hard to escape if firing came close. He'd once come across a Yankee sharpshooter hanging by his boots from the upper limbs of a tall cedar, arms dangling, face purple in death. A good tree was hard to find. An open canopy, cover, a line of sight.

Charlie had no idea what the troops on either side were doing, but he could guess. The Southerners would be elaborating on their breastworks, still digging, firing their artillery until the barrels were hot to the touch. They would be waiting as they always did, waiting for a Federal movement, and by the time it came, General Johnston would be striding back and forth like a bantam rooster, face red, arguing against the possibility of fighting an army twice the size of his.

Other scouts and sharpshooters crept into the wooded glen, which looked over a portion of the Union lines. Charlie had never seen such a bluecoat concentration, and he took a shot into the works, surprising the newer Confederates, who whirled and sighted him before they knew. No one fell across the way or heard his firing. Then: Some distance away, an advance from the Gray lines, and Charlie felt his pulse quicken. Probably Hardee and Hood, especially Hood, who had the sense of a mad dog when it came to war: Clamp on to your foe and fight until one was dead, and do it now. Charlie climbed a tree and fired, hitting an artilleryman in the groin. The man writhed like a worm on a hot rock.

"I've had enough of this," said Charlie softly. He climbed down, careful not to drop the Whitworth, and once down, he loaded again and moved north toward the bulk of the troops that were engaged with the Yankee center. The fighting there was terrible, and he would join it. But he could see it now, see the Confederate lines bend, then buckle, see the men fight back to their own works from the malignant field of fire. The shelling was louder. Union soldiers across the way were taking shots at him now, and he turned to face them. He thought: I do not even know the name of this place where I will be killed. He wondered what time it was. Surely midafternoon, possibly later. The minié balls sang past him, puffed up dirt at his brogans. Some whined and others buzzed as they passed, feral beasts bound to sting. Charlie looked through his rifle sight and saw what looked like a general. He shot an aide to the general who was trying to show him a paper, possibly a map. Then: *They are coming straight for me.*

Charlie turned his head a little as he reloaded. He fired at the coming soldiers and saw no one fall. Then he was running back toward the Southern lines, and he came up a rocky slope to the top of a tree-covered ridge overlooking a ravine, and none of the soldiers was familiar, though they helped pull him into their works.

"Damn if I ever seed a thing like that," said a red-faced boy with a voice high as a girl's. He was beardless, with a slender waist and narrow shoulders. His hands shook so badly he could barely rod the cartridge down his Enfield. "Out there in the middle of the battlefield standing there shooting back without no worry in the world. I never seed a thing like that. Would you look at that rifle."

The men leaned against the works, some shooting with their chests against the walls, others firing with both feet solidly on ground. Charlie had no more than six rounds left, and so he took his time. The Federal troops unrolled across the field toward them. Someone said the ridge must be held or the Yankees would flank them again. There was a movement from behind, and Charlie turned and saw, to his astonishment, men from Cleburne's Division coming up, Granbury's Brigade of Texans. The Union troops tried to come on, but the fire was thick as stones in a creek bed, though a few reached within twenty yards of the Confederate works before taking their deaths or wounds. Smoke, gunfire, blood, screaming, artillery shells exploding—the field had grown a crop of war, Charlie thought, and it was full and ripe. Nearly an hour later, with their dead in blood-running ranks, the Federal troops began to pull back into the edge of the woods, where they still received fire, and Charlie shot a man in the back from fifteen hundred yards. The man threw his rifle out, buckled forward in the middle, then fell like a child diving into a deep summer pond.

"We drove 'em back, boys!" cried a major, waving his arm in the air. The man's face was triumphant, wild, and the Texans began to scream so loud some were trembling with victory or rage. A wisp of cottony smoke drifted from the barrel of Charlie's Whitworth, and for a moment, he thought of running. He could not say what directed such pointlessness in the works, but he pushed the feeling back, choked it off. Some of the men coughed, but one kept coughing and began to convulse and vomit blood, and then he shuddered, said something inaudibly, and died. Others attended him. Charlie moved away, down the lines.

Then, incredibly, the Federals were readying for another charge, and this time they would die, all or most of them. *Some damned officer,* Charlie thought. Some officer ordering his own glory from a safe distance. Some did it for votes after the war, and others did it coldly, uncaring, as if the men were stone or wood, numbers in a store ledger. The Confederates reloaded and waited until the range was right and fired again, and the artillery found the range and blew gaps in the blue lines. He watched now, unwilling to waste the Whitworth rounds on such easy targets. The Yankees worked their way back up the slope, taking acrobatic falls, tumbling, sideslipping into sharp turns and rolls. A few turned and ran, then more, and finally all of them, but the Southern lines did not stop firing, and in twenty minutes, the few survivors made it back to the woods.

"The flank's done held!" said a very dirty soldier next to Charlie. His black hair was shaggy and plastered to his face with sweat and dirt. "The flank's done held! The war's over! We done won it for Bobby Lee!"

SOMETIME LONG AFTER DARK, the Federals went onto the field before the rocky ridge and gathered their dead and wounded, and the moans were piteous. Charlie did not look for food or water, spoke to no one. He saw a flock of Southern officers talking in rapid and subdued tones not a hundred yards away, and he knew the day was not ended. He once more considered quitting the war. He thought of finding a widow's house and eating his fill, bread with apple butter, roast pig, vegetables put up from the summer before. He thought of Shakespeare and Jack Dockery, and he thought of his mother and Martha. He had three cartridges left for his rifle. Something was happening.

Just after ten that night, the men began bunching with a knowledge of urgency, and Charlie did not ask what was about to happen. From the sullen darkness, Confederate bugles ripped apart the near silence, and the word from the bugles was for a charge down the slope, and Charlie felt the ramrod blood speed through his chest, into his springing legs, and he was running across the field screaming with the rest of them, attempting not to fall into shot craters or trip on dead men. The fire into them from the Union lines was weak, and they kept coming, screaming, a few stopping abruptly to fire their Enfields into the dark woods across the way. You could see the Yankees starting to understand that the troops opposing them were mad, that they would not stop until a death had been gained for them, for anyone. The Texans boiled past him now, running like boys in a summer footrace.

In less than an hour, they pushed back all the Federal soldiers, fired after them, screamed, pranced, stumbled over the dying, who gasped blood, cried for water. Then, after all that, they were ordered to walk back across the field and back up the rocky slope to their works, leaving only pickets behind.

CHARLIE MERRILL SLEPT IN the works sitting up. Some of Granbury's men were too elated to sleep and spent the night strutting out their victory, screaming curses at the Yankee invaders, sure this was a pivotal and telling victory. Charlie said nothing, but he had been in front of the lines since Dalton, and he knew this was a small battle, that tens of thousands boiled behind the lines, that Sherman was probably flanking them already.

He awoke the next morning and walked back from the Confederate works, away from the line of fire looking for the ordnance wagons, and it took him an hour to find the few that were left, the others having moved south already, an ominous development. Charlie got more rounds for the Whitworth and accepted a quarter pound of dried beef and a pone of cornbread in his turn from nearby soldiers. He wondered where Duncan might be. He was eating his beef when he recognized Tyree Baskins, from Govan's Brigade, coming toward him dragging a blood-bandaged foot and grimacing.

"Baskins is it?" said Charlie.

"Merrill," said Baskins painfully. He came on over. "My foot's done took a bounce of shrapnel, of all the luck. Of all the blessed luck. It feels like the bones is dancing in there of their own accord."

"Have you seen Duncan McGregor?"

"McGregor? No, not for a couple of days. I ain't seen nobody. Oh, Bob Rainey's dead."

"What?"

"He's dead," said Baskins. Then, louder, "He's dead! Shot through the throat last night in that goddamn charge." Baskins began to mutter, and Charlie wept as he had not done since Chickamauga. "He just sat down, and he wasn't making no sense, and I was beside him, and he was hacking and gargling and holding his throat. And I lit a match on my boot, and Lord God in heaven, what a thing. Lord God in heaven. Half his neck blowed away. And he was a good man. If God don't spare a man like that, then I don't know what to think. I just don't know.

"Then the canister exploded not far from me, white hot and crawling like a live thing on that field, and it crawled like a bolt of lightning across the field and hit my foot. Like God intended it! And for a long time it didn't hurt, then it was like a death in my leg, and now it's a thousand musketeers or swamp snakes, and I'd just as lief be dead with Bob Rainey." He was trembling hard now like a bullied boy. "I'd just as lief go on and get being dead over with."

He limped away, and Charlie thought of Bob Rainey as he walked down the lines, left them all, headed past the last picket and found a place on a high hill where he could see no troops at all, none from either side.

BATTLES WENT ON ALL that day, but Charlie stayed back from them. Cannon fire cracked and boomed. There was endless chatter of muskets. The ones farthest away might be crickets. Charlie tried to clear his mind of feeling and sentiment, but something was overcoming his resistance, a certainty that God was watching and that this bore meaning.

In the afternoon, a war-addled Yankee came wandering into the clearing before the tree under which Charlie sat. The man wore a bib of blood. He was unbearded and talked to himself.

"Talking of this. The lines and the firing. The lines and the firing. Talking of this." The man spoke the words over and over, sometimes adding a subtle variation. His wool coat was soaked in blood. Blood leaked down his arm and dripped from his fingers. He did not appear startled when the closest artillery began to roar without ceasing, did not stop talking when he fell to his seat. He struggled to rise again. As he came closer, Charlie could see that his teeth were red, and his tongue was red, and blood had spurted from his ears and dried in twin trails down his neck, black as snakes. Charlie cocked the Whitworth and waited. The man had no rifle or pistol or knife that Charlie could see.

The Yankee saw Charlie and stopped. He seemed to be considering whether to smile or not, and Charlie waited and watched him stumble in the ghastly heat. The air was motionless. Battles continued all around them. Someone was probably preparing a charge. Charlie stretched his neck and thought about rain, about great runnels of water running down the ravines to swelling creeks, about puddles and cornfields where you could almost hear the plants stretching with delight.

"Private Hiram Corn reporting," said the soldier. He fell to his knees. Charlie set the Whitworth on the ground and went to him and found he was a boy, no older than Charlie, perhaps even younger. A twist wrenched Charlie's heart. "Private Hiram"—the boy began to topple as Charlie knelt beside him—"Corn reporting."

Charlie caught him as he fell over, and he looked into his eyes and saw death coming on quickly, like clouds spreading storms before the sun. There were speeches to be made, but Charlie did not know them, could not spare the words. The boy's left shoe was undone, and the right was missing entirely, as if pieces of his clothing were leaving him to his sleep on the field.

"What's happened to you?" asked Charlie. "Where are you from?" Sharpshooters hit their targets from far away. This boy was here in his arms, looking up. He had no beard, just a matted cake of blond hair. He had bitten his fingernails. His features were delicate as a girl's, and Charlie wondered where he was hit, but by then the boy was in the shuddering of death and there was no reason to look.

"Ohhhhhhhhh," said the boy, shaking and gritting his teeth. "Ohhhhhhh. I want . . . Private Hiram Corn . . . there's a thing. Water. No. Over there. There it is. *My God.* There it is." Charlie struggled to hold him down, but the body, fighting its coming shape, struggled, then bucked like an unbroken horse, and Charlie whispered, hushed the boy, and then the shuddering broke into three great snaps of reflex or pain, and Charlie felt him weaken, look up, his brow knitting with confusion and a single question. His eyes were asking the question. Then his lips parted to ask the question, but his mouth was full of blood, and the boy turned away, then held up his right hand and inspected it as one does something strange and wonderful. He slumped dead in Charlie's arms. The firing of cannon and muskets intensified to the north.

For a long time, Charlie sat holding the boy, wondering how he could report the death of a Yankee boy named Hiram Corn. Others said that if your mother was alive when you passed away, she knew it instantly, that no other communion was needed to confirm that hideous loss. The soldier's blood wet Charlie's hands, and he went deathly quiet, then he looked outward, upward, crying as if his eyes had filled with blood, and he was letting go of it to die.

CHARLIE SLEPT IN THE dreamless woods. A great storm was breaking somewhere in the upper light, violent rain and wind, but it did not break here, and Charlie sat until the day was gone, watching the shape of Hiram Corn, whom he had laid out neatly in the pine straw, hands folded across his blouse. In the faint moonlight, the boy looked almost like Tom—the same hair, boy's fine hands on a man's hairy arms. Charlie would sleep and then awaken and not know where he was, perhaps on some height. He thought once of Jesus in the wilderness and His temptations, but no single idea held him for long, and he felt the airless night on his skin like a shroud.

In the morning, he knelt before Hiram and spoke a few words he remembered from the many funerals over which his own father had presided. He moved north again toward the skirmishing, which had already broken out. He came to the lines and saw a large group of Southern soldiers trying to carry their dead from the battlefield, but the Yankee sharpshooters and skirmish lines were driving them back, not even allowing this sanctity; night was the time for gathering the dead, and day was for dying.

Southern sharpshooters, none Charlie recognized from a distance, lay in rifle pits and fired desultory but well-aimed shots at Union officers and artillerymen. He walked another hundred yards. A bullet spun up the earth near him like a small whirlwind. He climbed a tall oak tree carefully, making sure the Whitworth was secure, and he seated himself in a crotch of limbs fifteen feet off the ground. By now, a trembling fear had come into him, but he looked through the telescopic sight and found an artillery battery. A man was ramming the long-handled barrel sponger into his cannon, and Charlie picked him off clean. The sponger stayed thrust into the barrel as the man fell. Charlie felt sick to his stomach, wept again.

The artillery, which had been sporadic, opened on both sides with a cough, then a roar.

"Damn fine shot, boy," said someone. Charlie jerked to his left, wiping tears.

"You damn got that right," said a voice to his left. He looked there, looked around and saw that the trees were full of sharpshooters plying their craft. He had the passing knowledge of something botanically arcane, the Grove of Soldier Trees, an Orchard of Sharpshooters. Not fifty feet away, smiling and nodding was Duncan McGregor, whose rifle would barely reach the Union lines, but this was better than being in the works, which were being shelled.

"You've turned into a rather poor scout," said Charlie. "General Cleburne is going to be ill with me for keeping you around."

"You're just befuddled because it's a battlefield," said Duncan. "The truth is that I'm the one who's keepin' you alive, Private Merrill. Our little detail has done great service. You in the sharpshootin' of the Yankees and me in the keepin' of you alive. I'd think the fair General would be pleased by such a thing."

"Merrill, where you been?" It was Walter Bragg, the Alabamian from his company.

"Down to the right," Charlie said, gesturing with his head. "Looking for the end of the line."

"You find it?" asked Duncan.

"Almost," said Charlie Merrill.

All day the artillery poured from both sides, and sometimes the musketry came in such sustained waves it sounded like a waterfall, and the sharpshooters resting in the tree crotches or sitting slung on limbs fired at officers and artillerymen, hitting quite a few. They took their time loading and firing since the cartridges for Whitworths and Kerrs were precious and not as abundant as the ammunition for the standard Enfields. Sometimes, in other battles, the sharpshooters would be put out even before the skirmish lines to cover the infantry as that great many-footed monster rolled out of the earthworks and bled screaming across the field of fire. Now they were left in the trees where they could take out Federal artillery officers, as good a duty as they might have.

A bullet cracked into the trunk of the oak not four inches from Charlie's head.

"Sharpshooter over there's trying to take you!" cried Duncan McGregor above the roiling din. Charlie was looking through the telescope of his rifle.

"I see him. He's in a tree, too." Charlie leveled his gun and fired back, and a limb splattered bark on the shooter, but the man was re-loading and did not fall. The next shot from the Yankee hit Charlie's coat, puffing up his shoulder and drilling a hole through it. Charlie slumped to the left and then sat back up sharply.

"Are you hit, son?" cried Duncan.

"Bruise."

Charlie reloaded and took his time, sighting the soldier. The shooter seemed neither young nor old, almost faceless, a poetic concept rather than a man. Charlie hit him square in the chest, and he doubled over in a sudden snap, dropped his rifle, then sat back up. Through the eye of his lens Charlie watched as the man's lower jaw slowly dropped and he fell from the tree. Others who had seen it through their Whitworth sights clapped and laughed.

"Damn if that weren't a fine shot," said a private named Howard Foote who shot a Kerr and was prone to weep when battles had ended. He would coolly pick off a dozen artillerymen or officers during the firing, and when it had subsided, he would hold himself and sob, but he could never say why. The others liked him enormously for it and took turns in their comforting.

All day they sat in the trees and fired, and the artillery cracked. Charlie's shoulder, which had borne the extreme kick and the loud pop the Whitworth made in fire for months, felt sore from the constant recoil. He had hung his canteen on a broken limb nearby, but his water was gone by late in the day, and he and most of the sharpshooters were running out of ammunition anyway.

"I'm getting down," Charlie shouted to Duncan.

"Praise God for that," said Duncan, who had fired his gun several times but knew he'd hit nothing. "I've scouted this position about all I can."

They moved together, now bent over to avoid the fire. Duncan did a small dance step and fell to the ground, then began to curse in a filigreed, baroque sentence.

"You hit?"

"Blast the luck, a goddamned bullet's bounced off the ground and bruised the bottom of my foot," said Duncan.

"Can you walk?"

"Aye, I can walk, and damn the lucky shot. That's the thing, Charlie. The lucky shot is what mostly gets you, not sharpshooters such as yourself and them othern. It's the shot in the air like an offerin' to the gods

that gets a man. Aimed at nobody or aimed at and missed and then doing its work when half spent. I saw a boy when we were in Kentucky
reach out with his foot and trying to stop a cannonball bouncing
through our lines, like it was a boy's ball. And it didn't seem to be going
no faster than that, but when it hit his foot, it pulled his leg clean off up
to the crotch. It took him no more than ten seconds to die, and he
looked at us like to say it weren't a thing to believe. The lucky shot."

That night, not beginning until ten, the Confederates made eight
successive charges at the Yankee lines in the lights of cannonading, and
the field was one of deafness and blood, and the wounded screamed for
water and their mothers, and the dead lay swelling. Charlie and Duncan
got as far left of the lines as they dared and poured fire from a slight enfilade into the Yankee position, but it was, Charlie thought, like spitting
in a river. Like schoolyard bullies who would not quit first, the armies
fought with every scream and shot until well after midnight. When the
firing finally dwindled, Charlie and Duncan moved through the ranks
and found that Cleburne's men had not made the charge but had been
behind it in the order of battle. The stench of sulfur lay like a rotten
blanket over the field, and there were no stars that Charlie could see,
not in any direction.

THE MEN SLEPT MOST of the next day, May 30, erupting with wracking
coughs, moaning and turning over in their works. Charlie and Duncan
found the rest of Cleburne's sharpshooter company, then slept, too.
Charlie dreamed of Sarah, as he often did, and he lay entombed in the
covers of his bed and she sat beside him dressed in blue, reading from a
book, but he could not hear her voice, only see the moving of her bow-
shaped lips. He strained to see the title of the book, but that was with-
held from him as well, and it could be a novel or poetry or a book yet to
be printed.

In the early afternoon, the men began to stir, and the stench of the
battlefield, of dead men and horses by the dozens, mingled with a lingering whiff of sulfur from the artillery to make the air hideous and
threatening. Men redressed their minor wounds or bathed their bruised
feet. Many were shoeless and walked on the side of their feet toward
their mess areas. Charlie awoke, jerking around and patting the hot
earth to find his Whitworth, which was lying between his legs.

"Now there's a hell of a fight for you, boy," said Duncan. He was sitting up smoking a short, stubby cigar. "When you look back on this war, you can say this was a hell of a fight. Thing is, don't nobody seem to know who won, if anybody did."

"Are they still over there?" asked Charlie, shading his eyes against the shock of sunlight. He pulled his forage cap low, but the light had the impact of a blast furnace. He realized he was hungry, smelled bacon cooking, a hint of coffee in the air.

"Aye, God, they're still over there, but nobody's fired a blessed shot, not even the sharpshooters or skirmishers or artillery batteries—not even your passing bird has so much as dripped a shit on us."

"This stench is terrible."

"We lost Bedgood yesterday."

"Oh, no."

"He was out on his own and came in after midnight when the fighting was still hot, and he had been shot through the knee, and he bled to death in the works. The lieutenant has taken his rifle for another man."

"I am sorry to hear of it. I cannot imagine why I am still alive. Every day when I awaken, I feel as if I have come through birth again."

"Then what a blessed morning you must have each day." Charlie was silent for a moment and burst out laughing. Together, weak-kneed and unsolemn, they walked to their mess and drew a small ration of bacon and cornmeal, and they sat with Cleburne's men and ate and drank the hot water that lay puddled in the bottom of their canteens.

LITTLE HAPPENED THE NEXT day, either, though the soldiers under flags of truce gathered their dead and entombed them in mass graves, placed with respect but rapidly. Many of the bodies had doubled in size, and arms tore away as they were lowered, like legs pulled from an overcooked chicken. Charlie wanted to head out and find a position or see if the enemy troops were moving, but the armies sat in their places, too exhausted for movement, letting the sounds of the north Georgia countryside reopen their damaged ears. This was nothing like Chickamauga, they said. A powerful battle, but nothing like Shiloh. A few who had been invalided home long before and just rejoined their regiments said this was nothing like Shiloh.

Charlie felt himself change, seeing the dying and the battles from another's eyes. This fight was going to end badly, and in the end, thousands would lie among the fields of fire, hugging death like a child his blanket. *Wrong,* he kept thinking now. *This is all wrong.* Somehow he took that feeling from Cleburne, though the general surely did not mean it.

Charlie had a few pieces of paper, and he took out the stub of a pencil and licked it and wrote:

Near Dallas, Ga.
May 31, 1864

Dear Mother,

I am so very sorry that I have written less than I should have on this campaign, but fighting has been fierce, and we have moved almost constantly. I take advantage of a cessation of arms to write you now.

First of all, please tell Martha that I am all right and that I miss her. I wonder all the time if she has changed, for I know that people change and sometimes it is for the good, and I wish it so for her. Also, know that I miss you terribly and that I would love to come marching through the streets of Branton again toward our home, and, God willing, I shall do it when my time in this army has ended.

We are engaged in a great fight, and I cannot say that we are winning it. I have seen friends torn to tatters before my eyes, and I have slain too many of the enemy to count. I am fortunate to have a fine friend in one Duncan McGregor, a Scotsman with a steady temper and a fine heart. He reminds me much of Jack in that way, and he has more than once saved my life, and I hope to save his when the time comes.

Mother, do not despair for me. During these months, the things I have seen could not be imagined by the most sensitive man or woman who has not been involved in them. The carnage and death are on a scale that dwarfs the imagination.

There is something in me that is sore and broken, and I do not know what it is, but I am discovering it a little more every day, and when I can name it, I shall know it.

I think each day of Tom and Father. My dear mother, only the knowledge that you and Martha flourish keeps me steady.

*But do not let such talk frighten you. I am well and doing
my job. I am a sharpshooter with General Cleburne, and I
know that he will protect all his men as well as possible, for
he is a great man and a fine general. My paper is used up
despite how tiny this writing is.*

*This comes with love and regret that I have written less
often than I should. We are but 25 mi. north of Atlanta.*

Love,
Charlie

May 16, 1862

☆ ☆ ☆

CHARLIE AWOKE TO THE sound of a single drumbeat. He sat up in bed, weak and disoriented, and saw that morning had barely rubbed the sun upon his windows. From down the hall, he heard his mother saying *Charles? Charles?* Charlie sat up and looked out the window, and far below in the silent pecan grove, a figure lay peaceably in the swath of grass.

Oh, my God, thought Charlie. He threw his legs over the edge of the bed and felt a strength spill from his face down his body and into them. He stood, and his legs felt capable of that burden. His nightgown fell to his ankles as he walked into the hall and downstairs. He could hear his mother putting on her housecoat. Martha would still be asleep in her room clutching her doll, Rose. Cephus and Missy lived half a mile away on the Traynor plantation and came to work every day like hired help. They would be present for another half hour. Charlie came through the back of the house and down the steps and into the wet grass. The day would be hot and airless. He felt capable of flight. A strength and sickness twisted his memory.

"Father?" he said. "Is that you, Father?"

Charlie ran toward the figure and then slowed down, finally stopping ten feet from the figure, a man wearing a black suit, lying face down, his head a mass of oozing blood. *Oh, sweet Jesus. Oh, sweet Jesus.* The back door opened a second time, and he turned and saw his mother, saw the certainty in her eyes, walking, her hands tented and half covering her face in prayer. He walked on to the body now and knelt before it and craned his face. His father's eyes were open and staring, and the back of his head was gone. Instead of retching or screaming, he felt a cold certainty came over him.

He remembered the day before, when they had gone to the hospital on the edge of town where Yankee prisoners were kept. His father had wanted to pray for them and had been turned back, furious, red-faced, sick at heart.

"Charles, Charles?" cried Betsy. Charlie stood, rigid with sorrow. He turned and walked rapidly toward her as she came toward her dead husband.

"He's dead," said Charlie. "He's gone. Don't go over there. There's nothing you can do."

"Charles? Oh, my God—what happened?"

"He's shot himself," said Charlie. "He's dead."

"Mama?" Martha stood at the back door in her flowing gown, eyes narrowed with fear.

"Go back inside, Martha, this instant!" she cried.

"Both of you go back inside," he said. "I'll send Cephus for the sheriff as soon as he comes. And Mr. Partain. Please go back inside."

"Charles," she moaned, her knees buckling. "Get up. Come on, get up." She smiled and looked with urgent hope at her son. "He's pretending. It's—it's a joke, Charlie. One of his jokes."

"Mama, he's dead," said Charlie. He turned her away from the body. Heat began to rise with the sun. The day would be suffocating.

"Mama, what's wrong?" said Martha.

"I'm coming, darling," said Betsy. "It's just a silly joke of his, Charlie. You know that." He took her in his arms and held her more tightly than he ever had.

"He has gone now," he whispered. He stroked his mother's hair as if she were a child. "He took his life. I will wait for Cephus and the sheriff and Mr. Partain. Go on back inside and tell Martha that he died. Don't tell her anything else for now. Do you understand me?"

"Oh, my dear God, what is happening? What is happening?"

Charlie helped her inside with Martha, whose eyes were wide with horror, and he walked slowly across the grove, realizing that a bitter strength was coldly flowing through his muscles. He could rip out trees by trunks and thrash the town down to dust.

✧✧

THE COFFIN LAY ON two sawhorses in the front parlor of Grace House, lid screwed tight, as a line of mourners filed past, touching the burnished wood and murmuring condolences to Betsy Merrill and her children. Martha's face was swollen, and she clutched a small twisted knot of a handkerchief. Betsy's face registered a dull shock. Charlie could not believe it was the evening of the same day. He imagined his father breathing. Perhaps the living always tried to bring back their dead through imagination, and that failure was unbearable because such a vanishing seemed unworthy of God.

"Betsy, we are terribly shocked and saddened . . ."

". . . we are bereft without our Reverend Merrill . . ."

"God's blessings and peace on you and the children . . ."

Charlie thought of Tom in Virginia, and how a bare few months earlier, he had been teasing Charlie as they walked on the Georgia Railroad tracks. Since then, all the world had been washed away in violence and darkness. *Sacrifice?* That was a boy or a man lying dead for no reason. This was not sacrifice; this was slaughter. If the shotgun's trigger had been squeezed by his father in literal telling, then who held the gun? Some ghost? Or was he carried home across the river by Jesus Christ himself? Could Christ approve of this slaughter?

Sheriff Jonathan Reed approached with a deep calmness. He held his hat in front of his chest like an offering of regret. His taut-faced wife, Annis, shuffled along a step behind him, wearing a black dress and a look of despair. The room was filled with murmurs, and Missy served tea, turning at times to wipe tears from her coffee-colored cheeks. Charlie glanced at his mother, and red streaks were spreading up her neck from below, flooding her face.

"This is a sad day for Branton, Betsy," Sheriff Reed said. He bowed stiffly and glanced with sorrow at the coffin. Despite the arts of Mr. Partain, the undertaker, a faint smell of the dead hung near the closed coffin. Inside, a bowl of aromatic salts lay on Charles's chest, and the mixed smells were hideous to Charlie.

Charlie had not noticed Sarah and her aunt and uncle coming in, and they were next in line. Sarah's face was pale as bone, and she wore a gray silk dress with a ruffled lace hem. The room had filled with his aunts, uncles, and cousins and with the town's richest—Craveltons, Potters, Syncoles, Jacksons, Westfields. Sarah could not take her eyes off Charlie as they came forward.

"Ah, most unfortunate occasion," said Dr. Sawyer Pierce. "Most unfortunate." His wife, Elaine, looked intensely sorrowful and hugged Betsy for a long time while Doc Pierce spoke on about his supposed grief. Sarah came to Charlie and stood before him, her eyes gray and rimmed with red.

"God grant you peace," she said simply.

"And you," said Charlie. Then, as he turned away from her and the sudden awareness of tears and was surprised to feel her closer, then in his arms, and he buried his face in her neck, in the nest of her hair, and he held her until she made the first move to break apart.

REV. ERASMUS BOWERS, MINISTER of the Athens First Baptist Church, stood in the pulpit behind Reverend Merrill's coffin, arms spread in obvious delight. He had trained down for the service, and now stood decked in glory before a packed sanctuary, his face red with sweat and inspiration, God-struck, free-rambling, enjoying himself enormously.

"I tell you my friends, that the world is a phantom, and we must never forget that fact. I tell you what is said in the Gospel of Mark: And it came to pass in those days, that Jesus came from Nazareth of Galilee, and was baptized of John in Jordan, And straightaway coming up out of the water, he saw the heavens opened, and the Spirit like a dove descending upon him: And there came a voice from heaven saying, Thou art my beloved son, in whom I am well pleased, And immediately! Yes, friends, immediately! The Spirit driveth him into the wilderness! And he was there in the wilderness forty days, tempted of Satan; and was with the wild beasts; and the angels ministered unto him.

"I say hallelujah, what a Savior, my friends! I say we hear the tramp of God every day upon the face of this earth, and no man can know when his time has come. We all spend our days in the wilderness, and why our dear friend Charles became lost in that wilderness, I cannot hope to know. But I can tell you one thing, my friends. Charles was a Christian! A Christian! And a man of God who is now returning to his God. Perhaps he is now already sitting at God's right hand, or perhaps he has a journey to make because of the manner of his passing.

"But I tell you this, he is rising on the wings of that dove toward heaven!"

Betsy Clark Merrill, veiled and solemn, leaned to her son, whispered to him rather too loud.

"Hot air."

Charlie felt a wild desire to laugh. If Tom were there, he surely would be laughing out loud, not caring what others thought. He looked around and saw Sarah sitting with her aunt and uncle, remembered that her brother Herman was somewhere in the field fighting for Union. Charlie glanced into the balcony and saw Cephus and Missy sitting side-by-side fanning themselves. Cephus chewed an unlit pipe fashioned from a corncob. Jack sat not far away with his mother and father, shifting from the pain in his foot.

Rev. Erasmus Bowers had leaped into the book of John, chapter twelve, verse forty-six: *I am come, a light into the world, that whosever believeth on me should not abide in darkness.*

Rev. Erasmus Bowers, tuned to the spirit, went on for another three-quarters of an hour as the sanctuary grew more stifling by the minute. Charlie closed his eyes and fell asleep instantly, and he was dreaming of rivers and great battles when he awoke to the congregation stamping, as it rose to sing "Amazing Grace."

THAT NIGHT, AFTER THE burial of the rapidly decaying body in the town cemetery almost behind Grace House, Charlie and Martha walked hand in hand through the shade of the pecan trees.

"I've shed every tear for my whole life," she said. "Are you are feeling stronger? Why do you think he did it?"

"He stopped believing that things could become better," said Charlie. "He believed that hope is a phantom. I think he was sick, too. Perhaps very sick. He never spoke of such things."

"Do you think so?"

"I believe what I see before me with my own two eyes," he said. They came to the railroad tracks, and he put his arm around his sister's shoulder. "You must believe Papa is happier now. That is the only consolation for us, Martha."

"I miss him so," she said. "I simply cannot believe I'll never see him again in this life."

"The whole country is bound to death now," he said. "Some day, I believe the Federals will come marching through Branton, and we will see hope vanish, and people will then know how thin the scaffolding of this life is."

"I don't understand," she said. "Yankees won't ever come here. We are far away from the fighting, from the war. How can you say that?"

"I don't know," he said. "But I almost see it, as if it were real." The sun faded downward. A long peel of orange tracks unwound before them. The sky looked alive with flame, as if the earth before them was falling away into hell.

June 2–26, 1864

DALLAS TO KENNESAW MOUNTAIN

EARLY THAT MORNING, RAIN began to spread over them in the trenches and rifle pits, a heavy, thick-clouded rain, drops sharp as ice, and a wind came with it, blowing off their forage caps and straw hats, forcing the water down their necks, soaking their coats and blouses until both sides seemed the same color of darkness. Charlie and Duncan moved through the rain, having left their company to scout. They came on through the small town of Dallas and found themselves near a hospital, and Charlie veered toward it.

"For the love of God, don't go there," said Duncan. "Can you not smell the death of it?"

"There," said Charlie hoarsely. "Look."

Outside, in the steady drip, was an enormous pile of arms and legs already filling with maggots, harried by flies and bees, and the stench rising from it exploded in them with a subtle violence. Many arms reached through the mass, hands bloodied and open, as if begging for help.

"Let's be gone."

"I want to see them," said Charlie. Duncan refused to go in, but Charlie walked into the hospital tent, which rippled with rain and wind, and moaning soldiers, their wounds half dressed or not attended at all, lay on the ground. Maggots crawled in their wounds, too, and the horror was beyond visceral, and Charlie felt his soul shrivel and edge toward darkness. One doctor came in bearing a saw that dripped blood and a yellow fluid, and Charlie backed out and walked across the main street of Dallas and found Duncan on a street corner and passed him, and they fell into an uneven step and quit the town, heading away from the firing.

THAT NIGHT, THE SHOWER turned torrential, and they sat in a grove of pines, having gone too far to return, with no dry tinder and only a little jerked beef and half a biscuit each. They could have been anywhere in North America, and the only sounds were the swishing of pine needles in the wind and the crinkle of rain.

"Are you going to die?" asked Charlie. "Do you think you're going to die? They say men know when they're going to die. You've seen it happen. They give away their possessions on the morning of a battle. I don't know if I'm going to die. I can't see it one way or another."

Duncan laughed and shifted to shade away the water from the boughs.

"You'll die. Sooner or later, you'll know it's time for you to die and you will, and or it will sneak up on you. Then you'll give your things away. Death to me is a living and breathing thing, not an accident, boy. It's a presence that hunts us. We are always hunted. Always. My wife and child were hunted hard for reasons I cannot know. I have asked God to explain this, but He has remained mute upon it."

"I can't imagine my own death in this war," said Charlie.

"I can imagine mine," said Duncan. "I can imagine it all too well. In fact, I know precisely *how* it will happen, just not *when*."

"How will it happen?"

"I will be gut-shot. I believe that is already written in the great scroll of heaven."

"The great scroll of heaven?"

"We need to gain you some fine Presbyterian learning, lad." Duncan laughed, but Charlie did not, and they did not talk again until darkness came, and they slept against the trunk of the tree, waterproofs tucked over them but doing scant good.

THAT WAS HOW THE rains began. Across north Georgia, rain spread like a malignancy, swelling creeks into rivers and rivers into lakes, washing away barns and a few mills, spinning their wheels so fast that millers had to shut them down. For a few minutes the rain would abate, and soldiers in their stream-struck works would look up, expecting a slash of blue in the sky, but it never came.

Sherman's troops on June 4 shifted strongly eastward through fields and on roads turned into a thick paste. Johnston's troops in turn withdrew again in their muddy beards, their butternut-brown coats gone to sheets of red clay so they looked to Charlie like figures from a nightmare play. He and Duncan had regained their old brigade with Cleburne's Division and marched along all day and through the night, for there was nothing special at which to shoot, and scouting was barely possible. The day before, the pickets of each side had been so close they threw rocks and even shovels at each other for amusement, but now everyone was moving. Perhaps the officers knew where they were going, but the soldiers did not. They never did.

The Confederate troops marched all night in the rain, and when a gray light rose on yet another day of rain, they were cloaked with mud, and only a whiskey ration kept them in line, and they quaffed it, swelling with the burn, strutting for that few minutes' solace and then collapsing. Charlie kept Sarah's letter as dry as he could, but the shape of her words was already changing in their neat lines. It was in his memory anyway, and he could repeat it then, he thought, and forever.

Charlie awoke just after noon to a scratching in his throat, and by mess time in the evening, he knew he was very sick with a trembling and a gagging cough. Thousands seemed to be coughing in the rain, humped over and shaking. A wavering stream of the sick was heading for the rear areas where they could rest and be sick, and even the toughest men, the Texans, had many sick hobble on south behind their present positions, stopping to grasp trees. Some leaked blood from their bowels or let hang out tongues dark with disease and coming death.

"Son, you look terrible," said Duncan. "I'm taking you to the rear."

"I'm tolerable," said Charlie. "I'm actually— I think I need— Could you help me get up, I . . ."

As Duncan lifted him, Charlie felt the small needles of illness prodding him all over in no direction, and he and Duncan walked in ankle-deep mud toward the rear, Duncan carrying both their rifles, and using them as one fifteen-pound walking stick. Charlie stopped to vomit in a puddle, and he was ashamed and wiped his face and would not look at Duncan. He thought of Bob Rainey and how much better it would be to take a bullet in the face, one sharp rap and then a descent into eternity. Not this again—not the bedclothes-sculptured life of an invalid. A man not far away fell face-first into a shallow puddle and lay there for ten seconds before a tall soldier without a coat or shirt lifted him out dripping by the neck of his soggy tunic. Charlie watched it amazed, for it seemed an echo of myth, the recreation of something long ago read by firelight and lanterns in Grace House when all of them sat and enjoyed their books and his mother played the piano softly. The half-naked soldier lifted the sick man full into his arms as one might cradle a sleeping child to bed, and he began to move hard and purposefully toward the hospital tents as well. Charlie was trembling when he passed, gaining speed.

BATHING HIS FOREHEAD WITH an alcohol sponge. On a cot beneath several extended tent flies with oiled cloth on their roofs that shut out the rain and the light. A cold wind whittling at the blankets, carving new scallops and angles. Coughing and spitting on the wet ground beneath him. Dizzy and thrashing with chills from side to side, and moaning for morphine, for anything, a cold that cannot be warmed, then a pan-flash of wretched heat, a summer day's battle.

Charlie felt himself slide into wakefulness and then back out of sight, down a chute and into an itching hell, and he tried to get his breath, but it would not come, then someone was propping him up and pouring a dram of whiskey down his throat, and it was fire and soured as it descended, and his stomach received it with gratitude then ejected it all violently, and Charlie lay back and wept from pain and frustration.

"Come on, boy, buck up as you can," said Duncan. Charlie moaned and turned and tried to respond but his words crumbled. A terrible taste rising in his throat and into his mouth. Terrible. He spat it out, but it would not go away. "My God, this ain't going to happen. Aye, God, it ain't!' Then Duncan was gone and Charlie slept and thrashed and awakened and thrashed, and someone wiped his forehead. Charlie sat up and looked around wildly, and someone was reading from the Bible: *I am the way, the truth, and the life.* Two pairs of hands folded for ten seconds and then carried a dead man from them to a trench, to tumble him in with the others. Charlie fell back and for the first time visualized his own death, and it was cold and impersonal and falling, and he realized that if he could imagine his death, he could yield to it.

✧ ✧
✧

A ROUGH JOSTLING AWOKE him in darkness, and two soldiers he had never seen were lifting him on a stretcher and carrying him out into the rain, and Duncan was walking alongside him. Charlie felt somewhat rested, enough to speak anyway.

"Where are they taking me?" asked Charlie.

"To a place where you'll be cared for," said Duncan. "This ain't no place for a man to die."

"Thank you," whispered Charlie, and the rain stroked and re-stroked his face and washed the hard material from the corners of his eyes as they passed beneath the waving arms of hardwoods and the benevolent needles of pine trees that thrust into the weeping clouds. When Charlie awoke again, he was in a large dry tent that was warm and light with lanterns and filled with arriving and departing steps that sloshed in the mud. He blinked, and a man was leaning over him, giving him a spoonful of a foul-tasting medicine that seemed familiar, and Charlie knew at once that something had happened, that he was being cared for, and he wondered if his mother might step in from the rain or perhaps Martha, bringing him books or letters. Duncan was not in the tent, but General Patrick Ronayne Cleburne was, and he pulled up a campstool beside Charlie's cot and looked down at him with a grave pity in his unblinking gray eyes.

"Your friend's quite the man, even if he is a Scotsman," said Cleburne. His eyes began to smile. The medicine sat well in Charlie's stomach, and he was no longer shivering uncontrollably.

"Something is breaking the rain," said Charlie.

"We're pitched under a beech tree," said Cleburne, glancing up as if he could see its limbs through the canvas. "Had to cut the lower limbs, but it offers some protection. Unless there's a lightning strike near us. I saw a sheer bolt of lightning hit the Mississippi River near Helena one time, Mr. Merrill. An awesome sight. Terribly awesome."

"I'm ill, General, and you should not be near me."

"I have been on sick leave myself," said Cleburne, nodding as if he understood. "I have not regained my duties after shuddering on that very cot for the better part of a week. This weather is a great misery, though I must say it reminds me well enough of home. I've come along as best I can. I am much better now but so very weak. Such an odd thing to be struck sick when one is needed for greater things. I have been treated well. How I grieve for the boys who are not. How I grieve!"

Charlie knew that he *did* grieve, that while General Cleburne foolishly believed in a single line of truth, and in that truth was the righteousness of the Southern cause, he was in the end a man of fortitude and faith, of absolute conviction and even kindness. Rare, thought Charlie. There were rumors in the ranks: Some said he had written a paper weeks before, arguing that slaves should be armed to fight for the South, and that those who did would thereby gain their freedom. Charlie scarcely believed it, but it could be true, knowing Cleburne.

"I regret your illness, General," said Charlie. "Did Duncan speak to you directly about me?"

"He did not, but he met my chief of staff, and he told me of it." As he spoke, two riders dismounted outside, and the sound of harnesses and rain and wind spun Charlie into a drowsy place, and he closed his eyes and fell through sleep and into dreams. Sometimes through the next two days, he would awaken and still hear the rain, and once during a lull he came outside, stumbling unshaven into a thin light and saw before him to the South the bulk of mountainous knobs, which someone said was Kennesaw Mountain, and Charlie knew that it was true. They were no more than twenty miles from Atlanta.

"Well, you're alive, though not necessarily looking the better for it," said Duncan, who was standing near him with a tin cup of steaming coffee, holding it with the soggy remains of a tattered sock.

"You don't look so well yourself," said Charlie.

"It's the bloody rain," said Duncan. "Aye, God, you look up and think it's about to be quit for us, and then it comes back in all its gloomy strands, and it ain't a man here can hardly stand it another day. But that's the soldier's lot, to stand it another day."

"What is the news?"

"The news? The news is that Sherman's whole army is out there sniffing for us, but they don't have no more spit for it than us in this mud. Our skirmishers can't even get their cartridges loaded afore the powder's wet, nor can theirs. You can't move a damned wagon, Charlie. You can't move a caisson. You can't even move a bleeding private. And the stragglers off and gone from us and they say from the Federals, too. And a line of sick men heading for the rear. And that damned mountain standing there looming over us like it means to block our way if we keep retreating, which outnumbered so much we will in the name of

God surely do. They're building works up there, though, and stretching our lines out for miles. If the bluecoats flank us this time, they can flank their way right into Scotland. Then there's no helping us."

"What do the men say of my being in the general's tent?"

"Ah, Charlie," laughed Duncan, "they say you're the general's bright boy and destined for an officer yourself."

"I'll never be an officer," said Charlie. "I don't want to be. I'd be a terrible officer."

"Ah, don't none of us know what we will do, son, not until we're in the situation to do it. Not a man alive can say that. Some will turn and run at the first rattle of musketry. We had a boy name of Hampton, who was afraid all through Shiloh, and then, in Kentucky, he picked up our flag and ran screaming into the face of the worst fire we'd ever seen in one massed place. And I saw his face, and it was lit up like God was inside his chest beating away. The Federals even cheered him just before they shot him to bits."

"A waste."

"No, Charlie. A sacrifice. We all sacrifice and are sacrificed, lad. Much of the time we never know to whom or what for. But it's a truth we dare not forget on pain of our mortal souls."

"I need to lie down."

"And get out of the bloody rain, for God's sake."

Cleburne's orderly brought Charlie a fine meal of fried bacon and biscuits and an apple, and he ate it sitting on his cot in the general's tent, looking at the chessboard, which Cleburne had set up. Neither position had changed and neither man had an advantage.

CHARLIE'S HEALTH SEEMED WORSE by June 9, the seventh straight day of rain, and he lay on the cot and looked out at the thin light. Cleburne, also still weak, lay on another cot sometimes, and though he remained on sick leave, coughing until his throat constricted with a gagging, he spoke all day to his adjutants and aides, kept informed of what was happening with the armies, which was very little.

That night, as they sat once again before the chessboard in lantern light, Cleburne seemed preoccupied, stroking his brown mustache and beard. Charlie could see, easily enough, the terrible wound to his jaw. Shot in the face, Charlie thought, just like Bob Rainey.

"I cannot for the life of me see what you are up to with these moves you have made," said Cleburne. "I half believe you are preparing to resign, and then I look again and see possibilities. There are possibilities in your thinking, are there not, Mr. Merrill?"

"Possibly," said Charlie.

"Never tip the hand," said Cleburne. "You should be in Richmond overseeing all this instead of Bragg." Charlie was startled: Generals did not denounce other generals to private soldiers. It was not done. "That being my private opinion that you are bound to keep private."

"General Cleburne, there's not a man in this army loved General Bragg," said Charlie. "Not the way they love General Johnston. General Bragg is missing something—maybe it's compassion. But they say he is ill. I don't know. His compassion for his soldiers has gone missing."

"You are astute for a young man," said Cleburne, who almost moved a pawn and then did not. "Well read. The best shot with a Whitworth rifle I have ever seen. Things do not quite add up in you, Mr. Merrill. Perhaps that is why I have taken an interest in your welfare. I am much the same myself. When I was but a small bit younger than you, I was learning to compound medicines in Mallow and was to have been an Irish apothecary all my life. I would marry and raise a family there in Ireland. Then I would be laid beneath the soil of my ancestors. Now I sit in a soaked tent in Georgia a general in the Southern army."

"I would never have thought to have become a soldier, myself, but then everything changed."

"It certainly did." Charlie realized that each was speaking for himself, and he let it go. Every native land was far away, if not from Scotland or Ireland, at least in its distance from childhood and sanctuary. In the end, Cleburne did not move before being called outside to speak with a rider from General William J. Hardee.

CHARLIE REJOINED HIS COMPANY of Cleburne's sharpshooters the next morning, June 10, wearing a new pair of boots courtesy of the general. Rain still drained from the low, heavy clouds.

"I can't bear just sitting here," said Charlie. "I'm going to head out and see what I can find."

"In this rain, for the love of God?" said Duncan. "Then I'll come and make sure you keep your recently sick head down. The general has asked me personal to keep a fine eye on you." Charlie turned and grinned. He was thin and pale, but he felt better, having shaved that morning in Cleburne's tent and had his hair cut by a regimental barber.

"General Cleburne wants you to watch over me? When did he tell you that?"

Duncan smiled and shouldered his rifle. "Some weeks back," he said. "Some weeks back."

They moved in the sullen rain, which slowed to a drizzle then returned in whipping lashes, moved through muddy and downcast lines of troops in their rivered trenches, walked past artillery pieces whose batteries had draped waterproof cloaks over the wheels and barrels and were sitting beneath them in cool puddles of rainwater. They walked west for a mile or more and did not come to the end of the Confederate lines, came slowly up a small mountain and heard, halfway up, the opening crack and roar of artillery from both sides.

"For the love of God, it's a sound I almost welcome," said Duncan.

"Let's find a place to see what is going on," said Charlie.

They came on up the small mountain and found an opening where they could see Federal caissons and troops moving toward them slowly in the rain. Charlie loaded his Whitworth and sighted through the scope and shot at a horseman, who lurched in his saddle and then sat upright again, brushing at his arm as if a bug had offended him. Charlie knew better than almost all of Cleburne's sharpshooters how to gauge distance, but his aim seemed off; perhaps his hands had grown unsteady with weakness and illness.

"Did you hit anything?" asked Duncan.

"Poorly, if at all," said Charlie.

He fired several more times during the barrage, and he did hit one man, a foot soldier who threw his rifle in the air and fell face-first into the mud. Charlie felt a mild sickness from it.

For the next two days, he and Duncan moved along and in front of the lines, but the rain was endless, rifle pits soon became muddy swales, and soldiers, unwilling to try to load their guns in the heavy downpours, sat and waited. Charlie shot once or twice, but his aim was no better and he let it lie. Once he ran into Tommy Wallace, the Texas sharpshooter, who had been working with a sergeant named Tunkins, also a Texan.

"I'm about aimed to walk me home," said Wallace, who was alone. "Did you hear about Tunkins?"

"No, I heard nothing about him," said Charlie.

"Dead of the bloody flux," said Wallace, glaring beneath the dripping brim of his slouch hat. "A soldier's lot, ain't it? Go through all this for so long, backing up all the goddamn way from Kentucky and then dying of your bowels. I'm about aimed to walk me home. A man can see a ways there." He turned and looked hazily in the distance. "He can see what's coming at him. Here you don't know what's going to come out of this goddamned jungle or when you get the bloody flux or pneumonia. I want there to be a goddamn battle. That's all I want. I want to feel like I was out here for something."

"There'll be a battle soon enough," said Duncan. "Sure as God, you can count on it."

"If there ain't, I'm about aimed to walk me home," said Wallace, almost shouting. He walked away, holding the Kerr rifle in the crook of his arm.

On June 13, the rain seemed even harder, and none of the soldiers made any pretense of scouting or looking to move. A disbelieving languor that often shaded into rage had crept among them. Small black mushrooms grew on the tongues of their brogans. Thousands of tents leaked and funneled rain down their necks, so they worked to keep fires sputtering in the downfall. Small streams that had watered the woods north of Atlanta came over their banks and grew into small rivers. New streams came down the hills, steady and red with mud, flecked in pine straw and spent bark.

"General's compliments, he'd like for you to ride with him to Pine Mountain," said Cleburne's aide, Captain Irving Buck. Charlie and Duncan stood in the rain. The aide sat on a large sorrel mare, and with his free hand he held reins on a squat gelding, brown and thick-waisted. Pine Mountain was a smallish peak a distance north of Kennesaw Mountain proper.

"Yes, sir," said Charlie. "Let me get my rifle."

"It's an observation party," said the aide. "You won't need it. We will have ample guard."

"Yes, sir."

"Maybe you can teach me to ride one of them things when you return, son," said Duncan, grinning. "I believe I've almost forgotten how to do so."

Cleburne's health was much improved, and Charlie recognized him immediately by his unimpressive horse, Stonewall. If the men had loved Cleburne less, they might have made more fun of his mount, a plodding, splay-footed animal who was more sturdy than swift, unable to change speeds rapidly. No one minded that Cleburne was not much of a rider.

"I want to see for myself what the disposition of the Federal lines is," said Cleburne. He still sounded a little short-winded. Charlie rolled into the rhythm of horse and man, refreshed and willing, but the rain was horizontal now, pelting his face, and his horse slipped often on the muddy path that led up the slope of the mountain. As they rose, Charlie began to see the earth's shape below him, Confederate lines from the foot of the mountain and upward, stretching as far as he could peer, east or west, and across the small valley their foes, arrayed and waiting. The rain must end soon. Everyone knew it. They came to a crest, and Charlie gasped at the scene's magnificence. A Confederate battery stood at attention as General Cleburne came to the point and looked across the way. A few skirmishers were cracking off shots far in front.

"They're down there in strength," said Cleburne. He looked right and left and sighed and shook his head. "There's going to be a battle here soon. God willing, this, our South shall triumph, and we will turn them back toward their own land."

"General, that's a pretty speech, but them boys over thar's got Parrott guns pointed up this way, and if they use they field glasses, they gone open on us," said a major standing at stiff attention. "Sir."

Cleburne got down and so did the others, and they tied their horses in a cluster of small white oaks at the back of the Confederate works behind five-foot-high rows of chopped timber. Charlie stayed fairly close, but Cleburne did not speak to him. The general paced back and forth, thinking, looking down the lines with a worried glance. He walked to the logs and climbed up a mound of mud, careful not to slip, peered over them, just as a cough erupted from the Yankee lines, followed by twin explosions. Two shells roared just past Cleburne and Charlie, making a whistling roar, exploding a hundred yards up Pine Mountain.

"Let's get out of this," said Cleburne. The horses were pulling at their reins, stamping, nostrils steaming like volcanic vents. "I have seldom known one to go where he had not business but that he got hurt."

Relieved, the party mounted and rode through the heavy cover back down the mountain and back toward their camp, and Cleburne was deep in thought, and Charlie did not speak to him, for there was nothing to say.

Toward evening, Charlie was napping in the tent when he felt a breeze flapping the slack canvas. When he awoke, feeling better than he had in days, Duncan's head was over him.

"Come out and see," he said. Charlie arose and sloshed through the ground beneath their tent, and he realized immediately that something had happened. Outside, the rain had stopped, and men walked around in dazed happiness, looking at slices of blue sky and a golden red sunset that was beginning to burnish the light. Charlie looked around. The clouds had pulled back from the knobs of Kennesaw Mountain, and he could see Confederate troop deployments, and he felt certain and strong.

"The rain has stopped," said Charlie. "What an incredibly beautiful sunset. Oh, how beautiful that is."

"You're a fine son," said Duncan. "A fine and gentle good boy you are, Charlie Merrill."

THE SUN ROSE BRIGHT and hot the next morning, and the ladies of Atlanta rode to the top of Kennesaw Mountain to watch the troops in their crawling lines below. Cool winds raked the valleys and the sharp rise of the mountain, and the fields and roads began to sponge off the running water from nearly two weeks of rain. Federal troops moved back there, parallel to Kennesaw Mountain, and the men murmured of flanking and firing and attacks. Confederate soldiers still headed to the rear in long lines with the coughing sickness, but many spread their blouses and coats and socks in the sun to dry. General Cleburne was off early, and word came late in the morning that a shell had just missed him. Confederate General Leonidas Polk, the bishop-general, was blown to pieces by shellfire on Pine Mountain in the morning. He had been standing with Hardee and Johnston when the Federal artillery found their range and fired. Two generals moved to the left, but Polk resolved to stand his ground. Hardee and Johnston had wept as litter bearers carried the body behind the lines toward the town of Marietta.

"Pardon the good General Cleburne's leadership skills, but he's going to get his fool head blown off like General Polk," said Duncan. He and Charlie had spent the day walking along the front looking for the end of the Federal lines and never came close to it. Now they sat by their fire eating bacon and cornbread. Charlie said nothing. He stared bleakly into the fire.

"General Polk was blown in two," said Charlie softly. "I can't imagine it. One moment you're whole and living and breathing, and the next moment you're split in half."

"You can't imagine being split in half?" asked Duncan. "Then it's a failure of the imagination."

'I've heard strange stories of men being cut in half. Things one must not believe."

Charlie finished eating and told Duncan he would go on his own to scout and shoot the following day.

"*Now?* You're leaving now, in the dark, for the love of God?"

"I'll catch up with you all some time tomorrow."

Charlie went alone into the woods. The sky was clear and cool, and filaments of clouds lingered over the last light. Crows remarked on his passing, and a whip-poor-will spoke with no special plans to stop. He smelled honeysuckle and pine, pushed back poke and blackberry, waded through a small meadow of moon-brushed wildflowers. He came past entrenchments and saw below him across the valley thousands of Federal fires, as if one man's fire differed from another's, and he calculated the pain of death and the pain of living and could not gauge much difference. His father or General Polk? Which death was the greater? Charlie knew his wounds were his illness and his love. There was little salve for either.

ON THE NIGHT OF June 16, Cleburne's men marched to a new line two and a half miles southeast of Gilgal Church, facing west. Charlie slept in the forest, arriving just after dawn when the men were digging new rifle pits. He had not regained his company when the cannonade opened between the lines, a deafening thunder of batteries, and Charlie found a tree and shot until his ammunition was low, and then he walked through the lines, not leaning over, thinking of the point of one shell boring for him, of General Polk's heart blown into the mud a few miles away. Charlie came to an artillery battery just as a shell struck. The concussion stunned him, but he stood and gathered his Whitworth back and looked down, and a lieutenant he did not know seemed to be fighting with the ground, grabbing grass, whipping like a bowed fish. Charlie sat down to gain his balance, then stood as litter bearers came forth. Men spoke in a hundred voices at once. The lieutenant's feet had both been blown away. Charlie followed the litter bearers and saw, not far ahead, General Cleburne standing in the lines and looking forward. He turned and saw the soldier whose bloodied stumps had been bound with cloth that leaked his life out.

"My God," said General Cleburne, and those around him were

shocked, for he rarely used God's name except in prayer. The lieutenant brightened and saluted.

"General," he said, "have I not won promotion today? I have always done my duty. Put my name in your report. At least put my name in your report." Cleburne wept. Charlie marched for the ammunition wagon, drew more cartridges and caps, then headed far forward of the lines, past the skirmishers and into a clearing where he knelt and shot an artilleryman.

He moved into a wood on his right and continued to load and fire, hitting three more targets before a Union soldier stepped from behind a beech tree along a small creek and pointed the barrel of an Enfield rifle in his face. Two others came and then three. Firing from the field pieces seemed suddenly far away, hollow as a drum, and Charlie smiled at them, breathing hard, eyes glistening with confusion.

"Goddamn, we got us a sharpshooter here, boys," said one of the men, who wore a wound across the bridge of his nose. "And a Whitworth rifle. The major's gonna give us all a furlough."

They were laughing. Charlie leaped at the man and began to choke him, and would have gone on choking if another had not hit him squarely in the back of the head with the butt of his rifle.

CHARLIE LAY IN A ditch with four other prisoners. Some time had passed, and it was raining again, and it was night. The ditch was filling with rivulets, and someone was pulling Charlie up by his collar.

"Don't get drownded, boy," said a man with a huge gray beard. Charlie windmilled, spluttering. "The boy's finally waking up whole." Charlie sat up in a gully of cold red water, and lightning cracked. Caissons and troops wavered off slowly, and wagons sluiced through mud inches deep.

"Let me go," said Charlie, fighting to escape the bearded man. The soldier dropped him, and Charlie fell face forward into the ditch and burst upward. Laughter and coughing. He sat on the edge of the works and found a rifle near his nose.

"Easy there, Rebel boy. Get a grip on yourself. We're marching out."

"What happened?"

"Your war's over, by the grace of God," said the gray-bearded soldier. "Who were you with? Bate? Govan?"

"I'm no soldier," said Charlie. More laughter and lightning. A brittle hissing seemed to snap the air, and a clot of thunder collapsed inward upon them.

"Then somebody's kidnapped you and put a gray coat on your back, boy," said the old man. "I don't care to watch you boys in this storm, but orders being what they is and all."

"I'm Paul Benefonce from Tennessee," said a younger man, dripping rainwater and extending his hand. The other two captives said nothing, merely glared straight out beneath their kepis. Charlie shook the young soldier's hand and then stood trembling in the rain. He felt very cold and was afraid. The air was not cold, though; it was a turgid soup of tropical air, so heavy Charlie thought he might swim through it rather than walk. The rain had not given them up after all.

"*Benefonce?*" said the old Yankee soldier. "Goddamn, what in the hell kinda name's that?"

"Well, what the hell's your name?" asked Benefonce.

"Ezrey Nutt," said the old man. All of the captives were suddenly laughing, and Charlie felt a hideous thrill and could not stem his own laughter, and Nutt grinned in the lighting strokes with them. Charlie's head throbbed as they walked, and they were in a thick wood, and they tripped over blackberry briars. Benefonce said something about snakes just before he fell into the briars, and Charlie and one of the others pulled him up, and he was spluttering and cursing. Charlie felt stupid for letting himself get captured, and he knew that he was still weak from illness and misdirection, that he could not bear the shipment north to a prison camp. There were stories of the prison in south Georgia at Andersonville, a place so vile that it invited retribution, but no one knew what to believe in but rain, and they walked back and forth to different orders, and their Yankee guards cursed their own officers more than the Confederates cursed them.

The next day, the rain assaulted both lines before Kennesaw Mountain. Now two miles north of it in a clearing, Charlie could see none of the mountain's knobs, which were enveloped in a wool blanket of clouds. No firing of cannon or muskets cracked the air. The Federals camped back here, tens of thousands, and Charlie, for the first time, knew that this campaign was hopeless.

"Well, boys, your friend up thar's done backed up again, and we be moving forward, and you got to come," said Ezra Nutt.

"The hell," said Beneforce. "A Tennessee man might be captured, but he's nought inclined to run away from this kind of fight."

Nutt held up his hand and turned to listen. Yes. They could all hear it. The *croup* and blowback of artillery, then the skittery clatter of muskets.

"My paw said a man who'd fight in the rain's liable to do anything," said Beneforce. Nutt laughed and spat.

"Well, they ain't no time left for you boys," he said. "This here's the end of you Rebel fellers. You're gone back up all the way to the ocean or you're gone be dead."

"My arse," said Beneforce. Nutt laughed and herded them forward, and they marched all day toward the firing, and when the Federals had gained their former lines, Charlie saw it was true that the Confederates had fallen back up Kennesaw Mountain, and he knew that whether the rain continued or not, a great battle was coming. They spent the day doing nothing. They sat in the rain and spoke sometimes, and Beneforce said that his mother was dead. He said it three or four times with increasing lamentations until Charlie turned away and watched the Federals touching off their Parrott guns, aiming high up the slopes of the last natural barrier but one between Sherman and Atlanta.

THAT NIGHT, THE PRISONERS moved into a cover of pine trees, and Nutt was their only guard, and soon the rain dwindled and everyone slept but Charlie. He was watching Nutt when he realized his breathing had changed into a ghastly hawking rattle. Federal troops crawled inside their tent flies, and the rain made thousands of fires sputter and hiss. Nutt began to wheeze and hold his chest, and then he was very quiet and frozen to a rivulet of muddy water. The ambient light from the campfires was pale and sickly, but Charlie saw the man's eyes had glazed with rainwater. His mouth was opening farther each moment. Charlie stood and walked to him and knelt and without testing to see if life still breathed in him removed his coat and kepi, put them on, and took the man's Enfield rifle. None of the others stirred as Charlie propped the dead Nutt up against the trunk of a pine tree.

A dream ensued: Charlie walked forward in his blue coat, slimy and moth-eaten but clearly blue over his gray, and he slowly passed through squad and company, through regiment and brigade, through division and corps. No one tried to stop him. The rain came again in violent gusts, and he knew that mountains held over him, and the odd sensation they might fall over and smother him drove him forward. God spoke to him now, whispering his name in the wind, and Charlie refused to answer, but then he said, "Father?" and he knew to whom he spoke.

Charlie walked as far as the picket lines out front and kept walking toward the Confederate front, finally swinging far left, tearing off the blue coat and hat, walking for several miles and then sitting alone at the edge of a rising creek, where he slept amid the keen of soaked night birds and the scraping of frogs and cicadas. He dreamed of Branton, the foursquare houses and clean-swept yards, the aging fragrance of boxwoods and the crinkled faces of widows in their gardens. He dreamed of the courthouse in the town square's anchored center, of the Branton River's stately autumn tumble south, of the creak and clatter of wagon wheels, the spinning of phaeton axles. He dreamed of grinning dandies and girls cloaked in blue gingham, and he dreamed of elixirs and sermons. Then he dreamed of the slaves, and some were content and waited and others looked one way and then another, with rage, as if for flight, and Charlie felt the shape of concern and knowledge in his heart, of a powerful evil, and he awoke to light rain and light.

Skirmishing continued behind him. He walked on east, finally throwing the Enfield rifle and his coats away to shed the weight and moved slowly through the trees, across a few open fields, then turned south. Charlie came to a small homestead above a rocky creek, and a woman stood in the doorway watching him, and two small children huddled like chicks, one on each side, and none of them moved or blinked, and he could not tell if they breathed or were painted there.

TOWARD NOON, HE ANGLED back west and began to hear the *poom* and *croup* of artillery, and the land rose beneath his feet, and he was walking up a mountain when a picket leaped out in front of him and demanded to know who in the hell he was.

"Charles Merrill, sharpshooter company, Govan's Brigade, Cleburne's Division," said Charlie. The picket had mounted the bayonet on his rifle and held it two inches from Charlie's breastbone.

"How come you ain't got a rifle then?"

"I was captured yesterday out front and then got away in the rainstorm. The Yankees got my rifle."

"Well, your peoples is gone be all kind of happy to hear that." The picket grinned and showed two rows of dark brown teeth. A short beard grew in spiky whorls along his cheeks, like an army confused for direction. "Get on with you, then. You don't look like no Yankee."

"How do Yankees look?"

"I heared they got tails," said the man.

Charlie made his way down the lines, walking through shellfire and the snap of skirmishing, and all day it went that way, but the rain came anyway, defiant and logy, and each step took power, for Charlie had a headache that left his ears ringing, his eyes pressed from their dark sockets. At nightfall, he was still not near his lines, and the rain continued, but skirmishing stopped. He slept badly against a bristling row of abatis, and all night two guards talked about women and their treacheries. In the morning, rain still fell, and Charlie tried to calculate, counting back: In the past twenty-one days, rain had fallen for nineteen. Firing resumed, but as if it were a hobby. Late in the day, he began to see familiar faces on Kennesaw Mountain, and then he glimpsed Cleburne not far ahead, speaking with his adjutant, and Duncan McGregor stood in front of him.

"Where for the love of God have you been?" asked Duncan.

"I got myself captured but then escaped," said Charlie. "What's happening here?"

"You've lost your coat, too. And your rifle?"

"Yes. I expect they should court-martial me."

"Let's see the lieutenant."

The officer sympathized but said there were no more Whitworth or Kerr rifles, and Charlie took an Enfield from a dead man and cleaned it by firelight, drew ammunition, and joined Govan's Brigade again as a regular soldier. Duncan went with him, glad to be back.

"I wasn't much for a scout anyway," said Duncan. "But you were a beautiful sharpshooter."

"My head hurts," said Charlie. Duncan took off his own coat and put it around Charlie's shoulders, and for the longest time after Charlie had finished cleaning the rifle, Duncan thought he was going to say more.

JUNE 26 WAS PENTECOST Sunday. The rain was gone, and a sharp sunlight spread up the mountain. Except for some skirmishing and cannonading on the right, the whole day was oddly quiet, and the foot soldiers ate and made sure they had drawn ample cartridges and caps. All knew the battle was coming on the next day, that the campaign for Atlanta was inexorably moving forward.

"I cannot say that I wish to die on this godforsaken lump," said

Duncan. Very late in the afternoon, a brilliant orange sunset painted all the western skies.

"Neither of us will die here," said Charlie.

"Bless the rightness of that thought. And would you look there, Charlie boy, look at that sunset. It surpasses even the one before. Did you ever see such a thing in your life? Here up this mountain it ain't like nothing but seeing the burning bush itself."

Suddenly, the skies were spread with a placid fire, russet and gold, and Charlie felt the breath of Holiness descend on him, and he wanted to see his mother and Martha worse than anything in this life, wanted to cradle Sarah to him. He remembered one evening when he had been very sick, and he heard Sarah calling from the ground below his window. Charlie had dressed quickly and walked outside into the dew-damp grass, and she was there, in the pecan grove, standing a hundred yards away holding a lantern. The wind waved the hem of her pale blue skirt, and it appeared she was spirit, without a foundation of flesh. She stood and waited for him, and as he came closer, it seemed the light passed through her, and her smile was slight and ardent, and the under-canopy filled up with fireflies and luminescent beetles. All the world seemed bent on praise.

He felt that way now. Men hushed to watch the omen of the skies. Some pointed, and one old man sang a hymn sotto voce. Charlie tried to remember the literal meaning of the word *Pentecost,* but it vanished before him. All day, women from Atlanta had been on Big Kennesaw looking with delight and horror at the ten-mile-long Yankee front before them. Now they had vanished, leaving the mountain to soldier work, and Charlie knew it would come soon enough.

Summer and Fall, 1862

JACK DOCKERY'S FOOT GREW worse in early June, and for a time amputation seemed likely, but the infection finally abated, and he was able to ride to Grace House on his horse, Sal. Charlie and Sarah were sitting on a blanket in the pecan-leaf shade when Jack dismounted and came over, a single crutch under his right arm. He perspired freely but smiled with such warmth that Charlie stood and waved. He and Sarah had been playing chess, and Sarah was resigned to loss.

Stonewall Jackson's Valley campaign in Virginia had been a glorious success, according to the newspapers, but the Federal army was swelling and spreading, and their resolve, if anything, grew, Charlie heard. The Confederate General Joseph Johnston had been severely wounded at the Battle of Seven Pines. Now in mid-July, the war in Virginia had turned into a field of blood. Betsy fretted about Tom, since his unit had been near Malvern Hill, a fierce battle on July 1. Other families in town were getting word that their sons were not coming home again. If Tom had survived, he had not written, which to Betsy signaled disaster; to Charlie, it simply sounded like Tom, too busy to bother with a pencil. The church council had told Betsy the family could live in Grace House for six months while they sought a new minister. The council would rent another house for the Merrills. Betsy nodded, broken. She visited her husband's grave twice a week with fresh flowers and whispered prayers.

Charlie grew in stature, and most days he seemed stronger and happier, growing toward war. He took long walks during the day and spent hours target shooting at cans and distant fence posts. His strength grew as his aim narrowed. On his cheeks, he felt the first threads of a beard, studied his face in the mirror and saw it elongating slightly, cheekbones more prominent, eyes darker and more sunken. As his body changed, he was afraid that it might not stop at adulthood but go forward into some monstrous shape from which he could not return.

A few days before, when a storm had settled over Branton for a day, he and Sarah had been in the parlor of Grace House, where Sarah had played Chopin with dreamy perfection, and Charlie watched her, broken with affection and desire. Betsy and Martha had gone to his Aunt Kay's house for the day, and with lamps unlit, the parlor was dark and cool, a steady wind waving the white lace curtains into the room. Charlie leaned back on the settee, and he wanted the day to last for years. If he had more courage, he thought, he would sweep her into his arms and love her.

"I know that one piece and maybe three more from memory," said Sarah. She slid next to Charlie, and her eyes sparkled into brightness. "They taught me French, piano, and a little geography, but no more. *Je suis une jeune fille. Oui? Mais oui, monsieur.* They were preparing me to marry a fine Boston gentleman. But they were too distracted in fighting each other to press my education very far. I've learned much through reading."

"I've gone to Mr. Marker's School since I was little," said Charlie. "And then Papa taught me, too. My French is poor, but I read Latin passably and a little Greek."

"I see." He could tell she was fumbling for words. He wanted more air. The room was cool and dark and enfolding, and he watched his hand reach for hers and take it, hold it. There seemed no volition in the act, as if his hand were seeking out a kindred shape.

"What do you think of me?" asked Charlie.

"You mean . . ."

"What do you think when you look at me? Do you feel sorry for me?"

"No. I think you have a number of fine qualities, and you have been a friend to me when few else would. To be from the North is worse than being a slave. At least people here seem to understand the colored. They look upon me as a species bred from stupidity and for hatred."

"I've never thought that of you."

"Of course, but you love me."

Their eyes locked. He thought: *It is true. I do love her, and everything slows when she is here, as if I am awakening from a grave darkness.* He held her hand more tightly, and she leaned toward him on the settee until their faces were inches apart.

"I *do* love you," said Charlie. The rain was harder now, and the room seemed to shade into night. "Did you know you are the first girl I have ever loved? I only wish you could love me back."

"How do you know I don't?" she asked.

They came together, each surprised at the enfolding, cheeks pressing tightly, arms fumbling for a place to cling. When they backed off slightly, he was going to say something poetic, something perhaps from Keats or Shelley, but her lips were slightly open and coming toward his, and he could smell her now, the fragrance of her soft perfume, the sweet insistence of her warm breath. Then they were kissing, and he felt himself somehow absorbed into her, one body and one beating, and he did not dare believe in her affection or her lips upon his.

"Oh, Sarah," he said when they broke.

"I love you, Charlie," she said. "I do so love you."

They held each other, trying somehow to get closer than possible, kissed often, whispered words that made sense or not, that spilled and flowed upon them. When she finally left, fetched by her uncle's servant in a surrey at noon, Charlie had stood in the doorway watching, and she had sat, turned toward him, until neither could see each other. That night, he had lay dazed in his bed, looking at his copy of Shakespeare's sonnets and touching his fingers to his lips, memorizing the contours of her bow-shaped mouth, the taste of her, the feeling of her mouth on his. *Sometimes too hot the eye of heaven shines.*

He lay awake half the night thinking of her until he went to the desk in his father's study, took out a sheet of paper and a pen, dipped it, wrote by candlelight:

> *You are the light that heaven does not know,*
> *Blistering the sun with sharper tones;*
> *You are the edge of greenery or snows,*
> *All seasons that mankind has ever known.*

When I think of hearts that dream apart,
I live the dream that brought you to my door.
When I think of love that rescues hearts,
I feel your yearning in the soul's sweet core.
Our lips have whispered out the other's name
In syllables too sacred to repeat;
Our hearts have dreamed the other's dream
And hold it silent as a secret when we meet.
We have seen our love among the stars, a night
That turns us from the shadow into light.

Charlie read it and reread it, and found it wanting in skill and craft, but when he spoke it softly aloud by the sputtering candle, he felt Sarah close to him, not far from his arms.

Now, Jack settled painfully on to the blanket Sarah and Charlie had spread beneath the trees, and Missy was nearing them with a basket of fried chicken and cornbread.

"Didn't know you was coming, but they's plenty fo' you," said Missy. "Cephus probably knowed it, but that lazy fool don't never tell me nothin'."

"Nobody knew it," said Jack. "I just took a shine to get out of the house. I've been ill."

"I knowed it, heard that you had been," said Missy. She set the basket down, along with three glasses and a large bottle of tea. "This here's near bout the last tea we got, and they ain't no more to be had in town, and coffee's gettin' scarce as hen's teeth, too, so I'd say you people enjoy while you can, you ain't gone have it much much longer if this war keep up."

She walked away talking to herself about war and food, but Charlie barely heard her, his eyes strong and held on Sarah.

"I bring you both greetings from Dockery's Mercantile, where the talk this morning is that Mr. Lincoln has sacked McClellan and has now installed General Halleck as commander of the Federals," said Jack.

"Are you all right?" asked Charlie.

"Not as good as you are physically, sir, but your superior intellectually," said Jack.

"More's the pity," said Charlie with a laugh. "What's the word on this Halleck, anyway?"

"He's supposed to be less incompetent than McClellan but not as competent as our General Jackson. Sarah, I see that Charlie is letting himself win in your chess game. That means he respects you. He always lets me win because he think I'm pathetic at the game, which is unfortunately true." Sarah's bright laughter spilled across the yard.

"He's let me win once or twice," she said. "Probably out of boredom."

"Charlie would have made a great general," said Jack. "He understands the tactical and the necessary. Half the time I have no idea what he's doing on the board until I find myself hopelessly cornered into checkmate. He's sneaky and mean and relentless."

"Charlie?" said Sarah coyly. "Now that you mention it, that does sound like him."

"General Merrill," said Charlie with mock pondering. "I rather like the sound of it. We could form the Brigade for the Sometimes Sick and the Often Crippled. The North would surrender by the millions."

They ate in silence, but Charlie only picked at his food, staring toward the railroad tracks and remembering the evening he and Tom had walked there, of Tom's long balanced walk upon the rail.

"I don't think they will ever get to Georgia, Yankees, I mean," said Jack.

"At least one has already," said Sarah. Charlie laughed.

"I mean the Federal army, Miss Boston," said Jack. "We're too far away. It's always Virginia *this* and Virginia *that*. People from Virginia all think they're carved out of marble."

"They are coming from both directions up and down the Mississippi, and if they break it, the country will be cut in half," said Charlie. "The press is full of small battles. Sooner or later, the armies will come together entire, and when they do, the death will be beyond anything we can imagine. It will be a great festival of death, and the blood will flow in the ditches like water after a storm. I half believe I could find myself in it."

Charlie saw Jack's eyes narrow. The air, which had been moving and hot, suddenly stopped, as if their picnic had frozen into a painting. The leaves lost their shimmer. Charlie thought the colors in the yard, all green and gray and brown, had gone slack and dull. He could imagine his words for the first time, lines of infantry firing from close in, artillery batteries blowing men to small bloody shreds, the cavalry riding hard, horses falling, shot and writhing beneath them. More than just *seeing* it, his imagination *gave* the *smell* to him, the acrid stench of gunpowder, the excrement of animals and men, the sweat of thousands gathering for death. The *sound* came to him as well, a ghastly turmoil of explosions, clattery muskets, the pitiful screams of the wounded and dying, calling for a God who would not save them or a mother miles away. The blood will flow in ditches like water after a storm. He felt an edge of some unexpected urgency and anger, thought of his father.

"Charlie?" said Sarah, touching his arm. "Are you all right?" Charlie caught his breath, exhaled, tried to keep from toppling. Jack was reaching for him, too.

"Wh—what are you looking at?" he asked. Then he laughed, a short explosion he hoped might rescue him from the awkwardness of it.

"You looked a little strange there for a second," said Jack. "All right now?"

"I'm all right," he said, looking down at the blanket. "Sometimes I feel myself becoming what I imagine. It's a strange thing. Probably from the illness."

"Well, imagine an end to the war," said Jack laconically. "I can be a cripple more easily in times of peace than in times of war."

The grove seemed to expand in color and shape, and the wind rose, and Charlie saw the greens deepen and become richer, the browns and grays take the shape of summer, and he felt the fear vanish, as if it might have taken flight before an advancing army.

THOMAS MATLOW, CORPULENT AND florid, stood in the parlor near the fireplace, clearing his throat and smiling and posing like the deacon he was. A lawyer too old to fight and too rich to worry, he smiled as if he had wonderful news for Betsy and Charlie, who were on the settee and Martha, who turned idly back and forth on the round piano stool.

"My point being that this house—home—is well situated, though farther from town, I fear," he said. "It has a good well that has never gone dry, and the amenities are such that I believe you will be comfortable, though the furniture is of the most, ah, basic type. It has not been announced yet, Betsy, but we have called Rev. Henry Finegan from Charleston as our new minister. You remember him from his previous visits here."

"He was a guest in our home—I mean this house," said Betsy. Charlie glanced at his mother, and her careworn face troubled him. She still went to the cemetery twice a week, but now that would be much more difficult.

"Ah, then you know what a fine preacher he is," said Matlow. "A fine Southern man who believes with his whole heart in our cause."

"What cause would that be?" asked Charlie coldly.

"This house—which one exactly is it?" asked Betsy. Martha twirled back and forth on the stool. Matlow told her, and Betsy cringed, for she knew it, a small, foursquare, very plain house so close to the railroad it shuddered when the trains came past twice a day.

"I've seen it," said Charlie. "It must have no more than four rooms."

"Ah, in fact, that is correct," said Matlow. Charlie studied his red face and thought: A secret drinker, though not so secret anymore. "But we will do our best to ensure your comfort. Now, you understand that Cephus and Missy are bound to the house here and cannot come with you."

"I understand that perfectly well," said Betsy coldly.

"You needn't trouble yourselves worrying about the move, either. By the way, there has been a battle of unparalleled proportions going on in Maryland near a town called Sharpsburg. It is unclear who has won, but General Lee is said to be coming with his troops back to Virginia. I know you have a boy up there somewhere."

"And I know that *you* do not," said Betsy. His son, Horace Matlow, had gone to Europe ostensibly to study in Germany. Matlow's florid smile turned sour at the corners.

"No. Anyway, there it is. We are sorrowful at this turn of events. The new minister will certainly inspire us as your husband did, Betsy." He bowed and walked quickly from the room, disappearing down the smooth front steps. Charlie thought his mother was going to scream, but she lifted her head and looked around the parlor.

"Let's be about it, then," she said. "No use feeling sorry for ourselves." Her face softened.

"I'm proud of you," said Charlie.

She smiled, but the only thing shining from her eyes, Charlie knew, was rank hatred.

CHARLIE DID HIS BEST to help with the packing, but fatigue sometimes washed over him. Sarah helped Betsy, and they spoke softly of the world and its sorrows. Betsy knew well enough that Charlie and Sarah cared deeply for each other, and she did not discourage it. The world was full of such manifold sorrows that the affection of two young people was a lovely thing. He had turned fifteen in April, and Sarah in May, and so they were not children anymore.

Betsy had Cephus and Missy help her make an enormous pile of unneeded households items on the wagon that belonged to Grace House.

"Take it to the Methodist Church and tell them it is to be given to the poor," said Betsy. Cephus scratched his head and nodded.

"Seem like to me *you* people gone be pore, if you don't take any offense from it," he said. "Everything change in the blink of an eye, that what the Bible say."

"We will be fine," said Betsy, smiling. "If you and Missy see anything you want, take it."

"Nome, I ain't," he said. "Well, maybe a little." He climbed into the wagon seat and grabbed the reins and looked around. "So much ain't hardly right. But you sending this to them Methodist is pretty funny."

"Thank you, Cephus," said Betsy.

Just as he was driving off, Mrs. Charles Layton Dobbs drove up in her light surrey, stopped, and jumped out blithely, holding a newspaper. The wife of a captain in the Branton Rifles, Mrs. Dobbs brooked no idle chatter and always made her points. She and Betsy had known each other since girlhood, and Betsy reasoned, knowing her, that people did not change. The sweet and the kind stayed the sweet and the kind.

"The battle in Maryland was worse than anyone could have imagined, if you have not heard," she said. "I have the newspaper, and the reports are horrifying." Betsy went stiff and had to hold to a pillar to keep from falling. She suddenly tried to focus on Tom's face, but it came to her at different ages—Tom as a ruddy child, Tom as a wisecracking young boy, his strength and good cheer obvious at every age. People do not change, she thought, but they pass. For the first time in several days, she thought of her husband.

"So it was a loss for our side?" asked Betsy.

"Apparently. General Lee has withdrawn from Maryland back into Virginia. Our men are up there somewhere—I believe from what I have heard that some of them were detached and went with Lee instead of staying in Virginia, but I can't be sure." She untied her bonnet, took it off, and shook out her hair. She had never been pretty, and unlike the other girls, she rarely wept.

"How bad were the losses?"

"The paper says total casualties are perhaps thirteen thousand killed and wounded on either side," said Iola Dobbs. "We had at least twenty-five hundred killed, maybe more."

"Oh, sweet Jesus," gasped Betsy. "Oh, sweet Jesus."

"That's not the worst part. Lincoln's decided that as of January 1, all the nigras in the South are to be declared free," said Iola. She read the paper for a moment, shrugged, and thrust it into Betsy's hands. "You know, they told us last year that the war wouldn't last until Christmas. Somebody lied."

"They didn't lie," said Betsy, trying clear the tears from her eyes. "They were just stupid." She paused and began to tremble. "Damn them, Iola. Damn every one of them who started this war. Damn them all to hell."

Iola, stunned, stared at said nothing for a long time then leaned forward and hugged her friend.

"You are mad from the sorrow, and I don't blame you, but don't worry," she said. "We have talked. All of us will be helping take care of you and Martha and little Charlie."

"Charlie is not little, he's fifteen," said Betsy.

"People say he's gone sweet on that Yankee girl," said Iola. "I thought you might want to know, but women are so gossipy. There's nothing to talk about with the men all gone."

"You may tell whomever you please that we shall fend for ourselves and do not need charity," said Betsy. "I shall sew. We will make do with what we have. After this winter, we will have a garden. Charlie will protect us."

Iola nodded, embarrassed, and kissed Betsy on the cheek, then climbed back into her surrey and drove off under a hot sun.

July 22, 1914

CHARLIE HAD BARELY TOUCHED his meal, and Mrs. Knight cleared his plate away with a snort. A brief storm cleared rapidly after it struck, and a rainbow, so sharp he thought he could almost hear it chime, stretched north from Branton toward Athens. He walked upstairs to his bedroom, slow on the stairs, trying to focus on his life and the singular Battle of Atlanta, not the falling back from Dalton but the engagement half a century before, when the air had been saturated with death. Afterward, he wondered if corn could grow in blood.

He was considering a nap when he heard a car arrive, slide to a parked stop in the long driveway that went from front to the back of Grace House. He knew who it would be, and when he walked across the hall and looked out the window, he saw her climbing out, lithe and strong, unbowed by age or disease. Her hair was gray and carved around her head like a hat, and she wore a pale blue dress, light against the heat and dripping sunlight. Steam rose in unfocused undulations from the top of her car. She walked toward the house without glancing upward; Charlie had noticed most people rarely looked up except when rain began. Now that the rain was over, there was no reason. He went back downstairs and met her in the kitchen as she entered. He was smiling and looked almost boyish, hands in his hip pockets.

"Don't tell me," he said, grinning. "You heard I haven't written the speech I have to give tonight, and you've come to see if I'm lazy or stupid."

"Catherine called me and said she was worried about you, that she didn't think you looked good and that you might be worried about all this hubbub," said his sister, Martha. Charlie looked at her with near-adoration. She had been his goad and conscience for much of their life, a woman of plentiful certainties who had four children and nine grandchildren of her own. Her late husband, Jack Wilkins, lay in the cemetery not three hundred yards from Grace House, struck down by apoplexy while singing a hymn in church, which most people considered a lovely death. Martha saw only irony, went on, lived alone in a fine home on the growing south side of town.

"I haven't looked good since 1900," he said. "I'm so glad you people have agreed to turn my slight concern over this event into a panic."

"You *don't* look good," said Martha. "Your skin is gray. If you're going to die, you have to wait until tomorrow. If you ruin the anniversary celebration, I'll never be able to attend church again without all the biddies thinking I'm pathetic and alone. Come on, let's sit in the parlor. I want to ask you something."

"It would be a great pleasure for me." A sudden tipping on the polished oak floorboards: Belle coming down the hall, Mrs. Knight rapidly coming after her with soft quick steps.

"I opened the door, and she come running in," said Mrs. Knight. "Dog has no manners and don't obey."

"It's all right, she's come to nuzzle Martha," said Charlie. "Belle's always loved her more than me anyway."

"She has," said Martha, who knelt and hugged the wagging dog. Mrs. Knight muttered back into another room, while Belle ran ahead of Martha and Charlie and sprawled panting on the cool floor. They sat in the old but excellent furniture, and Martha looked closely at her brother.

"I hear Mr. Josiah Biggs wanted to make a speech and is a bit peevish," she said. "But everyone knows he stammers. Mr. James Felden is said to be unclear whether it's his wedding anniversary or something else. And of course T. D. Varnell can't fit into his uniform. So that leaves you to be the sane and sensible one, Charlie. Plus they're more than ten years older than you are and in their wandery years. Now what I want to know is this. Are you up to this? Because I'd rather have you alive and here rather than dead on the stage at Ezra Atkinson Park."

He looked at his sister with quiet pleasure. She had suffered in this life and gone on without complaint, but until long after the war, he'd hardly known her. Their difference in age was great, but not great enough to hold back a deep love. She was gray and had a wen on her left cheek, but he could see the shape of a small blond girl.

"Now that half the town thinks I'm going to make a fool of myself in public, maybe I should go ahead and do it," said Charlie, tenting his fingers in mock solemnity. "Maybe I've already written the speech. Maybe I wrote it years ago. Or maybe I'll recite the Gettysburg Address. Mr. Lincoln seems downright popular these days. Remember during the war everyone said he was a baboon? Most of the Branton soldiers went to Virginia. There were only a handful of us at Atlanta. Ergo the present problem."

"I was too small to remember things like that," she said. There was a softening as she slid forward and took Charlie's hands in hers. "I don't care about the stupid speech. I just don't want you getting too exercised over this. Catherine's worried about you. *I'm* worried about you. And the fact that you've written all those books here or been printed in the *New York Sun* doesn't impress me because I knew you as a sick boy who crept around the house like a ghost for years. The very idea that you'd be giving this speech would have struck me dumb in 1862."

"That would make two of us," said Charlie. "I'm fine. Really. I keep forgetting I'm in the age of instant communication. We knew about battles in the war on the day they happened from the telegraph, and we all thought it was a miracle. Now, if I say a word at nine in the morning, the whole town knows it by nine-thirty. I'll make some notes, Martha. I'll sing 'Amazing Grace' if you want me to. Only stop mother-henning me or I'll do pig calling and try to juggle."

"I'd frankly prefer that to all the speechifying," she said. "Does it strike you as odd that we are glorifying a battle we *lost?* All these years, you never talked about the war at all—I don't even know what you did exactly."

Belle rolled on her back and Charlie rubbed her stomach with his shoe, and Martha watched it, eyes going kind and softened. He thought: There are some things in this life of which one can never speak. There are some sacrifices that are too holy to sunder in words. Charlie remembered the heat and the dust and the weeks of rain before Kennesaw Mountain. He remembered the unraveling of spring, the blood and the death, the marches and the flanking. Most of all, he re-

membered Duncan, and he remembered General Patrick Ronayne Cleburne, unexpected friend and chess partner, decent man far from his
beloved Ireland. He remembered the boy holding his entrails at
Chickamauga and begging Charlie for the love of God to spare him.

"Why does everybody want to talk about things," said Charlie.
"What did the doctor in Athens say about your kidney?"

"He said it hurt because it was sick," she said. "That cost me fifteen
dollars. And you're changing the subject."

"I'm an old man, Martha, very old indeed, and that in itself is the
miracle I shall celebrate," he said. "About the war—it's very hard to remember all that because it was a completely pointless slaughter. Boys
walking up line on line to be blown to pieces. And for what? For the
myth that it wasn't all about slavery. Slavery only existed because
wealthy men feared what they had created, both its presence in the
world and the penalty for its loss."

Martha exhaled sharply and stared at him with a level gaze.

"You're not going to say *that* are you?" she asked. "Not exactly a
way to honor the dead."

'I'll honor the dead," said Charlie, smiling and relaxed again.
"Don't worry about me honoring the dead."

BEFORE HIS NAP, CHARLIE wanted to check something in his mother's
diary. He kept it in a small box in the library closet, and the familiar
smell of leather and foxed pages washed over him. He knew the passage
he wanted to read.

Tuesday, September 30, 1862

*Oh my God! I have just received a letter from Vice
President Stephens saying my Tom has gloriously given his
life for the Southern Confederacy. And we sit in the ruins of
our home, packed to move. I am shuddering with sorrow and
locked away in the ballroom, crying my heart out for my
darling boy. The letter says that he was slain near Sharpsburg
in Maryland as were so many boys, though it does not say
how he died. As Mr. Stephens knew my husband, he wrote to
share his sorrow. Tom's body has been buried in Maryland.*

I want to scream, pound something into submission. In a

twinkling, Tom was gone to war, and now I shall never look upon his face again. I had asked God to vouchsafe me a comfortable life, and He has given me nothing but sadness and horror these few months. I blame the men who started all this, Mr. Rhett from South Carolina especially and Mr. Ruffin from Virginia. I hope this Confederacy falls in its ruins, collapses from the rot at the center of its heart.

Now I have what is left of my family here and in the counties around. And I must live for my stouthearted Martha and my gentle and damaged Charlie. I must tell them, with their comfort in my heart first, not my anger. For anger is a torch that lights entire lands, and when there is enough anger, there cannot be enough death. The killing shall not be stopped until the anger is satiated, and we are far from that.

I grieve that I was born into this time and this world. Better to have been a slave in Egypt building great monuments than the king of this fair ruin. But I shall not show this shattered heart to my remaining children. They shall see me unbowed, unbroken. But in my heart, the world is no more than ashes.

Charlie had read the passage many times, but now it struck him peculiarly, as a cri de coeur, and worse, a prophecy. He put the diary back and tried to remember Tom's laughter, the shape of his face, the strength of his character. But another face kept replacing his, that of the man who befriended him in time of war.

Winter, 1862–1863

BEYOND THE HOUSE THERE was an apple orchard and past that a
fallow cotton field. Fingers of apple limbs climbed the cold sky
toward a cluster of stratocumulus clouds. The day, which had
been reasonably warm, though edged with an irritated wind, was turning bitter as the sun fell apart toward Atlanta sixty miles west. Charlie
stood and watched the twin chimneys of the small house begin to cough
out smoke, thinking of his father and brother, considering the many
chambered vaults of heaven and wondering how the dead found their
families. Was love deathless, after all? What if you found your father,
and he had lost reason or recognition? After the Battle of Fredericks-
burg in December, more sorrow spread through Branton, even though
General Lee had won. The town, never wholly absorbed into the idea
of secession, turned sullen and shadowed.

Charlie did not try to shame himself with guilt. All he considered, as
the weather turned sharp, then bone-achingly cold, was Sarah
Pierce. Now, however, Jack was often ill, and Charlie had the iron taste
of fear and wondered what dark corners the light of reason might illuminate, and which ones it could never reach. Lincoln's emancipation
order was like a burned house, a place without shape but somehow familiar, and Charlie had tired of hearing local firebrands saying this was
somehow the best thing for the Confederates—a flame to the tinder.

Now the sun began to shade toward blood. Sometimes country hens laid eggs with red yolks, but this was unlike that, more like the first shudders of conspiracy or unexpected death. When they had moved into the house many weeks before, it was hot and stuffy, and rain sprayed through wall cracks; they damped down the puddles with old towels, and Martha, who feared storms, would sit rocking on the floor. Now, the wind howled beneath it, and the single fraying rug in the front parlor waffled with a sharp breeze, lifting as if spirits were mad to enter. Betsy kept flames in the fireplaces on both sides of the shotgun hallway, but the warmth extended only a few feet. Women from the Baptist Church brought charities, and Charlie turned quietly away or went for a walk when they came. Betsy, formal in breeding and Southern in manners, accepted clothing and food for her children. Mr. Thomas Mc-Combs, seventy and mild in politics and manners, paid for a laundry-woman to wash and iron, picking up on Monday and returning on Tuesday morning. The laundress was a silent old woman named Harriet Kilmarlin, whose eyes were as hard as her hands.

Death had wormed his way through the Branton Rifles, with wounds and disease rife. David Magruder, a young banker elected captain in the Rifles, died from pneumonia near Malvern Hill. Louis Vaught, a poor man seeking glory as a private soldier, took a ball in the face at Marye's Heights. Hunter Baldwin, a lawyer and city councilman, died from gangrene, which grew like an autumn garden on a slightly wounded foot after Sharpsburg. Though the Confederacy had reclaimed Galveston, it was shaken, and the town debated the war fiercely.

Charlie, fifteen, thought of the battlefield. Yet he could not abandon Jack, and his love for Sarah bound him with steel bands to the town and its manifold sorrows.

"Charlie! Supper's ready!" cried Martha. She was growing taller now, blond like Tom and sturdy, defiant.

"Coming," he said. The sky was lowering now, and he looked upon it, feeling like an Old Testament prophet, seeing auguries in the bloody streaks, messages from a God who had abandoned him long before.

When he was well, Jack worked alongside Charlie on the house, nailing and sawing, planing boards to replace the sagging front porch. Charlie scraped the buckled whitewash from the window frames and smoothed white lead paint, supplied by the church, around the sun-struck windows. Together, they levered up the spent shingles and replaced them, laughing as they made sly comments about fat wealthy men moving down the streets in their precious hacks.

"That rail wouldn't hold a flea on a crutch," said Jack, laughing one day. Charlie stepped back and looked at his handiwork, a lean strip beside the sharply ascending steps at the back of the house.

"You are to a carpenter as a goat is to a stallion," said Charlie, and he pushed the railing to show its strength, and it groaned once and slid over, falling slowly, like an old man. Jack howled in laughter.

Even when he was ill, Jack sat on a backless kitchen chair in the yard and watched as Charlie fired his rifle dozens of times in a row, honing the idea of weapon and target. Day by day, Charlie's eyes and hands become measures of symmetry, bearers of accuracy and pride.

BEING ALONE WITH SARAH in their small cold house was improper. But Betsy felt a black defiance to tradition, so when she and Martha left for the market and Charlie said Sarah would be coming by to visit, Betsy said nothing. She pecked him on the cheek, silently wished him love, the shape of kisses, something she would never again enjoy. Sarah was supposed to be driving to town as well, but when she pulled up in her own light gig, the horse's breath shot white on a sunny wind, she could barely hitch her before climbing down and running up the steps.

She wore a heavy coat over her pale yellow dress, and her bonnet rode back from her forehead, windblown. Her cheeks glowed red with the cold. Charlie let her in. She fell into his arms, and their mouths came together, tongues probing.

"Oh, God, this is a horrible time," she said finally as they broke. "Uncle is going around our big house wringing his hands. Pierce's Specific is being sold to *no one*. All of the old ladies have stopped pretending. They are drinking the last of their brandy straight or taking the very last of their laudanum or morphine and not caring who knows. The Specific let them pretend they were taking a medicine. He and my aunt are fighting all the time. My cousins are ill-mannered and stupid. We are drinking coffee made with okra seed and chicory, and it's bitter and vile. Uncle is afraid he will lose his house, and he keeps wondering aloud if I should join my father."

"Getting to Boston presents difficulties," said Charlie, feeling a heaviness in the pit of his stomach.

"He's no longer *in* Boston. He has gone to London and set up business there. My mother remained in Boston. Uncle says he might have to send me to London."

He came to her, held her in his arms, and she put her head on his shoulder, and he could smell a hint of scent in her thick hair. His lips slid along her neck.

"Don't say that it is a horrible time," he whispered. "I love you."

"I love you, but to what good?" she asked. "The world has separated from its senses, Charlie. And Uncle says that the real battles in the war have not even taken place yet. He says this will be an *annus sanguineus*. He wanders around the house saying that, and I want to run anywhere."

"Mama and Martha left not more than quarter of an hour ago," said Charlie. Sarah took off her heavy coat and dropped it on the floor. "You can't go to London. You *can't*."

Charlie felt strong, stripped of his illness, certain, uncaring for manners. He put his mouth on hers with a violent urgency, and he found his hands sliding down her back, fingers feeling for the cleft of her hips, finding it, tracing it downward. She tightened her buttocks but did not move away. They settled to the floor before the fire and lay upon the rug. Their eyes were open and calm as he moved his hand up her back then slid it around her chest, cupped her full left breast through the stays. She made small sounds of acceptance, breathed through her mouth. Her left hand toyed with the top button on his trousers, uncertain, wanting to move.

"I don't know," she whispered. "I want to, but I don't know."

"I would die for you," Charlie said. He immediately felt foolish, as if some line had been crossed, a code ruptured. He couldn't quite believe it when she closed her eyes and sighed, groaned, looked as if she might weep. He had never seen anything so beautiful in this life, kissed her again. Her right palm pulled his head closer, so close it almost hurt. Her left hand trailed down, down, then farther down, until it was loosely on his crotch. He groaned, and he reached down beneath her dress, brought his hand up rapidly beneath her skirts, aware she was whispering the word *yes* over and over.

He had tried to imagine vaginal shapes before, to separate boys' stories from anatomical truths. He knew there was a hole of some size in front, but he could not guess how high it might be.

"Not here," she said. She got to her knees and helped Charlie up and went into his bedroom and sat on his bed and began to undress, and he could not hold his breath. He thought she might slip out of her dress, lie upon the sheets in her underclothes, but she did not stop until she was completely naked, and he began to grapple with his own clothes. Her breasts were full, nipples hard and ringed from desire and the cold. A swath of blond hair began just below her navel and spread down between her legs, shining with wetness. He was embarrassed by his erection, but he finished undressing, thought they would lie side by side for a time. Instead, she took his hand, pulled him on top of her, reached down, pulled his penis lower and lower until he felt a warmth and wetness like nothing he could imagine. He was about to say something when he felt her shift, and suddenly, he felt himself sliding deep within her, then even deeper. He began to ask, then to warn, but her mouth came on his, and then he thought of nothing else.

Later, as he lay beside her, gasping for breath, she nuzzled close.

"Will you have a baby now?" he asked, almost choking.

"I doubt it," she said. "I don't care if I do. I need to use the privy."

"Okay." He couldn't think of anything else to say. They dressed, and she ran out the back door to the small double-seated shed, came back a few minutes later. Charlie followed her, inhaled the strange and maddening aroma of their bodies. He tried to think of the shame to his mother. Back inside, they sat before the fire, holding each other, looking into the small, almost pointless flames. They would glance at each other, kiss, stare back into the fire.

"What have we done?" he asked. The ecstasy of their coupling was fading, replaced by a gray guilt, the death-mask reproach of his father. "I can't believe that happened. I can't believe we did that."

"I'm *glad* we did," she said. "I've wanted to. I was going to. I don't care what anybody thinks. I don't care if they think I'm ruined. Some time, this damned war will be over. And the near-dead ones will come home and try to pretend it was about nothing."

"An abandoned mother and an injured father," Charlie said with wonder. "It felt so good, though. I never felt anything so wonderful. Did I hurt you?"

"I never felt a thing so wonderful, either," she said.

"Maybe we could run away and live in another town," said Charlie. "I could get a job. I could do something."

"Don't think about it now," said Sarah. "We have a little time to decide before he makes me go to London."

"My darling."

Sarah was gone by the time Betsy and Martha came home, and when Betsy was taking off her coat, she made a kind of half turn, almost a dance step, sniffed once, then closed her eyes and said a small prayer to God.

AS JANUARY SHOOK SNOW from its gray shoulders, then a cold rain, Charlie awaited news from Sarah, but she came less often, and his worry over Jack turned to panic on an icy Tuesday when Cephus rode up on his old mule and came into the cold house.

"Mist' Dockery done sent me fo' Mist' Charlie to say his friend Jack got the pneumoney and likely ain't gone last the night," said Cephus. "Lord, that boy done suffer more than any person ever done ought to."

"No!" cried Charlie. "Not this, not *Jack.*"

"You can't go out, Charlie," said Betsy. "You are too frail for the weather."

"Mama, don't let him go," said Martha, who was playing with jacks by the fire.

"Cephus, I'm going to take your horse," said Charlie. "She's warmed and saddled. Can you wait here?"

"Not wifout being axed," he said.

"Mama, don't let him go," said Martha, standing. Charlie was putting on his thick cotton coat, buttoning it to his chin.

"Cephus, come and warm up," said Betsy. "Charlie, go, but don't get too close, and come back before dark. Please?"

"Yes, ma'am," he said.

Outside and mounting the steaming horse, Charlie's head spun with a lack of balance, with a thousand unformed sentences. The sky spread before him, gunmetal and damp. The town was sinking in sentiment, and he understood why, but he had practiced shooting more and more, old men of the church sharing powder and ball, and his accuracy and aim had become consistent and willed; he could nip a target's notch at three hundred yards. Now, as he kicked Cephus's horse into a slow gallop, he thought of that summer night when he and Jack were camping beyond the railroad tracks near Grace House, when Jack had told him of the bisected man near Macon. The man's upper body had crawled away after he was sheared in half, crawled many yards from death and then written a note. How did you know when you were about to die?

Charlie thought of his brother and wondered if Tom had known when he was dying, that he'd never see his mother or family again. Tom's ghost probably didn't even know his father was dead. Tom simply disappeared from their lives and poured himself into the machinery of war. Maybe he killed a Yankee, but Charlie doubted it.

It was just after three in the afternoon, the sky was dark, and a few waves of sleet spattered on the rooftops as Charlie rode down Dixie Avenue, turned on First, and rode to the Dockery house, from which two huge tails of blue-gray smoke spread upward. He sneezed three times, slid off Cephus's horse, and tied it to the hitching post out front. Jack's mother, Delia, was stout and florid, and she held a crumpled handkerchief. Her eyes were painted round with redness as she let Charlie inside.

"He asked to send for you," she said. "His daddy's up there, been beside him these three days with his head in his hands. Hasn't eaten a bite, won't eat a bite. Dr. Dexter's given Jack palliatives and morphine, but he's wasted and is almost gone, son. His foot is fetid, too. It's a sore horror, Charlie. Dear God, sweet Jesus, my Jack."

Charlie felt the closeness of a sticky terror. The house was overheated and pretended to elegance, but a rot of disorder had set in, with wineglasses scattered about, crumpled and soiled handkerchiefs, even the slight but pervasive smell of chamber pots. Too few candles had been lit against the dark day, but the smell of tallow gave the air another tang, pungent and hopeless. He slowly ascended the terrible stairs, his breath shallow and painful. When he came into the room, he saw the fire had almost gone out, and before him was a tableau of grief: a small disordered room, lamp sputtering, Mr. Dockery motionless in his chair, and Jack lying on his back, mouth open, eyes staring at the ceiling. Charlie thought, *Oh, God, he died,* and for a moment, breathless, he felt himself swept into the past with the debris of all life, tumbled in the flood of things unsaid, undone. Jack's eyes shifted, and the motion startled Charlie.

"Charlie?" asked Jack weakly. A smell of putrescence, and Charlie knew it was Jack's foot, that he was dying from the leg up. Mr. Dockery rocked back, stared at Charlie without comprehension, his mouth slack. He had not shaved in perhaps three days, or bathed. The man reflexively pushed an unemptied chamber pot beneath the bed, but Charlie didn't care.

"It's me, Jack," said Charlie. "Are you being lazy again, young man? Maybe we should form our own company and be off to the war."

"Charlie Merrill, who has suffered also," said Mr. Dockery, and Charlie's eyes narrowed at the odd phrasing, at the distracted foolishness of it.

"I'll sit with him for a spell," said Charlie.

"If you think . . ."

"Go rest for a bit, and I'll stay with him," said Charlie. Mr. Dockery stood, leaned over, and kissed his son on the forehead and staggered out of the room. Charlie sat down, and a calmness descended upon him. Perhaps it was the cloak of God, or His guiding hand.

"I can't get my breath anymore," gasped Jack. He tried to shift in the bed, away from some pain, but he lacked the strength.

"Rest," said Charlie. "You are going to be fine."

"I'm dying," he said. "I know it." He choked for a moment, coughed, twisted in a sweaty redness. Charlie took his hand, held it. Jack's hand was hot and damp.

"You're not dying," said Charlie. "You can't die. Not you."

Jack settled, blinked, closed his eyes, and finally smiled slightly. "Last night I dreamed of the war, and I was charging across a field," said Jack. He waited for his breath to fill back up. "And I looked down. I could run. My feet—I was in one . . ."

"Save it," said Charlie. "Do you want some morphine or something? I don't see the bottle anywhere."

"Would you look at that," said Jack. "How strangely beautiful." He turned his head slightly and a quizzical expression played across his lips, then he lay still, his eyes almost closed, but not completely. Charlie stood, and his legs felt icy and unstable. He touched Jack's shoulder, lightly then harder, but Jack did not move. Charlie staggered out of the room. "Mr. Dockery! Mrs. Dockery!"

They came running up the stairs, Jack's mother weeping already, past alarm. Charlie tried to think of the proper words, but all he did was step back as they rushed into the room and threw themselves on the bed, moaning. Charlie went past them down the stairs and outside and sat in the sharp cold air of their front porch and wept. He had seen his best friend leave the earth, and it was nothing more than a last sip of air, a gasp, a step, then eternity. He felt staggered and terrified, and he wondered if Death were somehow stalking him like a sharpshooter, picking off those he loved one by one until It came for him, grinning blood and saying *Boy, now it's your turn.* He fell on his stomach and pounded his fists on the boards of the porch until his bones felt ready to snap.

He climbed back on to Cephus's horse and kicked it, found himself clopping slowly down bare-limbed streets, under a pale blue sky. He didn't realize he was near the Sawyer Pierce mansion on East Dixie Avenue until it loomed to his left. Smoke came only from one chimney, and great strips of white lead paint were flaking off, as if the structure had a skin disease. Charlie thought of Pierce's Specific and what Sarah had said about its failure. Her uncle Sawyer must not have the money to restore the house. In the months he had known Sarah, he had never come here because he was rarely well enough. Now, he felt angry and almost vile, wanted to hit something hard until it struck back or was hurt. He kicked the horse toward the front door, climbed painfully down, tied it to the Pierce's hitching post, then went up the front steps, knocked on the door.

For a long while, no one came, and Charlie looked through the leaded glass panes that lined the door and saw, coming down the hall, Mr. Pierce, limping oddly, as Jack had. The door opened with the reluctance of age.

"What do you want?" asked Dr. Pierce. He was foul, an unwashed mess, and a gust of colder air from the hallway exhaled with him. Charlie thought he stood in the mouth of some great monster, something risen from a lake bed or the ocean floor.

"May I see Sarah, please?" Charlie asked.

"Sarah is no longer here," said Doc Pierce.

"When will she be back? I have very bad news, Dr. Pierce."

"She won't be coming back."

"My friend Jack Dockery just— What did you say? What did you say?"

"She won't be coming back. She left yesterday morning for Savannah to ship to her father in London. My brother, I am sorry to say, has gotten wealthy off this war despite his marital problems, while I have failed utterly. Do you know what, Charlie Merrill, what it is like to fail utterly? Let me tell you something. That bastard Abe Lincoln thinks that he can solve this problem by freeing the niggers, and it won't work. It won't work." He stepped forward very close now, and Charlie could smell his breath, what might have been whiskey but was probably Pierce's Specific.

"She can't have gone without telling me goodbye," said Charlie.

"Appears that she did," said Pierce. "Liked her, did you?" He grinned maliciously. "She was spending too much time with you. You'll be dead soon, like your brother, so what good would it do her?" Doc

Pierce suddenly staggered backward and lost his balance and fell on his bottom in the hallway, and Charlie roared after him, wishing he had a long knife. He would kill the man. Books were stacked on the floor of the hallway, as if being prepared for shipping. Charlie picked up the top volume from one stack and knelt and hit Dr. Pierce four times in the head as hard as he could. Pierce tried to fend off the blows, but at least two landed level and straight.

"You bastard, you son of a bitch!" cried Charlie. "You sent her away?"

"I didn't send her away, goddamnit," he said. "Maybe she left of her own accord. Ever think of that? Took the train to Macon and then to Savannah. Would you like a sip of something tasty?" Then he fell over with a thud and began snoring heavily, and Charlie, too stunned and angry to speak, stormed out of the house and tried to get his breath back. He was halfway home before he realized he still had the book in his left hand.

CHARLIE TOOK TO HIS bed, frozen and staring, and Dr. Dexter said his illness had not returned, that this was something different. He stared blindly at the ceiling, let his mother read to him. Most days, he felt surrounded by a pale light, and Betsy told him how beautiful Jack's funeral was, that she was sorry about Sarah, that one day was cold and another springlike.

"I've never seen this book, *Resources of the Southern Fields and Forests,*" she said. "Would you like for me to read from it to you?" Charlie heard the title and did not open his eyes. He could not place the title. "The rest of its title is *Medical, Economical, and Agricultural, Being also a Medical Botany of the Confederate States*—then some other words. Published in Charleston this year." Charlie could hear her flipping pages and found himself vaguely interested. "Directions for collecting. All leaves, flowers, and herbs should be preferably gathered in clear, dry weather, in the morning, after the dew is exhaled."

She read on, but Charlie felt a small shiver of delight in that phrase: *after the dew is exhaled.* He wanted to awaken, but it was not yet time. He wanted to grow well, to go away, to be strong, to fight.

AFTER ALMOST TWO WEEKS, Charlie awoke one morning and opened his eyes. The windows in his small bedroom were open, and a warm breeze blew back the curtains. He thought of Sarah first, as he always did, then of Jack. The house seemed quiet, still. Bees buzzed near the window but did not enter the room. He pushed himself up and found that his mother had left *Resources of the Southern Fields and Forests* on his covers, and he picked it up and set it aside. He was not sick. Perhaps he never had been.

He walked to the window and looked out, shading his face from the sharp light. Trees had not yet begun to leaf, but jonquils and forsythia bloomed, and a cow somewhere near lowed insistently. For the first time in days, he knew that he was truly strong, that fear had left him. Charlie despised that fear. He walked to the mirror over the mantle and looked at his face, and then leaned closer, because he barely recognized the boy growing a fuzz of beard. He touched his face and felt the beard, watched the movement of his eyes. So now they were all gone, Papa, Tom, Jack, Sarah—lost to him for all time. Yet Sarah was alive. He knew that he would never be whole without her, but something was growing to replace her, a need for motion, a sense of marching.

He smiled, thinking his father would preach at him about now, probably from First Corinthians, nine, one, a favorite text: *Am I not an apostle? Am I not free?* Then Charlie remembered verse four: *Have we not power to eat and drink?* That power seemed to be pouring through him now, a leveling, a burst of resolve, of anger. He wondered what was happening in the war, if it had ended yet. Almost certainly not. In fact, spring campaigns were probably on the wing, and he wanted more than anything to stand in a clattering of musket fire. It would take months, but he would prepare himself and head for the nearest battle. Little was left to hold him. A shape of necessity drove him. Back at the bed, he sat and read from *Resources* for a while, examining "materials for brooms," and "Chinese sugar cane" and "glasswort." He scanned entries on native emetics and dyes, tanning leather, styptic oils. He found out that sugar could be made from the sap of walnut trees, that peach leaves could be used to substitute for vanilla beans. He read of the rose acacia, which grew in the mountains of north Georgia, which someone called "remarkably beautiful."

Suddenly there seemed before him a world with growing interconnections, a warm land of greenery that was useful and fruitful. He closed the book and felt a new strength flowing through him, as if spring had come to his bones. More than anything, he wanted to leave here, leave his mother and sister, escape Branton, head for another world, perhaps just in the South but maybe farther afield. He wanted to become lost in the woods and find plants like gravel weed and turnsole and clammy locust. He wanted to lose his relationship to the frail boy of childhood, bury him in the hard red clay of north Georgia with his ancestors.

He rose and walked to the window and spread his arms out, and a gathering wind spread his nightgown, billowed it, so that he appeared much larger, and the shadow he cast spread across the floor to the other side of the room.

LATER, CHARLIE WOULD REMEMBER, this was the day he knew that he was bound for war. With Sarah gone, Jack and Tom and his father dead, he felt a growing need for it. He was an expert marksman, his strength was growing, and he was no longer a boy. He spent two hours each day taking target practice and working on the house, firing, then shingling. But it was more than that: He bled a deep anger, not toward the North exactly, but toward the shape of this life, and toward how some in town would see this house as a family's fall toward poverty. He would fight against it. He would leave and make his way to Atlanta and then north toward the war. It would take a few more months, perhaps until the autumn of 1863, but he would leave, stand in battle, take his death if necessary. He would die as a man should, past sacrifice, among other men, not as a boy in his slumped and sorrowful bed. Jack would be waiting for him beside a stream in the gardens of heaven, grown perfect, strong enough to run.

June 27, 1864

KENNESAW MOUNTAIN

☆ ☆
☆

I N THE CLEAR, STAR-WASHED night, Southern men improved their
trenchworks on the slopes of Kennesaw Mountain and to its east
and west, and Northern men watched the slopes and prayed. Now,
not long before dawn, most of them slept, the Confederates in a great
arc, with Hood's Corps on the left, Hardee's Corps in the center, and
Loring's on the right. In Hardee's Corps, Cheatham's Division was on
the left flank, followed in order by Cleburne, Bate, and Walker. In Loring's Corps, French's Division came first, then General Walthall's and
General Featherston's.

Charlie had slept for three hours and awakened sorrowful and remembering, flexing and unflexing his hands on the barrel of his Enfield
rifle, patting his cartridge box and knowing he had at least sixty rounds
and fearing that today he must kill many men. In the faint trembling
light of a few campfires, he almost remembered the carnage to come.
This part of the battlefield wasn't even Kennesaw Mountain proper, or
any mountain, but a hill southwest of the knob they called Little Kennesaw Mountain.

"I'll have to say that all things being even, I'd rather be on a scout
somewhere and you in a tree," said Duncan McGregor. He sat up from
his bedroll. "Though the Lord knows them's magnificent works."

"They are that," said Charlie. The Confederate trenches were nine feet deep in places, thorned with abatis and spiked with cannon aimed with precise malevolence at the Union lines. The sappers had cut steps into the works so the gray-clad soldiers could step up and fire down. "This will be a murderous day if they come, Duncan."

"I think they will come today," said Duncan. "I believe General Sherman has run out of patience with the rain and the rivers and these mountains. I believe he intends to throw them upon us. Are you all right, son?"

"I feel unwell."

"I thought so, but you must buck up and do your duty." Charlie turned sharply on Duncan, and his eyes glistened with the small flames of a dying campfire.

"Duncan, something is terribly wrong here. I don't think we're meant to win this war. I have begun to think I want no part of it."

"Do you aim to skedaddle, then?"

"No. It's not that. I intend to do my duty."

"As do I."

"But I believe there's no accounting for the right. I can't see what's true here."

Others began to rise. Dawn spread from the east with clouds of rose and amber and a gentle and prevailing wind from the northwest, and a sweeter day Charlie could not imagine. But as the sun rose, the temperature began to swell like a living, breathing creature, and a vast and noxious beast feasted upon them, a predator, so that by seven-thirty, men were shedding their coats and watching officers for signs. Charlie ate nothing and found a good position in the abatis where he could see the slope before him, and he aimed and reaimed the Enfield and liked its heft. His father's cousin Joseph Bearden made Enfields at the Cook & Brother Armory in Athens, but most of these rifles had come from England. A muzzle-loader like the Whitworth, it was accurate only to four hundred yards, but deadly anyway.

"So how does it feel to be a soldier in the ranks again?" asked a very short man from Lowrey's Brigade who had slid down the lines looking for extra food. "You was a sharpshooter, but I heared you lost your Whitworth rifle. You's lucky they didn't tie you to a sour apple tree and shoot you."

"I'm lucky all right," said Charlie softly.

"Who the hell are *you?*" Isaac Kennon asked the man. Charlie had known Kennon in Dalton, a decent man who protected his friends.

"Name's John Brown, from Lowrey's." Several men giggled.

"*John Brown?* Hell, you're the one we orta tie to a sour apple tree and shoot."

"Go to hell, you son of a bitch, that was my daddy's name, too."

"We know, they hung him in fifty-nine," said Tyree Baskins, another man from Govan's brigade whom Charlie knew in Dalton. "And if you don't get back, you're gone get your goddamned head blowed off. If you do, then I'm personally gone stuff your head in a Parrott gun and fire your eyeballs at them Yankee brethren across the way." The man crabbed off cursing while the shifting soldiers laughed and took positions in their works.

"You *are* lucky," said Isaac Kennon to Charlie. "Every man spread from here across the mountains is lucky. We orta be dead from artillery or musketry or from the bloody flux or from pneumoney or typhus, but here we are, sitting in hell ready for another goddamn battle. And the ones who live out the day will be lucky and the ones who don't will be lucky. That's all I got to say on that matter."

"You done turned into a philosopher," said Baskins.

"Haw," said Isaac Kennon. "Better'n turning into buzzard food."

"Son, keep your head down," said Duncan, touching Charlie on the shoulder. Charlie did not move or seem to notice his friend's presence.

CHARLIE LOOKED OVER THE field of fire. The Dallas Road was on their far right, beyond Granbury's Texans. A branch of Ward Creek ran behind them. In front and to the left was a large hill on which Vaughan's and Maney's brigades of Cheatham's division spread in a sharp chevron to push back attacks like water pouring off a roof peak.

At precisely eight o'clock, fifty-one pieces of Union artillery opened up at once on the Southern lines, and the ground shook, and the sound was like a hard clap on their ears. Smoke erupted, and fused explosive balls and rifled projectiles all raked the Confederate lines. Logs splintered, and small pieces flew hundreds of feet. One six-inch-long shard stuck in the eye of a private from Tennessee, and he climbed down from the works in a desultory way, sat in the trench, emitted a single curse word, and fell over dead. Far on the right, across the Dallas Road, Yankee lines began to move forward toward Loring's corps, scrambling through a dense tangle of brush and briar, making little headway, as the barrage from both sides opened in full. Distant trumpets: heavy firing, screams, and yells.

Charlie and Duncan stood on the parapets and waited, watching the largely ineffective Union artillery strokes. A major had climbed up and sat boldly in the crotch of the abatis, using his field glasses to call out positions and movement.

"They've fixed bayonets," the major cried.

"Jesus Christ," said Isaac Kennon. "Not bayonets. We'll have to kill 'em all before they get here, then." A few laughed, but they said nothing. To their left, the assault was forming on Cheatham's men in their angle on the hill, and the firing was terrible and ceaseless.

"They're dying over there," said Tyree Baskins. "Them Yankees is dying in their hundreds over there. Goddamn it, I hope they come here."

"You're about to get your wish," said the major, who was scrambling down from the logworks. He began to speak again and this time spoke in syllables of blood, looked surprised beyond imagining, his eyes wild with knowledge, then he spoke again, and blood erupted, laced his face in red strands. He looked around for help, then fell gagging. He died there, and no one moved to pull his body from their footpaths.

Maney's Tennessee troops on the hill fired rapidly into the advancing Union lines, and hundreds fell, but no troops yet assaulted Govan's Brigade, and Charlie clasped and unclasped his hands on the Enfield and waited. A screen of brush and timber lay before them, and not until almost two hours after the battle had started did Charlie see the blue troops creeping forward toward their breastworks. Charlie glanced at Duncan, and a rush of affection for his companion came over him, and he knew that he had no better friend. The Union troops came to the barriers, three rows of increasingly impenetrable logworks, starting with a jumble the men called "tanglefoot," then pine logs sharpened and buried at forty-five degrees forward, ends axe-sharpened, and finally chevaux-de-frise, crossed logs with sharp stakes jammed in augured holes.

They swarmed forward, rising up the slope over the barriers, and as they lifted their bodies, the Confederates shot them. Charlie killed three men in the first two minutes of the Federal assault, one with each shot. All down the line the men poured murderous fire into the screaming Yankees, and they fell down in rows, some not moving at all, others wiggling in pain like just uncovered snakes.

"My God, they just keep coming!" shouted Duncan. Charlie glanced to make sure he was all right. Cleburne's artillery opened on the Federals, blowing one group of three into bloody hunks of meat.

Once, a near-spent bullet grazed Charlie's cheek, turning him back, leaving a small red mark the size of a cherry.

"Coming up on the left!" cried Tyree Baskins, and Isaac Kennon turned, and, without aiming, fired into the chest of a Federal soldier running forward with his bayonet held high. The bullet augured into the man's heart, and he fell straight down dead, and the rifle hit the hard earth dagger-first, and it stood up like a cemetery marker at the man's head. The stench of gunpowder scratched their eyes and rose in their nostrils like the sulfur of hell surfacing in the June sun. A malignant heat came as the sun spilled higher over Cleburne's troops. Charlie looked down the lines to the right, and as far as he could spy, the Federals were coming, charging up Little Kennesaw Mountain, up Big Kennesaw, up Pigeon Hill, up the nameless slope down to the left where Vaughn's and Maney's brigades of Cheatham's Division still bled back the fierce assault.

"This ain't no goddamn flank," said Duncan. "This time Sherman's bringing it."

Charlie said nothing, but the bluecoats sacrificed themselves on the works with stunning alacrity, and the thud of minié balls as they smacked into flesh was heard everywhere, so much that it became routine. A few Confederate soldiers fell backward in the trenches, picked off by Union sharpshooters across the way, but the dying was mostly before them, and the artillery became more fierce, and men came to the top spikes of the chevaux-de-frise and took death like a sacrament.

"Chickamauga! Chickamauga!" screamed a Confederate private, waving his Enfield above his head with a dark glowering of victory, and soon the chant spread down the line. Surely this was the end of Sherman and another signal victory like Chickamauga. Charlie said nothing and stared at them, incredulous. If there had ever been a pyrrhic victory, it had been Chickamauga, where thousands of Southern boys fell, even though the Union lines buckled and broke and flowed back north to Chattanooga. What had it gained? Only one season.

The violence increased, but now the Yankees lay on their stomachs before the logworks, not advancing or firing, and soon the cannon fire from both sides ignited fires in the brush before Cleburne's position, and the wounded began to erupt in flames. Charlie stopped firing and stared at the sight before him, and it was so like the images of hell in some of his father's books that he felt a thrill of horror, a trembling, as if some inner earthquake had begun to shake him with the violence of recognition. Now that the Union soldiers had halted this advance, their artillery opened up, and the Confederates held lower in their works, but the firing was wild, mostly far behind their lines, and the fires increased as the big guns from Hardee's whole corps—the divisions of Bate and Cleburne, Cheatham and Walker—opened in return.

"My God, they're burning to death out there," said Duncan McGregor. "The wounded are being burnt alive."

A lieutenant colonel nearby shook his head and began to say the word *no,* loud, then much louder. He took a white handkerchief from inside his coat and tied it to the end of his bayonet.

"Colonel Martin's surrendering us!" cried Tyree Baskins.

"He ain't surrendering, he's calling a halt to get them men out afore they're burnt," said Isaac Kennon. They looked over the works, and the colonel, whose name was Will Martin, from the First Arkansas, stood and screamed to the Union lines below.

"Come and get your wounded!" he cried. "They're burning to death! We won't fire a gun until you get them away! Be quick!"

The firing dwindled and then died. Charlie felt tears sting his eyes, and he set his gun down and climbed out of the works and walked into the hell of brush fires. The sun spangled them with a deathly stroke. Union soldiers rose from behind the chevaux-de-frise and came forward, and they all mingled suddenly, dozens from both sides, stamping fires, dragging men from them. Some of the wounded vomited blood. Others were dead and burning. The fires crept as if sentient, as if testing men to see if they breathed, to see whom they might roast alive.

Charlie saw a man whose face he knew: the rough Union soldier who had captured him and taken away his gun. The Whitworth was nowhere in sight, but Charlie knelt at the soldier before a Union comrade could reach him.

"You got any water?" the man asked.

"My canteen's off," said Charlie. The Federal soldier's eyes narrowed slightly, and he turned his head, as if recognizing Charlie. Blood flowed from his ears and the corners of his mouth. Charlie looked down and saw a ghastly wound in the stomach, pumping blood, and around it flies were humming already. A great smudge of smoke from the muskets and cannon blanketed the field, and smoke from the fires joined it, and the heat was murderous, and the screams bled around him like the cries of sick children.

The Yank's eyes rolled wildly. "Goddamn it, the rain's coming . . . I want to plow them fields." Then the man emitted a long, whistling sigh, and he trembled violently once and died. His eyes were staring up at the stinging light. A fly lit on his left eyeball. Charlie stood, staggering away from the dead man and balanced himself in the stench of the unspeaking and the rush of their fellows. After the wounded had been carried behind the lines, soldiers began to gather the dead, and Charlie helped carry a fat Texan from Granbury's Brigade back, a red-faced faro player who wheezed as he laughed when drunk, speaking of the flatlands, arroyos, and rimrock as if they had been his lovers. Now his mouth was open, and his left foot missing. What had he been doing out here? Almost all of the wounded, all of the bodies, were Yankees. Perhaps he'd seen enough and flowed into his own death, streamlike, certain. Perhaps he was one of those who had given his possessions away in the morning, prayed once, then resigned from the living to rush among his honored dead. The whole field seemed mythic to Charlie, connected to stories of Marathon and Hastings.

"Get back, men!" someone cried, and the Confederates who had come out to help left, but a few Federals were still plundering their own dead, and Charlie watched them in amazement as he climbed back into the works.

"Now why in the name of God did you go out there to look at some dead Yankees?" asked Duncan McGregor. "You can't do a thing for the dead but speed their souls."

"Dear God," said Charlie Merrill.

LIKE A GAME IN which fairness is desired by all, the firing did not resume until the bluecoats had dragged their dead and wounded back down the slope. The sound of repulse from the hill where Cheatham's men fought was violent and steady. Now the sun was higher, nearing ten o'clock, and the heat began to swell over them. Charlie felt the Enfield grow into his hands, and he missed, missed, then hit a Federal boy square in the forehead. He jerked backward in a halo of blood, fell dead. Charlie's hands began to tremble uncontrollably.

"My God, this is a slaughter," said Isaac Kennon. "A bloody slaughter. We're going to end this whole goddamn thing here at Kennesaw Mountain. Boys, we're in the battle of battles."

Charlie wondered where General Cleburne might be, and he knew he was too intelligent not to see the weaknesses in the Confederate lines. If the enemy's numbers are large enough, there is no flank that can be tended well enough. This would slow the flow of Federals toward Atlanta, but soon enough, they would arrive. It was clear, even back in March, that they would arrive. What then? Would they march east along the Georgia Railroad tracks to Branton only sixty miles away? Would they burn the stately mansions?

Charlie shot toward a middle-aged soldier who'd lost his hat. The man threw down his musket and stamped his foot in a blinding rage. Most of the Yankees were stomach-bound, pinned to red clay by shell-fire, and Charlie could not say he'd hit the man, for so many aimed at him. Shots turned him left and then right. Bits of blood and bone flashed away. Another shot spun him in a complete circle and still he danced angrily. A cannon blasted off his left arm at the shoulder, and great gouts of blood poured out, and still the man howled and shuffled his feet, but then he slowed and turned square to the Rebel lines and gave a look of contempt. Charlie counted five shots that smacked his torso with sickening meaty thuds almost simultaneously, and he fell forward and was dead before he landed heavily on the spike of a cheval-de-frise, and the spike split the man's chest and came out his back, and he lay there skewered. The gray lines cheered the man's courage. Charlie staggered back into the works and sat and shivered and felt as if he would vomit, but then he did not.

"You hit, boy?" cried Duncan in the din.

"No, Duncan. Are you hit?"

"No. You all right, then?"

"No."

The firing continued along the line, very far to the left and to the right. Charlie lay back and looked at the sky, which was almost white and cloudless, and the heat seared his face, and he wanted to go home. For the first time since he'd left Branton the year before seeking battle, he truly and clearly wanted no part of it anymore. He loaded his gun again and came back to the ramparts and stood and looked at the struggling Union lines, which had advanced no farther and would not, and he aimed his rifle, and from time to time jerked as if he had fired it, but he did not, and the only one who noticed that he was not reloading was Duncan, who fired but aimed high and waited for the battle to end. The concussion from artillery blasted Charlie's ears into deafness, and the muffled sound was like being in a shadowed place. He tried to think of how many men he had killed since Chickamauga, but he could not count them all. Surely thirty or forty, possibly a hundred. He could not say, but then he began to untangle their genealogies and their mothers and their children, spin tales of sacrifice and wonder, and he trembled.

He stood that way during the battle for a very long time and did not fire again.

July 22, 1914

✩ ✩
✩

CHARLIE SAT ON THE screened back porch of Grace House intensely reading from the single sheet of paper. He had placed it as an advertisement in seven Boston and New York newspapers. Belle snored at his feet as he rocked. The earth seemed to smoke, steam braising the grass and bare spots beneath the pecan trees. The heat was oppressive after the storm, and in the early afternoon sunlight, the yard before him seemed stunned, breathless with surrender, and insects hummed against the screen, a distant melody perhaps, like an unremarkable memory.

He closed his eyes, but sleep would not come as he rocked. Instead, he remembered a warm winter day when he and Sarah sat on a blanket in the pecan shade, reading Shakespeare's sonnets aloud to each other, sipping cold water, nibbling on crackers.

"When it comes down to it, slavery is the single issue," she said. As he rocked, he formed her face, her body, the bow-shaped mouth with pale pink lips, the tangled yellow hair. "You look at Cephus and Missy, and they work here during the day and then at night go back home to their plantation and probably live in a dirt-floored shack."

"Are you an abolitionist?" asked Charlie, half smiling. This was some time before he, Betsy, and Martha had moved from Grace House, though his father was dead, he believed. Yes, his father must have been dead by then.

"Of course," she said. "It's an immoral system. You must see that, Charlie Merrill."

"The Baptist church believes it is *highly* moral," said Charlie. "Look, I don't know. I know that I think about it a lot. It makes me sick. It's just that the people in the North hate us so."

"They hate slavery," said Sarah softly. "Would you like to be owned and have your family broken up at someone's whim?"

"I don't think so, but I don't want to talk about it."

"That's the problem. Even the people of good will don't want to talk about it." Her face had flushed, and Charlie found her passion attractive. The wind had a sharpening edge, as if a cold rain might not be far away. The old people could tell when weather was about to change, and perhaps the sunny warmth would fade in a day.

"You're red," he said. "You're getting yourself all worked up. They never let me get worked up because I was so frail. Every time I'd have a strong feeling, they'd cut it away like a tumor. Be quiet, you'll upset Charlie. Don't argue. Don't worry about what you cannot control. Here, read a book, dear. Except for what I read in books and target shooting, I never had a passion in my life." Charlie saw the irony: a bookish boy who also loved guns. Things, he knew already, did not always add up.

They were leaning close now, and he could smell her faint scent. Her eyes were wide with acceptance and an utter lack of guile. She narrowed her eyes, and he thought: *Yes, she likes me.* He could barely believe or understand it—a lovely young girl liked him very much, held his hand, whispered to him. They had kissed.

"And chess," she said. "Don't forget chess."

"I want to kiss you," said Charlie.

"You can't. Your mother might be watching from the window," said Sarah. She did not say it coyly but in a quiet, distracted way. "They might hang you in Branton for kissing an abolitionist."

"Sarah," he said, loving the shape of her name in his mouth. "Sarah."

"What?"

"I don't want you to go back to Boston," said Charlie. "I want you to stay here with me forever."

Her eyes grew wide, and she turned her head slightly to one side. Her lips were as moist as ripe peach halves. She looked down, then away, then back up at Charlie, and her eyes glistened.

"Nobody has ever wanted me before," she said. "My parents didn't want me. My aunt and uncle don't want me. I don't make friends easily. You're the best friend I ever had."

"Then we are just friends?"

"Dear God, I would die for you, sweet boy," she said, and Charlie leaned back, felt the sun on his face, felt it swell into his thin arms and legs.

Now, the same heat warmed him as he rocked and held the paper in his fingers. He looked at the back of his hands, and sparse white hair spread across them with age spots. Each day when he shaved, he knew the old man less and less. Perhaps he favored one of his grandfathers. His father's father had died before he was born, and his mother's father passed away from typhoid when Charlie was only two years old. Charlie was surprised at how fast life had gone, like some vast unraveling. So many of them were gone. So many had not survived the war.

Charlie again read the advertisement he had placed:

> Seeking Sarah Pierce, who lived in Branton, Georgia, during the early 1860s with her uncle Sawyer Pierce. Please come to festivities for 50th anniversary of the Battle of Atlanta, Ezra Atkinson Park, Branton, July 22, 1914. I will speak, and desire to see you again. Write if unable to attend. With kindest regards, Charlie Merrill, 16 Main Street, Branton, Ga.

He smiled at himself, a hunched and white-crested old man, sentimental and shot with phantom pains. He had spent more than two hundred dollars on the advertisements but had received no letter or telegram or any hint that she was still alive. *Of course*, he was seeking Sarah. All his life, through a solid marriage, through two fine children and grandchildren, through a superlative career and five published books, he had sought her. Thomas Jefferson had once written, "We love those best whom we love first." Yes, Charlie thought: a very smart man, Thomas Jefferson.

Unexpectedly, he felt as if he might cry. These days he wept easily. The young scorned crying, especially in men. They were a cocky lot, whizzing around the county in their new automobiles, laughter flying behind them, and they were largely sick of war stories, of lost causes and the bloody sacrifices. He had read many books about the war but had never written about it himself, not even in the *Branton Eagle* during all the years he owned it. The slaughter strained comprehension—

thousands of casualties at Sharpsburg before ten in the morning. Now Charlie remembered more gratefully what happened after Atlanta. He recalled a smooth-running stream, deafness, crimson-clotted hair, but also rain and pity and a return of hope. His head slowly began to lower as the tears came more easily now, and he knew what he would never possess again—youth, love, ardor, strength, time.

"Mister Charlie, are you all right?" It was Mrs. Knight standing next to him wiping her reddened hands on a small white towel. "Should I call the doctor?"

"I'm all right," said Charlie. "I was thinking of a small nap."

"I can call over to Miss Catherine's house and get her to cancel this speech right this minute," she said. "You ain't fit for making a speech you haven't even written."

"I'm fit enough," he said. He brushed back the tears, sat up straight, folded the paper and thrust it into his breast pocket. "Don't call Catherine. Don't call anybody. I'm fit enough. I'm just old. There's no remedy for that, is there?"

"None as I know of."

The idea came from somewhere. He couldn't quite imagine.

"Tell you what. Call up Tyrone at the paper and tell him I need him to drop here as soon as he can come by."

"Can I tell him for what?" Belle yawned and stretched.

"No, you cannot, Mrs. Knight," he said. "I'm of a mind to do something."

TYRONE STOOD BY HIS car and wiped the sweat from his face with a large white handkerchief.

"This is not a good idea, boss," he said. "You could catch pneumonia or something."

"For God's sake, Tyrone, don't," said Charlie. "I'm still man enough to make my own decisions."

They stood on the edge of Turner's Hole, a wide backwater in the Branton River a half mile north of town, and three small black boys screamed, swung out from a half-rotted tire swing, landed with giggling splashes in the sluggish brown water. The sun stroked Charlie's thin legs as he stripped to his union suit and waded into the cool water. Oak trees leaned over the river, dripping water from the earlier storm. He closed his eyes and thought of Tom, strong and grinning. He would dive into Turner's Hole and then swim across the river and back while Charlie sat bundled and weak in a one-horse buggy. Tom would come out clapping at his own achievement, summer brown, planes of hard muscle. The black boys pushed each other, tried out small oaths, looked with curiosity and amusement at the old white man wading into the hole.

"Don't slip," said Tyrone. He came closer. "I don't want anybody to know this, but I can't swim. I couldn't save you."

"You can't swim?"

"Never learnt," he said. "I was too scared to try and then too old to admit I couldn't."

"People get that way about a lot of things," said Charlie. The water, which he thought would feel fine, was too cold somehow, and he could feel an iron ice against his leg bones. He wanted to get out, wouldn't. He took two steps forward and suddenly felt the floor of the riverbank fall away as he slipped into a hole. He came up spluttering, and Tyrone Awtry shouted something, and the black boys splashed toward him. Charlie tried to find his breath, but it seemed to have slipped away, and he wondered if he should just sink, wash downstream, float on. A powerful peace swept him; the image of letting go, of passing away while floating downstream seemed suddenly attractive, even inevitable. Then two of the black boys held him under his arms, pulled him toward the shallow water, then on to the bank, where he sat in the grass, heaving for breath, looking around. Tyrone was pale. Charlie felt surprisingly calm, waited for the darkness to pull him down. Death was as familiar as his skin. From Dalton to Atlanta, he had never been very far from death.

"He okay," said one of the black boys. "There be a big hole there." He turned to Tyrone. "He be Mr. Merrill from the *Eagle,* don't he?"

"Yes," said Tyrone. "God help me, the town's going to think I killed you, boss. Please let me take you home."

"All right," said Charlie, slightly disappointed that he was not going to die.

"Did you even start on the speech yet?"

"I've got hours," said Charlie.

"He don't look too good," said one of the boys.

"You go tend to your own business," said Tyrone. Charlie turned and looked at them. They were burnished black, wearing cutoff, cast-off trousers that were several sizes too big, cinched by old belts. A glance of worry: a kindness.

"Thank you so much for picking me up," said Charlie. "I would have drowned. You are good boys. I thank you."

"Yes, sir," they said, one starting just after the other so the words were out of phase. They walked away slowly, whispering to each other. Charlie was silent on the ride back to Grace House, but he thought of Sarah again, and could imagine her scolding him for taking such a chance, but he was not sorry. He tested the pain in his chest and shoulder and found them acceptable, no worse, and for the first time gained a glimpse of what he might say at Ezra Atkinson Park in a few hours. It was important that he be alive and able, that he prepare well for his own passing. He did not want to see another war in Europe and the men it would consume. He was almost ready to fade into the history of one insignificant small town.

But not quite.

CHARLIE LAY IN HIS hot, quiet, still-air bedroom, flat on his back, dried from the plunge, seeking a newer depth in dreams. He had closed and locked the door, and lay naked on the freshly ironed sheets. He was still awake, thinking of Cleburne's chess game, hexagonal rifling, the dark mass of Kennesaw Mountain. Often he banished the images, shouted them down, filled hours with words and other memories, but now the war swept over him as he considered his speech. Going to Turner's Hole had been a splendid madness. He could count on Tyrone Awtry to tell everyone in town, and that would be fine; the legendary plunge, the salvation by two black boys. Charlie was not so sure of that help; perhaps a tragic and triumphant drowning would have been better, a magnificent vanishing. They say drowning is not such a terrible death. Far worse the sudden shell, the slap of a minié ball in the chest, the youth knowing he would die. Often they cried aloud for mother or for God. The night after the Federals' charge at Kennesaw Mountain, the Union wounded cried for water and death, and Charlie lay in his own works, weeping. He remembered the rain before that battle, three miserable weeks of ceaseless rain. He recalled hearing about Bishop-General Polk cut in half by a Yankee artillery shell, and the weeping and ground-pounding as they looked at his disintegrated remains.

No! No! Charlie thought of his beloved sister Martha, the rock of his life, a rough-minded and loving woman who had suffered loss and gone on. Charlie had rarely been well a day in his long life, and Martha had rarely been sick. If he had lived, Tom would have been the picture of health.

No! No! The rich men and their substitutes for war. Pale widows walking in a noble daze around the streets of Branton, past mercantile and fabric stores, past apothecary and hotel. The Rev. Charles Morgan Merrill standing in the backyard, beneath the pecan grove, lifting the shotgun, lifting lifting lifting lifting . . . *No! No!*

Charlie thought, as he often did, when seeking sleep, of that day with Sarah, when they had shared the secrets of their sex. He considered detail and word, air and aroma. He remembered her perfume and the scent of her crotch, warm and electric, the smell of them as they coupled. He could bring that smell up from memory, dawdle in it, exult in that love. *Yes.* Now, he felt himself slip toward sleep, and he hoped he would not awaken, for to awaken would mean never seeing her again. Each dream, when she came, would leave him with a shattering reluctance, unwilling to release her. He had always thought: *If I had been able to hold her one more time, kiss her one more time, I would have been able to bear her departure.* But not this. Not a lifetime of desire torn away. Brother, father, mother, lover, wife. They had all come and gone, disappeared into the mists of past-keeping. His parents lay in the Branton City cemetery, and Tom was buried in Virginia. Charlie's beloved wife rested in a twin plot not a hundred yards from Grace House, waiting his arrival. Soon, love. But what had become of Sarah? She had simply vanished. Sawyer Pierce and his wife and children had moved out west before the war was over; no one had ever heard from them again. Charlie had visited New York to speak with his publishers, gone on to Boston, searched for her, found nothing. Had his step into water over his head been an accident? Charlie smiled at the thought. They say suicides run in families. He and Martha had talked at times about their father, but she barely remembered him, and the suicide came to her as a vague dream, known largely in retellings. No, Charlie would not kill himself. He would make this ridiculous speech and pretend that he was as heroic as T. D. Varnell, James Felden, and Josiah Biggs were not. They had survived by accident.

Sarah. She is the one who will escort him to dreams, he thought. And then he was asleep, snoring lightly, his chest rising and falling evenly. Perhaps for some time he did not dream.

Suddenly, he was lowering himself into Sarah, and the length of his hardness slid along that corrugated track, and he was looking at her face, and she was writhing with joy, and her mouth was coming up for him, and he could not breathe for the love of it, for the closeness of her body.

CHARLIE JERKED AND AWOKE. He could see by the clock next to his bed that twenty minutes had passed, and he was feeling tired and sad. Yes, he thought, these were the themes of his life. He wanted to write now. More than anything, he wanted a pen in his hands.

July 21–22, 1864

ATLANTA

BEFORE DAWN, **CLEBURNE'S DIVISION** began moving south from the Georgia Railroad. Not three miles from the center of Atlanta now, they huffed in the wet air, not knowing where they were going or when they would take their place in line. Granbury's Texans were on the far right, and they finally settled, dug rifle pits, and waited. The day would not break for a while yet.

Charlie knew that in the next day or two Atlanta could fall finally, and the Confederacy split apart. Already the Federals were east of them and had cut the Georgia Railroad to Augusta—the road that ran through Branton and just behind Grace House. Charlie sweated through his shirt and into his coat and felt a deep fear shake him.

"Son, I've a dread of great proportions," said Duncan McGregor. "Maybe it's time I give you what I own in token of my coming demise." He laughed softly, but Charlie would not answer or look at him. They were in an area thick with brambles and blackberry bushes. "Then again, I've nothing to give you. I've already given you my coat. Keep that for me, then."

The day began to rise, and a violent heat swelled into them as the Federal batteries opened with a crash and a roar.

SINCE KENNESAW MOUNTAIN, EVERYTHING had gone precisely wrong for the Confederate soldiers. Two days after the furious battle on June 27, a truce had been called at the hill where Cheatham's men had fought so hard, and soldiers from both sides mingled on the field, ferrying off the carrion, which had gone fetid, swelling to the point of explosion overnight. Men vomited from the horror and stench. Charlie, who was detailed to help, took the arm of a Union boy to pull him on to a litter, and the arm came off in his hands. Staggered, blind with the fetid stench of rotting bodies, Charlie helped heap them into a mass grave where shovelers threw down clods of hacked-up red dirt on their upturned faces. The Union and Confederate troops swapped coffee and tobacco, drank from each other's canteens. By late in the day, they were firing at each other again, and to Charlie the war had taken on a sheen of madness. It was more than anything else like a boy's game played to the death.

The Federals were digging a tunnel beneath the Rebel works, hoping to stuff it full of powder and blow them apart. The Rebels soaked huge balls of cotton in turpentine, lit them afire, then rolled them down the mountain toward the Federal troops. For the next two days, skirmishing had continued, but the bluecoats made no further charges. A brief but intense thundershower cooled them late on June 30.

The night of July 2, the Union troops did what they had done since Dalton: began a massive flanking movement, and the Confederates abandoned their entrenchments on Kennesaw Mountain and fell back toward Atlanta. The next morning, Union men climbed to the top of Big Kennesaw Mountain and planted the American flag. Bands came up and played "The Star-Spangled Banner," and from that position, they could see the spires of Atlanta in the flatlands before them. At first, the Southerners took up new lines six miles south of Marietta near a Methodist meeting place called Smyrna Campground, but the fighting there had been brief before Johnston had ordered the fallback to continue. Charlie saw the new fortifications on the north side of the Chattahoochee River with fascinated horror.

"We're supposed to defend *that* for the love of God?" asked Duncan. Huge palisades had been erected, stretching miles, it seemed, almost as if in anticipation of an Indian attack. All day, the men knocked down the palisades and enlarged the fort until it resembled something that might be defended. Atlanta was barely more than eight miles to the southeast. On July 5 and 6, the Federals captured the town of Roswell

and burned its textile mills to the ground. Two days later, the Union
troops began to cross the river, planning yet another flanking, and on
the ninth, the Southern troops withdrew south across the Chattahoochee in the night, burning the bridges.

Atlanta erupted in a panic, and hundreds fled toward Macon in wagons and carriages, on horseback and on foot and by what few trains had
not been commandeered by the military. Once across the river, the Confederates, exhausted and dispirited, dug in at strong positions and
waited, but hundreds deserted. For a few days anyway, there was no
fighting, and men washed their filthy uniforms in the river, ate blackberries, and caught turtles to boil. The Union lines formed on the north and
south sides of the river, and all along it informal truces were held on the
picket lines. For most of a week, little had happened. Charlie took turns
on the line and sat in his rifle pit, quiet and frightened. He could think of
nothing but death and fire. Burying the mangled dead at Kennesaw
Mountain had bled his soul, and he knew he was no more than the sick
boy who loved books and music, who had been given the grace of Sarah
Pierce and had lost her. There was no plan to war; some lived and some
died, and generals played with death as if it were no more than a game of
ball.

The night of July 16, Charlie sat in camp, chewing on a blade of
broom sedge when Major Calhoun Benham, Cleburne's aide, rode up
and said the general would like to see Charlie in his quarters. Charlie
knew it was not far away, and he saluted, straightened himself, and
walked over. The ground beneath his feet was marshy, and an oppressive heat blistered his face into red welts. Cleburne looked terrible. He
was very thin and nervous, pacing in front of his tent. He tried to smile
when Charlie came up and saluted, but it was more of a grimace, and
Charlie took his ease and waited.

"Mr. Merrill, I am sorry that I have had no occasion to speak with
you since Kennesaw Mountain," he said. "I was pleased at your escape
from the enemy."

"General, I lost your Whitworth rifle," said Charlie softly. "I am
sorry of that."

"Better to lose a rifle than a life," Cleburne said, waving it away with
his hand. He chewed on a fingernail and looked around and sighed.
"This position is strong if we could but get them to attack us. We could
push them into the salient between the river and Peachtree Creek. Aye,
God, we could do that. So pray for an attack."

"Sir."

"I fear for my men."

"Sir."

"I am sorry that we were never able to finish our game of chess. I thought there might be a time when we could do so, but we officers are meeting constantly, and no one knows what shall happen next. But I wanted you to know how very much I have appreciated knowing you. We have shared many good words. You may be the only man in my command who can quote Shakespeare's sonnets with such a precise memory, or at all, for that matter. I have written to my Susan about you. She wishes to meet you after the war when we have married. Perhaps you will be able to attend our wedding."

"It would give me a great pleasure, General." Charlie felt an unspoken longing to confess to Cleburne, to speak of loss and sacrifice, to say how much he regretted this entire war. Winter camp in Dalton seemed a thousand years before, a moment lost in the mists of history. Cleburne crossed his arms and shook his head.

"Great battles are about, Mr. Merrill, and changes are in the air. I cannot speak of them, but I fear that we shall soon know the course of this war, and I pray that it shall not end as I fear."

Charlie said nothing. Cleburne's face turned into a sadness, and he shook his head. He continued. "I do pray it so fervently. When I was a boy and would walk along the River Bride in Ireland, I would dream myself into greatness. I believed that somehow I would become a great man, and I have failed, but I do not know what else we could have done. I do not know what else General Johnston could have done. No general ever cared as much for his boys." Charlie thought Cleburne was about to hug him. A wave of sentiment was passing between them.

"May I speak, sir?"

"Of course, Mr. Merrill. Of course."

"No one I ever knew was more kind to me than you have been. You have understood me and spoken with me and taught me more than I can repay. But somehow it is true that . . . I mean, I have in many ways . . ."

"Changed?" asked Cleburne. "Maybe the change in us happens without us seeing it, son. Perhaps it is of such a long duration that we do not see we have changed until long after."

"I don't know that I can ever get over what I have seen. I wish . . . I wish we had been able to finish the game of chess. I wasn't playing to win or lose. I just wanted to stay alive. Sometimes it looks like a clever attack, but I was just running away."

"So much death," said Cleburne, shaking his head. "We came from Ireland to remove ourselves from the starvation, and look what we have inherited on these shores. If I did not feel we were in the right, I do not think I could bear it. Now we are at the gates of Atlanta, and I cannot say where we shall go if we cannot hold this position." Cleburne seemed to realize he had gone too far in speaking so familiarly with a private. Charlie felt a crushing pressure in his breastbone, as if a stone lay upon him, immovable and edged with permanence.

"The men will always believe in you," said Charlie. "I have learned much from you, General. Much."

Cleburne laughed, and his gray eyes seemed almost merry. "If so, then you are welcome to it, for I cannot say myself what I have learned or taught anyone except to drill well, to hold discipline, to fight when one must. I cannot think what else I have taught any man."

"I will read your memoirs with great pleasure after all this is over," said Charlie. Cleburne's look of deep sadness returned, and Charlie understood for the first time: General Patrick Ronayne Cleburne knew that he would not survive this war, perhaps had known it all along. There might come a day when he would give *his* possessions away, mail the last letter to his beloved Susan Tarleton. She would hold tight his photograph, marry another, and legends would simmer through decades. Charlie looked down and fought against his sorrow.

"And I will read the books *you* shall write, Charlie," said Cleburne. Charlie felt a deep shock, for he could see a vocation stretching before him, one he had not considered before. He could write. He could be a journalist, and perhaps he might write a book. And yet the unmistakable message of death had not found him on the dawn of battle, and he did not feel marked by it. But he did not know if he could kill another man. He wanted to pray and weep and beg his own father to return in this life bearing smiles and homilies.

"General," said Charlie. An aide came for Cleburne, and Charlie backed away and saluted, and Cleburne returned it and walked off. Charlie had been gone for ten minutes before he realized this was the first time the General had spoken his Christian name.

✣ ✣ ✣

PRESIDENT JEFFERSON DAVIS SACKED General Joseph Johnston, commander of the Army of Tennessee, and replaced him with the dour and reckless Texan John Bell Hood. Men wept openly in the lines.

"I cain't believe they done took away our little General Johnston," said a private named Ricketts in Govan's brigade. He was a limping man who had been wounded in the cheek at Shiloh, and his face had a shriveled look as if he had been held underwater too long. "Our little General Johnston." The men knew Hood would not protect them; he would attack against impenetrable odds, move men into rows of death, sacrificing them for a salient without regret or hesitation. Charlie felt a shudder of disbelief that the commander of their army had been fired at the moment of their greatest peril.

"What in the name of bloody hell is our supposed president thinking, son?" asked Duncan McGregor. "No general ever cared for his men as much as General Johnston did. And to replace him with Hood *now*? All I can tell you is that a great blackness will rise from this city, and it will be the burning bones of Southern men."

"It doesn't matter anymore," said Charlie quietly. He sat staring at the hot red earth before him. "We are going to die anyway, and this city will be lost. The war has been lost for a year. People like Davis are trained in pretending that the impossible is real. They are children reading innocent books."

"You're speaking treason again," said Duncan. "Having come this far, it would at least be good of you to allow the Yankees to kill you rather than a firing squad of your own men."

There was no time for details of any kind, much less firing squads. With the heat withering their lines, the Confederates under Hood moved out into full battle near Peachtree Creek, but the fight was ill coordinated, slowed by dense underbrush, hesitant commanders, improper positions in the order of attack. Bate's division launched its attack and could not even find the Federal lines. Walker's division stormed the Federal works and suffered a killing repulse, and dozens died in their firing stances, blown into pieces by musketry and artillery, and still the Union army grew and spread out. Cleburne's men were in reserve, so Charlie aimed at nothing, firing over the Union lines, thinking of Cleburne and wondering when death would capture him, as he was sure now that it would.

✿ ✿ ✿

NOW, ON THE EARLY morning of July 21, with Charlie and Duncan side by side in their works near Decatur on the east side of Atlanta, the artillery opened with a violent noise, a ghastly drumming moan that seemed to roll like an ocean pouring over a cliff, bearing debris and stones with it, ten-ton boulders, whole continents. Charlie fired straight into the Union lines, had no idea whether his Enfield cartridges found their mark.

"We've got to back off this position or be overrun," a major was saying, then someone gave an order, and they were pulling away, and the Federals stormed to the crest of a bald hill, up which they pulled artillery and began to lob shells into the heart of Atlanta only a mile and a half away. In the city itself, the final remnants of the people, screaming, fled south as fires broke out.

Charlie held himself strong. All the men were exhausted from their night march, but they knew fatigue would mean a blooded death. They took new positions and began to bear down on the Union troops. Behind Cleburne's men were the scars of Atlanta's defense lines, a bristling series of redoubts spun with abatis and cheavaux-de-frise, but now they were of little use, and the fire of Sherman's army pinned them to the hot earth like botanic specimens on a board. Cascades of rifle fire raked the Confederate lines, and men collapsed or leaped backward in sprays of blood and bone, and a few were struck with solid shot from cannon and blown to pieces. A single shell killed seventeen of the eighteen men in one company. Troops moved out there, but Charlie could not see any order to the battle, only the smoke and stench of dead horses and men as the sun blasted higher over them, of men defecating in their filthy trousers, screaming and firing and sometimes just screaming.

Then Charlie could not even hear their screaming, the defiant Rebel yells mixed with wild-eyed shouts of fear and terror, and the battle seemed to move in stunned shapes. Duncan shouted something to him. But Charlie heard nothing, and he quit firing, did not even think of loading, and he held his ground and watched the slaughter with a slight disinterest and thought of Sarah.

Sarah. She came to him on the drifting smoke, arms outstretched, fingers slightly parted, and her lips were damp as dewy fruit, and her head was cocked, waiting for Charlie's reply to the most serious of questions. Charlie thought, *I am mad,* but he only watched as she floated now, and she was not impaled on the splashing lead, not disemboweled as a Georgia color-bearer just was moments before, his blood blasting gore on the red flag with its now dirtied crosses. She spoke one word over and over, and as she neared, he could see it was his name, and he reached for her. He would help her down before harm could sacrifice her to this war. He would be her savior. Then she was spreading her arms and was cruciform, and Charlie could see the stigmata in her palms and on the surfaces of her clean feet, and he was confused. *Are you the Christ?* Charlie asked. She spoke and he read her lips, and she said *Take this wound in remembrance of me,* and a sudden great knock rolled Charlie backward and into sleep.

"Boy, come around!" Duncan was slapping him when he awoke. Charlie shook his head and the sound of battle came back, but the roar was just less ferocious, and he felt the taste of pennies in his mouth, and he spat blood into the hot earth. Duncan was pouring water from his canteen on Charlie's face.

"What's happened?" asked Charlie. "Where is Sarah?"

"Sarah? Aye, God, son, you've gone to another world and come back," said Duncan. "We took a Napoleon ball in the line, and it killed five men outright and knocked you out, but you seem whole, praise God. Where does it hurt?"

"Praise God," said Charlie softly.

"We're in a bad position," said Duncan. "Drink this." Charlie took the sacrament of warm water, and it poured down his throat and revived him, and he wiped his face and looked around. The lines pounded each other with artillery and musketry, but no one seemed to move across the bloody field. The bald hill was not far away, and artillery officers poured shells into Atlanta at a brutal rate.

"We're going to die here," said Charlie. He looked at the sun and judged that late afternoon had come. There was the sound of hoofs in their sped rhythm now, drilling against the dirt, and they heard a great shout, as if a savior had entered Jerusalem. Just behind a few cavalry officers came hundreds of infantry now, Maney's whole division, which was being moved south of the bald hill, so that the Union troops could not leave it or stop their fire.

"Some general finally came to his senses," said Duncan. "I am not going to die here, and neither are you. Not this place. Are you all right in the bowels? Are you hit anywhere but from the concussion?"

"I don't think so," said Charlie. "My head hurts." He spat blood again, then spat once more, and the saliva was white and foamy.

"Then you are well enough, for a man whose head didn't hurt from this racket would be mad."

Charlie lay on the earth until his head cleared again, and he loaded his Enfield and fired once more toward the Yankees up the hill with the intention of missing all of them, and he was sure that he did.

AS DARKNESS ROLLED DOWN upon them, the rain came. A dense, drumming but brief thundershower, which fell in a small area only, blew among the troops, who almost wept with gratitude, and the firing slackened but did not stop entirely. Charlie's head now hurt far worse, and he wished for a morphine strip to chew, for a glass of laudanum, for any of the cures his mother had given him as a sickly boy, but he could only lie and feel the rain, and it was almost enough.

"I believe in God," said Charlie when the storm was blowing gales of rain beneath their caps and into their eyes. A miserable old horse had wandered into their line of fire an hour before and been shot to pieces, and its carcass bloated already, legs out stiff in death.

"You believe in God, sweet Jesus, so do I," asked Duncan. "This is a good time for you to be making such an admission to the Almighty if you understand my need, Charlie."

"I believe in my father," said Charlie blankly. "I have been in love like you were, Duncan. My love lasted no longer than yours."

Duncan looked at Charlie with profound sorrow and took off his cap and let the rain streak down his face, off the crown of his head, in runnels on either side of his nose.

"Then at least we've had a love, Charlie boy," asked Duncan. He looked out across the lines. "Sometimes I think I hear a higher calling in this world, Charlie, an order to things unseen. I think that I am about to understand the shape and function of this world, and I know then there's a truth behind the life we lead."

"Old stories seem true after a very long time," said Charlie. "I wonder, if I live, what I shall remember of Sarah and of this war? Everything is so terrible, Duncan. So terrible."

"No, no it isn't. Everything takes to peace in its own way, even war. If we could not believe there was an end to suffering, we could not bear the world, could we?"

"I am not sure I can bear more suffering," said Charlie. "In some pointless charge for a piece of land none of us even owns? I do not know what I believe."

"Believe in what we have shared," said Duncan, looking away. "Believe in walking alongside a good man for the greater part of your life.

There's worse ways to spend the balance of your days. I have grown quite fond of you."

Charlie wanted to be with Martha worse than anything in this world now, the only one left to whom he could be a brother, but there was only the plang and swish of firing, the occasional racking rumble of artillery.

SOME TIME AFTER DARK, the rain stopped, and the bright fire from cannon and rifle shots continued, and their yellow-orange sparks split the ink like massive fireflies.

"Moving out!" an officer cried, and there was a groan from the men, louder than the desultory fire, and they cursed and stamped, railed at Hood, gathered up in their companies or what was left of them, came to regiment and brigade. Cleburne's men, those of Maney, even Wheeler's cavalry, were posted for a wide sweep behind the Union lines to the east, then peeling back to attack them at dawn. Hardee's whole corps would enfold the Federals, and then the eastern half of Sherman's army could be annihilated in detail. Men in the lines knew nothing but marching, and they prepared, and Charlie could smell them, the stench of sweat and filthy clothes, and just beyond them, the dishonored dead, stray men who made useless leaps from their positions, shell-split mules, even one gutted black dog.

After an hour in the same position, a soldier Charlie could not see began to shout.

"Goddamn this war, and goddamn General Hood and goddamn Jefferson Davis, and goddamn General Sherman and goddamn the North and goddamn the South and goddamn the rain and goddamn the summer and just goddamn everything!" he screamed. Men laughed at him, and he threw his rifle down and told them to go to hell, and he walked off into the darkness.

"There's another patriot," said Charlie.

"Boy, you're beginning to annoy me," said Duncan McGregor, grinning.

They had not moved by ten o'clock, and an hour later they were still standing in ranks, the roads in the darkness clogged with moving wagons and artillery. Surely it was all going wrong again. They did not move until just after midnight on July 22, and then they marched all night in the swollen and fetid humidity of a Georgia midsummer night.

✿ ✿
✿

THE MEN BEGAN TO collapse around two-thirty, ragged and exhausted, cursing aloud, then falling. Some died where they sagged, wriggling into death as if it were a tight shirt. They moved slowly behind the congestion, mouths open to squeeze in a small amount of the heavy, sinking air. The humidity and heat seemed almost unbearable to Charlie, and he cataloged the ironies of it, that men who had been through such butchery for so many years could die from exhaustion like pack horses in the middle of the night with no objective seen, much less attacked.

"I'm about lost from air," said Duncan once, but he kept on marching, and there was no breeze, and the black outlines of trees spread beyond them, and they walked through forests and tripped in brambles, fell face-down in ripping briars. They seemed to swim through heavy woods, and the understory brushed them like catfish whiskers in a black river.

Bate's Division was somewhere far in front, and when dawn came, no one knew if they were in position or not. The men came to a halt, and not far away, Charlie saw General Cleburne and General Hardee mounted side by side and looking around sadly at the condition of men in Cleburne's and Maney's divisions. Some of the men wept with relief when they were ordered to fall out, and some collapsed, sleep coming before their bodies had properly met the earth. The others like Charlie and Duncan drew rations and ammunition and then dozed for an hour before they were ordered back into lines, and by now the groaning had stopped, for they were prepared to fight.

They trudged along in the breaking hot light. Charlie glanced at Duncan and saw what appeared to be a mild sheepish look spreading across his face. He was digging into his pockets for something, dug for a moment more, then brought forth a twisted and dirty envelope.

"Mail this for me if something—you know," said Duncan.

"Mail it yourself," said Charlie. He realized his voice was thick and dark, and he felt the madness coming back over him again.

"If I could have, I would have," said Duncan, now irritated. "And not able to do so, I ask that you do it for me."

"Why are you not able to do so?"

"You ask too many questions and have too many doubts for an educated boy," said Duncan. He thrust the letter into Charlie's hands. Charlie put the letter in his own pocket and said nothing and marched forward with the rest of Cleburne's troops.

✿ ✿ ✿

NOT LONG AFTER DAWN, the bombardment into Atlanta began once more, a clattery thundering that ripped the sky far and wide. Far ahead, Bate's troops stumbled into stinking mud and knee-deep water from a creek that Hood had supposed they might step across. Walker's troops suffered worse, finding their way blocked by an unmapped lagoon filled with dead trees, and officers wanted to have their local guides shot. Cleburne's troops crossed Flat Shoals Road and began to turn north, except for Govan's men, who stayed on the west side of the road as they went back up toward Decatur. The dawn attack never happened, and Charlie and Duncan like the rest of them fell through screaming briars and came back up with skids of blood along their sunburned arms.

Ten o'clock came, and then noon, but there was no Confederate assault until just after midday, and then it was far to the right of Cleburne's division. General Walker, looking through field glasses, was shot dead from his horse by a Union picket. Bate's men charged, but cannon fire turned their bodies red, and they ran back into the woods and then charged again and again, with fewer men each time. Wheeler's cavalry, meant to attack Federal wagon trains near Decatur, fared poorly as well. The coordinated plan of attack was falling to pieces, and couriers told General John Bell Hood of his plan's dissolution, and he received it with doubt and fury.

Just after two-thirty, when the news had not yet reached the Confederate lines that Union general James Birdseye McPherson had been shot dead by a Rebel skirmisher, word spread down Cleburne's men that their attack was imminent.

"I'm ready to die!" screamed an Arkansan, and those rough men spilled curses, shook rifles, trembled with the suppressed need to scream and run, to fire, to fall, to stumble upward, then fall again.

Charlie never heard an order to charge, but suddenly they were moving in the ghastly heat, and the minié balls whistled past, and the sickening sound of lead thudding into flesh, followed by the sharp exhalation from penetrated lungs, sang all around him. They crossed through brambles and across an open field, and Charlie saw that the Union men were dug in behind abatis and waiting, and when Govan's men got a hundred yards from the works, a single, bomb-loud explosion of musket fire ripped from the breastworks, and gray-clad chargers spilled down into the dirt, many motionless with death and some writhing as if burned by fire. Charlie knelt and fired into the works, and Duncan also, squinting and squeezing. They fell back through the lead stars, the swarm of lead balls, rank on rank, and many fell for-

ward, skidding head down into the steaming earth, into shallow puddles from the rain of a few hours before.

From here they fired all day, and some made reckless motions forward and were slain in biblical numbers or wounded so badly they
vomited blood and cried for death. One Confederate soldier two hundred yards away was bucking and screaming, and when he rotated
back, Charlie could see he was gut-shot more than once, and Charlie
felt an abiding pity for the man, a rush of clearheaded sympathy, and
he took calm aim and shot the man in the head. His skull snapped
back in a flame of blood. No one noticed, not even Duncan, firing at
his side. An aura of holiness descended on Charlie's shoulders, and he
thought: *God is entering me.*

God spilled into his arteries and veins and capillaries, through his
organs and muscle and bone, a lifting, and he saw before him stones of
light, mountains and hills, grave rocks and noble markers, and each one
was written in light, as if carved by the finger of Mercy and Grace, and
Charlie felt less like crying than ever before in his life. Stretched before
him was a life, a sacrifice, his shape on stained glass windows, but
mostly there were stones of light, and behind each stone was a living
memory, father or brother, mother, daughter, sacrificial friend, and
Charlie's face grew pale and strong, and he knew that he was different.
Thou art my beloved son in whom I am well pleased.

"We're moving!" cried Duncan, and Charlie saw that it was true.
They were moving at a double-quick march to the left, penetrating a
break in the Union lines, and the Federal skirmishers before the bald
hill broke and ran, and suddenly, impossibly, the lines bent back, and
the Confederates screamed and shot and stumbled forward in the
brightness of their exhaustion. They came past a huge three-story house
that had been shot into shards, and yet it stood, but the trees were
blasted, and the earth shook with ordnance. The Rebel lines shot forward until, suddenly, they stopped, and word came to fall back.

"*Fall back,* for the love of God?" cried Duncan in the din. "Now that
we have the advantage of the field? What madness is this?" Men
screamed with frustration and rage, but they fell back, and soon the Federals brought up four new brigades and twenty-eight cannon, and the advantage was lost. Enfilade fire began to rattle in upon Govan's lines, and
Charlie and Duncan held close to each other, not knowing which way to
fire. Charlie's face was blessed with light. A calm smile had etched itself
there.

"They're coming on!" someone cried. The Federals were charging now, and the field was fire and the field was blood. They battled on, and sunset came and still the firing was madness, and Govan's Brigade of Cleburne's Division of Hardee's Corps found itself before the bald hill once again, and there was nothing to do but charge it.

"Come on boys, for the love of country!" a major cried, waving his hat on his sword, and in their pain and exhaustion, they rose and ran up the hill and reached the rail barricade and fought hand to hand, and Charlie plunged his bayonet in the chest of a gray-bearded man who died without a grimace. Then they were falling back as the fire increased, and Duncan was by his side, clearly and terribly wounded, and the dead spread before them like flies on a dead cow, dead in their hundreds. Those left alive made it to a crust of woods and lay breathing raggedly.

Blood spilled down Duncan's neck in crimson runnels, and Charlie prayed, kneeling beneath the murderous flight of lead, that the convulsions and fear would end soon. The twelve-pounder Napoleons on both sides gnawed the air into tatters. Duncan blinked, coughed twice, spoke in bright red syllables. Charlie leaned close, heard nothing but Enfields and Springfields and artillery. He looked around helplessly for aid.

"Don't move!" Charlie screamed, but his own voice might have been the silence of graves. His fingers felt swollen from the heat. A drift of stench wormed its way across the field, horses and men, sweat, fear, gunpowder, blood, bone, excrement. Duncan's hair hung from his face in black curls. Minié balls displaced twin shrieks of air near Charlie's left ear. He felt the heave of tears, a shoving of the breastbone from inside, like a violent hand thrusting outward to catch or push.

The smell arrived and left, arrived once again with more urgency. The oven air swarmed with shot and the distant, then closer, crump of Napoleons and Parrott guns. Charlie knew he must stand and go for help, but the space above his kneeling form held a sea of fire, thousands of bullets, fused balls, shrapnel ripping through brambles, lifting earth upward in small spikes. So Charlie lay beside Duncan and held him and wept as one red claw rose from him, rose toward Charlie, touched him gently on the cheek, then fell on to the sweat-fouled shirt and held there motionless.

Men swarmed past him then, and one knelt over them and spoke, but the sound swam away in gunfire. Charlie rolled to his side and saw Duncan's eyes blink once, his tongue come out as if searching for water or speech. Then his eyes opened wider and stayed that way, dust already settling on the glazing eyeballs, and the tongue covered with the words of its own blood did not slide back. A small stream of blood spilled from the corner of his mouth and flowed just beneath his left ear, then down his neck.

"Don't move, Duncan," choked Charlie. He shook him gently, then with increasing urgency. "Don't move, damnit, don't you move, don't you move." The gray-coated men who had flowed past him were fleeing backward now, and one grabbed Charlie beneath his arm, pulled him up, screamed.

The air filled with angels. They were sentient, fair as young girls, with smooth skins and the song of morning. Charlie could not feel the ground with his feet, and he thought he might be drifting toward or away from something. Charlie felt fear release him. July knelt stunned with heat and noise. Broken bodies, bent into strange inhuman shapes, crowded around them. Down the blue line of Federal artillery, unbroken rows of men stood and fired, ripped ramrods out to reload, and the cannon spoke with a singular core of violence, a giant's roar, the prelude to earth's ending.

Charlie saw the world blue as water, green with renewal. Bushes brushed his shoelaces. He turned and saw that he was walking away, walking east, and he knew this was right. *This was how it should be.* He wondered where he was for only a moment, lifted by a great sense of exhilaration and buoyancy, by God.

Charlie stood back up in the middle of dying men. A motion went in all directions. Lines were gone, and the firing was beyond the edge of violence. An old bald man with a dripping beard stood next to him, then was blown in half by a shell. The upper half of his body crawled three feet before stopping. A lean and very tall man wearing a straw hat stopped and mumbled blood.

CHARLIE WALKED AWAY FROM the firing, swinging south and east, stumbling, praying, trembling for a while, sobbing more, thinking of God, of Duncan, hearing the cannon less distinctly and then the musket fire not at all, and still he walked forward, through forest and for a time on a small road, and not until it was very dark did he stop beside a small stream. He sat on a rock and tasted blood again, realized he'd been shot in the webbing beneath his left shoulder. The pain charged into him as he drank from the clear stream.

His hand shook as he pulled Sarah's letter from beneath Duncan

McGregor's coat, and he could feel blood upon it, knew the rain had blended letter on letter. But he did not need to see it. He knew the shape of each letter, every word:

Dear Charlie,

I write you with great sorrow from Savannah where I wait to board a ship for London. It was not my idea to leave with such urgency—this you must believe. I have wept the whole time, and now that an ocean will separate us, I can only hope Death will come for me soon.

It is not enough for me to say that I love you, dear Charlie. You are the star of my life, the only true joy I have ever known. I had no sister or brother as a child. When I was sent to Branton, I felt the most perfect hopelessness that it is possible to know. My uncle and his stupid Specific shamed me, and his loud ways were no better than what I heard in Boston.

I very nearly believe that I dreamed myself into your arms. I was alone and full of sorrow, and I asked God for a boy to take me as his own. At first, I asked God what He could mean—you were frail and ill and secretive with but one dear friend of your own. I loathed Branton, but then I did not mind it so much when God sent you to me.

This war is a kind of madness, as you told me. My father says that he shall not return to America because it holds war and my mother. I might have hoped he was leaving on some principle—abolition, unity—but in fact he left for convenience, and my uncle is sending me away for the same reason.

I wept when I was told. I said that I had to get to your house to tell you goodbye. Uncle said I'd spent entirely too much time with you already, much, he supposed, to my detriment. But, Charlie, it was not to my detriment. Even that moment when we committed such sin, I felt a light in my soul that could not have been condemnation. I cannot believe a just God would deny happiness to those such as us who are alone and broken in the world. If it was wrong, then I shall admit such when I stand before God.

I shall try to write you when nature manifests itself, but each day I cradle the thoughts tenderly, and I weep as I see your face before me. The only salve I have is that I met you at all. Perhaps it has been ordained that we meet and part, and that only in death will we be joined again. I will never forget the joy I found with you or the peace I saw in your eyes when we loved. My heart will ever be yours.

Now I must post this in haste for they are calling me to the ship, and I cannot know what will happen next. But as I sail, I will love you, and some day I will come back, and we will share that love God intended for us.

All my love,
Your Sarah

Charlie closed his eyes and listened to the frogs and cicadas, and he dreamed himself at the very portals of heaven, where the sunset crowned him like the golden-edged pages of a great book.

July 23–September 1, 1864

IN THE RAINLIGHT, CHARLIE'S eyelashes held beads of water. The brief shower was moving east, and he groaned awake on a stone and felt as if his bones were shod in ice. The wound under his arm oozed blood, and his head throbbed. He was in a glen, and water ran near him in a muddy trickle. He sat up, and he knew that the thunder he heard was shelling in Atlanta, some miles away now. He had quit the war, and Branton was to the northeast, perhaps fifty miles through forests and brambles. He stood and fell to his knees like a wax man, prone to melting as the sun rose.

He wanted to sip from the muddy stream, but it smelled foul with alkali or death, and so he found a dead limb of his own height and used it to pole himself along a pine-needled forest floor. He tried to untangle the battle of the day before, then he knew that Duncan McGregor was dead and that he had given Charlie a letter for safekeeping. He took out Sarah's letter, hand trembling, and it was a clotted mess, his blood shed, the sheet now brittle and almost illegible.

He hoped for a house, but none appeared, then he hoped for a road, but he walked for an hour and crossed none. He reckoned east easily enough, and with each step the shelling in Atlanta grew fainter. He stopped to spit blood in a clearing. He inhaled the terrible aroma of a dead mule, almost stepped upon it, lost and carrion now. Perhaps it had given up the war, too, wounded, and had wandered into these woods for a quiet death. That was the least God owed a man, the grace of a quiet death in his own bed. Charlie skirted wide and felt his head woozy, and his mouth was so dry that he wondered if he could bear it, and he thought he could, then he was sure he could not.

When he awoke again, late afternoon cast huge shadows from the trees, and Charlie got to his knees and coughed, wracked and trembling, a long bead of pink saliva hanging between his lips and the heated soil. He sat back and tried to clear his head. He uttered prayers, pulling himself up, and then he lurched forward unsteadily, robbed of balance and losing blood. There was a brief meadow, and above it, a red-tailed hawk rolled on the open air, seeking small movements in the broom sedge. The heat on his back grew intense as he came across the field, which glinted with flecks of mica and crystalline quartz. Into the shade of pines, he gasped, and blood trickled down his armpit and into his trousers, which were becoming stiff.

The stream was a breath-breaking surprise, a small rivulet running strong and clear over tumbled rocks, and Charlie thanked God and fell down to his knees and then his chest, and he drank long and deep, his throat moving with the flow of cool liquid. He was breathing very hard now, and he slept, and when he awoke it was nearly dark, and he was hungry, and a silent owl came gliding through the undercanopy, wings spread to catch the damp air.

Clouds blew against the last palette of rose sunset. A *mackerel* sky, he thought. He remembered God, the Old Testament shock of His revealed presence, and a burden broke from his shoulders, and he tried to pray, and at first it was no good. He shaped words in Elizabethan English, backed away from them. Charlie asked his father for the words, but none came, and so he did not pray but thought of peace and love, considered the balm of silence. He wondered if he would die this night, and he decided that he would not. All night he dreamed of Branton, and he walked through the mansions of the rich, but nobody was home, and each door he opened revealed splendor, oak sideboards with ornate carvings, baroque tea sets in brilliant silver, great gilt-framed portraits, but there were no people there, not in any house, not in any room.

He awoke just at dawn, and it was still very hot, and he drank again and felt as if he must find help or he would die. Soon the battlefield vultures, straying east, might spot his struggle and come to wait, patiently circling in a small company of black wings, angled in, eyes down.

Charlie stepped from the forest into a clearing, and a log house seemed to grow upon it, spreading downward, a bright strip of creek-lace foaming past it through a broad V of small gray stones. An old man wearing long white whiskers stood before a fire looking at him. A black iron kettle boiled up meat, and to one side a dog was humped and barking, but Charlie could hear nothing, and then he spoke, and his voice made no sound either. The man looked at him with slight surprise, and he brought his left hand to his mouth as if perplexed and deciding what he must do next. Charlie tried to speak, but there was a searing pain in his shoulder, and he broke down to his knees and then he fell over and begged the man with his arms and with his eyes. The man came over, and he knelt and cradled the boy, and Charlie could not believe the kindness in his eyes, the light that seemed to flow from them.

"I'm shot," said Charlie, but he heard nothing, and he was in the old man's arms, and there was a rocking motion, and then Charlie let himself go. The dog lapped at his face as he slid downward into a sleep without stories to guide him through it.

CHARLIE BLINKED THE LIGHT twice and realized he was on a bed with cotton ticking, covered by clean-smelling sheets. He wore a plaster that spread across his chest and beneath his arm. A quiet wind waved a pair of thin white curtains into the small room. He lay still for a very long time in his weakness and was drifting back into sleep when an old woman came into the room. She moved with a fluid grace and sat on the edge of the bed and placed her hand on his forehead and held it there for a time.

"You've a wound but it don't bear a bullet," she said. "I bathed you and put you in a bedgown and placed you down, and there's no shame in it. I raised three boys myself and I know of such necessities."

"Thank you, ma'am," said Charlie hoarsely.

"Was you shot over to Atlanta?"

"Yes, ma'am."

"Still shooting at one another all the livelong day over there," she said, shaking her head. Charlie saw that she was very beautiful or had been in her youth. She wore kindness in her eyes. "It's God's hope you walked this far from it, son. God's hope. For I don't have no truck with wars, and all three of my sons is gone these years, and I've not heard a word in that time. We figure them dead for a long time past."

"I'm sorry," said Charlie.

"We have the fruits of our garden," she said. "Praise God for the seeds, for we ain't had so much as a chicken these last eight months. My man's kilt a rabbit betimes, but it seems they ain't holding with us no more, neither. Everthing's gone away from the sound of it all. We'd leave, but we don't got no place to go."

"No, ma'am."

"You hungry?"

"I could eat a little something."

"Can you be up and about? The chamber pot's beneath the bed. There's no shame in it. Do what business you will. I will look after you until you can tramp back to your army."

"I'm not going back to the army," said Charlie. The woman's green eyes held him for a long time, narrowing with assent. She nodded.

"I'd wish that for you, son. I'd wish it. We will have you with us until health. Be assured of it. We will have you with us until health." Then she leaned down, and she kissed him on the forehead, and he watched her float from the room, and he divined a plain kindness but deep loss behind her affections. He tried to move and the wound pained him, and his head still hurt from its blows. The long muscles felt knotted and spun messages of sore pain, but he managed to sit on the edge of the bed, dizzy and warm. The plaster held to him by an intricate wrapping of thin old cloth. The room was very plain, with no adornments on the wall. A rough nightstand squatted by the open window, and through it, past the greetings of curtain cloth, he saw the old man splitting wood with slow precision, wasting no movement, each compact motion designed to fracture dead wood along its most favorable grain.

For the first time in months, Charlie put his hands beneath his chin and prayed in a faint whisper.

"Dear God, I present unto you the soul of Duncan McGregor, who was a good and kind man, whose losses were great and whose love was strong. I rejoice that he has come to you, though it breaks me to know this sacrifice. It is the third time I have lost a true brother, and I do not know if I could bear it again. There are many things I do not know that I could bear again. Take him into your kingdom and love him for eternity and grant him rest and grant him peace in his heart. And take care of Mama and Martha and all of my relatives. And dear God bring Sarah home to me. Amen."

He should not have said the last part, but perhaps it did no harm.

After a time, when he was back in bed, the woman, whose name was Emma Bondurant, brought him a plate of fried potatoes, rough bread, tomatoes, and boiled greens, and Charlie ate them with more hunger than he had imagined. She sat beside him in a straight, homemade chair and stood at times to wipe his mouth or brush back his hair. The old man, Thomas, clomped into the room as he was finishing, sweating into his white beard and looking pale and parchmentlike, though still strong.

"I see you've eat like a man," he said. "You couldn't find no better one to help than my Emma. She don't accept a sorrow. And a sorrow will not bind a man unless he accept it."

"I'm Charlie Merrill," he said to them both. "From Branton, up on the Georgia Railroad."

The old man came over and put his hand upon his wife's shoulder, and she reached back and touched it gently and then let her hand drop to her lap.

"Charlie was the name of our eldest boy," she said. She did not accept the sorrow she felt, and Charlie was more touched than he wished to show. "A stout boy of fine manners and a strong heart. What do your father do? Farm?"

"He was a Baptist minister, but he died a few years back," said Charlie. "My mother and sister live there now. I lost a brother to the war in Virginia."

She rose and went to the window and looked out as if she were expecting a visitor, holding the curtain back from its breeze.

"Oh, God, save us from this war," she said, her voice quavery with emotion. "It's done kilt us all. I'll have none of it." She turned and looked square at Charlie. "Not meaning no disrespect to your army, Charlie, but I'll have none of it."

"I'll have none of it, either," said Charlie. "Not now. Not anymore."

"We ain't gone speak of it no more," said Thomas Bondurant. "I'm aiming to boil sheets, mother. The fire's about up to it, I reckon."

"Yes," she said. She came and took the clean plate away from Charlie. "Can you sleep now?"

"I need to rest. Thank you for this. Both of you."

"There's no need to thank one for a kindness done. It's God's demand, and we accept it with pleasure. I will poultice that again afore night. Sleep now."

Charlie lay back and felt a rush of fear, and he wondered what was happening with Govan's Brigade of Cleburne's Division of Hardee's Corps of the Army of Tennessee, General John Bell Hood commanding. Charlie thought: *I was a soldier too long and have killed too many men, and now I want to run from that desperate horror. I cannot see it again without losing what little is left of my soul. God forgive me for what I have done. God forgive me.*

A WEEK PASSED, AND Charlie was up and around, hobbling in the yard, sitting for long spells in hard front-porch chairs and looking over the small yard tucked among the woods. A single-lane wagon road went north, but he did not ask where it led. The shelling of Atlanta continued, so Charlie knew the Confederates held out behind their chevaux-de-frise and abatis, but it could not go on forever. He had already decided to quit the war and walk home, but he was much too weak for it yet.

One night, as a thundershower cooled the dense air, he sat with the Bondurants at their modest table, and as he looked at them, he felt a deep sense of grief and dishonor. He stared out the window at the strands of rain. Life was too hard, and the fight was very grave, and he wanted a reason, a message.

"Boy, have you lost your appetite?" asked Emma.

"I was thinking."

"What was you thinking about?"

"About my friends and my father and my brother, and about what it all means."

"Meanings ain't in things," said Thomas. "They just is. Meaning is what we carve on them. If them Yankees come here, we will just up and go east. There's no help for the shape of this world. If a dog is throwed at, he runs. That's all meaning is."

"I want to know why I was sick all the time when I was young," said Charlie. "I want to know why I went to the war and found myself in the middle of Chickamauga and then came all the way to Atlanta and saw my best friend killed. I want to know why my friend Jack had to die as a boy or my brother Tom had to die in Virginia. Why did all that happen to me? Was that supposed to make me a better person? Why?"

"Eat up," said Emma.

"There was a girl," said Charlie. "And she went away. She's gone to England and I'll never see her again. What kind of terrible thing have I done to have this happen?"

"I don't believe in none of that original sin," said Thomas, now looking with a distant thoughtfulness at the rain. "I had me three fine boys out of my woman, and now they all gone into the ground like mules. I don't even know where they died. It was like they took a step and went oft the face of the earth. And I don't search for no message in it, but bad luck's found us even here in this country where we've lived to offend no man. Neither white nor colored have we held quarrel with. We hid here among the pine trees, and yet it sought us out. A man can't hide from happenings. And there ain't no meaning to it. That's all I want to say on it."

"Thomas," said Emma softly. She reached for him, and without looking at her, he reached back, took her hand, and he concentrated with fierce determination, and Charlie knew that the world *did* hold meaning, and that some of it was terrible and was endless.

ANOTHER WEEK WITH THE Bondurants, and he dressed to walk, cut a stout hickory stick, and carried food and a jar of water from Emma Bondurant.

"The Lord be with you and me, while we are absent, one from another," said Thomas Bondurant. He turned and went into the yard and split wood.

"I don't know how to thank you folks," said Charlie.

"Ain't no need," she said. "We will keep you in our prayers."

"And you will be in mine," said Charlie. Unexpectedly, the small woman came to him and hugged him fiercely, held him for a long time, and through his freshly washed shirt, Charlie could feel her chest rising and falling.

He walked east as he took it, through a wide field of a few spindly cattle and sun-struck birds that sang in folded wings. The world had changed him. He remembered telling Sarah that he didn't think about slavery. Now he knew well enough that it was evil, and that someone, in the end, is accountable for all evil. Charlie carried no gun and only a good hunting knife Thomas had pressed upon him. Duncan's coat was very warm, but Emma had cleaned it, and now he strode away from war still in gray and sure he would strike a road soon. What would his story be? Deserters could be shot, though so many were against the war in these parts he was not concerned. He was also just seventeen, barely the age of conscription, and after shaving and after Emma trimmed his hair, he looked that age or younger.

He poled through pinewoods with the hickory walking stick, and checked his pocket at times for Duncan's letter and for Sarah's, and their dry crinkle assured him of words. After a time, he came to a single-lane wagon road that angled northeast, and he walked along it for a mile before the sound of hoof-drumming arose behind him, and he ran off the road into a copse of red cedars and watched a detachment of Union cavalry pulse past at a gallop, probably seventy of them, heading north.

CHARLIE SAT IN THE darkness, listening to the wild cries of cicadas and tree frogs. He leaned against the trunk of a tulip poplar and tried to dream himself back to the Branton Baptist Church and into the hard smooth pews before his father's sermon. He could almost see his father's sweating joy, the bright eyes, the certainty before faith failed. What was his father saying? He was speaking from Psalms: *O Lord God of my salvation, I have cried day and night before thee. Let my prayer come before thee. Incline thine ear unto my cry. For my soul is full of troubles and my life draweth nigh unto the grave.*

No, that was not the one he wished to recall. Perhaps it was the Twenty-Third Psalm, but Charlie could see that one whole, and it was one different. Yes—the very next one in his tattered Bible: *Who shall ascend into the hill of the Lord? Or who shall stand in his holy place? He that hath clean hands, and a pure heart, who hath not lifted up his soul unto vanity nor sworn deceitfully. He shall receive the blessing from the Lord and righteousness from the God of his salvation. . . . Lift up your heads, O ye gates and be ye lift up, ye everlasting doors and the King of glory shall come in.*

Charlie Merrill put his face in his hands and wept softly for a long time before sleep came over him.

THE NEXT DAY AN old man hobbled by sickness gave him a potato and an ear of corn, and Charlie ate them as he walked. He stayed near the road going north but not on it, and though a few wagons came past, he saw no more soldiers from either side. He came to a small community of white clapboard houses, and there were three stores and a church whose paint had faded into long curling strips, as if caterpillars walked down its sides.

He came on into the street and stood before the general store, in front of which a dozen horses were tied near an empty water trough. Charlie walked to the horses, which nickered and stamped, and he looked at the saddles, and they had bold letters on them, U.S. Charlie backed away as the jangle of spurred boots came from inside, and half a dozen Union soldiers stood before him. They looked at each other for a moment.

"I'm a son of a bitch," said one of the Federals.

"Catch that bastard," said another.

Charlie dropped his walking stick and ran, and as his arms pumped, he felt the wound beneath his shoulder begin to leak blood down his side. He ran behind a house where a black stallion swished his tail at flies and tried to reach a green apple too high on a tree. Men came now. He could hear them running, but their boots and spurs would make catching him hard, then he could hear horses, so he fled into the woods.

"Yonder he goes!" cried one of the soldiers. An unexpected swiftness buoyed Charlie as he leaped a gully and fled into the deep woods, where trees held close together and no man could guide a horse. He crossed a creek and fell, scrambled up, smelled rain in the air. At least one was still coming for him, but Charlie did not look back until the man was so close Charlie had to pull out the hunting knife and turn to face him. The man was wheezing foam and had no rifle or pistol. He leaned against a tree and coughed, then spat. He did not even appear to have a knife.

"Don't cut me," he said. "I just ran because everybody else did. I didn't know I could run this far." He began to laugh. Charlie waved the knife at him and gasped for breath.

"I'm going home," said Charlie. "I don't want to fight anymore."

"Nobody does," the man said. He was no more than twenty-five, Charlie guessed, black-bearded and of no high rank. "I don't. I want to go home to Ohio." Charlie listened intently but heard no more men coming.

"Ohio?"

"We got bottom land. I want to go home. You go home."

"I will. I don't want a fight."

"Then let not winter's ragged hand deface in thee thy summer, ere thou be distilled," said the soldier.

"Sonnet six," said Charlie. "Shakespeare."

"I didn't even think you Rebels could read."

"I didn't think you all could feel."

"You better go on, now." The soldier held his side and wheezed, opening and closing his eyes. "I'll head back and tell them of the great fight we had and how I managed to whang you in the head with a limber stick. You can tell everybody in your town how you cut me with a great sweep of your knife. Go on."

"Obliged."

"I was David Draper. You remember that."

"Was?"

"I won't make it home," he said. "I never was going to make it home. I knew it from the first." He coughed and spat, and turned and stumbled through the woods, and Charlie ran forward, and he felt light in his feet, and he did not mind the blood that dripped down, for it was small and reminded him that he was yet alive.

TWO DAYS PASSED, THEN three, and Charlie saw no more soldiers, and kindly solitary women and bent and whey-faced men gave him small meals and aimed him toward Branton. He cut a new walking stick of sourwood from the edge of a bold stream, and he felt the strength passing back into his arms and legs as he saw the familiar land rolling beneath his stride.

He knew he was in Branton County now, and familiar landmarks built themselves almost holy in his sight. Why had he run away to the war? He wanted his mother's arms now, wished to kiss Martha's smooth cheek, to sleep under the sanctity of their roof. He tried to remember this road or that frame house, and finally he came to the railroad and knew all he had to do was walk it until sunrise.

With day only an hour above the horizon, he walked in the peach-colored light, heard the coughing crows and even a mockingbird, which seemed satisfied with each brilliant sweep of song it brought from necessity into creation. A black boy a hundred yards away sagged back and forth on the sweating flanks of a half-spavined mule, heading somewhere but very slowly. He saw a woman in a bonnet hoeing weeds from three rows of bushy beans. The bonnet was faded blue, and it was unstrung and the harness dangled on her chest. A dog ran back and forth, as if smelling or hearing him, and Charlie gauged that it must be blind or nearly deaf or both. For long stretches of the railroad, there was nothing but close-in forest and snaky thicket. He stopped to look for blackberries, but they had long since passed, and their canes bore only thorns.

For the first time in months, he considered what awaited him in Branton. His mother and sister, surely. God would not have submitted them to a terrible wrath as he had Charlie's father and brother. His wound had grown crisp with scar tissue, and even that had begun to fall away, and beneath it the open wound had disappeared into a dimple of broken flesh.

He walked onward through the forests, through the nights and the days.

A HUNDRED YARDS FROM his mother's modest house, he saw Martha standing in the side yard. She whipped dust with her skipping rope and counted aloud, looking down with delight at the speed of her feet. She glanced up grinning, and when she saw Charlie coming toward her, his face white with happiness, she tripped and dropped the rope, leaned forward, seeing the ghost in its gray coat step toward her, bearing a heavy walking staff and a glance of calm assurance.

"Sweet Jesus God in Heaven," she said, and she placed her right hand on her heart and pushed there involuntarily three times, as if to still her emotions.

"Martha, it's me," said Charlie. "I've come home."

"It can't be," said Martha. "Oh, sweet Jesus, God in Heaven, it can't be." Her arms went loose at her sides. She wept and trembled and shook her head, as if trying to dislodge the specter, but it was real, and it kept coming toward her.

"I'm home," said Charlie Merrill.

She ran to him and clung, crying and shivering, and he held her. The day was cloudless and hot, and he could smell the sure aroma of peaches in the air, cooking for pies or jelly. The smell was rich and familiar, and he kissed his sister on both cheeks and held her back to see her. She had grown considerably, but her eyes were bright with tears, and she spoke, but her words were indistinct. She was trying to say something, then she did.

"Mama," she said, as if calling, but the words was a veiled whisper.

Charlie saw the shadow at the corner of the house, moving into the sun, shading its eyes, standing back, and then coming forth. She was thin and small and had been wiping her hands on the saffron-yellow apron, which she bore aloft now before her. Her hair had shaded gray, and she had it piled above in a bun pierced through its center with a long shell pin. Pale scalloped clouds drifted on a hot wind, going nowhere, he reckoned. A young black man in a spring-shot wagon came past.

"Charlie?" she whispered.

"It's Charlie, he's home," said Martha, but the words rushed out like something from a foreign phrase book, vowels and consonants compacted. Betsy came slowly across the yard, then faster, and she was running, and he dropped the walking stick and took only two steps forward before she reached him, swept him up in the comfort of her tears. He would later remember this love, the surprise at having outlived the slaughter, questions of hunger and comfort, the touching once, then twice, to see if he were real.

I THOUGHT I'D NEVER see you again," Betsy said a few days later as they sat in the front parlor. Charlie had been telling her stories. "They say Atlanta is still holding out but that it is a matter of time before she falls. I cannot believe after all this suffering that we shall have lost the war."

"It isn't lost yet, Mama. But it's going to be lost, I fear. They have more of everything than we do. And I'm weary of it, weary to hoping it just ends."

"I hope we do lose," she said bitterly. "This war has taken my husband and my eldest son, and the husbands and sons of so many here." She told him of the Union cavalry raid on the town a few days back, during which a visitor from New Orleans had been shot and killed. "The minister of your Papa's church from Charleston had just said aloud on the courthouse square that there were no Yankees within fifty miles of Branton, and that he'd eat any within ten miles. Just then five horsemen in blue came dashing around the courthouse chasing one of our soldiers on his old swaybacked gelding."

"But they left again?"

"They did. They set the depot on fire with cotton bales and robbed some of the homes. They robbed the communion silver from Grace House. But then they were gone. Yankees on the streets of Branton. If your father had been alive still, he would have welcomed them with the Stars and Stripes. Mr. Curtis on the Athens Road has flown that flag during the entire war. Sentiment here against it grows, but we are still part of things we cannot change."

"What about Doc Sawyer Pierce?" asked Charlie, looking down at his hands. He sat in a ladder-back rocker and made small motions forward then back. Betsy smiled sweetly at Charlie.

"Gone, too," she said. "Moved out west. Did you ever get any more letters from Sarah?"

"None," said Charlie. "I wish I knew what happened to her."

"I know you do. So do I. We must be grateful for what we have and endure what we have lost. One morning, we will all awaken in heaven to the footsteps of those we loved and who loved us. We cannot live if we don't believe it. I cannot live if I don't believe it."

Charlie was no longer sure in what he believed, but it was not in this war.

HE WAS DOWNTOWN IN early September, driving a wagon to which he'd tied the family's old carriage horse, Liza, dickering to buy some corn-meal and lard. A rider hastened into town and dismounted, shouting, and a crowd clotted around him, and the old men turned away bearing fists. One woman in a bonnet laundered white pressed the fingertips of both hands to her mouth.

"What's happened?" asked Charlie. Robert Butler, a tall, thin man with a gray beard so long it waved in the breeze, walked on the stilts of his thin legs, then stopped.

"Atlanta's fell to the Yankees," he said. "It's gone. Sherman's in Atlanta."

"Then the war will be over," said Charlie.

No one in Branton had thought the less of Charlie for coming home from the war because of his age and wounds. The local conscription office had closed, and he was comforted by women and blessed by men for his service to the South. The word of his friendship with General Cleburne had spread, and a few would ask of the Irishman and his stories, his demeanor.

"I'd say that's a certain truth," said Butler. "I'd of give all my life for it not to have happened a-tall. I'd of give all my life to have them boys back, North and South. To have done this slaughter is a blot." He sternly shuddered. He looked away. "It is a blot that we cannot unspill. God is my witness for this."

Charlie walked slowly home, past Grace House, and he tried to dream himself back to its storied joists and rafters, to the sound of Sarah's footsteps on the stairs, but he was here and now, and all was breaking or broken, and there was nothing to do but go on. He walked for a long time on the tracks of the Georgia Railroad before heading home.

July 22, 1914

⁂

NO ONE HAD ENTERED the ballroom on the third floor of Grace House since the death of Charlie's wife, for it had been her sanctuary and aerie. A walled-off attic space had been added at one end two decades before. Charlie had risen slowly up the stairs and now stood in the ballroom and saw the sewing machine, dress forms, half-filled scrapbooks, stacks of photographs, clothes trunks, dusty bolts of fabric. The heat was oppressive, but Charlie did not notice or think of it.

"Amy," Charlie whispered. "Amy." He remembered how he first realized he cared for her as he stood outside the office of the *Branton Eagle* after the war. He watched as she and her father, Burton Chandler, walked slowly down the sidewalk, arm in arm, heading toward him. They had clearly eaten, since Mr. Chandler's big-bellied swagger showed an obvious lack of urgency. He was a short man who radiated success, through insurance, land holdings, and Branton's largest livery stable. Amy was his oldest daughter, having just turned nineteen, and she walked with an easy grace, secure in the shape of her stride. She and Charlie spoke often at church, more often at town picnics and even government meetings, since her father was a councilman. She always seemed to be finding Charlie by accident, though he had long since lost his belief that anything in the world happened that way. Burton Chandler was giving a speech to his daughter, the kind that makes grown children cringe, looking down as they walked, gesturing with his free arm. Charlie waited. A softness erased the light from the sky.

"Ah, Charlie Merrill, our increasingly famous newsman," said Mr. Chandler, gesturing with his free hand.

"Mr. Chandler, Amy," said Charlie, bowing slightly. As they neared, he saw Amy's eyes fixed upon him, pale green and intense, a slight smile, curled brown hair that held to her shoulders with an ornamental insistence. "Pleasant evening, isn't it?"

"Pleasant, indeed," said Mr. Chandler, tsking. "Yes, our Charlie is an intelligent man, my dear. And knowledge of our own land is power. Did you know that, Charlie? What you do is not the sharing of information but the sharing of power. The man who *knows* all may *own* all."

"Oh, Father," said Amy.

"I prefer to think that the *Eagle* is a literary vehicle," said Charlie, grinning. "There's a vanity that must be served in yours truly." He bowed.

"Oh, Charlie," said Amy.

"See, she slays both of us!" said Mr. Chandler, looking with mock surprise at his daughter. "But I take your point, Charlie. Each man approaches the world for different reasons. I am amazed always that some men have no interest in wealth and power."

"And I am amazed that some men have no interest in love and art," said Charlie. He was clearly relishing the duel by now.

"Ah, love and art," said Mr. Chandler. "There are subjects fit only for a woman. Be that as it may, our town takes pride in your success, Charlie, and I can only say, as I must on this fine evening—well done!"

The entire conversation seemed to Charlie like an elaborate hoax, or perhaps a ritualized Punch-and-Judy show. Mr. Chandler with his pot-bellied fatuousness was not truly praising him at all. He was congratulating himself on living in a cultured small town that had survived the dark times of the war.

"Thank you, sir," said Charlie. As they resumed their stroll and passed, Amy reached for Charlie's sleeve, touched it gently, looked into his eyes. Her glance was deep with intent, and Charlie felt buoyant and alive to the possibilities.

Now, alone in the home of his old age, Charlie's voice was dry and hoarse, and he was unsure whether he could go through with the speech at Ezra Atkinson Park after all. Oh, dearest Amy. Gentle, kind, thoughtful, she moved through life like a swimmer through calm waters. Their girls, Catherine and Martha Jane, were a father's pride and a mother's grace. Martha Jane and her husband Terrence Jacobson lived far away in Maine, where Terrence owned vast tracts of timber and was vice president of a railroad. He was a shy man, with a refined temperament. Charlie had not seen Martha Jane since her mother died two years past, but she wrote once a week, letters full of love and joy and stories of her four sons, all of whom were growing toward adulthood with the rowdy enthusiasm of Maine woodsmen. Catherine called her "my Yankee sister" without a hint of irony. At least Charlie had two grandchildren in Branton, Marianne and Lewis, and they visited often, and he would speak family histories, stories of hilarious aunts and dull uncles, of Branton's origins in Indian days, of their grandfather's sermons. At the cusp of her final illness, before she had yet told Charlie of her pain, they had been up here one evening dancing alone to a gramophone record. Branton had been wired for electricity in 1892, but sometimes they would light the candles in three quintuple sconces and step to the flickering of a faded past.

"Did you have anyone before me? A boyfriend?" asked Charlie. Amy had giggled and looked up at him.

"Of course. Everyone has someone before someone else. But he was just a boy. I don't think it's salutary to speak of old loves. Besides, we did no more than hold hands. He was awkward and pomaded with a part like a hatchet-mark." Charlie laughed out loud. Amy could do that.

"Who?"

"David Muntz, I'm afraid." He was a squat man with a foul temper and a belief the world had isolated him from all others to be cheated. "I heard stories about you and a Yankee girl. I never asked you about it."

Charlie stopped dancing, and a clouded, distant look passed over his face. Amy cocked her head slightly as if to urge him to say more.

"There's nothing to tell," said Charlie, thinking, *Liar, there is everything to tell.* He had never stopped thinking of Sarah or wondering of her life and where it had taken her. Perhaps she was stout and gouty or long dead from disease or mischance, but she also might be lovely and strong and thinking, in her quiet hours, of Charlie. "She was the niece of a man who sold an alcoholic specific for old women. Her name was Sarah Pierce. Her Uncle Sawyer Pierce and his wife lived here, but they moved out west during the war. Sarah's parents were getting divorced in Boston, and she moved to England to be with her father. End of story."

"That doesn't even sound like a beginning," said Amy. "What was she like?"

"Ugly," said Charlie. "I was an invalid, and she was ugly and she came and read to me. It wasn't pretty." Amy smiled, knowing he was lying and not caring. They danced again, and for a while she stepped lightly, but then she brought forth a groan and doubled down her thin torso, then rose with sweat dappling her upper lip, and that was the first time Charlie knew something was wrong. Lasting love was not the residue left when hatred had been banished; it was stronger and deeper, infrequent and impenetrable.

He walked across the ballroom now, thinking of the fiddle dances that must have been held here in the magnificence of the 1840s, the women in their long dresses, curled tresses bouncing along their shoulders, dreaming of husbands and endless lives, seasons turning, Christmases and children, a natural order of word and action. Charlie sat in a chair, and he knew that it was hot, but he was barely perspiring.

All afternoon he had been thinking of sacrifice, but perhaps that was wrong. Others had sacrificed for him but who received his own sacrifice? In those three weeks of rain before Kennesaw Mountain, he had sacrificed nothing but a Whitworth rifle and the health of his head from several bashings. Was love earned, or did it just arrive like a letter, full of sweet confusion and delight? Charlie thought of the thousands of men and boys who had died on the Atlanta campaign and the dozens he had shot coldly, as if picking off cans in the backyard. He knew that the casualties on the Atlanta campaign were heavy but not as bad as the slaughters at Sharpsburg, Gettysburg, Cold Harbor, and Petersburg. Those passions seemed intractable then, and they seemed quaint now. Was love the same?

He walked across the ballroom and came to the attic door, and opened it and went inside. Ghosts filled the oppressive air. There, where he knew it was: the coat of a Confederate private on a hanger and dangling by a stretched wire. He knew that it was Duncan McGregor's coat, and he thought of Duncan and his sacrifice. Charlie's third novel had been about Duncan, though he'd called him Thomas Conwell. The misters Biggs, Varnell, and Felden were supposedly wearing their coats in this heat to Ezra Atkinson Park, but Charlie would not. He walked at a limp slowly into the attic and touched the coat, and it trembled on its wire, turning shoulder to shoulder in the hot quiet light from twin dormer windows.

"Duncan," said Charlie. "A proud Scotsman."

Then, unbidden, Atlanta itself rose before Charlie in its hideous cannonading and musketry, the fires and screaming, troops moving, feinting, slashing, crumpling in death by ranks, as if ordered to fall in some ghastly drama. The brush caught on fire, and the wounded writhed and screamed and begged for escape or death, not caring which came first. Generations had conspired to create these ranks that plowed themselves under, and a generation back home would wonder where they died and how that death came about and pray for illusion and victory. Charlie remembered the courage of soldiers in blue and gray and how they carried comrades through fields of death to trenches, the magnificence of such love, unexpected and deeply moving. Then he thought of Duncan again and realized how much like Jack he had been, selfless and expecting little of life, having been torn through the death of his own wife and child and yet coming to perform a duty as he saw it.

And yet it had all been wrong. Slavery was an obvious and impenetrable evil. So little had changed, too, with the hungry still the same, the poor still the same, the mistreated still the same. Slavery, at least, was a monstrous history, though Charlie doubted its stain would retreat soon.

Oh, Duncan McGregor, thank you, my friend.

Charlie hugged the coat to him and tried to scent the aroma of the past. He had become an artist with a sharpshooter's rifle, and if God passed out warnings and omens, He had done so before Kennesaw Mountain when Charlie had been captured in the storm and lost his Whitworth. Now Charlie held the coat. He wept, knowing he had done some small good in this life, but not enough, that if love lasts, it does so only in the heart.

He loved Amy more than life, begged God to spare her, sought specialists from as far as Charleston, but she faded into stone anyway. Now, the only breath of love that might live was Sarah's, and he wished he could pray himself back into their tender age and her arms. But she would not be coming. An old man's follies are embarrassing. He wept and left the attic and the ballroom and went back downstairs where it was cooler and went into his bedroom.

It seemed like a century since morning, when he'd awakened to the train moving west through Branton County. He lay on the bed and hoped that he might die before he must speak to the celebration. They did not know what the Battle of Atlanta meant or the dark edge of war and the harsh mornings of corpse-strewn fields of fire. They could not even guess.

July 22, 1914,

5:00–5:30 P.M.

☆ ☆
☆

CHARLIE FELT GROTESQUE, A circus fool. He lay on his bed and listened for the late afternoon train on the Georgia Railroad tracks, which would come any time, rattling the windows, purring through its heated groove toward Augusta. The idea that Sarah had seen the advertisement, was even still alive—that she would rail south to be with him on the day of a speech he could not even give properly now—was preposterous. An hour before, in a damp wall of heat behind Grace House, he had burned the pages he had written earlier in the day, turned their fine sentiments to ash. He would simply rise and say a few words of thanks, say them as a farewell to Branton and to this life at the same time. Perhaps he would just say thank you and sit down. The other veterans, Josiah Biggs, James Felden, and T. D. Varnell, would be cupping their ears, would have heard only the rattle of a plate, a cough in the crowd.

Ghosts flowed around him. Jack Dockery, Duncan McGregor, General Patrick Ronayne Cleburne. And there was his father, pleading for love from the podium, asking sinners to come forth in the name of the Lord. There were soldiers like Tyree Baskins and Isaac Kennon. Bob Rainey, shot through the throat, whispered greetings from the dead. Warren Prather, from whom he had bought the *Eagle,* stepped forward in his death lineaments. Charlie recalled the Bondurants and how they had saved him from the sickened cramp of wounds, how Mary Emma had loved him back to life.

He thought mostly of Sarah. He closed his eyes as he lay on the bed and thought of her voice as she read Dickens or Byron, as she spoke of her hopes, the loss of her family in Boston, the shadow of pain and sorrow. He thought of her warm lips pressing his own urgently, warmth on warmth. He spoke the name of Martha Jane, his other daughter, too far away to come, and her husband and children, and their love for him.

The door creaked back on its hinges, and Belle swayed into the room, her tail wagging, her tongue hanging out. Charlie sat up on the bed and threw his legs off.

"Just sitting in here feeling sorry for myself," he said. He went to the broad window that looked away from the sun, and long shadows crept from Grace House toward the cemetery. Belle nuzzled his leg. "Should have gone ahead and drowned in Turner's Hole this afternoon. That would have wrecked their celebration of battle." Belle wagged at his voice. Then a slight drumming that grew louder. Belle's ears arched, and she ran from the room, into the hall, and down the steps. Charlie came slowly after her, breathing heavily with each step. The front door was open, and a young black man of about sixteen peered through the screen.

"Well, Jim, I was wondering when you'd drop around to see if I was still alive," said Charlie.

"I ain't come around to see if you was still alive," he said. Charlie smiled. He was very glad to see him. "Mama sent me to see do you need anybody to help you with anything before you talk this evening."

"Have you ever sat on the gallery up there?" asked Charlie. He pointed to the balcony above them that ran the length of the front porch and looked out over Main Street.

"Not as I know of," said Jim.

"Come on then."

Charlie ascended the stairs slowly, Belle attending him like a nurse awaiting a fall. Jim ran two steps, waited, ran two more. They came to the top of the stairs and then turned around them and walked slowly to the glass-paned doors that gave on to the gallery. Charlie opened the doors and went out, and they sat side by side in heavy rockers and looked at the swaying hum of cars that passed below them in the street.

"Hit's a grand house," said Jim.

"Your grandmother used to look for me at supper time," said Charlie. "Probably my mother would have called to me, but I would be out here reading or playing with my lead soldiers, and I'd look up, and your grandmother would be standing there with her hands on her hips, shaking her head. She never did understanding my playing with toy soldiers, but then, when I got sick, she was a second mother to me. I loved her and your grandfather, too."

"I only knowed her this little bit before she passed, and I didn't know my granddaddy at all," Jim said. He was sweating heavily, and streams of liquid flowed down his lampblack temples. "She told me to trust God and not to be bitter about nobody."

"Good advice, especially coming from someone who knew slave days, who knew what they were like."

"So is you okay? You going to be ready to go to the park and make you talk?"

"I'm okay, Jim. It's been a very strange day for me. Do you know what slave days were like?"

"Nothing but what I hear from the old folk, that some was good but most was evil and whatnot, and nothing you did made no difference. My mother say Mr. Lincoln the best president we ever have."

"Your mother is right," said Charlie. "He was a man of great sorrow. Suffering is the mother of atonement. Do you know what I mean by that?"

"No, sir, I don't have no idea what you talking about."

"We all suffer, but it is only made noble if, through it, we add grace to the life of another."

"That don't mean nothing to me, neither, Mr. Charlie."

"No? Well, it may not mean anything to me, either. I'm just an old man, and old men keep talking because they're afraid of stopping. We're afraid that if we shut up, we'll die. We think that if we keep talking people will love us and take care of us. Old people are fools that way."

"You ain't no fool," said Jim, shaking his head. "I don't know much, but I know enough to say people in this town think you the greatest one ever lived here."

"What?" Charlie stopped rocking and leaned forward. A stout wind arose and brought a cooler edge to the day, and the sun began to reach the treetops in its descent west toward Atlanta. "What did you say?"

"Don't you know that, Mr. Charlie? That people say you the greatest man in the history of this town? They say you give more, done more, seen more than any man. That you axed little in return, that you are a good and famous man. My mama says you was born with a good heart, and that there ain't a colored person in this county don't know it. That you was borned with suffering and that you have bore it up for us on the wings of a dove."

"The wings of a dove?" Charlie's voice was husky and high. Belle snored lightly at his feet. He tried to remember all those newspaper columns, how he had spoken of sacrifice and truth and honor and love. He had told stories of the common man and woman, small tales of lives well lived. He stood and walked to a support post and looked at the traffic as it came past Grace House, young men in their dusters and goggles, old women steering slowly among the ruts.

"In a way of saying it. Grandma told me afore she passed that I was to help look out after you. She said you was a man of you word and that you come from good people."

Charlie felt the tears grow behind his eyes like a sunstruck crop. He wanted his mother to come to his bedside bearing a bowl of chicken broth and a book, his father to stand before him, watch fob strung across the width of his belly, his brother Tom to wink at him, then push him down the railroad embankment.

"Missy was my mother, too," said Charlie. He remembered how he visited her once after the war.

He had walked slowly down the dirt path along Main Street in the glow of gas lamps, from light to light, shadow to shadow. He carried a paper sack whose heft and swing was difficult to balance. He forced himself along, like a man climbing ice crags. He turned off Main and walked three blocks in the faint moonlight, passing solid lamp-lit houses. Once, a horse in someone's backyard whinnied and stamped, but Charlie did not turn toward the sound. He curved on to Dixie Avenue and then slid down an unnamed alley and found himself among a row of sagging shacks, on whose concave front porches old men sat behind the glow of their pipes and cigars. The air was chill. He stopped before the third shack and walked across a bare yard and on to the front porch, which sagged with each step. He rapped on the door. There was a movement inside, a creaking of floorboards, and then an old woman's voice.

"Who that?" she asked.

"It's me, Missy," said Charlie. The door opened, and Missy smiled as Charlie walked inside. A small fire burned feebly in the grate. The wind was rising, and it puffed out the newspapers Missy had tacked against the walls as insulation.

"Mist' Charlie, thank the Lord, spring coming," she said. "I ain't gone live through another winter if it be like this one."

"I brought you some candied sweet potatoes," said Charlie, handing her the bag. "I know you always had a sweet tooth."

"Is that right? Is that right? I declare. You always bringing me things. I declare. That's so good of you."

"Before long, you can plant your garden. Before long."

"That's right. I does plant my garden, and I will if I ain't too weary for it. But you know, I'm weary, Mist' Charlie. I've had the wearies for so long. You get to be old, you give up thinking anybody but the Lord Jesus gone come save you, because they ain't. It's just life, but it's hard. Lord, it's hard. Sometimes I think about all them peoples of mine back from slave days that's gone, and I can't get my mind around it. I can't get my mind around folks who go on to heaven. But couldn't none of us white or colored bear this life if they wasn't some promise of rest. That's the sight I keep before my eyes, rest in a weary land."

"I hope you find rest," said Charlie.

"I hopes you does, too," she said hoarsely.

Now, with Missy gone for years, a distant clattering arose, and it was the train, and Charlie closed his eyes and waited a long time as it came past, and it was a very long one this time, bearing cars east toward the gathering darkness.

"Well," said Jim. "I got to be going if there ain't nothing you need."

"There's nothing I need. My daughter and her family are coming by to pick me up around six-thirty to take me to the park. I've got to make a little speech, and then I'll be through." He held to the rail and looked at the green world. "Then I'll be through."

"Then you take care of youself," said Jim.

"You as well, son," said Charlie.

July 22, 1914,

5:45–6:30 P.M.

✡ ✡
✡

DRESSED, SHAVED CLEAN, CHARLIE sat in the parlor of Grace House holding in his lap two letters, each blood- and water-stained, brittle with age and handling. Mrs. Knight was gone already. The first he only glanced upon, for he knew the shape of each letter as he knew the spike of his own pulse. He had shed his blood upon Sarah's writing, and this is all he would know of her in this life. The other was worse somehow, for he had promised to mail it for Duncan, but it had come into Charlie's keeping with no address. After the war, he had tried, with many letters, to find Duncan McGregor's parents, his hometown. Finally, after years of it, one night he told Amy that he would open the letter with ceremonial propriety and read it aloud in memory of his war-dead friend.

"Maybe you should just burn it and let the words fly back to God," said Amy. Winter had cloaked Branton in a lovely moon-bright frost. The children slept beneath blankets upstairs, and their fire was banked for the night.

"I want to read it out loud for Duncan," said Charlie. "Words don't seem real to me unless they are made into the shape of a voice."

"Honey, do what feels right," she said. "I'm here with you." She sat close on the sofa before a full fire, and Charlie got the letter from his burled-walnut secretary and sat next to her, close enough to feel her breathing in the hollows of his neck. Charlie opened it ceremonially.

The handwriting was in pencil and quite neat—neater than he would have suspected.

Near Atlanta
July 19, 1864

Dear Ma,

We have done the best we could, but we aint been able to hold no line for too long, and I think Atlanta will be lost soon. There is not a thing to regret for this fight, for we don't have near the numbers of them Yankee, and they can flank us out to the sea. Ma I have praied for you but you do not need to pray for me. It has come to me of late that I will not end this war in life so I am not afraid no more. I was afraid for so long. I was afraid at Shiloh Ma. I was afraid in Caintuck, and I was most terrible afraid at Chickymaoga (howsever you say that) but I am not longer afraid Ma.

You see there come a time when there aint nothing left to be feared for. This world can take and take and take from a man then there aint a thing left. I would not be happie leaving you Ma in this world but you will know I am with Godd and waiting for you. Me and Pa will have cut fresh wood for a fire if it be cold. My wife and girl will be standing and waiting for you, and I will wave so that you can see me. And ther won't be no pain nor sorry and no more dyin for ever.

If there be one sorry left to me, it is to leave my friend Charley, whom of Ive done wrote you before, Ma. He is a fine boy. I never had a beter frient, and he has save my life on more time than onct. Life has dealed him biter blows as it has me, and so we know the long shadow of the hart, but he is good in the deep part of his Nature. I will regret to leave Charley to find his own way. That is all I can say now as we are moving soon, Ma. I do not think to write again because Godd has told me that in this world I shal be no more. But come on when you can and watch out for me waving. I will stand in the light so you can see me.

Your loveing son
Duncan McGregor

Charlie had broken down when he spoke Duncan's name, sobbing, his face on Amy's shoulders, and she had let him go on for a long time and then hushed him and said she was there. Amy was always there. He had walked on to the front porch for the air, and a frosted moon held over Branton, and the air was sharp and extremely cold. A brisk wind arched the leafless limbs, and they scratched the clouds that blew low from the northwest. Sentiment was a weakness, he knew, and he pushed it back.

Why had he lived through that war? Was it by design or accident? He wanted to see a shape to time, for it to have a plot, a central meaning, but there were only episodes, spilled words, loves and losses.

NOW, HIS WHITE SHIRT was damp against his chest as Charlie reread Duncan's letter and smiled, slid it back into the envelope, and replaced it in the walnut secretary. He sat back in his chair and took out his pocket watch. Not that long before Catherine would pick him up. Not that long before he would speak at Ezra Atkinson Park. What should he say? Perhaps he might tell the truth only, that slavery was a vast wickedness that could not have stood on its own. There would be a respectful silence as they ushered him away at the end. Some might say he meant well. Others would emit the Rebel yell and go plan revenge on whomever they chose. No, he should not provoke with his last public utterance. They wanted to hear about the Battle of Atlanta on its fiftieth anniversary. They knew he had been wounded and had walked home, still a boy, and none blamed him for it. They could not know what such death was like, the bodies twisting in the pain and heat of battle, screaming for mother or water and shortly not knowing the difference between them in such writhing agony. They could not imagine a man blown into three clean pieces by rifled canon fire or a friend shot through the neck, singing blood until he died, begging for help that could not come. They could not know the rising horrors of chevaux-de-frise and abatis, the stunned look of men who knew their works were insufficient for life. Nor could they understand sitting in a tree with a Whitworth rifle and shooting an artilleryman in the chest at sixteen hundred yards.

He could not tell them of General Patrick Cleburne and the arrant stupidity of his death at the Battle of Franklin, near Nashville late in the war, yet another John Bell Hood massacre, pointless and improbable. Cleburne was imperfect, a man of contradictions, but he loved his countries, the South and Ireland, with equal ardor, and in his death he lost both long after the war was truly over. Charlie could not speak of the hundreds of thousands dead, the restless ghosts that swarmed battlefields across the country, nor could he point out that Atlanta was lost before Dalton—as inevitable as death.

They wanted mythology. They wanted Perseus and Andromeda, Valkyries, Atlas, Greek tragedies and white columns, happy slaves and cavaliers. How could he tell them that we plan our pasts more carefully than our present? That battles are the least important currents of history? He should have finished the game of chess with Cleburne: For miles they would hunch over the same board, make one move, study, think on it. Neither wanted to lose, but Charlie always knew that that neither wanted to win, either. The game was not designed for victors but for survivors.

Charlie got up and ascended the stairs to his bedroom and poured a basin full of water from the pitcher and washed his face with it. He thought: We wish to hear our old men speak because we pretend they are wise, but no one gains wisdom with age, only knowledge. And knowledge can give shape to wisdom but is not its mother. Perhaps he could craft a new essay. No. He was too old to start another book, and it was just as well. Everything in this life was just as well.

He went back downstairs in time to see the young man standing before the screen door, peering in. He wore a faux military uniform and was holding a piece of paper.

"Mr. Merrill?"

"I'm here," said Charlie.

"It's me, David Nicholson, with a telegram, sir," the boy said. Charlie opened the door and came on to the porch.

"Fine evening," said Charlie.

"Yes, sir. A telegram, sir." He handed Charlie an envelope, and Charlie reached in his pocket and pulled out a quarter and pressed it into the boy's hand. David looked at it with wonder and gratitude, tipped his hat, and walked down the steps to his bicycle, was gone. Charlie sat in a rocking chair and the front porch and looked at the telegram for a moment, then opened it.

He read it once, then twice, and a broad smile spread across his cheeks.

DEAR DADDY STOP I AM SO PROUD OF YOU TONIGHT STOP I
WOULD GIVE ANYTHING TO BE THERE AND I AM THERE IN
SPIRIT STOP I WILL ALWAYS BE THE APPLE OF YOUR EYE MARTHA
JANE

He folded the envelope and put it in his coat pocket and smiled. A mockingbird began to string unrelated arias together, repeating none of them over the course of the several minutes Charlie listened. Joy came to him as it always did, planned for, worked toward, yet entirely and stunningly unexpected. He took out the watch and looked at it. There would be time for him to walk to the cemetery to Jack Dockery's grave, to speak over his loosened bones, but he did not have the strength for it.

He stood and looped his thumbs in the black suspenders and looked around as if to begin a speech, but words failed him now. He thought backward to his childhood, wondered why his life had passed so rapidly. Surely he would awaken to find these years but a dream and Sarah at his bedside reading Dickens in her soft, even voice. He would hear his father coming home from a visit to a sick man, a woman who had borne a child with no husband, from a drive to select tomatoes at the farmer's market in Branton. He would smell the meal cooked by Missy, brought up by Cephus to him. Jack Dockery's slow limping footsteps, cousins, uncles, the braid of family, a skein of friends, and all life before him, years and lovers. He could not awaken from it, nor did he know what he would say. He was still standing that way when his sister Martha pulled up in her new car, a boxy Lexington that puttered and sneezed with effort.

Martha: afraid of nothing, not even learning to drive an automobile at her age. She pulled into the circular driveway in front of Grace House and stopped by the front stairs, climbed out. She wore a high-necked dress of an older fashion, held up the hem as she walked rapidly, staring at Charlie with an unasked question as she came on.

"Catherine's fetching me to the park, if that's what you're wondering," said Charlie.

"What I'm wondering is if you managed to write a speech," said Martha. "I didn't have Mrs. Knight over here all day keeping an eye on you. Somebody said you were up swimming at Turner's Hole, and I said even *you* weren't that foolish."

"Surely it would take a great fool to swim in the middle of summer," said Charlie.

"Don't mock me," she said. "Have you written the speech or not?"

"I wrote a speech," he said.

"Let me see it," she said. "You're not going to go off on one of your shrill tangents, are you?"

"That's amazing. The title of my speech is 'Shrill Tangent Against the Confederacy.' How did you know?"

"Go ahead and mock me, but I can't let you go out there and make a fool of yourself. Where's the speech?"

"I sort of memorized it," he said. "I mean I did write one, but then I had to burn it in the backyard. It has been an interesting day."

"You wrote your speech and then burned it in the backyard? Are you crazy?"

"Possibly," he said thoughtfully. "I've been thinking over my life today, and it's occurred to me that I didn't learn anything in all these years. That I'm just the same as I was when I was little."

"Don't say that," she begged. "At least make some notes. Say something nice about the South and the men who died defending Atlanta from the Yankees. That's what they're expecting you to say. Talk about your general friend, that Cleburne. You could do that. Something to make them wave their flags and then shut up. Do you know they had a reenactment of the battle today at Stone Mountain and the South won?"

Charlie laughed and walked back and forth on the porch. Only Martha could retrieve him from utter gloom.

"Victory has many mothers," said Charlie. "It wasn't that way in 1864. Everybody was trying to find somebody to blame. The soldiers all blamed Davis for getting rid of General Johnston and replacing him with Hood. I was only in the war by accident in the first place, and when I took a small wound, I left and walked home. The end. Not much of a story."

"They want you to be a hero," said Martha. "They want you to say that all these men and boys didn't die for nothing. You could say that. Just stand up there and say it like you believe it."

"They didn't die for nothing," said Charlie. "They died to keep the country together and rid it of slavery."

"They don't want to hear *that,* Charlie," she almost shouted. "They want to hear that we were attacked and all we wanted was to be left alone, and the North wouldn't leave us alone. A matter of states' rights."

"No state has a right to enslave anyone," said Charlie. "The South was wrong and has paid for it bitterly."

Martha put her hands on her hips and shook her head.

"Well, at least speak inaudibly," she said. She was beginning to smile as she walked back down the steps toward her car. "If you have to be heretical, do it to create the least ruckus, brother. And make sure when you step from the dais, wobble so they may think you're unsound in the head. Just give them a little reason to think all this dying wasn't for nothing."

"I'm thinking of just doing Lincoln's Second Inaugural speech," said Charlie.

"Goodbye, heretical brother," she said, waving. "I'll be moving to Monroe after this to save what face is still on my skull."

"Goodbye, Sister Conscience," said Charlie, waving back. "I shall do my best to embarrass you and all others related to us this evening at the park. Fifty years. Quite a long time, isn't it? But not long enough for the truth to change."

"Nobody wants to hear the truth," she said, hand-cranking the car with the élan of a twenty-year-old. "They just want stories. Just stories."

CATHERINE AND HER HUSBAND, Richard, would be by to pick up Charlie in ten minutes for the ride to Ezra Atkinson Park. The sky held the color of apples, yellow and pale red. A few doors away, someone was playing a ragtime tune on a piano, missing notes by the handful but having a fine time anyway.

Charlie walked inside and down the hallway and into the kitchen and drew himself a glass of water from the tap. Well, what *would* he say? Should he speak of being captured and escaping? Of losing his fine Whitworth rifle? Or should he tell of the salmon sunset that Pentecost Sunday before the Battle of Kennesaw Mountain, when so many gave up their souls to God? Or should he aim at the heart of political discourse, speak of the rights self-determination, of states and individuals to decide their own destiny without coercion?

Perhaps he should talk about the Negroes after all, those black people who still lived in shacks along the railroad track and had been invited to none of the events at Ezra Atkinson Park. Or what about Ezra himself, drummer boy and steady shadow through half a century, the first small sacrifice? Charlie remembered his father reporting that loss in the coffin-shaped sanctuary of Branton First Baptist Church. The gasps and moans. Surely someone would pay for this loss. But all along, Branton was different, a conspiracy of moderation among them. What was the name of that man who flew the Union flag over his house all during the war? And no one even asked him to draw it down?

Or perhaps he should not recall the Battle of Atlanta at all, but the events of that November, long after Atlanta had fallen, when Sherman's northern wing under General Slocum had strode through the streets of Branton in their thousands. He had watched, glum and sick again, as the conquerors in their cinched blue coats came down Main Street, smelled the small fires they set, saw them dashing among the houses to steal silver, but, in all, doing little damage. They had been in town only one full day, turning south for Milledgeville where they would hook up with the rest of Sherman's men on his march to the sea.

CHARLIE AWOKE ON THE polished, sun-scrubbed floor of the kitchen, lying in a puzzle of shattered glass. His face felt numb against the floor, arm wedged beneath him, bright with pain. He groaned and licked his lips, blinked around in the spilled water, felt it cool and wet beneath his heart. He sat up and fell back against the knotty pine cabinet with its black iron pulls. He saw his arm drizzling blood on to the floor, and he stood unsteadily and held it in the sink, testing his heart for pain, finding none. He stood for a long time and ran cool water over the slice, and he felt a stunned glow in his skull, bits of memory coming rapidly in no order. He tried to remember what had befallen him, but no signs appeared. I must have fainted, he thought, fallen dead away on the floor. The cut on his arm was small, and he pressed a towel to it for a minute, and the leak had stopped. His shirt seemed unstained at least. He dropped the towels to the floor and soaked up the water, then fetched the broom from the kitchen closet and swept the splinters and slices of glass into the corner where they could do no more harm.

Charlie tottered back into the front parlor and fell heavily to the sofa and thought: *I cannot give a speech tonight.* Then, more ominously, *I may not live until morning.* Was the day of his own death arriving? Should he pin his name to his shirt as so many did the morning of great battles, give away his possessions? He was starting to feel better, but he knew now that this day had been one last gift of memory and so he should not squander it. Belle scratched at the door. He let her in, and she stood before him, puzzled, questioning.

He felt his heart beating just as it had when he walked away from the Battle of Atlanta.

July 22, 1914,

6:30–9:30 P.M.

⭐ ⭐
⭐

CATHERINE, CHARLIE'S DAUGHTER, SAT in the front seat of the landau, Lewis by her side, and her husband, Richard Phillips, driving the disciplined pair of chestnut roans. Charlie, black-coated and formal, sat behind them in the seat opposite his grand-daughter, Marianne, whose hair floated golden and dense around her shoulders. The coach had been Catherine's idea, a gentle glance back to what a few were already calling simpler times.

"Granddaddy, what does it feel like?" asked Marianne, who was eleven. She wore a lovely blue dress and white gloves and had her Grandmother Amy's deep blue eyes.

"What does *what* feel like, Cricket?" asked Charlie. He was better now but still weak, and he was trying desperately to order some thoughts for his speech. Richard drove them through town for the sheer joy of the ride, and the horses pulled the landau easily but unwhipped and very slowly.

"Being so famous," she said softly. She fumbled with her gloved hands. The buildings here in town had held different trades when Charlie was a boy: Dockery's Mercantile, Calhoun's Embalmer's, Garfield Insurance, the Blue Diamond Company.

"I'm not famous," said Charlie.

"You are, too, famous," said Marianne. "You are the most famous man in the history of Branton. Everybody says it. And tonight you're giving a speech. That makes you famous."

"Marianne, don't bother your granddaddy with such questions," said Catherine.

"Leave her alone," said Charlie, smiling. Catherine had turned and looked at her father, and his skin seemed translucent, gray as morning in winter. A sorrow passed through her. "Being famous is for politicians and fools, honey. I just live alone in a big house and think back over a long life. That's all I do now. Maybe someday you'll be famous."

"What could I be famous for?" asked Marianne.

"For being stupid," said her brother Lewis from the front seat.

"That's enough," said Richard Phillips. "Haw now, Jim. Haw, Jim."

The carriage turned south.

"You could be famous for being a singer or a composer or a writer," said Charlie. "You could be anything you want to be."

"I couldn't be famous," said Marianne. "You're famous. Tonight you're famous."

"Well, maybe I am for tonight," said Charlie. "Maybe I am."

They clopped along the streets now, heading west, then north again, finally reaching Main Street, where Slocum's troops had marched that cold November of 1864. Who would have thought that thousands of Yankees might come straight through Branton?

The great houses passed by, and a few cars came around, spooking the horses that Richard held at short reins. Ezra Atkinson Park was only a mile away. A few old women who were not going to the anniversary party stood on their front porches and waved at the sight of the carriage. Charlie, who wore a flat-brimmed straw hat, doffed it at them and nodded, thinking: *This is my final journey through these good people and I should enjoy it. There is no reason I should not enjoy it.*

"I forgot to tell you I got a sweet telegram from your sister," Charlie said to Catherine. When she turned, Charlie's daughter for a moment looked just like her mother, the same kind wisdom spread across her eyes, the glowing cheeks, the light of happiness.

"From Martha Jane? How wonderful."

"I thought so," said Charlie. He was feeling much better now, and he was beginning to feel rhetoric rise in him, the shape of a speech.

The horses' hooves cupped out: *Will she be there? Will she be there? Will she be there?*

⁕ₒ⁕

EZRA ATKINSON PARK WAS a green swale on the west side of Branton, now fragrant with barbecue pits and pinned on one corner by a two-story-tall statue of the drummer boy Ezra atop a marble pylon. He was perpetually poised in mid-strike, drumsticks above a skin of Vermont marble. A decade before, vandals had broken the original stone sticks off, but the boys had confessed in a glut of corn liquor and been sentenced to a year in jail. Public subscription bought another pair, which a sculptor from South Dakota crafted back into the stern boy's frozen hands. On the pediment were the words "For God and Country" and below them "Little Ezra Atkinson, Branton's Brave Drummer Boy." Charlie glanced at the statue, but he could not miss the crowd—at least a thousand by his reckoning, spread out around a rough-hammered stage draped with Confederate battle-flag bunting.

"Would you look at that," said Catherine. "Would you just look at that."

"My heavens," said Charlie. "I had no idea it would be so many."

"It's an important anniversary," she said, turning to her father and smiling beautifully.

"What would they have done for a battle we actually won?" asked Charlie.

"Granddaddy!" squealed Marianne. "You are so strange!"

"No, just old, Cricket. Just old."

"You're not *that* old," said Marianne. Richard kept driving the landau down the hill toward the stage, and Charlie realized for the first time that this was a planned entrance. His heart sank. "The other three are much older than you are. Somebody said Mr. Felden seemed to think it was his birthday."

"I was only a boy when it all happened," said Charlie. "I wasn't all that much older than Ezra Atkinson. But he never killed anybody." Charlie looked across the landau and saw Marianne staring at him pensively.

"Did you *kill* people?" she asked. She was asking him to say he had not, that this was another ancient joke they could share.

"Here we are," said Catherine, turning to fuss with her daughter's hair. Charlie tried to form a sentence, any response, a gesture of kindness and sorrow, but words failed him. He reached over and touched his granddaughter's cheek, held it for a moment and smiled, as if to say, *Someday this may make sense to you, but probably not.*

Charlie catalogued the wildflowers that spread out from the main barbecue pit just east of the stage: spurge nettle, drum-head, violet wood sorrel. They had been trod down, and one man, kneeling before a steamy hank of pig, wore their petals on the soles of his boots.

"Mr. Charlie! Mr. Charlie!" voices cried. He looked around him and saw Mayor John Allen, a waddling man with many grinning chins, and A. J. Butler, the county's state senator. Butler walked with his thumbs stuck in his lapels, as if he were an ambulatory orator, a great speaker. Even though he had a high voice that rose to a squeak when impassioned, the men of the county had elected him to office for three terms now.

"John," said Charlie, nodding as he climbed out of the landau, Marianne and Catherine giving him a hand. "If we had had this kind of turnout in 1864, Atlanta might never have fallen."

"Did you hear? Did you hear? They reenacted the battle at Stone Mountain this afternoon, and we won! This time, the South won. It must have been glorious."

"Glorious?" said Charlie.

"Glorious indeed," said Senator Butler, his voice rising through half an octave. The Branton Brass Band, which sat thirty yards away, broke into "Dixie" as its director, a fat, sweating, clean-shaven man named Leslie Bunt, smiled at Charlie through the fog of thick glasses.

"Glorious, then," said Charlie. Men and women crowded around him, some familiar, others not, wanting to see him, shake his hand, touch the hem of his coat. James Felden, wearing his neatly washed butternut coat, wandered back and forth on a secret path in front of the stage, steered by his gray-bunned daughter Hannah. The heat felt very close, and the smell of roasting pig hemmed Charlie in. He began to look around, craning right and left, looking close, then far away with his hand across his brow.

"Are you looking for someone, Daddy?" asked Catherine.

"No, just looking," said Charlie. But even if Sarah had come, how would she look? She would be an old woman now, spent, even wobbly. She could stand right before him, and he would not know her. If only. If only once. Charlie smiled at his aged self. He looked across the crowd, but they seemed distant and mist-bound, and he took out a pince-nez and clamped it to his nose and stared again and saw hundreds he did not know, but their faces somehow spoke of kinship to others. The band came to the end of "Dixie" and struck up "The Bonnie Blue Flag," and a few men shouted from their spread blankets in the still-hot early evening.

Lightning bugs seemed to illuminate the tableau with faint and pale yellow light.

"Granddaddy, look!" cried Lewis. He danced among the trembling wings, the off-on of a thousand campfire lights.

"Light without heat," said Charlie softly. "That's their beauty, Lewis. They make light without heat."

". . . fine evening and one of the most important in the history of . . ." The mayor was orating, and Senator Butler nodded. Great runnels of sweat poured down his neck into the dark suit. Leslie Bunt, his glasses opaque with fog, mouth open for air, looked disappointed that Charlie had not nodded thanks to the band again. Charlie smiled, thinking how much he hated these songs and their invocations to slaughter.

"Mr. Charlie, may little Annabelle have the honor of giving you a copy of the program for the evening?" asked Emma Cushing, a city councilman's wife. Charlie looked down at Annabelle, who dripped with perspiration and looked miserable. Charlie knelt before her and pulled her close.

"I'd rather be playing," he whispered. "Hadn't you rather be playing?" Her eyes went glassy bright.

"I have a speech for you," she said.

"Don't give a speech," he said. "Give me a program. There. You did your job. Go catch some lightning bugs in a jar, Annabelle."

"You're nice," she said. She was not pretty, but the smile shifted the contours of her face until she seemed pleasant. She curtseyed and walked off, her mother speaking her name with increasing urgency at her back.

"Take care of him," Marianne said.

"Oh, don't you worry about Mr. Charlie," said Mayor Allen. "He's indestructible."

He steered Charlie away toward the pits where barbecue was being served, and all the way, Charlie looked to one side and then another, thinking: *Will she come? Will she come?*

Cousins crowded him. Barrington Avery from the *Branton Eagle* stepped up and asked if he could have a copy of his speech *now*. Charlie smiled and winked at him and followed the mayor and senator to the barbecue pit. Barry shrugged and shook his head. Mrs. Knight and her ne'er-do-well son Nathan stood not far away waving. Charlie doffed his hat toward her and half bowed.

"I've got a little of the good old stuff in a bottle in my car, if you're so inclined," said the mayor. Charlie was not inclined. He read the program, his legs feeling heavy and somewhat unsteady beneath him:

FIFTIETH ANNIVERSARY, BATTLE OF ATLANTA

1. INVOCATION—REV. HOWARD OATES, BRANTON FIRST BAPTIST CHURCH

2. WELCOME—MAYOR JOHN ALLEN

3. POEM ESPECIALLY FOR THIS OCCASION—MR. LESLIE BUNT

4. SELECTIONS FROM THE BRANTON BRASS

5. PRESENTATION OF RESOLUTION IN HONOR OF THE HEROES— SEN. A. J. BUTLER

6. KEYNOTE SPEECH—MR. CHARLIE MERRILL

7. CLOSING PRAYER—REV. THOMAS SILFING, BRANTON FIRST METHODIST CHURCH

Charlie felt queasy and only nibbled at his plate and sipped from a tall glass of sweet tea. He looked right and left, through the center of the crowd, saw a few women wave, but no one searching for him as she would. The light was soft, and it would all end before darkness.

He tried to think of a speech, to understand, to consider words alone. And they were beginning to come now, to shape themselves into sentences, and he began to know what he would say. He began to feel the presence of his own days rushing into a single evening. Catherine was close, as was her husband. Marianne and Lewis twirled and played with other children, and serenity began to paint its velvet motions over Charlie, and he understood that Sarah was present through the shadow of memory, the shadow of stones. Jack Dockery was here, too, as was Duncan McGregor. Even poor lost Patrick Cleburne was here, away for a short hour from his beloved Ireland. Peace fell over Charlie like a loving shadow, and he felt a quiet joy in the thousands, in their love of country, misguided and lost in myth though they surely were. A man, thought Charlie, can be entirely wrong, and still love his land. Maybe that explained much. The sun had settled behind a stand of longleaf pines, and light sifted through the green spokes like the rays from a crown. A rising wind soughed, breathing among the oak leaves and new stems of flower and shrub.

"Did you ever think of anything smart to say?" It was his sister Martha, and radiance seemed to pour from her eyes. Charlie felt gratitude that they had shared this long life together. "And if you're wondering what I'm drinking, it's not tea or sasparilla. It's water and a very fine Kentucky whiskey that I bought at a fair price from the mayor. The man understands politics, Charlie. Would you like a gulp to increase your loquacious manner?"

"I'd be happy for five minutes, then fall backward off the stage," said Charlie, laughing. "But I approve. I approve of all anodynes, from laudanum to liquor."

"There is no cause to suffer as I see it," said Martha, sipping from her glass. "And now, by heavens, I'm in the mood for some oratory and any musical concert that does not include 'Dixie.' It's a fine old song, but you hear anything enough, it becomes tawdry."

"Especially speeches from old men."

"You intend to improvise, do you not?"

"Doesn't everyone?"

"Well, wahoo. I knew you before you were a great man. I knew you when you spent years in bed being waited on hand and foot, Charlie Merrill. Nothing you do could impress me. I just want you to know that. Give General Washington's farewell to the troops, and I will not love you the less."

"My compliments to your distiller," said Charlie, taking off his hat and bowing. Martha curtseyed and walked off on slightly unsteady legs.

T.D. VARNELL'S DAUGHTER HAD to lead her father to his seat on the dais. He got up and waved toward a spitted beef that smoked slowly on a low fire. She helped him back down, and he slumped, his gray coat tight across his chest. Josiah Biggs, frail and skeletal, tottered up by himself and sat, saluting the crowd, which was growing quiet now. James Felden's daughter stood behind his chair and leaned forward sometimes to gently and sweetly wipe the spittle from his lips. The ministers came up with their chins elevated toward God, then Leslie Bunt, hands trembling on the sheaf of his commemorative poem. He wore a bandmaster's blue coat, fraught with braid and brass. Charlie came last, walking stiffly up the four steps, which had a freshly sawn aroma still clinging around them. An ebbing wind riffled the Confederate bunting. Miss Kimberly Malting, vice president of the United Daughters of the Confederacy, sneezed loudly in the front row of viewers, who were seated on the warm grass. Miss Malting was past eighty but shy of ninety, and she was bitter and defiant, but her hatred of Yankees was beginning to seem almost quaint.

From the three-foot elevation of the stage, Charlie scanned the crowd. The Branton Brass, by some prearranged signal, played a fanfare and flourish, and Reverend Oates rose and came to the lectern. Charlie inhaled and realized that he had never felt so happy or content in his life. This was his land, these, his people. The shadows of all he loved stretched long and deep here. He was blessed and admired. The war had been wrong. Slavery had been far worse, a deep evil. But death could whisper his name now, and he would look past that phantom for his mother and father, for his beloved brother, Tom, for dear friends and sometime lovers. The town drunk, Henry Brown, would be there, standing amazed in the presence of something holy.

Charlie did not know that Reverend Oates had even started the invocation until he said *Amen,* and a cascade of repetitions rumbled through the crowd. James Felden had fallen asleep, and his daughter behind him held his shoulders and smiled at him with deep love and pure understanding, and Charlie found himself unaccountably moved.

"We are here on the fiftieth anniversary of the last great battle in the western theater of the War Between the States," said Mayor Allen. For a moment, he lost his place, shuffled papers, cleared his throat. "The Battle of Atlanta was a time of sorrow for this great state, but it was also a time of honor and duty and sacrifice. So many died to help preserve our right to self-determination." Marianne and Lewis and several other children far to one side threw a baseball and laughed softly, and Charlie watched them with a transcendent delight. "The men who sacrificed much in that battle from Branton have mostly gone to their final reward, but a few, uh, are left among us, and they are here this great evening to be recognized. I, ah . . ." He shuffled papers again, and there was a riffle of burnished giggling from the crowd, and Charlie tried very hard not to smile.

There, near a tree, not forty yards away, a woman with graying hair down. Could that be Sarah? No, it was Ida Doane, a vapid busybody who attended every funeral and wept, even if she had not known the deceased in life. Charlie mocked himself silently. Now, Leslie Bunt stood and came to the podium, and his hands were trembling worse than before, and his voice at first did not carry, and there were shouts, and so he spoke his poem more loudly:

> *We come tonight to honor the war*
> *And the battle that once they fought.*
> *We all understand just what it was for*
> *And why they all did what they ought.*

Charlie felt a shiver of horror at the silliness of the lines, their lack of even moderate craft, but the crowd was respectful for the first minutes of its length, growing restive only after Leslie had finally finished with a burst of solemn and sentimental rhetoric. He left the dais and went to conduct the band, which played "Kathleen Mavourneen," "Lorena," and "Dixie" once again. Charlie floated along on the discords, the pungent sourness of good intentions, and somehow the music soothed him. Peace, like a patient and enduring light, was settling on him.

Senator Butler spilled parts of campaign speeches for five minutes before reading the resolution honoring Branton's surviving veterans of the Battle of Atlanta, and the old men stood and looked somewhat confused, all but Charlie, who still scanned the crowd and saw that she was not there and that it was good. The raw passage of ghosts from a life can lift us, he thought.

"We have now come to the part of the program that I know you have most looked forward to," said Mayor Allen. "I hardly need to introduce Mr. Charlie Merrill to his own hometown. He is without question the greatest man ever to arise from Branton, and his many books and his work in the newspaper business attest to that. His columns, with their joy of life, their stories, not of himself but of others, helped shape who we are." Charlie heard the drone go on, but his mind was elsewhere, and he realized with a start that he did not know where he might start or what he might actually say. Maybe he would just say thank you and sit down. Then they were standing and applauding, and Mayor Allen had his arm curved toward Charlie, and he knew it was time. He stood, tested the fragility of his heart, then came forward and grabbed on to the lectern as the crowd settled down. Lightning bugs lilted across the meadow, and the serial squeaks from ice cream churns sang behind him.

Charlie stood silently for perhaps thirty seconds, and he closed his eyes and tried to dream himself into the Battle of Atlanta, the scars of abatis and chevaux-de-frise, the deafening eruption of artillery and the popping of musketry, but it was no good. The memory faded from him, as if it were something book-learned and now evaporating in its full dress of details. He finally opened his eyes and looked back and forth over the men and women, past the children to Main Street, on which a few cars spun past.

"My dear friends," said Charlie. Catherine watched him with slight alarm. Martha was next to her, grinning, head cocked, not appearing to care if Charlie was a prophet or a fool or perhaps both. "I come to you this evening, this fine summer evening, among distant sounds, distant shadows. I . . ."

He paused for a long time, looking down, shaking his head.

"If I listen closely some nights when I awaken," he said, "I can hear the sound of trumpets in the far distance, and the creak of caissons and the clank of canteens and tin cups against the belts of troops who move in darkness." The gathering had grown utterly silent. "I can hear the orders of officers who will soon lie in the twisted inhumanity of death. And I can hear the dying shout of grown men for their mothers or for water or for lovers they will never see again. I hear the wind in the pine trees and the rain on tent roofs, and I know that the soldier coughing in the next tent will be dead by morning.

"I can hear the laughter of boys at cards or dominoes, the casual after-sound of a joke told and understood. I can hear the sound of old men collapsing in their bootsteps, apologizing even as they curl up to die in terrible heat. I can hear thunder and I can hear the sound of splintered oak trunks when the artillery opens up.

"And I can hear my own father's voice from the pulpit, the injunctions for justice and the blessings from a God he trusted so deeply. I can hear the sound of my brother Tom's swift feet on the rail-strewn stones or the winter drizzle on tarpaper shacks."

Charlie felt exalted, and he no longer scanned the crowd for Sarah. He gave her up to time, and felt her disappear from his arms.

"If I think harder in the nights when I awaken, I can see a small town with its square and churches, its squires and ladies rising and then falling in majestic sequence. I can see my mother's hands as they reach to comfort me in illness and sorrow, and I can see her eyes as they grow calm and accepting of loss and pain. I can see a boy my own age limping in constant pain and never complaining about it, then dying on the sad second story of a home where he was well loved.

"I can see Union soldiers at Chickamauga falling over and over and then over again in a murderous fire. I can see men half starved and eating terrible food or being shot down as they swam rivers to escape the onslaught. And I can see the ridge near Dalton and a Scotsman there who became my finest friend, with his kind sorrow, and his refusal to die from a loss that would have torn most men apart. I can see a sunset at Kennesaw Mountain on Pentecost Sunday that was brighter than the burning bush on Sinai, and all the men around it bowed down, many knowing it was their last day to celebrate on this earth.

"I can see General Patrick Cleburne and his gray eyes, and how he gained animation when he spoke of his beloved Susan Tarleton and how he believed in what was lost already, either in this South or in Ireland. And I can see Atlanta dimly, a dream of smoke and blood and multiple agonies where I was wounded and from which I was bound to flee."

The children had stopped playing now and stood and listened. A few in the audience wept. Charlie barely felt their presence, and he wanted to stand here forever testifying.

"I can smell the open cookfires and bacon frying over them, and I can smell the new leaves of spring and the sweet blossoms of honeysuckle. I can smell the stench of death and sweat and misery that was without end. I can smell three weeks of rain and its terrible rot and mud, but I can also smell the blessings of sun when the rain stopped, the odor of sweet cedar and pine and wildflowers along riverbanks. I can smell the smoke of artillery and muskets, acrid and persistent. I can smell the lavender scent of women as they pass, and the fresh insistence of their hair. I can smell the Branton River at flood tide and freshly turned cotton fields in the spring, rich and lovely. I can smell the aroma of harvest, from pumpkins and wheat and tomatoes and corn. I can smell a hog roasting in the fall after killing time, when life freshens, and men and women dance with joy at the end of heat."

Charlie glanced at Catherine, and her face was turned on itself in a rush of tears, and she sobbed quietly, her hands tented under her chin in a gesture of prayer.

"Some nights when I awaken," he continued, "I can taste the salt of tears and the dust from a tramped road. I can taste the meals of my life, from the bounteous at home to the meager in military camps. I can taste the winter wind and its hints of ice and a hundred hearths, and I can taste all the seasons as they have passed by and through me. I can taste a lump of candy or the bile of sickness."

Charlie felt a wave of nausea come over him, and he gripped the lectern to steady himself. After a moment, he felt better again.

"But I cannot touch the soldiers whom I knew and loved so well. I cannot touch my mother or my father or my dear brother, much less my beloved wife. The past flashes to us so quickly, my friends, that we hardly know the present has occurred. Suddenly, the defining time of one's life wears a half century of freight, and we start to claw back toward it, but we never reach it again, and in so doing we suffer. We cannot touch the love we shared, the sorrows we suffered, the miles we walked, the ones whose sacrifice for us endures. I cannot, then, touch that past. I cannot bring you a victory that it was ordained we should never have in the Battle of Atlanta. I cannot touch mythologies that we construct to explain such loss, and I dare not. We invent the past to suit our present, but there is no truth in the present, for with each breath it is drawn backward into history. It is not the present in which we act, but the past that we attempt to rearrange. All our loves, our losses, the men and women who walked with us, the children lost, the sorrows borne in the night—these we reshape until they become stories that make sense and hold us by our childlike hands.

"And so I wonder what it is we celebrate this day, as another great war is near in Europe in which thousands will die. Already, they will be inventing reasons for deaths to come, slights and treasons that can lead only to extinction. If we celebrate anything this day, it is that we have learned something from the misery and sorrow of our own war, the mothers whose sons never came home, wives whose husbands turned to names upon a roster of the storied dead. We celebrate the shape of loss and the turning of our faces from unity to tragedy and back to harmony once again. We must understand our own wounds and find some way to forgive those who wounded us.

"We must on this day celebrate not a way of life lost"—Charlie looked down and was silent for a full ten seconds—"but great love, sustained and sanctified."

Charlie looked down and, realizing he had finished, walked slowly back to his chair and sat, and for a moment, in the silence of the park, there was a deep silence, a stunned peace. Then, as if on command, the crowd erupted in such a frenzy of shouting and applause that for a moment he thought some great catastrophe had occurred. In the time of one breath, everyone stood and applauded, screamed, cheered. Many wept. Charlie could not quite believe it and looked around his townsmen and saw that they understood, and for that he felt pleased. The cheering lasted for a very long time, but he neither stood again nor acknowledged it. He looked ahead and wondered if she would outlive him, if she had already fled among the honored dead. *Those we love best are those we love first.*

REV. THOMAS SILFING OF the Branton First Methodist Church delivered the closing prayer, and the Branton Brass struck up "Dixie" again, but Charlie didn't listen and only nodded politely as men and women crowded around him as he descended the step from the stage and felt Catherine in his arms.

"I'm ready for home now," said Charlie softly.

"You were wonderful," she said. "You were always so wonderful."

"Sweet Catherine," he said. Marianne and Lewis had arrived and were tugging on his coat.

"I told you you were famous," said Marianne. "Next time listen to me."

"Marianne!" said her mother.

"I will, Cricket," said Charlie.

"I want to drive the horses," said Lewis.

"When you're older," said his father.

"Nobody will *have* horses then," said Lewis.

They crowded back into the landau, and Charlie felt a deep weariness, a need for his bed and the solitude of Grace House. The air was damp and hot, but all the way home, lightning bugs snapped sparks against the darkness like small campfires on a thousand hills.

July 22, 1914
9:30–Midnight

CHARLIE'S SON-IN-LAW PULLED THE carriage to a stop in front of Grace House. Far behind, they could hear the pop and hiss of fireworks in Ezra Atkinson Park. Richard had lit the landau's lamps, and they threw a pleasant glow on the street. Catherine and both her children were in the coach proper now, and Richard sat alone on the driver's seat.

"Did you mean to leave the lights on?" asked Catherine. "I worry about you. Don't you want to come spend the night with us tonight, Daddy?"

"Stop fussing over me," said Charlie. "I'm fine. And yes, I left the lights on. I always leave the lights on in the front parlor at night." He kissed Catherine and his grandchildren good night, then shook hands with Richard and walked slowly up the sidewalk to the front door of Grace House, stopping to turn and wave. In all, he felt only relief that the day was finally over and that he could now fade away, a book in his hands. Perhaps there was another book to write, but perhaps not. The horses strained against their burden and pulled the carriage down the street, turned a corner, and soon faded into silence.

Charlie went on to the porch and realized he was very tired and might barely be able to drag himself up the stairs to his bedroom. He felt as if a light fog or a haze of battle smoke enveloped him. Very strange. Who was he? From where had he just come? He tried to turn and look at Main Street and saw, through the tall oaks, the sparking fireworks that revelers still fired at the park. It took a while, but then he stood, or seemed to, and Belle came, and he scratched under her neck, then took a deep breath and opened the unlocked door and came slowly inside and stood for a long moment looking at the floor. Why had he planned nothing and then spoken so splendidly? Perhaps it was the adventure, but he felt the words were decent, that they conveyed some of what should be remembered on such a day. He could not have made a rousing defense of the Confederate States of America, nor would Branton have wanted one. All he could do finally was speak of the joys and sorrows that attended those days or any days. Perhaps no man could do more. *If I could do it again, I would have spoken more of love,* he thought.

He again felt enveloped in a distant silence, and his mind was full of shadows and memories. A sound came from somewhere in the lamplight. A sudden chill of recognition swept through Charlie, and he rubbed his forehead with the fingers of his left hand. Then his feet were moving, and as he moved, his strength seemed to return, a lightness afoot that startled him. Years bled away. The smoke was so dense he could barely see through it. He could not feel the ground with his feet, and he thought he might be drifting toward or away from something. By the time he reached the back porch and the grove filled with fireflies, he was young again, all muscle and promise, with years spreading before him.

SHE WAS STANDING IN the moonshadow holding a lantern, quite still as he descended the steps and walked through the damp grass toward her. She turned at the soft squeak of the screen door and held the light up to her face, and Charlie saw the outlines, the shape of her cheeks, the gray hair upswept, blue eyes glittering with refracted light. He felt himself rising toward the canopy, strong with disbelief and hope. And then he was ten feet from her, and he could not believe it for a very long time, then he did.

"Sarah?" he whispered.

"Charlie?" she answered. "Is that you?"

"Sarah?"

"Yes. It's your Sarah."

"Oh, dear God," he said.

He came closer, then closer again, and she was an old woman with eyes like shattered mirrors, full of light from all directions. She wore a pale dress around which the lightning bugs seemed to hover. The lantern glow spread through her chest and face, changing her into something sea-borne, translucent and bearing its own light. A few fading rockets crumped against the black night like artillery from a distant battle, as far as memory.

"I am so sorry we were late. We—did you see the man inside?"

"I did."

"He's my son. My husband passed away last November. I saw your advertisement and wanted to surprise you. We had to take a car for hire from Atlanta."

"Your son," he said. "Sarah. Is it you? Can it be you?"

"I'm sorry I missed your speech," she said. "I wanted so much to hear what you had to say. Surely it was wonderful. I have all your books. We live in Boston."

"I hardly believed it could happen. In fact, I did not believe it could happen. I have thought of you for so many years."

"As I have thought of you, Charlie. Look as us. We've grown old."

"You were the first girl I loved."

"And you were my first boy."

His face drew close to hers, and he could see the shape of her girlhood, the sharp cheeks, the turn of her hair, the curve of her hands. She set the lantern down on the grass, and they stood for a long time, and he touched her face with wonder, then took her into his arms. He could feel her breath against his neck and closed his eyes with wonder. The copse began to tremble with the dry rattle of cicadas. She kissed his ear and put her face in the hollow of his shoulder. They rocked slightly. Sorrow's deepest lines faded; all was swept away in the river of time, replaced by names upon a stone and the few stories of immortal deeds.

"I called for you."

"And I came here," she whispered. Charlie cleared his throat and spoke in deep, even tones.

"I write you with great sorrow from Savannah where I wait to board a ship for London. It was not my idea to leave with such urgency—this you must believe. I had wept the whole time, and now that an ocean will separate us, I can only hope Death will come for me soon.

"It is not enough for me to say that I love you, dear Charlie. You are the star of my life, the only true joy I have ever known. I had no sister or brother as a child. When I was sent to Branton, I felt the most perfect hopelessness that it is possible to know. My uncle and his stupid Specific shamed me, and his loud ways were no better than what I heard in Boston.

"I very nearly believe that I dreamed myself into your arms. I was alone and full of sorrow, and I asked God for a boy to take me as his own. At first, I asked God what He could mean—you were frail and ill and secretive with but one dear friend of your own. I loathed Branton, but then I did not mind it so much when God sent you to me."

Sarah stood back and looked at him, and her eyes were filled with tears, and she canted her head slightly.

"That's what I wrote you when I left. And you have remembered it all these years?"

"How could I forget you, Sarah?"

Their faces were very close, and his lips came to hers, and in that moment, he felt transcendence, a sacrifice that he had made, that had been made for him, and he gloried in the shape of its arrival.

IN THE DARKNESS, CHARLIE sat up in bed and looked around the room. Moonlight washed through the curtains of the tall windows. He reached for Sarah, formed the shape of her name upon his lips, but she was not there. Of course, he thought. All the world seemed to lie before him, bright as noon, boys and girls, soldiers, fathers in the garb of love, and all seasons spun in a whispered cycle, from gold to ivory, and there were ancestors and descendents, streets and country lanes, whirring phaetons and automobiles, the sweet flanks of horses and the affection of comrades. He looked around for Sarah—surely she must still be standing right here, where she was a moment ago, fast in his arms and faster in his heart. Surely she must have spoken his name only a moment before. The floor planks glowed with an opal smear of moonlight.

He gave away his memories, his uniform, his books, his children, old loves, streets, towns, his own country. He gave away the breadth of fields, the river with its dark enfolding pools, summer childhood days. He gave away all his possessions and nestled downward toward a name engraved in stone.

This might have been the edge of battle, but Charlie Merrill was not afraid.

November 1918

I SHOULD HAVE CALLED *the old woman to stoke the fire when I woke two hours ago, but there is sanctity in these sheets that should hold me alone, as in my dreams. Through the tall windows I can see the softness of a sky lowering for flurries. Church bells rang deep into the night, and I know another war has ended, though blood will run from it for years to come. My gown is bunched around my knees, but I shall not move to straighten it, not yet. Soon, I will rise and walk to the window and look out and watch the train come cutting through the city and place my memories in order once again. The blood from all wars stays damp, will not evaporate or soak into the shattered soil.*

I feel so very old, and quietness is entering me, a grace even, and yet I cannot make peace with this life of yearning. I cannot. I have long since expected to awaken without old love on the front porches of memory. I want to take forgetfulness with my coffee, but I dare not forget beauty. Of all the things we may lose toward God, the last should be beauty, those moments given to us when the world opens toward symmetry.

I can see the birds in my leafless oak tree, trembling with cold, knowing it is past time for flight south—to the enduring warmth and wonder of latitude. They bring color to the last seasons of my world. Lives, too, have seasons, I have learned, and in spring one should love intensely, feel the world whole, as if it breathed and moved at a touch. So many have their unloved lives to mourn at the end, their childless days, their happiness. I cannot bear the sorrow of those lost lives in Europe, dead not of shellfire and mud but of human stupidity and malice. If there is a heaven for most generals, it is shallow and distant, and all who live there defy orders and move away from grief.

Such philosophy from the old is tolerated. I may lie here in these twisted damp bedsheets waiting for the train to slice through Boston and be called the Old Woman of Beacon Street. They believe they know me, understand my heart, but they are wrong.

I rise now and walk to the window, and it shudders with the cold, and below me, there in the breathing city, are the bundled young already working, selling automobiles, cutting fabric, marking patterns for dresses and shirts, waving their endless banners and wondering when the boys will come home. This room is very cold, and the air billows out my gown. But even the soldiers who come home, who step down gangplanks in the harbor to the brass bands and tears, will never again be whole. Once we are broken, the healing comes only in dreams.

I speak across the years to you, Charlie. You know I am speaking to you. I will speak to you until the light of escape gathers me inside with its deathless charity. I will make a person of these bones and speak the words, as though sentences may grow sacred through their ordering.

I did see your advertisement in the Boston Globe, *but I was ill and thought to come later. Then I read that you had passed away the very night you spoke, and I wept for days. No one knew why, and I could not say, but by ways known only to God, I sent a message that I pray has found its way to your heart.*

Our child, a son I named Charles, was born in England. My father was not in London when I arrived, and so I was able to invent a husband who died of disease. I thought that when I sailed back for Boston, I would come with an infant in arms, but our child was small and did not thrive. Now he lies at eternal rest in another land, and I pray that he has found you in heaven. I did not know a girl could bear so many tears as I shed for him. He would have grown into an honorable man, Charlie, and he looked so much like you that I ached for years at such losses. And oh my Charlie, how beautiful his eyes were! But time moves us onward, and I married a man named Simmons, and he was a good husband to me until his passing last year. I bore him three sons, and the eldest bears your name.

In all of these years, I never forgot your sacrifice for me. Alone and nearly a foreigner, living in a land that had grown strange with hatreds, you loved me. And I can say with all my heart that I loved you. Because your death notice was printed in the Globe, *I know that you married and had children, and for that I was most humbly grateful.*

How I wish I could have been there for your speech, Charlie! I did read your books and your newspaper pieces, and in them I saw your soul, the light cast from a tender and wounded boy, and that glory fell around me like stardust. I always believed that your gentle nature would cast off a slow fire, and I know that it will burn for a very long time.

Mostly I believe that our love was not wrong but somehow sanctified, and that you would have been most proud of your son, and the sons and daughters he might have given us; that you, also, would have loved him. I believe that such love will go onward and that it will make some mark upon this sorrowful world. I am very old now and so tired. But when I look deep in the mirror I can see the girl I was.

Some days, the streets are packed with soldiers, Charlie, and they fill their boots with pride, but their inheritance is sorrow. I see black faces on boats in the harbor, and I wonder what they have yet gained. Love, I now know, outlasts all wars, will set shame on their battlements.

But Charlie, I will speak no more today of such regrets. May I speak of our enduring gifts? I see below me a boy kissing his sweetheart with delicious stealth, and they both grow smiles of joy. Do you remember the day we first kissed and knew? I close my grateful eyes and turn backward toward Branton, and I am riding in a carriage with you, and we are wearing lap robes, listening to the slow clop of our horse, feeling the faster passions of youth. I can see your grief upon a father's passing, and I accept as real the pressure of your hand in mine. I recall the war talk, my dread uncle's alcoholic terrors, the battle news, my rushing ride to Savannah and then onward by steam to England. But more, I remember the afternoon that we created a son who by now has surely found you, attracted by the kindness and familiarity of your face. Your heart rushed into mine, and we saw that passion can also bring peace. It does not always presage wars.

I have had a good life, Charlie, a life of books and reading. Sometimes old people have memories instead of life, and they sadly try to dream the long-gone decades back into their hands. But old age is not a sorrow for those with loving pasts. It is a tower from which we can see, with deep delight, our first loves in the far distance, still tender, always blessed.

I must have the fire stoked, for it is freezing in here. There is much to do today. As always, this message is for you alone, my gentle Southern boy. This is from your Sarah. Know that she loved you always.

Author's Note

I HAD BEEN WORKING for many years on research for this book, unsure of its shape and direction, when a footnote in a Civil War history changed the focus of the narrative. The book was *Sherman's Horsemen,* David Evans's magisterial retelling of the Union cavalry operations in the Atlanta campaign of 1864. Evans's book was crammed with detail I'd never heard, even though I grew up in Madison, Georgia, a town through which a part of Sherman's army came on its March to the Sea. I was reading Evans's book when I came to description of Major General George Stoneman's cavalry raid in July and August 1864, part of which involved Madison.

Evans told stories I'd never heard, and in a footnote I found that he'd used information from an article by Rev. J. R. Kendrick, published in the *Atlantic Monthly* in October 1889. Kendrick in 1863–1864 was pastor of the First Baptist Church of Madison, and his article, twenty-five years after the campaign, gave a startling view of Madison as a town in north central Georgia that had a sizable minority of men and women who opposed the war in all aspects.

I had grown up knowing that an antisecessionist named Joshua Hill, before the war a U.S. representative in Congress, and after it a senator, lived in Madison and helped save it because he was a friend in Washington of General W. T. Sherman's brother, John, a congressman from

Ohio. What I didn't know what how pervasive that anti-Confederate sentiment was in Madison.

Kendrick's article ignited my imagination, and I was able to focus on the story of a boy in a Georgia town that was never strong for the war and doubted its wisdom. One man did, in fact, fly the Stars and Stripes over his house for the entire war, without reprisal. I renamed the town Branton, because I wished to change certain physical facts of Madison, but in large part my research focused on Madison.

My writing about the Civil War was, in fact, personal as well. My great-great-grandfather Joseph Bearden made Enfield rifles at the Cook & Brother Armory in Athens, Georgia, during the war, and was part of the Athens Home Guard. When Sherman came through Atlanta, the Guard was sent south because it was felt the Union troops would certainly be headed for the armories at Augusta (they weren't). Almost by accident, Sherman's troops ran into a group of Confederate soldiers that included the Athens men, and in the Battle of Griswoldville, just east of Macon, my great-great-grandfather was wounded in the leg. (Another great-grandfather, Solomon Smith, was in a Georgia unit that saw action in numerous battles, including Antietam and Gettysburg.)

The Battle of Griswoldville was yet another pointless charge that ended in a lopsided Southern loss, and Joseph Bearden decided he'd had enough, and after healing somewhat, he walked home from Macon to his farm in northwestern South Carolina. When I met Charles Frazier at an autographing I gave in Raleigh in 1997, we swapped stories, over a beer, of our ancestors who had quit the war. His led, of course, to *Cold Mountain.*

My story revolves around the pivotal, life-changing events in the youth of a sensitive boy who later finds himself in the campaign for Atlanta. This, then, was the genesis of *A Distant Flame.*

During the decade I spent writing and researching this book, I spent many happy hours, working with period letters, diaries, and newspaper accounts. I read, as well, dozens of books, monographs, and web sites devoted to the Civil War era in general and the Atlanta campaign specifically.

Far and away the most important book in my research was Albert Castel's *Decision in the West* (University Press of Kansas, 1992), a superb history of the Atlanta campaign. From this and numerous other sources, I developed an almost hour-by-hour timetable of that campaign from March to late July 1864. Anyone wishing to know about the campaign for Atlanta can happily read Castel's marvelous book.

There is no way to list all the sources for this book, but among the most important are *The Siege of Atlanta, 1864* by Samuel L. Carter III (Ballantine Books, 1973); *Getting Used to Being Shot At: The Spence Family Civil War Letters,* edited by Mark K. Christ (University of Arkansas Press, 2002); *Cleburne and His Command* by Capt. Irving A. Buck, and *Pat Cleburne: Stonewall Jackson of the West* by Thomas Robinson Hay, ed. (McCowat-Mercer Press, Inc., Jackson, Tenn., 1959); *Stonewall of the West: Patrick Cleburne and the Civil War,* by Craig L. Symonds (University Press of Kansas, 1997); *One of Cleburne's Command: The Civil War Reminiscences and Diary of Capt. Samuel T. Foster, Granbury's Texas Brigade, CSA,* ed. by Norman D. Brown (University of Texas Press, 1980); *Sherman's Horsemen: Union Cavalry Operations in the Atlanta Campaign,* by David Evans (Indiana University Press, 1996); *Company "Aytch"* by Samuel R. Watkins (Times Printing Company, 1900); *A Diary from Dixie* by Mary Chesnut (Houghton Mifflin, 1949); *This Terrible Sound: The Battle of Chickamauga* by Peter Cozzens (University of Illinois Press, 1992); *The Diary of Dolly Lunt Burge, 1848–1879,* edited by Christine Jacobson Carter (University of Georgia Press, 1992); *The Plain People of the Confederacy,* Bell Irvin Wiley (Peter Smith, 1971); *The Civil War, A Narrative,* Shelby Foote (Vintage Books, 1986); *Confederate Georgia,* by T. Conn Bryan (University of Georgia Press, 1953); "A Non-Combatant's War Experiences," by J. R. Kendrick, *Atlantic Monthly,* October 1889; Civil War Talk (online): "Long Arms of the Civil War"; Army of the Cumberland dot net: "Breech-Loading Rifles of the Civil War"; *Berry Benson's Civil War Book,* edited by Susan Williams Benson (University of Georgia Press, 1992); *Civil War Sites Advisory Commission Reports: Battle Summaries,* National Park Service; *Soldiering: The Civil War Diary of Rice C. Bull,* edited by K. Jack Baver (Presidio Press, 1997); *The Life of Johnny Reb,* Bell Irvin Wiley (Doubleday, 1971); *The Life of Billy Yank,* Bell Irvin Wiley (Bobbs-Merrill, 1952). In addition, I did considerable research in *The Official Records of the War of the Rebellion,* the huge multivolume U.S. government publication that is the standard source for all Civil War writers.

I also want to pay tribute to the inspiration I drew from *The Civil War,* Ken Burns's epic documentary that I still believe is one of the greatest programs ever aired on American television. The companion book by Geoffrey C. Ward, with Ric Burns and Ken Burns (Knopf, 1990), was also a great help. While the texts above are some of the main ones I studied, there were many, many others. Since more than 80,000 books have been printed about the American Civil War, I am aware of only a small portion of them. I think that is probably true of real historians as well.

Finally, readers are entitled to know what in such a historical novel is true and what is fiction. This book is a work of the imagination, not history, and I am not a historian. Spending ten years on research, which I did, does not make me a historian. I have tried, however, to be faithful to the history of the time both in general action and specific detail. The sections of this book dealing with the Atlanta campaign are as correct as I can make them, down to the weather on specific days. It goes without saying that General Patrick Cleburne almost certainly did not have a friend like Charlie Merrill, and such a friendship might well have been impossible given the times. Still, Cleburne was one of the most interesting Confederate commanders of the war, and I believe I have drawn his character properly, based on numerous sources.

As the reader has no doubt noticed, I did not attempt to write a history of the Atlanta campaign using an omniscient narrator. I wanted it to unfold through Charlie's eyes and actions—through the limited vision of a single soldier. Much of the time in the Civil War, soldiers in the ranks had little idea what was transpiring—something often true of the officers as well. I have used enough detail to keep the reader oriented, however, to know the shape and movements of battles, without trying to explain their importance or wider significance. Again, if one wishes to know the history, read Castel.

I was also fortunate to rely on the expertise of my father, Marshall W. Williams, who for many years has been the county archivist for Madison and Morgan County, Georgia. On many occasions, I would call him with questions, and his vast knowledge helped me constantly. (Madison, for example, had electricity in 1892 but didn't have city water until 1908, facts he had at his fingertips but which had importance to my narrative.)

I would like to thank my friend Scott Berry, sheriff of Oconee County, Georgia, for teaching me to fire black powder weapons, including his beautiful .50 caliber Hawken.

For reading and commenting in depth on this manuscript, I am eternally indebted to the noted Civil War historian Dr. David Evans. He saved me from many blunders, but any mistakes are mine. I am also pleased to thank my agent, Bill Contardi of Brandt & Hochman, for excellent advice that greatly helped this book, and my editor at St. Martin's/

Thomas Dunne Books, Peter Wolverton, for his brilliant help in shaping the final manuscript.

Final thanks, as always, go to my wife, Linda, and our children Brandon and Megan. I am especially delighted to thank Brandon and his wife, the wonderful Laura Boyd, for the marvelous gift of their son, Caleb, our first grandchild.